Holy Ground

Karl F. Hollenbach

Published by internet marketing KY, LLC
d/b/a Books Authors And Artists
Louisville, KY, U.S.A.

Enjoy!
Karl Hollenbach
July 2014

Published May 2014 internet marketing KY, LLC, Louisville, KY, USA

CreateSpace ISBN: 1497421705
CreateSpace ISBN-13: 978-1497421707

ENTANGLEMENT: The entangling of two or more microscopic particles that, even though spatially separated by great distance, can be used for instantaneous signaling.

~*The Quantum Zoo*

Something we do here can be subtly entwined across space and through time with something that happens over there.

~*The Fabric of the Cosmos*

DEDICATION

For M.

TABLE OF CONTENTS

ACKNOWLEDGMENTS

Acknowledgements are due to the following for their help and assistance:
Ray Bennet,
Reverend John Bruington,
Dr. Charles Davis,
Dr. Charles Conley,
Spencer Harper, Jr.,
Pardy Withers,
the Meade County Library,
the Hart County Historical Museum of Kentucky,
and my wife, Martha Jean.

~KFH

The publisher is indebted to Shae Thoman for assistance with the front cover, and is grateful for the proofreading and editing.

Shae used images from Wikimedia Commons as elements in the front cover. The Ouroboras (snake swallowing its tail) is a photograph by Sebastien Wiertz of a carving from a cemetery door found online at:
http://commons.wikimedia.org/wiki/File%3AOuroboros_on_a_cemetery_door.jpg
By Swiertz (Own work) [CC-BY-3.0 (http://creativecommons.org/licenses/by/3.0)], via Wikimedia Commons. The only modification to the image was cropping and replacing the interior with an image of a house which Joshua Applegate may have built for Fannie.

The image of the house is from morguefile.com, is titled housePhillips.jpg, and was created by "taliesin" over eight years ago. The image URI is:
http://mrg.bz/CLhWP0
Little did "taliesin" know that after thousands of views and downloads a photograph she created would be perfect for a mystery/suspense book. Thank you very much.

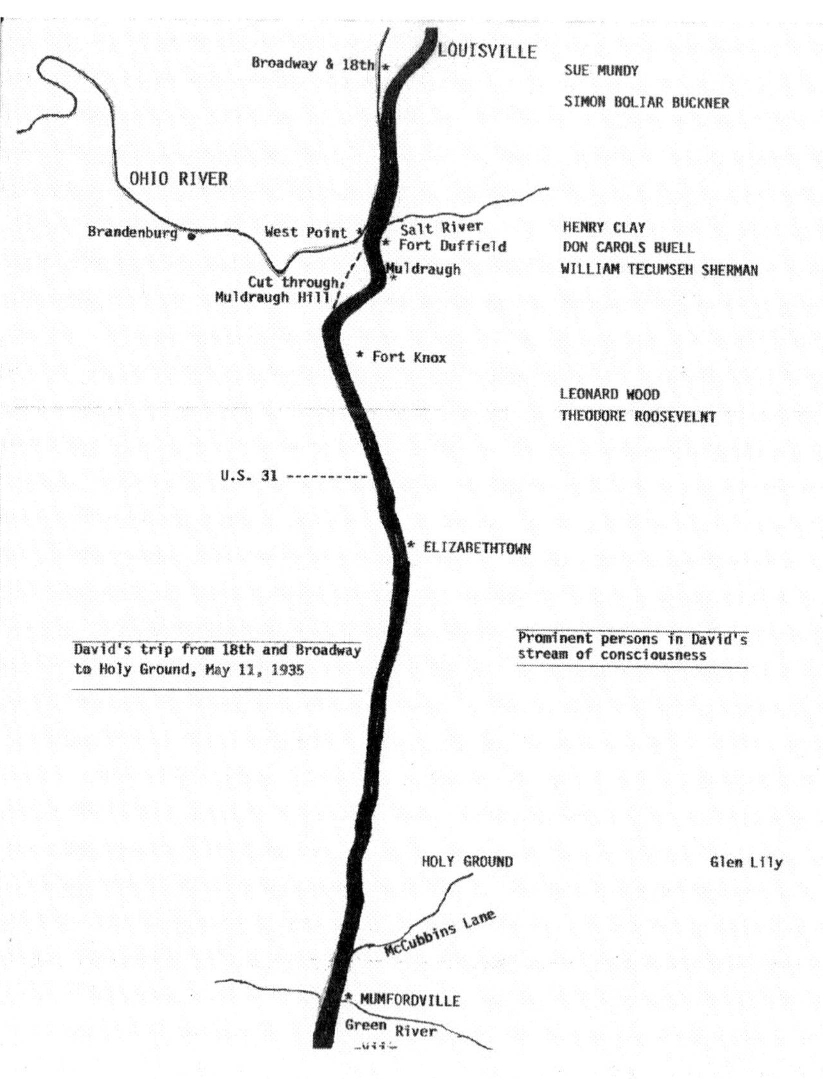
LOUISVILLE
Broadway & 18th
SUE MUNDY
SIMON BOLIAR BUCKNER
OHIO RIVER
Brandenburg
West Point
Salt River
Fort Duffield
Muldraugh
Cut through Muldraugh Hill
HENRY CLAY
DON CAROLS BUELL
WILLIAM TECUMSEH SHERMAN
Fort Knox
LEONARD WOOD
THEODORE ROOSEVELNT
U.S. 31
ELIZABETHTOWN
David's trip from 18th and Broadway to Holy Ground, May 11, 1935
Prominent persons in David's stream of consciousness
HOLY GROUND
Glen Lily
McCubbins Lane
MUMFORDVILLE
Green River

PART ONE

DAVID

CHAPTER ONE

SATURDAY, 11 MAY 1935, 6:30 A.M.

If true, we're puppets on this stage,
'Twould help to hold the strings;
For then we could manipulate,
And bring about strange things.

Two entangled particles instantly respond to each other though they are light-years apart. The same response may occur between two souls separated by time and space. Such is the case of attorney David Crist when he receives a cryptic message from his uncle: Come to Holy Ground tomorrow. I need you professionally.

"I'll need him professionally." That's how David's Uncle ended his telephone message to David's secretary.

Why would his uncle need a lawyer? wonders David, as he turns on the key to his new 1935 Ford.

"Tell David to come to Holy Ground tomorrow morning. It's very important that he comes." That is the first sentence in the message his secretary wrote down on the memo-pad that David takes out of his shirt pocket and reads again. What is so important that a legal problem is involved? He shifts into reverse and backs out of his garage.

Ellen stands at the kitchen door and waves to David. He gives a slight touch to the horn and waves back, and then gives another short toot of the horn to Bobby, who waves from the kitchen window. They had planned this Saturday to go to Crescent Hill swimming pool, but Uncle Bob's message changed their plans. They could go next week, promised David.

Swimming is no longer a problem for David. As an adult David has become reconciled to the red birthmark on the upper part of his right leg. The long shorts he wore as a teenager brought some laughs, but the shorts covered the ugly, red spot. The shorts he now wears bring no laughs but sighs of admiration from women and the lifting of eyebrows by men who envy David's athletic body.

The drive to Holy Ground will take over two hours and, like Bobby's switching from WHAS to a distant radio station and then back to WHAS and then to another station, David's thoughts and images switch from his uncle's message to some sudden thought, then back to his uncle, and then again to another thought.

The sun is beginning to rise over the row of trees, and this early hour has a chill he has never experienced before in May. He is glad that his new car has a heater.

"Need him professionally." comes to mind again. It's Saturday and his office is closed, so he has the whole day to visit Holy Ground. He wishes his uncle and aunt had a telephone, but he is glad that they finally got electricity two years ago. At first his aunt didn't want "electricity running all over my walls" but the benefits enabled her to tolerate seeing black wires stretched from the base of her walls to the center of her ceilings.

It has been nearly a year since David and his family visited his aunt and uncle. They receive a Christmas card each year from David; but their name and address come from a long list, and David's secretary signs his name to look like his signature. To the card Ellen mails is added a few comments about the family, but she insists that David sign his name. It never occurs to David that he sends two Christmas cards to his aunt and uncle each Christmas, and his aunt and uncle both think it wonderful that both Ellen and David each send cards.

He notices that the lights in Peggy's Grocery Store brighten the street corner, while a block farther, the new A&P Grocery Store (The Great Atlantic and Pacific Tea Company) is still closed. These new chain stores have lower prices but they don't give credit. David wonders if A&P, Piggly-Wiggly Stores, and the chain of Louisville Steiden Stores can succeed without giving credit. He remembers that Ellen shops at the new Steiden Store: "I like their fresh vegetable and fruit department," she says.

David likes the lay-out of streets in the newly developed West End of Louisville, that portion of land within the curve of the Ohio River that had been farms for decades. Two blocks to 42nd street and less than six miles to his office in the Staburn Building in the heart of downtown Louisville.

David's father, Andrew C. Crist, of the law firm MacDowell and Crist, negotiated the financing of the Starburn building in 1922, the same year David obtained his law degree and joined his father's law firm, now in the Starburn building. His father had become a partner with Colonel Andrew Jackson MacDowell, after marrying his daughter Angelica, who was named after her mother, Angelica Louise. The law firm became Crist and Crist after 1925, and when David's father and mother retired to Florida, primarily because of her poor health, David retained the firm's name Crist and Crist with the expectation that his newly born son would someday be a partner.

During his last year of law school, David courted eighteen year old Ellen several weeks before suggesting marriage, speaking of marriage as an event in the near future, but not a proposal. It had been David's habit to make such a suggestion to all the girls he dated more than three or four times, and, in his opinions, it proved fruitful. For their first luncheon together, David took Ellen to the new French Village in the basement floor of the Starburn building.

The restaurant was designed like a French Village, with cottages painted on the walls among trees, vineyards, and open fields, and with waitresses dressed in the sparkling colors of French peasants. More interested in Ellen than in food, David ordered sole, one of the several 95¢ entrees. New to being courted at lunchtime and determined to "make no mistake" Ellen ordered what she thought David had ordered: the sole platter. She did not notice that the sole platter, a combination of three fish entrees, cost $2.10. But David did!

Ask them to marry you, and they immediately begin to spend your money, he thought to himself, the "they" being Ellen. That evening, their second date of that day, David had decided he must be sure of Ellen's feelings.

"This afternoon I told you of my plans to take you to Europe and other parts of the world, and of course, we'd have to be married. Will you marry me?" asked David.

David was not totally estranged from his previous courting techniques, and a simple "yes" from Ellen would have sufficed. She, however, looked up into David's eyes, lingered for a second, and then, in a soft, loving voice, said, "yes."

It hit David! This was for real. "I'll buy you a wedding ring!" he exclaimed.

"Oh no!" She had not completely departed from the "being pinned" ritual, which was an understanding about an understanding about getting married.

The next day David bought an engagement and wedding ring combination and that evening placed the engagement ring on the finger of a very happy girl. A month later they were married.

Having earned a sizable fortune, David's father turned the law practice over to David and retired in his sixty-third year with his wife Angelica to Florida, where Henry Flagler (who had helped create Standard Oil) early in the century had established the Palm Beach "season" that had begun to attract permanent retired couples.

Stopping for a red light, David glances at the two books Ellen asked him to give to his cousin Jane, when he stopped by her and her husband's home and general store in Elizabethtown, on his way to Holy Ground. The two books were *Anthony Adverse* and *Gone with the Wind*. Ellen couldn't understand why David didn't want to read these two war stories, since that was his major interest after law. He explained again that his interest was the Civil War. Besides, *Anthony Adverse* was about the Revolutionary War and *Gone with the Wind* was more of a love story than about the Civil War. The light turned green and David wonders what if he hadn't become lawyer? Would he have become a history teacher?

David had considered becoming a minister when he attended confirmation class at Saint Matthews Evangelical Church in 1915. The class met every Friday after school and was conducted by the church minister, Christian T. Richter. David thought calling the minister Christian rather than Reverend was "too religious" but later discovered that "Christian" was the minister's first name.

The issue of military preparedness had been introduced into public debate with the beginning of World War I, and Reverend Richter had explained to David that if he became a minister, he would not have to go into the army, if the United States entered the war.

His father told David that a person entered the ministry for one of two reasons: for one's own spiritual concern or for the spiritual concern of others. If David became a lawyer, he could earn a good living, which would allow him to indulge his own spiritual needs and help others at the same time. David didn't think it proper to enter the ministry to keep out of the army and liked the idea of making a lot of money. He'd become a lawyer, he decided on his fifteenth birthday.

Another stop for a red light and another glance down at the two books. He'll take Ellen and Bobby for her birthday to Stebbins's Grill and then see the new movie with Clark Gable, "Mutiny on the Bounty."

He smiles and shakes his head, realizing that he wouldn't have made a good minister. His early spiritual inclinations had introduced him to Soulcraft and to the publications of the Association for Research and Enlightenment. William Dudley Pelley, a professional writer, had founded Soulcraft, and Edgar Cayce, with his psychic ability, founded The Association for Research and Enlightenment.

On a memorable spring night in California, Mr. Pelley had undergone a completely unexpected and uninvited out-of-body experience. His article "Seven Minutes in Eternity" printed in the *American Magazine* of March 1929, resulted in thousands of letters from readers stating similar experiences. In Noblesville, Indiana, Mr. Pelly began his own magazine and published his own books about birth, life, death, and the realities of Spirit.

The prophet, Edgar Cayce, a native of Hopkinsville, Kentucky founded The Association for Research and Enlightenment in 1931 to research and make available information on ESP, dreams, holistic health, meditation, and life after death. As a youth Cayce had displayed powers of perception that extended past the five senses. Entering a trance, Mr. Cayce "gave readings" in which spoken information would come through him from high spiritual sources in answer to questions. These readings about health questions, meditation, dreams, reincarnation, and prophecy, were made available to the general public through the A.R.E. Headquarters that had been established in Virginia Beach.

David thought it was interesting that Noblesville lay 150 miles north-east of Louisville and Hopkinsville lay 150 miles south-west of Louisville. He was "in the middle" he would tell himself.

With his unorthodox spiritual interests, he would not have been a proper evangelical minister. But a lawyer, yes.

"Is my uncle Bob being sued?" suddenly came into David's thoughts. That seems unlikely. Uncle Bob and Aunt Sarah need to get a telephone. He turns right from Broadway and sees two lines of telephone poles on each side of 18th Street, merging and disappearing far ahead.

Called the Salt River Road, when Louisville was still a small town at the falls of the Ohio River, 18th Street, two miles south-west of the town and part of U.S. 31, becomes Dixie Highway. With the Louisville and Nashville Railroad running parallel, it is also called the Louisville-Nashville Road. The vacant block on the south-west corner at 18th and Broadway is still used for circuses, and David recalls each time he turns on to 18th Street that Sue Mundy was hanged there a few days before the Civil War ended.

David's grandfather, Andrew Jackson MacDowell, served on the army court that tried Mundy and always added more detail each time he told young David about Mundy's exploits and capture. Sixteen when he enlisted in a Confederate Brigade on 15 August 1861, Marcellus Jerome Clarke became Sue Mundy, Kentucky's most notorious guerrilla during the closing months of 1864 through the publicity generated by George D. Prentice in the *Louisville Daily Journal* to embarrass the Union authorities. In March of 1865 Mundy and several of his companions were ambushed by local Home Guards and took refuge in a tobacco barn in Meade County. Surrounded, they surrendered and were taken in chains to Louisville to be tried in a military court.

David's grandfather, a brevet Lt. Colonel assigned to the Adjutant General's Department, embellished the trial and hanging of Mundy after every, "Grandpa tell me about Sue Mundy." Reminding his grandson that Sue Mundy was only a few years older than David, the Colonel told him what Mundy did after being informed that he was to be hanged the next day (March 15). Mundy wrote four letters, enclosing a lock of his hair in each. One was to his sweetheart.

"My dear Mary,

I have to inform you of the sad fate which awaits your true friend. I am to suffer death this afternoon at four o'clock. I send you from my chains a message of true love, and as I stand on the brink of the grave, I tell you I do truly, fondly and forever love you. I am truly yours.

M. Jerome Clarke."

The more times David asked to hear about Mundy, the longer became the story as well as the several versions of the letter. David often wondered how his grandfather could remember all of that. It was the hanging that mesmerized the young grandson.

Mundy was conducted from the Military Prison at Tenth and Broadway to the state fairgrounds at 18th and Broadway where 10,000 to 12,000 onlookers were assembled to witness his execution. After being read that he was to be hanged, Mundy was allowed to say a few words.

"I am a regular Confederate soldier and have served in the Confederate army four years. I fought under General Buckner at Fort Donelson. I have assisted and taken many prisoners, and have always treated them kindly. I could prove that I am a regular Confederate soldier, and I hope in and die for the Confederate cause."

A white hood was placed over his head and the order given to set the trap door "ending the life of Kentucky's most infamous guerrilla," said his grandfather. David had felt a certain sympathy for Mundy, being so young, to die—not yet twenty; but now a lawyer, David accepts the verdict as just and deserving. He enjoys reading more about the major personalities of the Civil War than of its human tragedies, and that reminds him of General Buckner.

In 1914 David had chosen Simon Bolivar Buckner for his junior high school term paper about Kentucky Governors. Buckner, who had died that January, had been elected governor of Kentucky in 1887. Reading that Buckner had been born near Munfordville in Hart County, Kentucky, David had asked his grandfather, Andrew Jackson MacDowell who had been born near Munfordville, if he knew Buckner. Did he ever!

In his mind's eye David remembers his grandfather sitting comfortably in a large wicker chair on the veranda of his colonial home in the east end of Louisville, sipping a cold glass of lemonade, and taking the entire afternoon to tell David, sitting on a footstool in front of his grandfather, about each time he had met Simon Bolivar Buckner.

David's grandmother and Buckner's mother had attended school together. When Buckner graduated from West Point in 1844 and was commissioned a brevet second lieutenant, his parents had invited their friends and neighbors, including the MacDowells, to Glen Lily, their family estate near Munfordville. Young Andrew, age eleven, had gone with his parents to Glen Lily and met Buckner, dressed in his formal lieutenant's uniform.

"I want to be a soldier like you," exclaimed Andrew.

"Well, Andrew," said Buckner, "ask your father to contact our senators to obtain an appointment to West Point when you finish high school. You'll make a good soldier."

For the next five years Andrew's father had written and called on successive Kentucky senators to no avail. In 1851 Andrew became a cadet at Virginia Military Institute. After graduating from VMI as a second lieutenant, Andrew had served one year at several army posts in the West. Returning to Kentucky, he had entered law school and joined the Kentucky Militia. Early in 1861, with the succession of several southern states, Andrew's regiment had been placed on active duty in Paducah, Kentucky. When Ulysses S. Grant, who had been promoted to brigadier general in August 1861, occupied Paducah that November, Andrew was assigned to Grant's headquarters and promoted to captain.

In early 1862 Grant captured Fort Henry and laid siege to Fort Donelson, not knowing that the two senior confederate officers had escaped from Donelson and unaware that they had left General Buckner in command. When Grant received the request for the terms of surrender, his reply was for immediate unconditional surrender. Buckner accepted what he called Grant's "un-generous and un-chivalrous" demand, and signed his name as the commanding officer of Fort Donelson.

Grant was surprised to discover that Buckner was in command. He asked Andrew if he knew Buckner, since both of them were from Munfordville.

Andrew told Grant that their families had been friends and when he was about twelve, he met and talked with Buckner.

"Andrew" began Grant, "General Buckner and I have been friends since our West Point days. Some years ago, shortly after I had resigned from the army, I had a financial problem, which General Buckner helped me to resolve. I didn't know he was in command when I sent - what did he call it? the "un-generous and un-chivalrous" demands for the surrender of Fort Donelson. He's right, of course, but my duty as commanding general of our Union army is greater than any personal obligation to General Buckner.

"What I'm telling you, Captain MacDowell, is personal and confidential. I'm taking you with me to receive the surrender of Fort Donelson from General Buckner. After the formal surrender I shall offer him my financial help, but I can not allow my personal feelings and obligations to interfere. I'm appointing you to accompany General Buckner after his surrender to help him and his command where we can. Buckner will pretend that this war is a sort of medieval tournament, and he'll likely present me with his sword. That will help him play the chivalrous soldier. I'll take it, and then you can return it."

"I said I understood" said David's grandfather, "and we headed for a small farm house outside Fort Donelson."

A stop light at Northwestern Parkway allowed David time to read the billboard across the street: "Go on to better prices at Shilito's." When his grandfather leaned back in his chair and stopped telling about his encounters with Buckner, David would yell out, "Go on! Go on, Grandfather!"

Pleased with his grandsons enthusiasm, his grandfather would remind David of the painting of General Buckner surrendering his sword to General Grant that hung in the living room, and then his grandfather would continue.

Grant accepted Buckner's sword and handed it to Andrew. "General Buckner", said Grant, "I've assigned Captain MacDowell to help you and your command while you are held prisoners at the village of Dover. I understand both you and the captain are from Munfordville." Exchanging salutes with Buckner, Grant and his staff departed, leaving Andrew with Buckner and his smaller staff.

"Andrew isn't it?" asked Buckner.

"Yes General. Andrew Jackson MacDowell."

"I remember. You wanted to become a soldier. You followed my advice, I see."

"I graduated from VMI, not West Point." replied Andrew.

"A Southerner and a VMI graduate! You're on the wrong side, Andrew," said Buckner. His tone was matter-of-fact, not hostile.

"Southern and a VMI graduate I may be," said Andrew, "but at heart I'm a Union man. I'm sorry we've met again under these circumstances, General Buckner."

"Andrew," said Buckner, leaving with his two staff members through the door Andrew held open, "this war isn't over yet."

Each time David's grandfather got to this part of his story, David would ask "Did he go to prison? Did you see him again?" and his grandfather gladly continued.

Buckner had been sent to prison and been kept in solitary confinement a little over five months before being exchanged for a Union officer. David's grandfather had been wounded at Shiloh the following April, spent the next six weeks in the hospital, and then was given leave to recuperate at his home.

In early September of that same year, fully recovered except for a slight limp, newly Brevet Major Andrew Jackson MacDowell was assigned to Colonel John Wilder's command at Munfordville, Kentucky. On the 13th of September Confederate forces struck at Wilder's position. Three days later, after a series of furious attacks, Wilder informed Confederate General Bragg that if satisfactory evidence was given of Bragg's superior numbers, and to avoid the waste of further human life, he would entertain terms of an honorable surrender. Bragg wrote back that he had "20,000 men ready to attack" and gave Wilder one hour to decide.

Early on the 17th, Wilder told Major MacDowell to come with him outside their defense, where both were blindfolded by a Confederate soldier and brought into General Buckner's presence. The blindfolds removed, Colonel Wilder told a startled General Buckner that he had come to get advice about surrendering. He said he wasn't a military man and had been told that Buckner was a gentleman and would not deceive him. He had come to find out from General Buckner what he ought to do. He introduced Major MacDowell, "whom" he said, "I believe the General knows."

David's grandfather said that he was as shocked as General Buckner must have been. "Colonel Wilder hadn't told me why or where or who we were going to see when we were blindfolded. When our blindfolds were removed, my eyes met those of an equally surprised General Buckner," said David's grandfather.

"General Buckner was too honorable a man to deceive Colonel Wilder" said David's grandfather, "and all I could do was listen to General Buckner's reply. His words are still imprinted on my memory."

"Well, Colonel," began General Buckner, "I cannot advise you about that. You are in command of your troops, and you must decide for yourself what you ought to do; but I will give you some facts for which I pledge my honor as a soldier and a gentleman: At this moment you are surrounded by a force of not less than twenty-two thousand men who have orders to open fire at daylight. It is for you to judge how long your command would live under that fire."

Colonel Wilder, looking very solemn, was silent for several minutes. "Well, it seems to me, General Buckner, that I ought to surrender."

"No, Colonel," said General Buckner. "You appealed to me, and I must tell you frankly everything that I think a soldier ought to do." The General said it would be wrong for Colonel Wilder to tell him his strength, and besides, Buckner knew it to be a force of about 5,000 men.

Wilder would have to judge whether he could live under the fire that would be opened on his forces; but should he have information that sacrificing every man would gain his army an advantage somewhere else, it was his duty to do it.

"Wilder whispered to me." said David's grandfather, "'I know of no such information, Andrew." I agreed. "I believe we should surrender," he added. "I concurred."

General Buckner took us to General Bragg to arrange for the surrender. "Well, Andrew, we meet again under different circumstances," said General Buckner. There was no hint of sarcasm in his tone, merely a statement of fact. "It would seem so, General," I replied.

"The surrender was formal," said David's grandfather, "with our 4,000 men drawn up facing the Confederates and each of our men stepping forward and laying down his arms. Colonel Wilder and I were not paroled but exchanged, and I was assigned to the Judge Advocate General's Department."

The sun was high enough, keeping David from squinting his eyes. He checked his gas gauge and decided he'd fill up after he left Elizabethtown. The slow steady stream of traffic allowed him to indulge memories of his grandfather and relive the excitement of listening to those Civil War stories. When the red light turned green David automatically stepped on the accelerator and continued reminiscing about his grandfather's further encounters with General Buckner.

After General Lee's surrender to General Grant at Appomattox and General Joseph E. Johnston's to General Sherman in April 1865, the remaining Confederate resistance was in the West. On 4 May General Taylor surrendered the remaining Confederate forces east of the Mississippi. The remaining troops of General Kirby Smith's Trans-Mississippi Department in Texas had turned into "mobs of disorderly soldiery, thronging the roads, interrupting travel and making life and property exceedingly insecure." Smith learned that General Buckner, his own chief of staff, had gone to New Orleans to arrange terms of surrender.

General Grant had heard that General Buckner had urged his troops to accompany him to Mexico, but the troops did not respond to the idea. Grant wished to end all resistance as soon as possible, including preventing any Confederate forces from entering Mexico. A telegram informed him that General Buckner had made communication with the Federal Authorities on the 20th of May. Grant thought of MacDowell: a lawyer, soldier, and from the same town as Buckner.

Andrew Jackson MacDowell, now a Lt. Colonel serving in the department of the Judge Advocate General, was temporarily attached to General E.R.S. Canby's Command to "advise" the General in obtaining the immediate surrender of General Buckner and his forces in New Orleans. Three days later, Colonel MacDowell was in New Orleans, shaking his head at this seesaw confrontation with General Bucker, one time as the victor, then as the vanquished. Andrew, sensing that General Canby did not appreciate or want an "advisor" obtained Canby's approval to talk privately with General Buckner before the official surrender talks.

David's grandfather enjoyed retelling this encounter with General Buckner, not only because it officially ended the Civil War, but it had also allowed both him and General Buckner to resume a friendship no longer under the shadow of hostilities. With each telling, David noted, the story became longer.

"It appears you are to write the last chapter, Colonel MacDowell," said General Buckner, sitting at one of two chairs in a small room provided for their private conversation. Acting as if he were the host, General Buckner motioned with his hand for Andrew to sit down.

"The last of only one chapter. There are many more chapters in the book, General" said Andrew. Appreciating Andrew's sensitivity to the circumstances, General Buckner raised both hands as a sign of acceptance of what fate had degreed.

"General Grant wants me to assure you that you will not be prosecuted, and the terms of your parole will allow you to return to Kentucky after three years" said Andrew.

"I could have left the country at any time in a clandestine manner," said General Buckner, "but it is not suited to what I regard as the true dignity of my character, to sneak out. It's been almost five years since I've been to my home, Glen Lily. Three more years? You must visit me there, Colonel MacDowell."

David's grandfather would stop at this point and say that he never did visit Glen Lily, much to his regret, although he met Buckner two more times.

David turned the windshield wiper on to remove a few drops from a drizzling rain. He remembered always asking his grandfather to tell him about those two meetings, and, satisfied that his audience of one was listening and interested, his grandfather did.

Running as a Democratic nominee, Buckner won the governorship of Kentucky in 1887. He made clear his intention to veto the numerous special interest bills passed for the private gain of legislators or those of their constituencies. Governor Buckner vetoed more special interest bills than had been vetoed by the previous ten governors combined.

Andrew MacDowell, a Republican, had established his law firm in Louisville and represented a group of individuals interested in the passage of one of the special interest bills. He decided to talk personally with Governor Buckner about the bill, hoping that his and the governor's past encounters might prove helpful.

Governor Buckner personally invited Andrew to lunch, welcoming him to the governor's office. "Finally we meet not as combatants," said the Governor, extending his hand. They reminisced about their encounters during the war. Buckner commented that he had had the "honor" of being the first Confederate general to surrender and the last Confederate general to surrender: First at Fort Donelson and then at New Orleans. Andrew reminded him that he too was at both surrenders, and they both laughed.

They compared tactical points. Andrew believed that General Bragg should have allowed Buckner's regiment to contain Colonel Wilder's forces at Munfordville and march the remaining Confederate forces north and seize Louisville, an important military objective, before Union General Buell, coming from Bowling Green, could reinforce Louisville. Bucker smiled and said Andrew was a better tactician than Bragg. "Louisville was the gateway to the South, and we should have done everything possible to seize and hold it," said Buckner.

As far as the bill of interest to Andrew's clients, Andrew spoke about it at some length and Buckner listened. Their meeting ended cordially, but the bill was vetoed.

Andrew had represented the Kelley Axe Factory, the largest axe factory in the country at the time, in a case some years before. He asked them to make a ceremonial "Veto Hatchet" which he then asked the Republican speaker of the house to present to Governor Buckner. Not to be outdone, Buckner wrote Andrew that he hoped his new "Veto Hatchet" would not separate their friendship.

At the 1896 Democratic National Convention in Chicago, the sound money Democrats, who opposed the nomination of William Jennings Bryan and the free silver platform, formed the National Democratic Party, or Gold Democrats. At their state convention in Louisville they nominated Buckner as their vice-presidential nominee. Andrew, a supporter for gold, attended this convention. At the close of the convention, Andrew congratulated Buckner on his nomination. "Finally, General," Andrew said "we're on the same side."

Buckner whispered into Andrew's ear, "We've always been on the same side, Andrew."

David had been so captivated in remembering the Civil War stories that his grandfather told him that he nearly misses seeing the

West Point sign as he enters this river town located where the Salt River enters into the Ohio.

David thinks about the first buffalo that began this trace, which ancient Indians and later European settlers followed along this route that he has just completed in less than one hour. He puts the various names of the route in sequence with some difficulty, remembering first the Salt River Road, the Louisville and Nashville Turnpike, Dixie Highway, and now U.S. 31. Slowed by a horse driven wagon in front of him, David imagines the wagon to be any early stagecoach, while the several vehicles behind him magically become pre-World War I Camp Knox tanks and other military vehicles.

Patiently driving in first gear behind the wagon, David remembers the first time he read about "going up Salt River" and wondered what it meant. His father could give him no help except "Ask your grandfather."

Grandpa knew. It seems that during the Presidential election of 1832, Andrew Jackson and Henry Clay were both candidates. Clay's key speech was scheduled for Louisville and was expected to give him sufficient votes to win the election. In those days gentlemen enjoyed taking a weekend trip up Salt River, playing poker and drinking mint juleps. Clay took the packet boat ride up Salt River, not knowing that Jackson's men had bribed the captain into delaying the return trip long enough for Clay to miss his scheduled appearance in Louisville. Clay's supporters apologized for the famous orator's failure to return to Louisville in sufficient time by saying he had "gone up Salt River."

David crosses the Salt River, one of the more narrower tributaries of the Ohio, and slows his speed to 20 miles-per-hour as he drives through the busy main street of West Point.

In 1903 the government held large-scale maneuvers in the area around the small river port village of West Point on several thousand acres of leased land. These maneuvers proved suitable for a military installation and the government purchased 40,000 acres, calling the base Camp Knox in honor of Major General Henry Knox, chief of artillery for the Continental Army during the American Revolution and later the nation's first secretary of war. Because of the problem of flooding from the Ohio River, the center of activity for Camp Knox located ten miles further south.

A favorite anecdote David enjoyed telling, when conversation turned to the Civil War, concerned General Don Carlos Buell's army's entrance into West Point in their mad dash to protect Louisville from the advancing Confederate army of General Braxton Bragg. On the 22nd of September, 1862, Buell's entire force of 13,000 men sought billets in and around West Point. Buell himself rode up to the hotel operated by Mrs. Ann McCoy and gave the following orders: "Prepare food for 75 men and be damn double quick about it."

Sympathetic to the south, Mrs. McCoy, a cousin to Confederate General Stonewall Jackson, was not disturbed by Buell's terse military order, and slowly, but politely, replied, "You will get your food for 75 men, but I don't know how double quick it will be."

Every time David told this anecdote, a discussion followed about Buell's terse order. David always enjoyed being able to end the discussion to everyone's satisfaction. "Some years after the war," David would say, "Buell travelled through West Point and visited Mrs. McCoy, apologizing for his ungentlemanly like behavior."

No major Civil War battle was fought in West Point, but the area played a vital role in preventing the Confederate army from claiming Kentucky. Lincoln had said that the loss of Kentucky was nearly the same as the loss of the whole game. West Point was known as a major boat town, supplies, unloaded from steamboats at West Point, were transported south by wagons along the Louisville and Nashville Turnpike.

Union General William Tecumseh Sherman had realized that protecting the turnpike was critical, for it was his only supply route to his southern front. He had constructed a fortification on the bluff that looked over West Point and onto the Ohio River. Located on Muldraugh Hill, the 1,000 foot-long fort served as Sherman's headquarters.

David's grandfather had taken him to visit Fort Duffield when David was in junior high school. Abandoned after the end of the Civil War, Fort Duffield's ramparts, gun emplacements, and structures were overgrown. With his grandfather's skill of description, David easily visualized the fort as it had been during the Civil War.

Civil War fortifications were precisely designed, explained his grandfather. Every angle, mound of earth, and slope were designed to allow infantry and artillery to sweep all the ground in front of the fort. No foe could take refuge in any "dead space."

The romantic, youthful David hoped someday that Duffield would be restored and maintained as a fort, with grassy slopes replacing dense thickets, and with duplicates of the cabins that had been built during the Civil War.

Leaving West Point and glancing to the top of the bluff, David's thoughts flash a particular scene to his inner view, one that he visualized several times after he had read General Sherman's *Memoirs* On a slight rise of land, Sherman sits erect in his saddle with the reins in both hands. As time went on, this returning vision seems to come from a long forgotten memory.

General Sherman is David's ideal of a professional soldier. Besides Sherman's two volume publication of his memoirs, David has read numerous Civil War books which included details of Sherman's actions. When his son was born, David named him after his uncle Robert and General William Tecumseh Sherman: Robert William Crist. David wanted to name him Robert William Tecumseh Crist, but his wife said no!

David considers General Sherman to have been beyond personal ambition and devoid of pride. He admires and, when necessary, attempts to imitate Sherman's fortitude when, under a cloud of ridicule, Sherman was relieved of his command, only to return several months later and prove time after time to be a charismatic leader and brilliant tactician. David's father, grandfather, and Sherman formed a trinity of mentors in David's pantheon of heroes.

Sherman had been supervisor of the Louisiana State Seminary of Learning and Military Academy for a year when Lincoln was elected president in November 1860. When Louisiana followed six of the southern states in seceding from the Union, Sherman tendered his resignation. That March he accepted the presidency of a bank in St. Louis and a few days later was offered the rank of major as chief clerkship. Believing his abilities as a graduate of West Point deserved more than the clerkship position, he declined the position and moved his family to St. Louis.

The following May Sherman was commissioned colonel of the 13th Regular Infantry, which, when filled, would consist of three battalions of eight companies each. Sherman resigned his new position as president of the bank and shortly thereafter went to

Washington at the request of General Winfield Scott, the aged commander of the U.S. Army who was making preparations for defending the capital. Serving Scott in inspection duty, Sherman assumed command of the 3rd brigade of the First division in June, 1861.

In July 1861 some of the men in Sherman's command had become so mutinous that he had to threaten them: if they dared leave camp without orders, he would open fire on them. An officer told Sherman that he was going to New York and asked if he could do anything for Sherman? Sherman asked how he could go to New York, as Sherman had not signed a leave for him. The officer said he did not want a leave. He had already served more than the three months he had signed for, and, being a lawyer, had neglected his business long enough, and was going home.

Noticing the number of soldiers paused about them and listening, Sherman knew that if this officer could defy him, they also would. He turned to the officer sharply. "Captain, this question of your term of service has been published in orders. You are a soldier, and must submit to orders until you are properly discharged. If you attempt to leave without orders, it will be mutiny, and I will shoot you like a dog." Sherman's hand was by his breast under his overcoat and the officer looked hard at him, paused, and then turned back to camp. The men scattered, and Sherman returned to his quarters.

Later that day Sherman met President Lincoln and Mr. Seward riding in a carriage. They had heard of the mutinous atmosphere that Sherman had dealt with and came out to see the "boys." Standing up in the carriage, Lincoln gave a moving address, at one point receiving cheers. "Don't cheer, boys," said Lincoln. "I confess I rather like it myself, but Colonel Sherman here says it is not military; and I guess we had better defer to his opinion."

Lincoln told the men to appeal to him personally in case they were wronged. The officer that Sherman had berated earlier that day forced his way to Lincoln. "Mr. President," said the officer, "I went to speak to Colonel Sherman this morning and he threatened to shoot me."

Lincoln looked at the officer and then at Sherman. "Well," he said, "If I were you, and he threatened to shoot, I would not trust him, for I believe he would do it." The officer turned about and disappeared and the men laughed at him.

The carriage drove on and Sherman explained the facts to Lincoln. "Of course I didn't know any thing about it," said Lincoln, "but I thought you knew your own business best." Sherman thanked him for his confidence and assured him that what Lincoln had done would help maintain good discipline.

The following month (August, 1861) Sherman was promoted to Brigadier General of Volunteers. That same month General Robert Anderson, a native of Kentucky and the commander at Fort Sumter when it was attacked by Confederates, was offered command of the Department of the Cumberland, which comprised Kentucky and Tennessee. Sherman had served as a lieutenant under Captain Anderson at Fort Moultrie from 1843 to 1846. General Anderson wanted Sherman to be his right-hand man.

In his conversation with Lincoln, Sherman had told him he wished only for a subordinate position, in no way desiring a superior command. Lincoln jocularly remarked that his chief trouble was finding places for the too many generals who wanted to be the head of affairs or command armies. Sherman, along with Generals Don Carol Buell and George Thomas, became part of the Department of the Cumberland under the Command of Anderson.

In September the action of the Kentucky legislature amounted to an adherence to the Union instead of joining the already-seceded states. This became a signal for the rebels under General Albert Sidney Johnston, another Kentuckian, to cross into Kentucky to Bowling Green, and then dispatch General Buckner toward Louisville.

Anticipating that General Buckner, who was familiar with the ground around Muldraugh Hill, was aiming for a position there, from which to operate against Louisville, General Anderson ordered General Sherman to secure possession of Muldraugh Hill before Buckner could reach it.

Several thousand Union soldiers used shovels and picks to create an intimidating military installation. On three sides were embankments and trenches and on the fourth, a sheer 300-foot cliff, making the installation no easy target.

Named after its commander, Colonel William Duffield, Fort Duffield served as General Sherman's headquarters.

The next month (October 1861) General Anderson informed Sherman that he no longer could stand the mental torture of command. Three days later General Anderson resigned. By reason of his seniority, Sherman became next in command, a position he had repeatedly told his superiors, including President Lincoln, that he did not want.

A week later, Secretary of War Cameron came from St. Louis to speak with Sherman about the problems he confronted. Cameron and several of his party met with General Sherman in a room of a Louisville hotel. "Tell us your troubles," he said to Sherman.

Sherman requested that their conversation be private, but Cameron said the individuals with him were part of his party, and for Sherman to speak freely. Sherman did.

If General Johnston chose, he could march to Louisville any day. Cameron was astonished to hear this. Sherman stated that his command was responsible for defending twice the line of defense as in the East and West combined, and while both the commanders in the East and West had 100,000 troops each, Sherman's Department of the Cumberland had only 18,000.

Cameron asked Sherman what forces he needed. Taking out a map, Sherman showed that he would need 60,000 men to defend Kentucky and 200,000 men for an offensive into the heart of the Confederacy. Unbelieving, Cameron asked where Sherman expected to obtain such a number of soldiers. Sherman replied that was not his concern; it was the War Department's concern.

From someone in Cameron's party, the newspapers obtained Sherman's estimates and, taking them out of context, called the general crazy, insane, and mad in his demands for 200,000 men to defend Kentucky. General Buell arrived the following month (November 1861) and relieved General Sherman who was then assigned to the Department of Missouri and ordered to report to General Halleck at Saint Louis.

Sympathetic to Sherman's distress at unfounded attacks on his sanity and bitter denunciations of his competency, Halleck told him to rise above such criticism. Understanding that the cares, perplexities, and anxieties of the situation had unbalanced Sherman's judgment and mind, General Halleck assigned Sherman to a post where he might more readily recover. Three months later, on the 13th of February, 1862, General Sherman was placed in command of Western Kentucky and headquartered in Paducah.

Leaving Fort Duffield behind, David admires the character of General Sherman, a dedicated man of duty, who was abused unmercifully and suffered a mental breakdown, only to rise in the ensuing three years as the commander of the Union forces that "marched to the sea."

From West Point David follows U.S. 31 up Muldraugh Hill, passing through several small villages. He wonders if he will have to shift his new Ford into second gear as he ascends the curving road to the top of the hill. Nearing the top of the hill, the strain on his new car's motor suggests David shift to a lower gear, which he does.

He had read of engineering plans to cut through Muldraugh Hill, which would reduce the drive on U.S. 31 by ten miles. That's the progress promised at the Chicago World's Fair, designated "The Century of Progress" in 1933, to which David and Ellen took Bobby.

Another progressive step was having a radio in your car. He turned his Arvin radio on but could only receive station W.H.A.S. in Louisville. The news continued the reporting about the Stresa Conference that had been called by France that April to consider action against German rearmament. The month before, Adolph Hitler had startled the world by denouncing the clauses of the Versailles Treaty that provided for German disarmament.

The Stresa Conference, the radio commentator said, also called for further guaranties for Austrian independence from a possible Nazi take over. While this had been supported by Italy, continued the commentator, the Italian Dictator Benito Mussolini's designs on Ethiopia complicated the attempt at guarantees.

David turns the radio off. Let the Europeans fight, if they must, but the U.S. must stay out of all conflicts, he had concluded long ago. David had been nineteen when World War I ended, and he was not called up for service. Bobby would be thirty in 1955 and too old to be subject to the draft, should serious hostilities result from the demands of Hitler and Mussolini.

David still thinks it is a good idea for Bobby to enter the Junior R.O.T.C. in high school, as he reads the sign "Chaffee Avenue," that leads to the entrance into Fort Knox.

After land was purchased in 1918 for establishing Camp Knox, the towns, schools, churches, farms, and businesses became only a memory. Farms held through five generations were purchased, and the owners sent to seek new homes and livelihood elsewhere. Battle grounds of Native Americans and settlers as well as Civil War skirmishes had no visible evidence of their past except for 119 cemeteries that contained the remains of over 3,800 early settlers.

The headquarters for Camp Knox was located in the area where the town of Stithton had been, all the residents of Stithton having left by 1932. The Stithton Baptist Church and many of the wood frame houses remained, the latter becoming quarters for army officers. In 1932 Camp Knox became Fort Knox.

A mile south of the main entrance into Fort Knox, David sees on his left the beginning construction of the United States Treasury's gold depository, which he understands is to be completed next year. David smiles at the story going around that modern man has advanced to the point where he digs up gold from deep within the earth and then constructs expensive buildings to bury the gold deep within the earth.

What if there's a problem with the title to the farm? Abruptly comes to David's mind. He remembers years ago hearing Uncle Bob talking with his father about a 99 year lease the previous owner, a Joshua Applegate, had been offered by the original owner, J Martin Talmadge, for the fifty acres that became Holy Ground.

David reflects on what he remembers hearing about Joshua Applegate. Applegate had purchased Holy Ground shortly after being discharged from the Union Army when the Civil War ended in 1865, He built a small cabin in the woods in the center of Holy Ground and then some years later added the house.

David's aunt and uncle built the porch with Greek columns and finished the three upstairs rooms after buying Holy Ground in 1901 (two years after Applegate died) from the Church of John the Baptizer, the beneficiary in Applegate's will. Aunt Sarah converted the cabin that was attached to the house into a pantry, where she allowed Uncle Bob to have his work table in the corner.

A month after Aunt Sarah agreed to have electricity installed in the house, Uncle Bob bought her a new refrigerator, which replaced the old ice box in the opposite corner of the pantry next to the entrance to the kitchen.

His uncle had shown David the animal cemetery Joshua Applegate maintained in the woods some distance in front of the house. Several dozen stone markers were stuck in the ground, but only a few of the painted names on them were recognizable. The

"Bea" stood for Beauty (Mrs. Applegate's favorite cat), and "Gen'l Grant" was Applegate's old hunting dog. The largest mound, larger than a human mound, had the largest stone with the word "Hayseed" still visible. David's uncle discovered that Applegate had raised mules, and Hayseed was a favorite. David is sure that he would have liked Joshua Applegate.

Applegate lived at Holy Ground for thirty-four years. and David's aunt and uncle have lived there thirty four years. David dismisses the suggestion of a faulty title. He had asked his secretary if his uncle sounded upset when he called.

"No, not at all," she had replied. "He sounded excited, as if he had won a prize."

Uncle Bob is an eternal optimist and may be making more of something than it is, thinks David. He remembers the stories his uncle would tell him about the war trophies attached to the wall behind his desk: An Apache red bandana and settler-style jacket, a string of wampum beads, an Apache war club, a Cuban machete, and a colorful, Spanish fan made of ivory.

His uncle's desk is a roll top, which David's Aunt Sarah insists must always be rolled down when not being used, so that all the hodgepodge of notes stuck in the cubicles in the back of the desk and the boxes and stacks of papers on the desk are concealed. Periodically she reminds Uncle Bob that this room is a parlor, not a den. David thought of the inside of his Uncle Bob's desk as a treasure trove of adventure and would insist, when he was a youngster, that he be allowed to strike the small Chinese gong on the desk top.

Both David and his cousin Jane spent a week at Holy Ground during each summer before they began high school. Being three years older, David loved to tease Jane. He observed that the cranes always broke up their V-formation, fly about, and then reform, when they were over Holy Ground. David would tell Jane that the cranes did this because some bad person below disrupted the earth waves guiding the cranes, and Jane was that bad person.

Like all young boys, David thought he "understood" girls, but, of course, he didn't. Even though Jane was three years younger, she wasn't taken in by David's taunting into thinking she was bad, let alone that the cranes broke up their flight pattern over Holy Ground because of her. She did, however, ask her uncle why the cranes always changed their flight pattern over Holy Ground.

Her uncle hadn't given much thought to the recurrence of cranes breaking up their formation above and near Holy Ground. He had read portions of Alfred Watkins' book about ancient track ways, which he called "Ley lines" that were alignments created for ease in trekking during Neolithic times, and since these alignments might be oriented to sunrise and sunset, birds, such as sandhill cranes might use these alignments in their migrations.

David pictures in his mind helping his uncle feed the pigs, milk the cows, rubdown the mules, and, when he was older, plow the field. He liked to lord-it-over Jane when he brought in a pail of fresh milk, gave it to his aunt to separate the thick cream from the rest of the milk, and then poured the cream into the butter churn for Jane to operate. "You may make the butter," he'd declare courteously with some air of superiority.

Again, in his youthful innocence, he had thought Jane's quiet manner was a form of submission, but, of course, it was Jane's tolerance of his childish bravado. The rhythmic up-and-down motion of the butter churn handle, magically producing butter, assured Jane of her womanly importance and of David's unknowing. The last step—pressing the butter into a wooden mold and obtaining a round, yellow ball with a leaf design on top—proved, at least for Jane, that woman had the "final say."

The Elizabethtown sign changes David's childhood memories of Jane to the present attractive wife of James Morgan and the doting mother of Trudy Morgan. He drives into the city square and turns left in order to park behind Morgan's General Store. He picks up the two books and decides not to take the umbrella, for the drizzle has become more a fine mist, but the sky is still cloudy.

David's brother-in-law, James Morgan, waits on a customer but nods and smiles in recognizing David, and then motions with his head for David to go to the back of the store. Astonished by the variety of items in the store, David notices a glass enclosed case of knives on the back counter. Resting on a base, the case can be turned to display all four sides, each showing a different variety of small pocket knives. Nostalgically, David turns the case of single blade, double blade, and multi-blade knives with ivory, wooden, metal, and even rabbit-foot handles.

He recalls pleading with his parents when he became ten to be permitted to carry a pocket knife, a sign among his peers of "being a man." Their response "When you're a little older" was repeated a year later and then a year after that. By then, other symbols of manhood satisfied the mores of the "gangs" at school and David, far past "a little older", forgot about owning a pocketknife.

Bobby's ten, but seems to have no interest in owning a knife, David suddenly realizes. Bobby has been pestering his mother to let him wear long pants rather than knickers. "When you're a little older." said Ellen. So now its knickers rather than a pocket knife, thinks David. He decides to speak with Ellen.

After ringing up the sale on the cash register, James Morgan walks to the back of his store. Six-foot four-inches tall with a thick, black moustache, James Morgan is always addressed as James, never Jimmy. His infectious smile disarms others' apprehension of his size.

"What brings you here so early in the morning, David?" asks James, extending his hand.

"Bob called my office yesterday and asked that I come," replies David. David notices James' receding hair line and James is envious of David's full head of brown hair, neatly trimmed and combed compared to his own disheveled hair. "He said he might need me professionally," continued David. "Do you have any idea why Bob would need an attorney?"

"No. He came to town the first of this week to pick up several rolls of linoleum I ordered for him. He's replacing the old linoleum in their panty," says James.

"Is Jane upstairs?" asks David.

"She and Trudy are upstairs. They're going to Holy Ground this afternoon," says James.

He walks to the door in the back corner of the store and yells out, "Jane! David's here." He motions with his head for David to go upstairs as he walks to the front of the store in answer to the jingling bell on the front door.

At the top of the stairs David is greeted by Trudy. "Hello, Uncle David. Mom will be out of the kitchen in a few minutes. This is a surprise."

"I'm on my way to Holy Ground and stopped by to give your mother two books from your Aunt Ellen," says David. He notices on the dining room table the school project Trudy has made from cardboard. "What's this?" he asks, walking to the table. "It looks like a Greek theater."

"It's the Theater of Dionysus. It's a special project for my English class," says Trudy. Thirteen, but going on twenty-three, Trudy Morgan's red hair belies her calm, deliberate manner, and her plain dress contradicts her creative ability and her taste for the exotic.

David bends down to observe the circular seats, made through the arduous task of pasting layer upon layer of cardboard as the half-circle of seats rises from the orchestra. "I'm impressed, Trudy. Were you assigned this project?" asks David.

"No. I chose it," said Trudy.

"Dionysus is the god of wine and wild festivals," says David, admiring the pen work on the architectural background to represent statues, doors, and openings.

"Yes, I know," says Trudy, "but Dionysus is also the god of the cycle of life, like the yearly return of flowers. The theater of Dionysus is the prototype of all Greek theaters, you know."

David nods his head yes, astonished at this sophisticated, young cousin of his. He is concerned that Trudy treats the frenzied dancing and singing of a Dionysian festival too lightly, for the worship of Dionysus was centered in two ideas far apart—of freedom and ecstatic joy and of the savage brutality of the Maenads.

The Maenads were women, frenzied with wine, who rushed in fierce ecstasy through woods to worship Dionysus, ripping the wild creatures they found to pieces and devouring the bloody flesh. David remembers reading how ancient Greeks sent their thirteen and fourteen year old daughters into the forests to release their inherent, primeval wild nature. After centuries, had it evolved into a creative nature and been passed on to future generations? He wondered.

Spirit emerges into visible forms as soon as a channel is open though which it can flow. A spark within the deep recesses of "the mind of God" has merged into the maturing child Trudy, who, at a deep subconscious level, knows that all life is cyclical and not terminal. Woven into the fabric of our minds, eternal recurrence emerges as a truth from those for whom the veil of forgetfulness is not complete. This emergence is for Trudy as normal as is her budding womanhood, and her childlike innocence enables her easily to change the direction of their conversation.

"Mother told me how you used to tease her about the cranes changing their flight pattern just because of her," says Trudy. Before

David can respond, Trudy continues. "Come with me into the living room, Uncle David."

She sits down to the piano. "I'm going to hold the peddle down and push middle C without it making a sound." which she does. "Now I'm going to push hard on C above middle C," which she does. "Do you hear middle C now begins to vibrate?"

"Sympathetic vibration," said David, not sure where Trudy was going.

"I'll do the same thing again to middle C, but this time I'll push hard on D, not C, above middle C."

"Middle C doesn't vibrate," says David. "It's not in harmony with D."

"And maybe there's something out of harmony with the cranes when they fly over Holy Ground," says Trudy in an unintended triumphant mood.

"You're up early on a Saturday," says Jane, taking off her apron as she comes through the door.

"Bob called my office and left a message that he might need an attorney and for me to come to Holy Ground. Do you have any idea why?" asks David.

"No. Trudy and I are going there for dinner today," says Jane.

David remembers that dinner in the country is lunch in the city. "That's great! I may need you."

"Trudy and I can leave earlier, if you think that will help."

"It will. I'll leave now and you follow as soon as you can. This drizzle may stop soon," says David.

Matter-of-factly Trudy says, "The sun will be out before noon."

"I hope you're right, Trudy," says David. "Oh! Ellen sent you two books, Jane. They're on the dining room table."

"The Civil War and Revolutionary War books?" asks Jane.

"Yes, but they're more about romance than war," says David as he begins going down the stairs.

"You should read Tolstoy's *War and Peace*, David," says Jane as David steps onto the first floor.

He turns and says, "I have. It's more than romance and war."

The "more" is what David discovered in Tolstoy's character, Pierre, with whom he readily identifies. A prisoner of Napoleon's army in Russia, Pierre experienced an epiphany that assured him that he was his eternal soul, which David feels reflects Tolstoy's own spiritual experience.

Not a religious man, Tolstoy had gone to the near Orthodox church after his epiphany, only to discover that the church did not understand the experience he had had. He became aware that spirituality is individual, and a religion is founded on a saintly individual's spiritual experience. This resonated within David.

David reaches the first floor and walks to the side entrance. He waves to James, who is helping a customer, and walks to his car.

A block from the town square, David pulls into a Standard gasoline station and asks for ten gallons of gasoline. The attendant, in his green uniform and green peaked hat, pumps gasoline into the glass-container portion of the pump at the top of the red base until it reaches the ten gallon line. He then releases the valve and allows gravity to fill the car's gas tank with the ten gallons.

He wipes off the dried drizzle spots on David's windshield, checks the tires, and after checking under the hood, carefully lowers it. David gives him a dollar-and-fifty cents, assuming the penny more per gallon than at home is because he's in the country.

While absentmindedly viewing the gasoline rise in the glass portion of the pump, David's thoughts had skipped from wondering if the earth's magnetic lines cause disruption in the sandhill cranes' flights over Holy Ground to whether his visit there would be just that—a visit. He would be there in less than half-an-hour, and the image of his Uncle Bob, sitting in the big arm chair by the side of the fireplace, brings back memories of the great war stories his uncle told him during those magical summers of his youth, about the Apache Indians in 1886 and the Spanish in 1898.

The stories never changed, becoming neither less nor more, so they must have been true, believed the youthful David and now reasons the attorney David.

Uncle Bob's father encouraged his son to become a lawyer, doctor, or engineer; but Robert, seventeen and not academically inclined, enlisted in the United States Army in 1885 for three years by stretching his six-foot two-inch muscular body and stating he was twenty-one. Robert was stationed at Fort Huachuca, Arizona and participated in the last campaign against Geronimo in 1886.

It was during this campaign that Robert gained the friendship of Leonard Wood. Lieutenant Wood had taken a position as an Army contract surgeon in 1885 and was stationed at Fort Huachuca. His company had sighted the small band of Apaches under Geronimo and given chase, only to be decimated in an Apache ambush. All the officers except Lieutenant Wood had been killed in the hand-to-hand combat with the Apaches.

Lieutenant Wood, the only remaining officer, had Corporal MacDowell run through the sparse line of troopers to tell them to shoot their wounded horses and lay behind them to fire at the attacking Apaches. A fierce looking Apache with his hand grasping a lance, raced towards Lieutenant Wood just as an exhausted Robert returned. Wood's pistol misfired before the Apache jerked his arm back to throw the lance. Robert fired at the horse. It somersaulted forward, throwing the Apache over its head. Landing on his feet, the Apache raised his war club—a long sheath of rawhide in which a heavy round stone had been sewn—and raced to the defenseless Lieutenant Wood. A second shot through the forehead and the raging Apache lay dead at the feet of Lieutenant Wood.

Lieutenant Wood picked up the rifle of a dead trooper and added to the fire of the remaining troopers as the Apaches withdraw. Aware that his troopers were too exhausted to follow the Apaches, Wood ordered them to assemble and return to the Fort. He singled out Robert.

"Corporal, you saved my life to day. I much appreciate that," he said.

"It were my pleasure, Lieutenant," replied Robert.

Eight years his senior, Leonard Wood befriended Robert and looked after him like a big brother, writing him even after he became personal physician to Presidents Cleveland and McKinley. It was during this period that Leonard Wood developed a friendship with Assistant Secretary of the Navy Theodore Roosevelt.

With the outbreak of the Spanish-American War in 1898, Wood and Roosevelt organized the 1st Volunteer Cavalry regiment. Popularly known as the Rough Riders, the regiment consisted primarily of western cowboys and gentlemen sportsmen from the east. Wood, who became colonel of the regiment with Roosevelt as second-in-command, feared that the jovial manner of the cowboys and the gentlemen sportsmen with their lack of military training needed a small cadre of U.S. sergeants to "shape them up." He wrote Robert, who had retired from the army after his three years were completed and had joined the local militia, asking for his help and offering him the rank of master sergeant and assignment to Wood's staff. "Hostilities will be over in three months, and then you can return home," he concluded in his letter.

After his discharge in 1888, Robert had accepted his uncle's offer as a bank clerk at the First National Bank of Munfordville, where his uncle was president. Robert courted the petite blond Sarah Lou Cummings, who worked at her mother's restaurant in Munfordville for the last five years, and asked her if she would marry him at the end of his three month's enlistment. She said yes and he joined the Rough Riders in Tampa on the 5th of June.

He discovered an army undisciplined and unready. A single train track was backed up for miles outside Tampa. No one was there to tell the Rough Riders where to camp, and for twenty-four hours there was no food for them. Officers provided their own men out of their own pockets. Filthy camps had been set up by earlier arrivals and one had dug latrines just windward of the tents.

Under Wood's orders, Master Sergeant MacDowell and the other regular army sergeants quickly established discipline and set up tents and kitchens. During this "rocking chair period of the war," officers and foreign military attaches gossiped in the Tampa Bay Hotel, a Moorish monstrosity, where peacocks strutted in the exotic gardens. After two weeks of mishaps, the Rough Riders saw the blue-green mountains of Cuba from their ships and were informed that they would land the next day.

Having disembarked at Siboney, Cuba, ten miles from Santiago, the Rough Riders marched into an ambush. Robert stood among the small group of Colonel Wood's staff who were trying to see from where the shooting was coming, but they could only hear the Mauser bullets cutting through the air. Robert observed "Old Icebox," their commander, Colonel Wood, completely cool but fully aware of the danger, give orders for the men to stop swearing and start shooting.

Colonel Roosevelt, Robert noticed, jumped up and down, divided between joy and running away. Colonel Wood steadied his deputy and ordered Roosevelt to take a squad into the bush, signaling to Robert to go with him. Roosevelt's initial panic gone, he led the men into the jungle, staggering momentarily as his sword got caught between his legs.

Robert suddenly pointed to Spanish troops down in a valley, and Roosevelt gave the order to pepper the valley with shots. The Spaniards leaped from their cover and disappeared over the hill. To their right Robert heard cheering, for they had bumped into the advance guard of the Second U.S. Infantry. With the Spaniards breaking ranks and fleeing, General "Fighting Joe" Wheeler, the old Confederate cavalry general, yelled, "We've got the damn Yankees on the run!"

Colonel Wood was promoted, and Roosevelt inherited command. Wood ordered Robert to remain with Roosevelt. "When it comes to fighting, Colonel Roosevelt is perfectly cool and collected and may disregard his own safety," said Wood. "Watch over him, Robert."

Robert observed artillery pieces being wheeled to the top of El Pozo, which overlooked the San Juan Heights that were two miles from the forts guarding Santiago. He spoke to the young man who was sketching artillery pieces, a Frederic Remington who, like himself, had served with the Army against the Indians.

A corporal pointed Robert's attention to an artillery officer. "That's Jacob Astor," he said. "Worth millions. He bought his commission as well as his artillery!"

Early the next morning the American guns opened up and the Rough Riders marched down the valley to the San Juan Heights. Soon they were in the position that they couldn't move forward into the exposed grass at the base of San Juan Hill and couldn't move back into the flood of troops still coming down the road, slippery not from rain but from moisture that was blood.

His first orderly overcome from heat, Roosevelt summoned another to act as orderly. After receiving orders from Roosevelt, the newly appointed orderly saluted and pitched forward, shot through the neck.

Robert heard Bucky O'Neill, the Arizona Sheriff that had joined Roosevelt's Rough Riders, answer the sergeant that implored him to lie down and not get shot. "Sergeant, the Spanish bullet isn't made that will kill me." He turned and a Spanish bullet entered his mouth and tore through the back of his head.

Mounting his horse, Roosevelt found a man cowering behind a bush and ordered him to stand. The man hesitated. "Are you afraid to stand up when I am on horseback?" yelled Roosevelt. The man stood and immediately fell, shot with a bullet intended for Roosevelt.

Five hundred Rough Riders moved into the tall grass at the foot of a hill. Roosevelt waved his hat, swearing and joking, ridding back and forth to rally his men. He realized they would not be able to take the hill by firing. Only a rush would succeed. A half-mile long line of Rough Riders and other troops began to move forward along the base of San Juan Heights.

The only commander spurring his men forward, Roosevelt reached a wire fence only forty feet from the top of Kettle Hill. He jumped off his horse and turned it loose. Two orderlies having fallen away, only Robert remained at Roosevelt's side. He too jumped from his horse and let it loose.

Suddenly two Spaniards emerged from their trenches and began to kneel before firing at Roosevelt. Robert stepped in front of Roosevelt and fired twice. Both Spaniards fell, each shot through the head.

Roosevelt and Robert were soon joined by a melee of men from different regiments. Roosevelt, with Robert behind him, ran down the hill that separated Kettle Hill from San Juan Heights, and two of the handful that followed them were hit. A hundred yards farther and Roosevelt realized that no one else was following him and Robert.

Roosevelt returned and obtained permission from higher authority to advance. He rallied the Rough Riders and the other troops and led them into the valley and up the San Juan Heights. Reaching the heights, they saw the last Spanish soldier fleeing.

Several dozen Rough Riders had gathered around Roosevelt, waiting for a photographer to take a picture of their victory at San Juan Hill. Roosevelt yelled to Robert, standing near the photographer, to join him. Robert did, but shook his head "No" when Roosevelt told him to stand at his right side. He stepped behind Roosevelt instead.

From his perspective nearly four decades later, David doubts that his uncle became aware after San Juan Hill of the emergence of an imperialistic United States. Discharged the following month with Wood's personal thanks, Robert returned to his position at the bank, married Sarah Lou the following week, and two years later purchased Holy Ground. David feels sure his uncle did not realize then that the once great Spanish Empire, that had ruled most of the new world and with it's Hapsburg cousins half of Europe, would soon fade into the history books. In school, reading about the fall of Santiago and the destruction of the Spanish fleet by the United States Navy thrilled David.

The large maps that rolled down over the blackboards in David's elementary school showed British "pink" possessions scattered all over the world. David had wondered then why the United States, always colored "green" on school maps, didn't have more possessions than the "green" Philippine Islands and the few dots of green scattered in the Pacific and in the Caribbean? Now he feels discomfort at such imperialistic views, seeing them emerge in Europe.

In high school David had discovered the interesting fact that the original colonies, and later as the United States, had been in a war once during every twenty-five year period, beginning in 1675 through the Great War during the period 1900 to 1925. He showed this cycle of ten wars to his college history teacher who commented on its coincidence.

Intrigued by such a coincidence, David calculated the average length of the ten wars to be six years. A future war lasting six years would have to occur within the fifteen years remaining in the period 1925 to 1950. David took the middle of the remaining fifteen years—1942—as the middle of a suppose six-year war, obtaining the period 1939 to 1945.

He recognized the naiveté of such prognostication and tossed the paper with his calculations into the wastebasket. In the middle of a depression and the horrors of the recent Great War still fresh in people's memory, there was no way that nations would begin another war, felt David. The cycle was coincidental.

For David the Spanish-American War was more a skirmish when compared with the Civil War, and the Revolutionary War was too distant in time. The twenty-two month war with Mexico was confined primarily to Mexico, and the Great War contained little of the chivalrous and romantic aspects of the Civil War, dear to the hearts of young men. These reasons and the encouragement from the many stories his grandfather told him, David concludes, explain his deeply inherent interest in the Civil War.

Logically, and as a lawyer, David refuses to consider such interest comes from a previous life. But his unconscious spirit, the spirit that lingers deep within his soul, does, even though his environment and inherited culture had buried that spirit at the moment of his birth.

Like the energy released from an ignited log, that spirit will be released unknowingly within David this very day, under circumstances that only that unconscious spirit, deep within him, can understand.

Turning left onto McCubbins Lane, David drives the quarter mile to the entrance of his aunt and uncle's farm. Painted black in old English letters, the faded white sign that David's uncle has nailed to one of the two entrance posts proclaims his farm to be “Holy Ground.”

The overcast weather still remains and David feels uncomfortable as he adjusts to the stillness of the woods, with only an occasional crackle of a crow. He suddenly realizes how alone he is at this moment. The dirt road that follows the base of the hill atop of which his aunt and uncle's house sits, vanishes ahead in the morning mist. He steps on the accelerator, the sooner to see his aunt and uncle.

CHAPTER TWO

SATURDAY, 11 MAY 1935, 9:40 AM

Matter's mostly empty space,
There's not really much of us;
Yet, for this short-lived body,
We do make an awful fuss.

In the world of Spirit, where matter dissolves into massless, subatomic energies and galaxies spiral out of space and time, only unity exists, and joy and life are eternal. David has no awareness of this transcendental world or any desire at the moment to explore it. He, therefore, is subject to the duality of the world of matter, where he emerges from an ordinary but pleasing journey down U.S. Highway 31 into a natural but frightening concern for the lives of his aunt and uncle and a challenging but unexpected mystery.

David parks his new car in front of the house rather than drive to the rear, where the road is rough and filled with farm equipment, goats, cats, and General Pershing, the aging, last of a litter of four coonhounds. The abrupt change from the hum of the car motor and soft, melodious radio music to the serene quiet of pristine nature early in the morning startles David's random thoughts into a keen awareness that something is not right.

Stone steps lead to the house up a slight incline and remind David that he needs to exercise more. The newly painted white front door contrasts with the flaking white columns that support an added porch, the tin roof of which also covers the remainder of the house and has replaced the shingles on the old cabin that became the pantry. Lace curtains obscure two narrow windows in the door's top panels. Long, side windows frame similar curtains with the same filigreed design.

The door is partially open to allow a breeze through the house, assumes David. He hears voices coming from in the house and yells out. "Uncle Bob! Aunt Sarah!" He pulls on the screen door but the hook is fastened. He knocks on the screen door and yells again with no answer. David decides to walk around to the back porch door. He hears talking from within the house, which interrupts the silence that pervades the woods and fields on all sides of the house.

Small stone steps lead from the front porch along the dining room windows to the old attached cabin that his aunt and uncle converted into a pantry. Chickens roam the open space between the barn and the house, and a few goats "maa" within their large enclosed area past the barn. The continual talking becomes louder, which David realizes comes from a radio.

David sees General Pershing sleeping on the porch "Hello, old buddy," says David, taking the single step onto the porch. The old coonhound lifts his head and grunts, and then goes back to sleep. The kitchen door is open and the daily farm report is being given over the radio. David looks into the kitchen at the same time he grabs the screen door handle, calling out for his aunt and uncle with no reply. The kitchen screen door is latched.

David remembers that his aunt always locks the screen doors of the house at all times. Long ago Aunt Sarah came into her kitchen and found her neighbor, Florine Skruggs, pouring sugar from Sarah's sugar bowl into her own large cup, and later, found Florine had entered the kitchen and poured half of Sarah's fresh cream into her pitcher. Upset with such unwelcome behavior, Sarah asked Bob what she could do to stop it. "Keep the screens locked," he said. And she has ever since.

Bending close to the screen, David sees two coffee cups, a glass of what David assumes is orange juice, and two small plates on the table, each with a slice of cake. This time he yells loud. Still no response. He goes to the barn and finds part of a coat hanger. He bends the hook portion and inserts it into the screen just below the latch. A slight lift of the hanger and he unlocks the latch.

David turns the disturbing noise from the radio off and removes the blue and white porcelain coffee pot from the wood stove. The charred wood is no longer hot after boiling the remaining coffee from the pot. A few egg shells near the side burner remind David that his Aunt Sarah always mixes egg shells with the ground coffee beans to keep the coffee grounds together when the coffee is poured.

The coffee cups are still warm and the glass still has two tiny pieces of ice, from the ice cubes made in Sarah's new refrigerator. The cake in front of the place where his uncle always sits (the only chair with arms) has a piece of cake missing with the prongs of the fork resting on the plate. On the counter sit two cakes on pottery cake plates: part of a yellow cake with chocolate icing (Bob's favorite) and a whole Jam cake, Sarah's contribution to the church congregational dinner that Sunday.

On the other side of the table, next to Bob's chair, is an open Figaro cigar box that had been popular in Europe and by 1848 had become popular in the United States. Like all major Havana brands and all handmade cigars, the Figaro box or *boite nature* was made of cedar, which prevented cigars from drying out and furthered the maturing process. Looking inside the cigar box, David sees photographs, letters, papers. A sudden tinkling of glass, caused by a breeze shaking the glass beads hanging from a silver cord in the hall, compels David to step into the hall.

Both his aunt and uncle's farm hats and jackets hang on the coat rack in the corner of the narrow hall. They'd wear their hats and jackets in this morning's breeze, if they went outside, he reasons. They're in the house somewhere. Why don't they answer?

David enters the dining room after calling out their names again. Atop the mantle sit two kerosene lamps. He remembers how Jane would have fun cleaning the chimneys, which he considered dull work, preferring to help his uncle with the livestock. The two windows as well as the single kitchen window are locked from the inside.

He steps into the vestibule and opens the front door all the way, allowing a greater breeze to blow several small slivers of leaves off the hooked rug into the corner where the stairs are next to the wall. He looks at the stairs, recently covered with blue carpeting, then turns to the entrance to the living room.

The large ten-by-eighteen-foot carpet, an oriental rug that "came with the house" when his aunt and uncle bought it, nearly covers the entire living room floor. For a moment he becomes absorbed in the intricate diamond in the center of the carpet, as he did when a youngster, and is again intrigued by the ornate, geometric designs that suggest a lush garden of exotic flowers.

He surveys the room, beginning in the corner with the winged chair, which David pretended was a throne when he and Jane played, and next to which stands the ornate Chinese teakwood table, on which rest a crystal setting for two. He picks up a glass. Dry, as is the other glass.

Cold embers lie in the fireplace, and the desk next to it has the roll top open all the way. This is unusual, David realizes, since his aunt always insists that his uncle always close the desk when he is finished. An 1880's style cigar box, smaller than the one on the kitchen table, sits on the desk. David lifts the lid, which is decorated in soft pastels with pretty girls, and finds more letters, papers, photographs and a leather bound copy of *Marcus Aurelius Meditations*, with the inscription printed on the first page: "From the Library of J. Martin Talmadge" and, in hand writing, "For Joshua Applegate, April 3, 1869."

The carpet bears no discernible marks. A push upon the green drapes on each of the four windows pulled back with golden cords proves that nothing is behind them and all four windows are locked from within. The old upright piano, opposite his uncle's desk, has a stack of music on the piano stool, something unusual for his aunt to allow.

Opposite the fireplace sits the short, red velvet sofa, with one arm higher than the other. As a boy, David never understood why this meredienne sofa should have two different size arms—one higher than the other—and only became more confused when told it was a fine example of French Empire style. On the side by the higher arm, rests the pillow with the figure of Gambrimus, holding a stein of beer and relaxing under a tree, while a spider crawls up his leg. The embroidered caption above his head states, "I should worry?" David looks under the pillow, finds nothing, and, thinking of his aunt and uncle, whispers, "I should worry!"

He now has to face his fear of going upstairs: finding his aunt and uncle unconscious. He resists further thoughts. The stairs creak and the banister shakes as he puts full weight on the first two steps. David finds the door to his aunt and uncle's bedroom is closed when he reaches the top of the stairs. "Uncle Bob! Aunt Sarah!" he yells.

Slowly he opens the door, flips on the light, and looks into the large bedroom without stepping into it. The two beds are made up. A closed bible and a small glass of water sit on the table between their beds. He notices both his aunt and uncle's slippers neatly placed under their beds. Cool nights do not require open windows, and all four are locked from within. The bathroom is at the other end of the bedroom.

The only sign of recent use in the bathroom is the light that is still on over the medicine cabinet, which he turns off. A tube of shaving cream on the washbasin is open with gel oozed out. Hesitating, he looks behind the shower curtain and, relieved, finds only a dripping faucet, which he tightens. The bathroom window is locked from within.

David notices the window at the top of the stairs is locked from within, as he walks through the hallway across from his aunt and uncle's bedroom and enters the first of two smaller bedrooms. The larger of the two had been Jane's and the smaller, David's, when they visited during the summer. David would scratch on the wall between his room and Jane's and make squeaky sounds, until he discovered that Jane, unafraid, slept soundly, while he was awake, making strange sounds and scratching the wall. Both windows in both bedrooms were locked from within.

Before going down the stairs, David counts in his mind all the windows and two entrances of the house, and is sure all were locked from within before he entered. He has checked all the closets.

The attic!

The square opening to the attic is in the ceiling at the top of the stairs. Too high to reach, David gets a small ladder from the barn and looks for the flashlight that sits on top of the refrigerator in the pantry. The flashlight is not there. He looks to see if it has been placed somewhere else in the pantry.

In the pantry, only tools are on Uncle Bob's work bench, which has been moved to the center of the room. The old linoleum under the work bench has been pulled off the floor and lies separated from the linoleum under the refrigerator, in front of which lie a hammer and a screwdriver.

David sees only jars and cans of food on the shelves Uncle Bob built against the east and south walls of the pantry for Aunt Sarah. Nothing is around the old, potbellied stove that sits in the corner next to the window. Jane used to feed long strips of newspapers into the stove and watch them burst into flame. David liked to spit on the red-hot stove and watch the spit sizzle. The only window in the panty, on the east side, is locked, and on the floor are three new rolls of linoleum and a can of glue and a brush.

David carries the ladder up the stairs, hopeful that he'll find the flashlight he remembered being in the drawer of the night table between their beds. The flashlight is there and beams a bright light. He also sees a box of cuff links, a small metal box of Bayer aspirin, a purple velvet jewel case, and a mishmash of oddities.

Turning the flashlight on and stepping carefully up the ladder, he unhooks the latch holding the square door covering the opening to the attic. The low roof allows only a few feet for moving about the attic. The flashlight and the ventilators at both ends of the house give sufficient light to show nothing but empty space, except for one wooden beam that was, apparently, forgotten during construction and rests upon the set beams.

He puts thc flashlight back in the draw and carries the ladder down the stairs. I've checked the entire house and there is no sign of them, he says to himself. The relief in not finding them hurt or, at the worst, dead, has the bitter-sweet opposite of dreaded uncertainty. Where does he look now? What does he do now? He hears a car drive to the back of the house.

David walks out to the back porch and greets Jane and Trudy, each of whom is carrying a package from the car. Trudy hands her package (a large, covered bowl) to David and rushes to General Pershing, who has gotten up on all four legs, waiting to be rubbed under his neck.

"I'm sure glad you're here, Jane. I can't find Uncle Bob or Aunt Sarah anywhere in the house," says David, as he and Jane enter the kitchen. Trudy continues romping with General Pershing.

"They're outside, somewhere," says Jane, nonchalantly, putting her package on the kitchen table and taking the covered bowl from David and putting it in the refrigerator.

"I always bring a bowl of potato salad—German style," said Jane.

David ignores Jane's change of conversation. "They were in the house just a few minutes before I came, Jane. All the windows were locked and both screen doors were locked from the inside. I unlatched the kitchen screen with a coat hanger. Their coffee cups were still warm."

"David, if they're not in the house, than they must be outside. I'll look through the house, David. You and Trudy look outside," said Jane. Her original light hearted response changed to concern. David goes outside and Jane enters the living room.

Jane's concern is that her uncle and aunt are outside and something is wrong. She hears David calling their names out by the barn and Trudy yelling on the other side of the house. In a normal voice she automatically calls out. "Uncle Bob? Aunt Sarah?"

She picks up the coffee pot, its burned aroma still lingering, and places it in the sink. She opens the drapes in the dining room and the light reveals nothing unusual. The slight breeze has blown the bits of leaves into the corner by the stairs, and she decides to go to the living room first.

A careful viewing of the left side of the room reveals only Uncle Bob's open desk being "out of order." On the right side the sheet music piled on the piano stool draws her attention immediately, but her interest is drawn to a single, folded sheet on the piano stand, where the sheets on the stool usually rest.

The sheet, yellowed by time, crackles, when Jane takes it in her hand and unfolds it to reveal a Civil War song titled "Sherman's March to the Sea." Underneath the title is written "By S.H.M. Byers, composed while a prisoner at Columbia, South Carolina." She places it back on the piano stand and walks upstairs.

There is a musty smell in her uncle and aunt's bedroom and Jane unlocks and opens the windows at both ends of the room. She looks under the bed on the side her aunt sleeps and does not find her aunt's work shoes.

She opens the chifforobe and does not find her aunt's housework dress. "Aunt Sarah isn't dressed to go somewhere," says Jane under her breath. Nothing appears changed in the other two bed rooms or the bath room.

Nothing in the house indicates a hurried exit or disturbance, concludes Jane. They must have left the house intentionally. Why?

She goes downstairs to the kitchen just as David and Trudy return to the house.

David enters and sits down at the kitchen table, in Uncle Bob's chair, while Trudy begins to romp again with a not so willing General Pershing. "We should call the sheriff, Jane," says David. Jane shakes her head in agreement. "I'll drive to Perryville and use the phone at the grocery," concludes David.

"Ask Joe Fletcher if Uncle Bob used his phone yesterday," says Jane. "You did say Uncle Bob called your office yesterday afternoon, didn't you?"

"Yes. That's a good idea, Jane. I'll be back in less than thirty minutes."

"There's no bologna in the refrigerator," says Jane. "Bring a half-dozen thick slices for lunch later."

David, leaving through the front entrance to avoid interrupting Trudy and General Pershing, notices that the sun has come out. He looks at his watch; it's a few minutes before eleven o'clock. He remembers Trudy's prediction that the sun would be out before noon. He smiles. Maybe it wasn't a prediction.

He carefully turns his car in the opposite direction and goes slowly over the rough road before turning onto McCubbins Lane and then onto US 31. A mile further and David cautiously parks his car as far as he can from the two old trucks parked in front of Fletcher's Grocery.

He pulls on the metal sign attached to the screen door with the name "Honey Crust Bread" and walks in the grocery, the two old farmers sitting around a table made from an old barrel eye him suspiciously. It has been over two decades since David has been in Fletcher's Grocery, but little has changed, even with the advantage now of electricity. He looks at the man behind the counter.

"Mr. Fletcher?" asks David.

"Yes," says the old man, raising his glasses.

"Mr. Fletcher, I'm David Crist. Robert MacDowell's nephew."

"Bob's nephew!" He extends his hand over the counter. "Good to see you, lad. It's been many a year since you were in the store. You haven't come for candy again, have you?" He laughs and the two old farmers sitting at the table snicker and return to their checker game, now that the stranger has been identified. David ignores the humor.

"I'd like to use your telephone, if I may, Mr. Fletcher."

Mr. Fletcher points to the corner of the store. “Help yourself, son,” he says. Returning to the list he was going over, Mr. Fletcher turns his good left ear towards David, to hear what David says: “Sheriff's Office? This is David Crist. My aunt and uncle (blurred) an hour ago (blurred) off McCubbins Lane.” He hangs up, and Mr. Fletcher pretends not to have listened.

“Owe you anything for the call, Mr. Fletcher?”

“Not a cent. Your uncle was in the store yesterday late afternoon.”

“He called my office in Louisville yesterday and left a message with my secretary,” says David. Not wishing to give any details, David asks, “Mr. Fletcher, did my uncle seem anxious, or ... disturbed?”

Now why would he ask a question like that, thinks Mr. Fletcher. “No he didn't. Came in. Used the telephone. Left, after thanking me for the use of the telephone. He seemed happy: like a man who won first prize in a turkey shoot. Is something wrong?”

“No, Mr. Fletcher. I came to visit my aunt and uncle this morning, but they aren't at home now. If you see them, well, tell them I'm at Holy Ground.” Mr. Fletcher nods his head, that he will.

“I need six thick slices of bologna, Mr. Fletcher.”

Five minutes later David parks in the same spot in front of the house and walks up the steps to the front entrance.
The screen door is not locked. Jane and Trudy walk toward the house when they hear David's car and enter the kitchen.

“We've looked in the barn, the old ice house, the root cellar, and even down the well, David,” said Jane. “The animals have been fed and General Pershing has eaten most of the morning table scraps.” She puts the bologna in the refrigerator.

“What about the cemetery?” asks David. Jane shakes her head no. “Come on. We'll all take a look.” says David.

A hundred steps in front of the house and inside the woods surrounding it, the cemetery is overgrown with tall grass, bushes, native cedars, and is shaded by surrounding maple trees and one large oak. David leads the way into the wooded section, trampling the tall grass to make it easier for Jane and Trudy to walk.

“There are the Applegates' graves,” says David. “Mr. Applegate's mound has sunk a good deal, but hers is in good shape,” says David.

"I can't read Mr. Applegate's headstone," says Jane. "The vines have covered the inscription."

"Mother Nature is more gracious to Mrs. Applegate. Her headstone is in good condition after thirty years," says Trudy, noticing her death in 1897. "Dorothea Shelton Hamilton Applegate. Long name. What are all those little figures over her name, Uncle David?"

"Little cherubs looking over clouds," says David. "They were popular on tombstones back then—a means to show how much the deceased was loved."

"Mr. Applegate must have loved her a great deal." observes Trudy.

"There's nothing helpful here," says David. "We better go back to the house."

Twelve paces to their right, as they return through the path David made, Trudy notices a number of wooden crosses stuck in the ground.

"That's the animal cemetery, Trudy." says David. They stop and David points out that each cross has a name. "Mr. Applegate was fond of animals and buried his pets and other animals he owned here. Uncle Bob buried his dogs here also. There! That new one, marked 'Jennie.' That's General Pershing's mama."

"Mr. Applegate's grave ought to be cleaned up, Uncle David." says Trudy as they approach the house.

Ready to rest after the search of the farm, they sit down to the kitchen table and David pulls the open cigar box towards himself. "This box was on the table when I entered. It may have something to do with their disappearance. But what?" says David.

"I noticed a smaller cigar box on Uncle Bob's desk." says Jane.

"I've seen that box before. Uncle Bob kept it in the bottom shelf of the right stand of his desk, with the Indian relics, odd-looking rocks, and other things he found." says David. "When he showed me the Indian relics one summer, he had to take the box out first, and I noticed the cigar box had "Property of Joshua Applegate" penciled on it. I glanced into the box this morning. We'll look at it also. Trudy? Go get it. It's on Uncle Bob's desk."

David removes a faded envelope from the large box. He holds it up to the light so Jane can read to whom it is addressed: Lieutenant Robert Patrick Henry~ 33rd Kentucky~ Second Brigade~ General

McCook's Division, Department of the Ohio. He removes the folded letter, opens it and reads:

> "24 March 1862
> Dear Robby,
>
> How I miss you! Love you! Robby, please take care. You know I'll wait forever my precious darling.
>
> All my love,
> Angelica Louise"

David hands the letter to Jane. "That's our grandmother's name, Jane. What's the return address?"

"210 Limestone, Lexington, Kentucky." says Jane.

"That's in downtown Lexington. I remember our grandmother lived on Limestone. That must be she, before marrying Grandpa," says David. "That explains how Uncle Bob got his name: She named her first son Robert Henry after Lieutenant Robert Patrick Henry."

"And she named mother (her first daughter) Angelica, after herself; and her second daughter (Aunt Louise) also after herself," says Jane.

"Probably grandpa wanted his two daughters named after their mother," says David. "Angelica Louise didn't wait long for Lieutenant Henry," says David, smiling.

David places the note and envelope on the corner of the table and retrieves another faded piece of paper from the cigar box. Trudy enters the kitchen and places the small cigar box on the table and sits down.

"This is written in ink with a hurried hand. It's dated 9 September 1862. Munfordville. Kentucky." says David:

> "Attention U.S. Army Pay Master;
>
> The chest and contents of wrapped greenbacks was discovered in a barn near Munfordville, Kentucky. Give receipt to Lt. Robert Henry.
>
> Major A.J. MacDowell
> Colonel J.T. Wilder, Commanding

"A.J. MacDowell. That's grandpa!" exclaims David.

"Here's our Lieutenant Henry again. This is becoming a family affair."

"Or a triangle affair." Says Jane.

"I doubt that." says David. "I know our grandfather didn't know our grandmother until after the war was over."

David touches two small slips of paper, each the size of two rectangular stamps attached at the narrower sides. They each have two holes made by small pins. He holds one up to the light, the faded writing barely visible.

"Lieutenant Robert Patrick Henry, Glenbrook Farm, Lexington, Ky." David holds the second slip up to the light. "Sergeant Peter O'Conner, Morehead, Kentucky." He lowers his hand and explains. "During the Civil War there was no official identification for each soldier, so most of them wrote their name and address on a slip of paper and fastened it to their clothing for identification if they were wounded or killed. I wonder why Applegate would have kept them?"

"Maybe he intended to write their families," says Jane.

"That would have been the army's responsibility. He should have given the identifications to his captain."

"Why would Mr. Applegate have the lieutenant's identification, our grandfather's note, and the love letter?" asks Jane.

"The lieutenant was probably killed and Applegate took them from his pocket," says David. "It was probably during the Battle of Munfordville that followed, which took place about that time. The battle doesn't compare with later battles or with the staggering loss of men in later battles, but it kept the Confederates out of Kentucky."

"We're not finding anything that will help us locate Uncle Bob and Aunt Sarah, but we're learning something about Joshua Applegate." He reaches into the box.

"What have we here?" asks David. "A list of names with a dollar amount opposite each name." He shows the list to Jane and then reads:

"February 3, 1865, Charlie Brumley, $25; February 15, 1865, Jacob Dobbs, $50; March 2, 1865, the Straubs, $300…why there must be a hundred names listed and a considerable amount of money. The last entry is 1874: Tim and Mary Shackelford, $400."

"Gifts?" asks Jane.

"Apparently. No other markings to indicate payment—just a list," says David. He makes a quick calculation of the total. There must be several thousand dollars recorded. I wonder where Mr. Applegate obtained that much money to give away?" The list ends. David subtracts 65 from 74 in his mind—nine years later. "Why did the gifts end?"

"There's more in the box," says David, removing a photograph in the brownish hue of early photography: A young girl of seventeen or eighteen looks over her shoulder with a coquettish smile and "For my darling Josh" written below. It is signed "Fanny." David hands the photograph to Jane and lifts his eyebrows.

"Let me see," says Trudy. "Humm!"

Next, a faded blue hair ribbon.

"Fanny's?" asks Trudy.

"Fanny's," say David and Jane, each smiling.

"What's this?" says David, holding a packet of wrapped greenbacks. The faded, brittle wrapper cracks and a hundred bills wave like a fan in David's hand. "They're all fives, with a 1862 date, this is five hundred dollars!"

"The greenbacks mentioned in the note to the army paymaster?" asks Jane.

"Must be," says David.

"The money for the gifts!" says Jane.

"The note to the paymaster said 'wrapped greenbacks'," says David. It may have been a payroll. Certainly thousands."It would appear the paymaster did not get the greenbacks but Joshua Applegate did." He places the bills in front of the other items.

David looks in the near empty box. He sees something wrapped in a white handkerchief. He removes it and unwraps a small, ornate black handled knife in a black scabbard, six or seven inches in length. Silver designs decorate the tip of the scabbard, and an oval silver band is attached to the knife where it fits into the scabbard. A silver crown with a jewel at the top covers the pommel, and a silver crest is fastened on the grip. He withdraws the blade. The upper part of one side is serrated and the other is sharp.

"It's a hunting knife." says David. As an afterthought, "And a weapon, if necessary." Wouldn't I love to have owned a knife like this when I was a boy, says David, silently to himself as he hands the knife to Jane.

She refuses to take it. She doesn't want to touch it. Trudy reaches for it and pulls the knife partially from the sheath. She studies the several silver designs and then gives it back to David. He holds a single greenback taken from the box, not part of the wrapped package of greenbacks.

The bill is crumbled and torn. David turns the bill over. "Listen to this," he says and reads: "Corporal John Tafel and Corporal Josh Applegate. Galt House Oct 1 1872."

"The Civil War ended in '65," says Jane. "That date is seven years later."

"It's a pledge to meet after the war is over. People do that all the time. I agreed to meet ten years later with three of my buddies after high school graduations at West Baden Spring in Indiana. That would have been a year before the depression. I forgot all about it, until I found the dollar with our four names in an old school book several years later. Probably Mr. Applegate forgot about his 1872 meeting also."

David tilts the box, reaches in, and removes an open envelope. "This is all," says David, as he removes the letter in the unaddressed envelope. He unfolds the letter and scans it. "It's our Lieutenant again," says David. He reads aloud:

"September 9, 1862

My darling Angelica,

I go on a special detail early this morning and am taking a few minutes to write you now. More to follow when I get back.

A large Confederate Army faces us and I look forward to my first battle. I've tied your white silk scarf you gave me around my neck for extra protection. Thank you, my darling. I shall make you proud of your future husband. I put a kiss on the ring I placed on your finger last month, a kiss for you, my own dear Angelica.

"We will hold off these rebels until General Buell sends us reinforcements. You will ..."

"The lieutenant's letter ends there," says David. "He was probably called to report for duty immediately and put the letter in his pocket to finish it later, but he was killed in battle."

A car drives up to the front of the house.

"That's probably the sheriff," says David. "See if it is, Trudy."

Trudy walks to the front door and yells to the kitchen. "It's the sheriff. He's coming up the walk. He's a big guy, Uncle David. (She emphasized big.)

David goes to the front door and steps out onto the porch. "I'm David Crist."

The six-foot-four-inch sheriff is all business: no smile, no initial small talk. A firm jaw on a square face with a handsome but cruel countenance, the sheriff has two faint streaks running from the top of his right eyebrow to the curve of his lip, as if two claws scratched him. David initiates the conversation. He sees the name identification on the sheriff's form-fitting, highly starched shirt with two fine creases, each passing over the hidden nipples. The shiny name plate is meticulously placed parallel with the top of his right shirt pocket with the center of the plate exactly over the single button. His tan campaign-style hat with its broad brim is cocked forward, so that he always appears to be "looking down" at the person or persons to whom he is speaking—something that his dark sun glasses reinforce.

"Come inside Sheriff O'Connell."

They enter the living room, and David points to a chair, which the sheriff ignores and remains standing. "You reported your aunt and uncle missing. When did you determine this?" asks the sheriff; his eyes slowly observing the walls and furniture of the room. His few minutes with David confirms his initial feeling that he does not like David Crist.

David describes the events of the last three hours, stressing that he found the house completely locked from the inside. Trudy and Jane enter and David introduces them to the sheriff, whose only acknowledgement is a nod of his head.

"How old are your Aunt and Uncle?" asks the Sheriff."

"They're in their late sixties."

"If they are not in the house, as you state, Mr. Crist, then they must be outside," says the sheriff. "They've gone visiting and will be back soon," says the sheriff, in the condescending manner of a pedant.

"They were in the house, as I said, only minutes before I arrived and both the screen doors were locked from the inside," says David, containing his annoyance.

"You thought they were both locked. That's usually the case," says the sheriff. "I'll drive down McCubbins Lane for a mile or so and I'll inform my deputies." He turns and walks to the door.

David feels a visceral hostility towards the sheriff. He follows the sheriff to the door. "And if they don't come back?" he asks in the cold tones of an attorney.

The sheriff concludes that his first impression was correct: this fellow will prove to be a problem. "Then call me before five o'clock," says the sheriff, tipping his finger to the brim of his hat and nodding to Jane and Trudy, before leaving the house.

"He's not very helpful," says Jane.

"I don't think he likes you, Uncle David," says Trudy.

"The feeling is mutual. I don't trust him. I know his kind. He thinks he's God. He'll go by the book. Nothing more."

"You speak as if you know him, David," says Jane.

"I do. I come across his kind in court every day."

"I think it's more than that, Uncle David," says Trudy.

Trudy's words jar David from his negative, primeval feelings to his professional, rational thinking. "My Trudy is atop Mount Olympus again," says David, smiling, as he pats her on the shoulder. But inside David, something says she's right. He has a deep hatred for this man whom he met a few minutes ago for the first time.

Like all worldly mysteries not explained through conventional knowledge, David's unreasonable feelings of hatred can be understood only through transcendental wisdom; which, however, is something foreign to his classical education. David takes both Jane and Trudy by their elbows.

"Let's look through the other cigar box," he says.

David feels certain that this larger cigar box – or more properly, the contents of the box—is the cause of his uncle's telephone call. What they have found inside the box does not warrant his uncle asking David to drive to Holy Ground. His uncle, however, may have taken something from the box that does.

All three sit at the kitchen table with the small box in front of David and the larger one and its contents to the side of the table.

"Do you see a difference between the two cigar boxes other than size?" asks David.

"The small one seems 'crisper' than the larger one," says Trudy.

"The large one has a musty smell and a moldy look," says Jane.

"I agree with both of you," says David. "The small box has been in uncle Bob's desk for years: a nice, warm place. It's become 'crispy'. Uncle Bob must have recently found the larger box—maybe yesterday—probably in the ground, possibly in the old section of the barn," says David.

"And they've gone back to see if they left anything behind!" exclaims Jane.

"Right!" says David.

"Wouldn't they have left a note for you, Uncle David? And it's been three hours," says Trudy.

If they left to find something left behind, Uncle Bob and Aunt Sarah should be back soon. If not, David, Jane, and Trudy will have to wait until five o'clock.

"You're right, Trudy. They would have left a note if they expected to be gone some time, certainly three hours. We'll have to wait until five to call the sheriff's office. That's plenty of time for us to see what's in the smaller box."

David takes a small book from the box. "I found this copy of *Marcus Aurelius Meditations* this morning. It's a gift to Mr. Applegate from J.M. Talmadge, whom, I assume, is an ancestor of our Uncle Bob and Aunt Sarah's neighbors, the Talmadges at Twelve Oaks," says David.

"Did you notice the folded sheet of music on the piano stand, David?" asks Jane.

"No, I didn't. I did notice the stack of music on the piano stool. That surprised me; something Aunt Sarah would not approve," says David.

"Trudy? Go get that sheet of music," says her mother. Trudy leaves and Jane continues.

"It was an old Civil War song about Sherman's march to the sea," says Jane. "I'm sure it must have been in this small box, and when Uncle Box discovered the larger box contained things belonging to Mr. Applegate, he looked through this small box, maybe for the first time. My guess is he put the sheet of music on the piano stand for Aunt Sarah to play later, and then put the other sheets of music on the stool."

"How could Aunt Sarah sit on the stool with all those sheets of music?" asks Trudy.

"She didn't," says David. "They probably began looking through the larger box, and Uncle Bob forgot about asking her to play the tune."

"Well, Joshua Applegate seems to have collected a great deal of things about the Civil War," says David. "It's possible Uncle Bob found something in this box that precipitated his call to me." He takes out a single sheet.

"Another list," says David. He glances over it for a moment then smiles. "This is a list of names and burial location of the animals Applegate buried in the animal cemetery. Listen to some of the names: Sherman, Sheridan,—there's the Civil War again— Skillette, Toulette, Bobo, Sal. These must be all dogs. There are several names under mules: Ted, Billy, Gertrude.

"This is odd. About a dozen names under stuffed: Willie, Jamie, Gus, and Bushy. I guess stuffed means taxidermy." David places the sheet opposite the sheets from the larger box and takes out a scroll-like sheet from the box.

"A marriage license!" exclaims David. "Joshua Clay Applegate and Dorothea Hamilton Applegate, dated November 22, 1874. Didn't use her other middle name. What was it?"

"Shelton," says Trudy.

"That's right. Maybe she was a widow when she married Applegate," says David.

"According to the tombstones she was two years older," says Trudy.

"Didn't the list of cash gifts end in 1874?" asks Jane.

"I think you're right, Jane," says David.

"She is, Uncle David. It was 1874," says Trudy.

"That's probably not a coincidence, but I'm not sure it helps us," says David. He places the marriage license with the list of animal names and pulls out a printed form that proves to be the deed to Holy Ground.

David reads the deed to himself. "It's a deed for fifty acres, transferred from Jose´ Martin Talmadge to Joshua Clay Applegate, dated February 10, 1865," says David.

"Wasn't the Civil War still going on then?" asks Jane.

"Yes, until April," says David.

"Mr. Applegate wouldn't be buying property while still in the army," says Jane, more as a question than statement.

"He'd probably been discharged early. By the end of 1864 and into early 1865 the Union no longer needed a large army," says David.

"I assume Uncle Bob didn't call me about any problem with the deed to Holy Ground." David places the deed on the beginning of the pile of material from the small box. He pulls out a document.

"Here's his discharge," says David. "Sergeant Joshua C. Applegate, 6th Kentucky Voluntary Infantry ... discharged January 2, 1865."

"He was home the first of the year then," says Jane.

"He certainly didn't waste any time to buy land," says. David. "He may have received a bonus with his discharge to buy land. A number of reenlistments promised a bonus after discharge."

David takes a leather cigar case from the box. It is personalized in gold: Joshua C. Applegate. "Rather fancy," says David. Probably held five cigars. Most men smoked cigars then."

He takes two items from the box: a medal and a piece of material. The bronze medal is attached to a purple ribbon with a pin attached. It's inscribed For Valor and has crossed rifles on one side. The other side is blank. No note is attached.

David unravels the material, a strip of red with the letters "ssippi" in white. "Part of a rebel flag, probably a Mississippi regiment," says David. "Both the Union and the Confederates would tear off strips of a captured enemy flag and keep it as a war souvenir."

A daguerreotype, with "1874 Dorothea and Joshua wedding" printed in a beautiful script on the back shows a handsome Joshua, sitting in a chair and Dorothea standing behind him. His serious expression contrasts with Dorothea's gentle smile—she's pretty, but not beautiful.

David gives a sheet to Jane. It is a list of furniture with a date and dollar amount for each item. Jane reads aloud; "Dresser Jun.

1868, $50; poster bed Oct. 1868 $79; cabinet, Mar. 1869, $45 ... why there must be twenty pieces of furniture listed, David. Where did he put it?"

"Maybe he sold it." says Trudy.

"The dates stop in 1874," says Jane.

"When he married." says David.

"Dorothea probably had something to do with it," says Jane.

David looks in the box and brings out two sheets of paper and a small notebook. One sheet is from an attorney informing Joshua that Mr. J.M. Talmadge in his will gives ownership to the 10 by 18 foot oriental rug at Twelve Oaks to Joshua C. Applegate.

"It has to be the rug in the living room. It either came with the house when Aunt Sarah and Uncle Bob bought the house or they purchased it separately," says David.

The other sheet is a note from J.M. Talmadge, which David reads aloud. "*War And Peace* is a great book, Joshua, and I present it to you on your birthday. It is really two stories: One, the War of 1812, when Napoleon invaded Russia; and the second, concerning the several families and their problems in Moscow at that time. The author, Leo Tolstoy, like you, experienced an afflatus in his youth, and this divine imparting of knowledge changed his life. Wishing you many more Happy Birthdays. August 17, 1884. JMT."

"Well, that's interesting. Joshua Applegate must have experienced some beatific vision," says David.

"What does "afflatus" and "beatific vision" mean?" asks Trudy.

"It's the awareness by some gifted individuals of the whole universe," says David."

"It's a state of oneness with God, Trudy," adds Jane.

"This tattered, black notebook is the last item in the box," says David. He looks and scans several pages while Jane and Trudy look at Mr. Talmadge's note about *War And Peace*. Jane suggests that Trudy see if the copy of *War And Peace* is on Uncle Bob's bookshelf, which she does.

"Listen to this Jane," says David. "These are thoughts that Applegate wrote down through the years, beginning in 1875, shortly after he was married and probably about the same time he had a religious experience.

"'Every spiritual lesson I need to learn today is contained within the experiences I will have today.' He wrote that in 1876." David continues to read. “God is not an explanation but an experience.” David hands the book to Jane. “That’s good. He wrote it in 1882,” says David.

Jane turns several pages and reads: “Knowledge is seeing the parts: wisdom is seeing the whole.” She gives the notebook back to David. “Interesting,” says Jane.

David places the notebook on top of the other items taken from the small box and leans back in the chair. Trudy enters and places a large worn book on the table, with “*War and Peace* by Count Leo Tolstoy” printed in gold on the faded, green cover. She opens to the first page and points to: “From the library of Joshua Clay Applegate.”

David scans the pages. “Full of notes, written in the margins,” he says. He stops near the end of the book and reads to himself words written along the margin.

“What does it say?” asks Jane.

“Did you ever read *War And Peace*, Jane?” asks David.

“It’s too long. No I haven’t,” says Jane.

“Pierre is a major character in the book. Listen to what Applegate wrote on the margin about him. ‘Pierre’s experience of an epiphany assured Pierre that he was his own eternal soul. This reflects Tolstoy's own spiritual experience, as it does mine.’ Applegate is becoming an interesting individual,” says David.

David continued, “Epiphany, in this context, is another word for divine awareness, Trudy. Applegate read *War And Peace* at least once.” He pushes the book to the side of the table.

“There's a piece of paper in the bottom of the box," says Trudy.

“Hand it to me, Trudy,” says David.

“This is a note from the Church of John the Baptizer to Pastor Joshua Applegate ... in appreciation for ten years of faithful service,” reads David. “Apparently it accompanied a gift. Applegate's spiritual experience must have led him to the ministry.” He hands the note to Jane.

“All of this material tells us a good deal about Applegate, and I think he or something from the larger box that Uncle Bob must have found the day before calling me is the cause of him and Aunt Sarah not being here now,” says David.

“Uncle Bob and Aunt Sarah were looking through this large box on the table,” says David. He speaks his thoughts without necessarily addressing Jane and Trudy. “They must have left the house voluntarily, probably because of something in the box, which they probably took with them. They apparently didn't expect to be away long." He looks at Jane and Trudy.

"What's caused this?"

PART TWO

JOSHUA

CHAPTER THREE

WEDNESDAY, 10 SEPTEMBER 1862, 7:30 AM

We dream we are a sinner,
And wake to find it true.
We pray we live forever,
And then are born anew.

The soldier's life of endless drilling, marching, waiting, is overshadowed by the ever existing possibility of impending battle, and death becomes his constant companion. The recruit balances his feelings between proving his manhood and avoiding permanent injury, death being something that happens to others, but not to him. The Union recruit, Joshua Applegate, not yet eighteen, willingly accepts a soldier's daily routine but prays that the bullet, shell, or bayonet has not been made with his name on it, nor will it ever.

As a virgin, he considers it the greatest wrong to be killed before ever having loved a girl.

It is 7:30 in the morning, on Wednesday, the 10th of September, 1862, four months since he enlisted in the 33rd Kentucky Infantry, the detachment (to which he belongs) being assigned as scouts by Union Colonel John T. Wilder, since they were not equipped with arms.

Colonel Wilder assumed command of the troops at Munfordville, Kentucky on Monday, the 8th of September. Informed that Confederate raiders had destroyed the bridge over the Salt River in his rear, Wilder sent out foraging parties to scout the country for bacon, flour and other necessities, should his supplies from Louisville be cut off.

The morning is crisp and slightly fogy, as Joshua and the other scouts south of Munfordville extend the distance between each of them by several hundred yards. Finding no trace of enemy soldiers and hearing no artillery or rifle fire, the walk through lush fields and over crude fences becomes a morning stroll, allowing Joshua to reminisce.

Joshua's joining the Union Army began with the election of Abe Lincoln. Like most Kentuckians, Josh considered himself a Southerner as well as a Union man; and, although he was too young to vote, he supported John Bell, the Constitutional Union Party nominee for president, who condemned the two sectional parties. Again, like most Kentuckians, his heart would have voted for the southern nominee, John C. Breckinridge, while his reason would have required him to vote for the Democratic nominee, Stephen A. Douglas; but fear of hostilities, led him to support Bell, who carried only Kentucky and the two other border states.

The Kentucky legislature resolved in May of 1861 to be neutral, after Lincoln (who said he hoped God was on the Union side, but he had to have Kentucky) assured the state that no troops would be sent to Kentucky if it remained peaceful. A further assurance was Lincoln's statement that the war was fought to preserve the Union, and not to free the slaves.

On the 3rd of September, 1861, Confederate forces crossed from Tennessee into Kentucky, occupying Hickman and Columbus. Three days later Ulysses S. Grant occupied Paducah, Kentucky. The Kentucky legislature then declared Kentucky a Union state, and the struggle for the possession of Kentucky began.

During this time Joshua helped his uncle-in-law, Hank Bonger, raise, sell, and deliver mules to the Union. His uncle would gladly have sold mules to the Confederates, but when they blew out one of the piers of the railroad bridge across the Green River at Munfordville, they took several of his mules and reimbursed him with worthless script.

Joshua had a way with mules. He'd saddle up slowly to the side of the mule, facing in the opposite direction, eye to eye. He'd hum and whisper soft, soothing sounds into its ear, and then gently stroke the mule under its neck. Within a few minutes the mule would do what Josh wished it to do—most of the time. He had better results with female mules, but most of the mules his uncle bred were the sterile male mules. His uncle told Joshua he'd make a good teamster.

The soldier on Joshua's left, Jamie Cutler, pointed to a barn and burned down house with only the brick chimney standing, several hundred yards ahead of them. He motioned for Joshua to check it out. Jamie's brother, Ben, had been killed at Shiloh that April—the first casualty from Hart county. That's when the war first came home to Joshua. The following May, when he and his uncle took a dozen mules to Elizabethtown for the Union, Josh determined to enlist.

His 5' 10" height and dark face-stubble gave credence to Joshua's statement that he was twenty-one years old. The sergeant who enrolled him in the 33 Kentucky only looked up to Joshua when he told him to sign his name. That night he told his Uncle Hank and Aunt Mary that he had enlisted and would leave the next day.

"Keep your feet and clothes dry and in good condition all the time," said his uncle. "Drink only good water, and don't drink too much at one time after a long march. And, Josh, stay away from scarlet women—wait for that when you're older and at home," said his uncle late that night.

"Write, when you can, Josh," said his aunt. "Don't swear or mingle with them that does. Keep clean – inside as well as outside. Treat all young ladies as if they were a sister. Keep an extra pair of socks and underwear," said his Aunt Mary the next morning before giving him a kiss on the cheek and a bag. Later that afternoon, Joshua opened the bag and found a sandwich and dried fruit and a pair of socks and underwear.

Half way to the barn Jamie had pointed to, Josh reaches down to his right sock and feels the knife concealed there. He smiles as he remembers receiving it from his aunt when he was twelve.

It was during recess, when he was the only fifth grader in school among fifteen other students, that he found a small pocket knife hidden among the tall grass. He saw Fred Schradder, the only seventh grade student, looking around the playground, asking everyone whether they had seen his knife. When Fred asked him, Joshua shook his head no, considering not saying anything kept him from lying.

The next day Joshua's teacher, Miss Blanch, came to his house after school and spoke with his aunt, while Joshua was helping his uncle. That evening during supper, his aunt asked Josh, "You have a new knife?"

Unprepared for such questions, Josh nodded his head, yes, and asked for more potatoes. His aunt took the bowl to the stove and filled it with more potatoes. Placing the bowl in front of Josh, she continued her questioning.

"Did you find it?"

"Yes." That was the truth. He gave his attention to the potatoes.

"Does it belong to someone?" she asked.

"I guess it does," seemed a safe reply.

"Who?"

This question didn't provide much wiggle room. "I don't know" would be a lie. "I think Fred Schradder."

"Then you should give it back to him." His aunt returned to the stove and nothing more was said about the knife or about Fred Schradder. The next morning before school began; Joshua met Fred Schradder before they entered the one room school. "I found your knife," said Joshua. He handed the knife to Fred and walked to his desk, sad, but refreshingly relieved.

On Joshua's twelfth birthday, his aunt gave him the knife now tucked in his sock. "Your grandfather Wallace brought this knife with him when he left Scotland," said his aunt, handing him the ornate knife with its handle carved from black bog oak. "Scottish Highlanders call it sgian dubh , which is Gaelic for black knife. The word black probably means secret, since it was usually a concealed weapon, hidden under the armpit or worn in the sock. Your grandfather Wallace would want his only grandson to have it, Josh, on his twelfth birthday." Proudly, Joshua hid the scabbard knife in his right sock.

Suddenly Josh senses something alive ahead. Like the lion who lifts his head to sniff his prey, Joshua's intuitive sense is drawn to the barn. He hears the bray of a mule from inside. One of the two barn doors is not closed, allowing Josh to slip into the barn and see a mule hitched to a wagon.

He whispers gentle sounds to the mule and stokes her under the chin, for it is a female and more submissive to Josh's attention. "Are you abandoned, old girl?" says Josh. "I know that feeling." Joshua's mother had died when he was five, and his father left for California, abandoning Joshua. His mother's sister, his Aunt Mary and her husband, Hank Bonger, had no children and had welcomed him into their home.

His attention is drawn to a chest in the middle of the wagon with a rope tied around the middle. "What are you hauling in this wagon, Jennie?" says Josh.

He steps onto the wagon and unties the rope. The chest is about two-foot by fifteen-inches and about fifteen inches high. The lock has been shot away. He lifts the hinged cover. The chest is filled with bundles of greenbacks, each wrapped with a band around the center. There are no markings on the chest, which is reinforced with metal bands and has a grip on each end.

Josh closes the lid, pets Jennie one more time and leaves the barn. In the far distance he sees Captain Fillmore on his horse. He yells "Captain!" The captain gallops toward Josh . "What is it?" yells the captain, reining in his horse.

"There's something you better see, Captain," says Josh.

The captain ties his horse to a small tree near the barn and follows Josh, who opens the barn door wide. The captain gives Josh a quizzical look. Josh points to the chest in the wagon. "You have to see what's inside." They both climb onto the wagon.

Josh lifts the lid.

"Holy Jehoshaphat!" says the captain. He removes one of the bundles of greenbacks and flips through them with his thumb. "Ones" he exclaims. "This bundle must be a hundred dollars." He replaces the bundle back in its place. "There must be several hundred bundles here."

"The chest was tied up with that rope," says Josh, pointing to the pile of rope by the side of the chest.

"Tie it again, private," says the captain. "Can you handle this mule and wagon?"

"I worked with mules before joining up," says Joshua.

"We'll take the wagon to headquarters in Munfordville. Don't tell anyone what the chest contains," says the captain. He unleashes his horse from the tree and mounts it. "Get that mule and wagon out of the barn and follow me."

Joshua ties the rope around the chest and covers it with the tarpaulin he found under the seat of the wagon. He leads Jennie out of the barn and follows the captain. It's two miles to Munfordville. Joshua begins to multiply the one hundred one dollar bills by the several hundred bundles. Maybe some are five dollar bills! "Wow!" he whispers.

In 1801 Richard Munford settled on the Green River at a natural ford and buffalo crossing. The following year Munford established a ferry and nine years later an inn accommodated weary travelers. In 1830 the L&N Turnpike brought more people while others arrived on rafts and riverboats on the Green River. With the coming of the L&N Railroad in 1859 Munfordville's importance increased and it became the target of both Union and Confederate armies.

Joshua's aunt and uncle had frequently attended the Presbyterian Church, a block west of Main Street in Munfordville, and had taken Joshua with them. The church, built in 1834, was a joint effort of the local Presbyterian congregation and the Green River Masonic Lodge, the congregation using the first floor and the Masons the second floor. Joshua's uncle belonged to the Green River Masonic Lodge. Joshua, therefore, was familiar with Munfordville.

Crossing the Green River the road becomes Munfordville's Main Street. The recent rain has left the dirt streets a quagmire, and the hundreds of trampling soldiers make the road impossible to walk on. Jennie is having a hard time pulling the wagon, and Joshua is glad to see the captain motion for him to turn west off Main Street on to South Street. On his left, in the middle of the block, sits a beautiful old home. Horses and men fill the front lawn. "Take the wagon to the back," orders the captain. "Put it in the carriage house."

The drier road leading to the back of the house makes pulling easier for Jennie. There are less than a dozen soldiers and civilians in the back of the house, and only a young boy with a hoop seems curious about the wagon. The carriage door is open and Jennie obediently enters. She is rewarded by water, hay, and sweet talk from Joshua, who proudly stands guard over the wagon's treasure.

Joshua marvels at the carriage house, which is larger and "more beautiful" than his aunt and uncle's four room frame house. The back of the mansion (that's what Joshua calls the house) looks as courtly as the front.

F.A. Smith, who built the house in 1835, is a staunch Union man and refused to sell any products from his meat processing plant, located west of the town, to the Confederates when they had occupied the town earlier. Smith's friendship with Confederate General Buckner kept them from confiscating his goods. The Smith

House, Joshua has been told, had been occupied by General John Hunt Morgan in the Fall of 1861. Joshua observes the captain leaving the house with a major.

Joshua stands at attention and salutes as the captain and major enter the carriage house. Returning the salute, the captain picks up a step-up box by the nearest stall and places it at the back of the wagon. Joshua can hear only bits of their whispering: "...scouting south...in a barn...chest..." After the captain and major step onto the wagon floor, the captain removes the canvas tarpaulin, unties the rope, and raises the lid of the chest.

It surprises Joshua that the major does not seem impressed—he makes no comment when he first sees the bundles of greenbacks. He picks up a bundle, flips through it. "Fives," he says, and places the bundle back in the chest. The major steps down from the wagon and takes a pencil and piece of paper from his pocket. Using the floor of the wagon as a desk, he writes a few words and then hands the paper to the captain.

In a deep, strong voice—there is no longer need to whisper—the major orders the captain to "have this chest taken to the Union paymaster in Elizabethtown immediately. Put Lieutenant Henry in charge and give him the note. It will give him something to write about to his father in Frankfort, and something his father can tell the governor at a cabinet meeting. He's a honest, reliable young man," says the major. To himself he thinks, and may be a little naive.

The major looks at Joshua. "What's your name son?"

"Applegate, sir. Private Joshua Applegate."

"Can you handle this mule and wagon, Joshua?"

"Yes sir!"

"Better have an old non-com go along," says the major to the captain.

"Sergeant O'Conner ?" asks the captain.

The major does not like Sergeant Peter O'Conner personally, but admires his professional, by-the-book attitude, and his command of soldiers. The major considers him someone who would never steal your wallet, but if he found it, he would not return it to you. "Sergeant O'Conner will do fine, captain," says the major. "See that they're on their way in an hour and return immediately. We'll need every man we have in a day or so." The major returns to the house after exchanging salutes with the captain.

In less than an hour the special party of three leaves Munfordville on the road to Elizabethtown thirty miles away.

A special mission brings together these three disparate Union soldiers, each for what they may contribute to success: the lieutenant for authority, the sergeant for experience, and Joshua Applegate to drive the wagon. They have seen each other before but have never spoken to each other. Other than soldiering, they have little in common, other than to complete this mission.

From Lexington, Kentucky, Lieutenant Robert Patrick Henry, a descendant of Patrick Henry, is the grandson of Gideon Henry, who came to Kentucky on a flatboat six years before General Harrison defeated Tecumseh's brother, the Shawnee Prophet, at the Battle of Tippecanoe in 1811. Settling in Lexington, Gideon Henry amassed a fortune and built Bedford Park (his palatial home on a thousand acres of rich Kentucky bluegrass), where he raised thoroughbreds and privately hosted political gatherings of the new Republican Party.

Gideon Henry opposed Kentucky Governor Magoffin's efforts to unite the slave states in demanding the protection of the institution of slavery and the dividing of the national territories at the 37th parallel between slave and free. Magoffin wanted Kentucky to join the growing number of succeeding states and called for a special session of the General Assembly to convene on January 17, 1861. Influenced by Henry, the State Unionists refused to call for the convention, and that June, Unionist candidates won nine of the 10 seats in a special election.

After the August 5, 1861 election for members of the General Assembly, the Unionists had veto-proof majorities in the House and Senate. Magoffin retired and James Robinson became governor with Gideon Henry serving in his cabinet. Gideon had two sons, the younger being Robert's father. Young Robert, therefore, was given every opportunity in life to add to the fortunes of the family. He graduated from Centre College and then Transylvania University law school in June 1861. He received a brevet second lieutenancy immediately after graduating from Transylvania and was assigned to the 33rd Kentucky.

Bright, handsome, with raven black hair and dark brown eyes, his slim figure made his medium height appear taller. Where his grandfather was astute, Robert was naive; where his grandfather was firm, Robert "understood" and while women respected his grandfather, they adored Robert! He was by nature faithful to his betrothed Angelica Louise, with whom he intended to have a son to carry on the family fortune.

Sergeant Peter O'Conner was the opposite. Tall and beefy, his red hair cautioned about his fiery temper when sober but promised his jovial camaraderie when drunk. Where Lieutenant Henry was trusting, Sergeant O'Conner was skeptical; where the lieutenant was naive, the sergeant was knowledgeable; and where the lieutenant wished to serve, Sergeant O'Conner manipulated to receive. His professional soldiering masked his bitterness at life, the cause of and his justification for such bitterness occurring during his army service in the Southwest.

Serving a second three-year enlistment, Sergeant Peter O'Conner had been stationed at Fort Ellis in Montana. In August 1854, a Lakota Indian killed a wandering cow in Wyoming. Afraid to look for the cow, the owner reported that the Indians had stolen it. Twelve US soldiers under the command of Lieutenant Joseph Garrison, son of the powerful Senator from Massachusetts, and Sergeant Peter O'Conner, went to the Lakota village to forcibly reclaim the cow.

The young chief offered to meet the lieutenant alone. Agreeing, the lieutenant rode his horse towards the several dozen Lakota Indians mounted on their horses and extended in a line behind their chief, who sat haughtily on his speckled horse, resplendent in his colorful animal-skin shirt and pants, with his bonnet of white feathers trailing behind.

Sergeant O'Conner ordered the men to extend their line into a semi-circle behind the lieutenant. He had told the lieutenant not to parley alone with the young chief, but the lieutenant merely brushed the warning off with a wave of his hand. Sergeant O'Conner noticed, as the young chief rode to meet the lieutenant that he held the reigns of his horse with his right hand while his left hand pointed, without bending, down to the ground.

The two horsemen stopped a few feet from each other. The lieutenant raised his hand saying "Wah Hay" (Hello) as the chief raised his right hand. Suddenly the chief threw his left hand up, yelled "Yayaya!" and from his sleeve came the head of a tomahawk.

Grabbing the other end of the tomahawk as it came through his sleeve, he thrust both legs into his horse and smashed the tomahawk into the head of the lieutenant, cutting it in half through the neck.

Immediately after the chief yelled, the Indians behind raced towards him, yelling, holding their lances high, and then hurling them at the dead body of the lieutenant.

In those few moments before the Indians would attack the troops, Sergeant O'Conner turned his horse abruptly around and ordered, "Troop! Follow me!" Although they were followed half the way to Fort Ellis, the entire troop of twelve men and Sergeant O'Conner reached the fort safely.

The first commendations for saving the entire troop soon changed to condemnation for leaving a wounded officer. That the lieutenant had been instantly killed was ignored by the court-martial that could not allow any blemish to be attached to Senator Garrison's only son.

Sergeant Peter O'Conner, thirty-five years old, was court-martialed and reduced to private, with the loss of three months pay. With his second enlistment ending shortly after the three months, he returned to civilian life, bitter, resentful, and prepared in the future to serve only himself. Returning to his home in Kentucky, he enlisted in the 33rd Kentucky and was given the rank of sergeant in early 1861.

Rank prevents Joshua any comradeship with the lieutenant and age, with the sergeant. Unlike the lieutenant, who hopes for some commendation for the success of this his first "command" or like the sergeant, who wonders how he might profit personally from whatever is of value in the chest, Joshua wants only for Jennie to obey him for the next two days and pull the wagon and hopes to be given his own rifle when he returns.

With a two day supply of bacon, hardtack, and coffee in the wagon, the lieutenant, mounted on a restless horse, lifts his hand high in the air. "Forward!" he yells; "Ho, Jennie!" shouts Joshua, snapping the reigns; And Sergeant O'Conner, sitting to the left of Joshua in the wagon, shakes his head in unbelief.

The road is crowded with army wagons and columns of soldiers for the first twenty minutes out of Munfordville and gradually becomes deserted. Jennie's rhythm of travel requires nothing from Joshua and she and the wagon she pulls set the pace for the journey. The lieutenant lets his high-strung horse trot back and forth in front of it, occasionally prancing off the dirt road to investigate some motion among the bushes or chase a groundhog or raccoon.

"Do you think we'll run into any trouble, Sergeant?" Joshua had heard that the sergeant had been court-martialed from the regular army several years ago, but the sergeant's experience and "by the book" command has earned him the respect of Joshua and the rest of the troops.

Thinking about the chest, Sergeant O'Conner doesn't want to engage in unnecessary conversation. "No," he says.

To pass the time, Joshua tells the sergeant that he was born not far from where they are, that he lived with his aunt and uncle, that he helped his uncle raise mules, and that he actually will be eighteen on his next birthday.

"What's in the chest?" asks the sergeant.

The sergeant's abrupt question startles Joshua and he answers without thinking. "Greenbacks. Full of them." He had assumed the sergeant knew. Well, he knows now. But the sergeant says nothing else and assumes the role of the disinterested passenger.

Joshua ends the lull that followed with more personal details. "Up yonder is a hole in the ground that me and my buddy Zac Tompkins discovered last year. It opens into a big cave that must be at lest eight feet high. Zac got kicked in the chest by one of our mules a few months after that and died. So I guess I'm the only one in the world that knows about that hole into the cave."

The sergeant turns his head to Joshua with an encouraging look to continue, but a blank expression belies a calculating interest.

"We'll be coming to McCubbins Lane soon. The cave isn't too far from McCubbins," says Joshua.

"How wide is the hole?" asks the sergeant, matter-of-factly as if making the effort to continue the conversation.

Joshua considers the question merely one of many that contribute to a long conversation of little meaning. "About two feet across," he says. "This whole area is full of caves and passage ways underneath the ground with lakes, and rivers, and waterfalls."

"There's McCubbins Lane," says Joshua, pointing to a narrow dirt road, on the right. As they pass the entrance to McCubbins Lane, the sergeant stands up and looks around the area. "How far is it from here?" he asks.

"A mile or so," says Joshua, pleased that he now has a conversation going with the sergeant.

Sergeant O'Conner sits down and disappoints Joshua by saying nothing more. For the next hour Joshua begins a monologue about learning to work with mules, his ambition to own a farm, and other trivia dear to a seventeen year old boy.

The lieutenant takes another departure from the dirt road to a patch of woods on the right. Joshua observes the lieutenant from the corner of his eye, searching among the grass and brush, when his horse suddenly neighs and rears on his two hind legs, throwing the lieutenant off and onto the ground.

"Hee, girl!" Joshua yells, pulling on the reins. "The lieutenant's fallen off his horse, sergeant," he says. The sergeant turns his head. "Go see if he's hurt," he says.

Joshua runs to the frightened horse, grabs the reigns and ties them to a branch. He then runs to the lieutenant, who lies on the grass, a trickle of blood appears on the rock upon which his head rests. His face has become ash blue.

The sergeant approaches Joshua. "He's dead, sergeant."

Sergeant O'Conner takes hold of the lieutenant's chin and moves it a quarter circle to reveal the back of the caved-in skull. He stands up, looks around, seemingly undisturbed by events. "Bring the wagon over here," says Sergeant O'Conner, as he begins to remove the scabbard and saber from the horse.

Jennie obligingly brings the wagon to where the lieutenant's body lies, and the sergeant and Joshua lift it onto the wagon. The sergeant pulls the saber halfway out of the scabbard, looks at it for a moment, thrusts it back in the scabbard, and then throws it next to the lieutenant's body. "Turn around and turn down that McCubbins lane," says Sergeant O'Conner.

An hour later, Joshua is ready to turn onto McCubbins Lane. "Shouldn't we be going to Elizabethtown, Sergeant?" Sergeant O'Conner does not answer. "Hadn't we better go back to headquarters?" adds Joshua.

"Just follow my orders," says Sergeant O'Conner, with a slight emphasis on "my."

A hundred steps from and out of sight of the road to Elizabethtown, the sergeant tells Joshua to stop. "How far are we from the hole?" asks the sergeant.

Both cautious and fascinated by the emerging realization that the sergeant intends to hide the chest in the cave, Joshua answers. "About half an hour."

Sergeant O'Conner steps onto the wagon behind the board they are sitting on. He fumbles in the pockets of the dead lieutenant. "Here we are!" He takes a small box from the lieutenant's inside pocket. "The benefits of wealth," he says. He returns to the seat next to Joshua.

The sergeant takes out two cigars from his pocket. "Do you smoke?" he asks Joshua.

"Occasionally," says Joshua. He takes the cigar offered him.

Sergeant O'Conner takes a match from the small box, noticing the small print: "Manufactured by Alonzo Dwight Phillips at Springfield, Mass." followed by the patent number. He strikes it, lights his cigar, and then extends it to Joshua. "Light up, Josh!" says Sergeant O'Conner with a big smile.

"A lot quicker than flint and steel," says Sergeant O'Conner. "Of course, you have to be wealthy to afford these phosphorus matches." He stops, inhales his cigar and eyes Joshua, whose body movement indicates his interest in hearing what Sergeant O'Conner has to say.

"That chest of greenbacks is rightfully yours, Josh. It was lost and you found it. There's no name on the chest. It doesn't belong to the US paymaster anymore than it does to some southern rebels," says Sergeant O'Conner.

"You're going to be several years older when this fighting is over, and your enlistment bonus won't buy the farm you want," says Sergeant O'Conner.

"You want to put the chest down into the cave," says Joshua, devoid of emotion, excitement, or anticipation.

"Smart boy!" says Sergeant O'Conner. "We'll let the horse and mule loose and get rid of the wagon, and tell Captain Fillmore how some southern renegades bushwhacked us, killed the lieutenant, and took the wagon and chest."

"What about the lieutenant?" asks Joshua.

"We'll given him a Christian burial!" laughs Sergeant O' Conner. "Private and secret."

"Then what?" asks Joshua.

"After the war, we come back here and split it."

"Half and half?" asks Joshua.

"Of course, Josh!" exclaims Sergeant O'Conner. He reaches over and pats Joshua on the shoulder. "If I get killed, you'll get it all," he says. This is the first time Joshua sees Sergeant O'Conner smile, He has two missing bicuspids.

Sergeant O'Conner extends his hand to Joshua. "Agreed?" he asks. They shake hands.

"Now let's get to that hole in the ground," says Sergeant O'Conner.

Joshua first ties the horse to the back of the wagon, and then has Jennie take the wagon up McCubbins Lane for fifteen minutes before turning left onto a level strip of land that follows the base of a hill covered with brush and trees. Slowing ascending, they reach the top of the hill, which has an open field surrounded by thick brush and cedars. Joshua ties the mule to a tree. They walk through thick brush some hundred steps until they come to a small opening among the trees. The wild grass reaches their knees. Joshua stands still and searches the rim of trees. Sighting the tallest, he steps several paces towards it, looking carefully to his left. "Here!" he exclaims.

Sergeant O'Conner steps to where Joshua is pointing.

The hole is covered around its edge by overlapping tall grass. Two thick branches cover the part of the hole not hidden by grass.

"You covered it?" asks Sergeant O' Conner .

"Zac and me wanted a place to hide our treasure."

Sergeant O'Conner gives Joshua a quizzical look?

"Zac had an old revolver and his grandfather's musket, and I had the head of a tomahawk and an assortment of Indian arrows. We never got around to it, though," says Joshua.

They clear the grass from round the edge of the near circular hole and determine that the chest can be lowered into it with the rope in the wagon. Jennie brings the wagon closer to the hole. They tie three of the four fifteen-foot ropes in the wagon, that were used to make a tent with the tarpaulin, into one length and circle one end several times around the nearest tree.

The chest is removed from the wagon and dragged close to the hole.

Sergeant O'Conner takes the kerosene lantern that is hung from the side of the wagon and lights it with a match. They attach the lantern to the rope and lower it down the hole.

"The chest can go over there," says Sergeant O'Conner, pointing to a spot in the cave that is partially hidden from the hole. "It'll be hidden from anybody who might find the hole. You'll have to go down in the cave to untie the chest after I lower it into the hole."

In their new relationship, the sergeant has no official command over Joshua, but habit prevails and Joshua agrees. The prospects of future wealth begin to cloud his caution.

Joshua pulls up the rope and unties the lantern. He lowers himself into the hole and grasps the rope, while O'Conner slackens the other end of the rope as it slips around the tree, lowering Joshua by steady jerks. Joshua touches the rock floor. "I need that lantern!" he yells.

Sergeant O'Conner pulls the rope up, attaches the lantern, and lowers it to Joshua. Again, the rope is pulled up and tied to the rope round the chest. Tying it tight, Sergeant O'Conner lowers the chest until it touches the floor of the cave.

Joshua unties the rope and pulls the chest to that part of the cave hidden from the view of the hole. He opens the chest. "God amighty!" he yells. Reaching in the chest, he takes a bundle in each hand and holds both up in the air. "We're rich! Sergeant! We're rich!" he yells.

He looks at the denomination of each bundle. One is a bundle of one dollar bills and the other of five dollar bills. He tosses the bundle of ones back into the chest and grabs a handful of five dollar bills from the other bundle, stuffs them in his pocket, and throws the remainder of the bundle into the chest. He starts singing as he walks to the rope:

"Rainy days are gone forever;
I'm rich beyond all measure.
More sadness in my life—never!
I've found the only treasure."

It doesn't occur to Joshua that the church song he learned is not about worldly treasure. As he ends the verse he prances on one foot and then the other. He looks for the rope.

It's not there.

"Give me the rope, Sergeant!" he yells.

The rope is not thrown down to Joshua. Only Joshua's voice echoes through the cave. Not a sound nor voice comes from above the cave.

"Damn it, Sergeant! Throw down that rope. Do you hear me?"

The quiet focuses Joshua's thoughts: He wants me dead! "You son-of-a-bitch! For God's sake; throw down the rope!"

Joshua hears O'Conner's heavy breathing. Suddenly something covers the hole. It falls to the floor. It's the lieutenant. Stunned by the grotesque, contorted body, Joshua turns his head. A clash of metal hitting rock brings Joshua out of shock, as he sees the lieutenant's scabbard with the saber inside fall across the body.

Sergeant O'Conner starts to throw a canteen of water down the hole, but considers that it will only prolong what he wants to end. It takes about forty days with no food, he had read somewhere. About a week with no water. Perhaps a little water dripping from the walls of the cave might add a few days. He tells himself he isn't doing this to have all the greenbacks for himself. The kid talks too much. In a week the entire squad would know, and the next week, the entire company. He has no choice. He gathers long branches and begins covering the hole.

An hour later, tired from gathering the coverage now over the hole, Sergeant O'Conner sits down by the wagon, leaning against a wheel. He decides to fry some bacon and brew some coffee.

The yelling from the cave has stopped. O'Conner tries to stop thinking about what he has done, what he is doing. Memories of his childhood resurrect his buried conscience, which he attempts to placate by affirming his only action has been pulling up a rope. He attempts to erase from his mind the image of Joshua, soon to be in total darkness, alone. Totally alone. An uncomfortable chill runs up his spine as he flips over the bacon.

Tomorrow he'll release the horse and mule after dumping the wagon in some near crevice. Later that afternoon he'll walk back to Munfordville. He takes some hardtack with the bacon and washes them down with hot coffee.

A chill is in the air as the sun nears the horizon. He takes the lieutenant's and Joshua's bedrolls from the wagon - it being too bloody to sleep on - and with his own, makes a comfortable bed on the ground by the side of the wagon. He smiles at the realization that he finally deserves his court-martial. Moonlight filters through the trees and Sergeant O'Conner falls into a deep sleep, facing the flickering fire.

"Thank God I didn't tell O'Conner about the cave entrance," says Joshua aloud. The cave extends a quarter of a mile before ending in a small entrance, big enough for a man of average height to enter by stooping over. Exiting requires a high "step" up to the entrance. Zac and Joshua discovered the entrance and followed it to the hole later.

He prays that the kerosene lamp keeps burning until he gets to the cave entrance. He sees light coming through the cave entrance, but walking on the rock floor of the cave is made easier and safer with the lantern. The uneven floor and the rock obstructions make the walk to the entrance tedious and long.

From the dampness of the cave to the chill of the evening, Joshua watches the last rays of the sun filter through the trees as it nears the horizon. He sits on a boulder and touches his sock, feeling the outline of his knife. He'll wait until O'Conner goes to sleep, for he doesn't expect him to return to Munfordville until later the next day.

His hunger and thirst awaken the beast ready for the kill. He rests after putting the lamp out, for he must not make any noise nor have any light that will reveal his presence. Revenge has a power all its own, and Joshua's only desire is to thrust his knife deep into the heart of Sergeant O'Conner.

His sense of direction has always been good, and his intuition always proves helpful, but what would be a fifteen minute walk during the day, takes three times longer. His eyes, adjusted to moonlight, he immediately sees the glimmer of a small fire. Carefully feeling the earth with his feet before putting them down, Joshua creeps within twenty paces of the fire now nearly burned out. Sergeant O'Conner lies on his back, snoring.

Joshua becomes aware that he must be on top of O'Conner to plunge the knife into his heart. He sees a four-foot long limb three inches thick. Quietly he picks it up with both hands and moves it back and forth as if parrying an opponent's thrust. He puts the knife back into his sock.

He steps from the bush into the open area where O'Conner is sleeping, now turned from the fire. The last glimmer from the fire outlines O'Conner's body, and Joshua stops one pace from it, lifting the limb high above his head, as he hears O'Conner snore and turn his head again to the fire. O'Conner opens his eyes in horror as Joshua brings down the limb with all his strength, smashing in the right side of Sergeant Peter O'Conner's head and face.

Exhausted, Joshua drops the limb and slumps to the ground.

Four hours later Joshua wakes from a deep sleep, famished, weak, suffering from bruises and wounds, and beginning to fathom the horrible events of the last eighteen hours. He forces himself to search the body of Sergeant O'Conner, avoiding looking at his bloody, mutilated face. He finds the box of matches in O'Conner's pocket.

A few twigs and dry grass are ignited and added branches produce a small fire. His trembling is more from the trauma he has experienced rather than from the chill of the night. He warms his hands over the flames.

The provisions are under the wagon. He takes out his knife and slices off a strip of bacon, puts it in the frying pan after throwing out what O'Conner had left, and places it on the fire. The sizzling sound is pleasant to his ears. He grabs a handful of hardtack and begins to eat one. He empties O'Conner's cup, adds coffee and water, and places it next to the frying pan. Army food never tasted better.

Refreshed, he smokes one of the several cigars he found in the sergeant's pocket. With his eyes closed, he goes over in his mind what he needs to do.

He'll throw O'Conner's body down the hole. The sergeant can keep the lieutenant company, thinks Joshua, grinning. Next he'll put rocks at the cave entrance to keep out varmints before hiding the wagon. After letting the horse and mule loose, he'll walk back to Munfordville.

Full, warm, relaxed, he falls asleep again. Five hours later, dreaming he is hunting with his uncle, he awakes to the sound of birds.

After removing the branches from the hole, Joshua ties rope around the ankles of O'Conner and drags the body to the edge of the hole. Stepping opposite the hole, he pulls the body until the legs are over the hole. He removes the rope and lets the two legs dangle into the hole. To avoid looking at O'Conner's face, Joshua ties the rope around the body's waist and pulls. Gravity completes Joshua's task when the upper half of the body slips down the hole, cutting the brow as it scraps the side of the rock, and falls to the rock floor below.

Placing several thick branches over the hole, Joshua folds the tarpaulin into a four-foot square and places it over the hole, covering it with the branches and twigs that previously covered it. He leads Jennie and the wagon over the rough ground towards the cave entrance.

Several hundred paces farther from the cave entrance is a pond, and near the pond is as grove. Taking the wagon as far into the grove as possible, Joshua unharnesses Jennie from the wagon and ties a rope around her neck.

Returning to the cave entrance, he fastens several large boulders with the rope and has Jennie pull them to the entrance. The boulders cover more than the bottom half of the cave entrance. Placing several dozen smaller rocks on top of the boulders, Joshua hopes to closes the entrance to large animals.

He takes another path back to the hole hoping nature will soon cover evidence of human activity. He scatters the dead fire, and uses a branch as a rake to make the trampled grass to appear natural again.

On the morning Joshua left for the army, his aunt had given him a "money belt", a small pouch attached to a cord which he could tie around his waist under his clothing. "Inside is a prayer I writ for your protection, Joshua, and also three dollars," she told him. She insisted he wear it when he left. He has worn it every since, and now places the roll of five dollar greenbacks and the box of matches inside, before again tying it around his waist.

He cuts another strip of bacon with his knife, cleans the frying pan out with a handkerchief from the lieutenant's haversack and starts a fire. He crumbles the hardtack and adds it to the grease left in the frying pan after taking the bacon out. When it gets thick, he flattens it with his fingers and turns it over, adding a pinch of salt. Hot coffee adds to the feast.

He takes the underclothing and socks from the lieutenant's haversack, being his size, and wraps them in his bedroll. He takes the rest of the lieutenant's and Sergeant O'Conner's personal equipment and buries them in the bushes some distance from the hole.

Leading the horse and Jennie down to McCubbins Lane, Joshua ruffles the grass where the wheels of the wagon have pushed it down, until it blends again with its natural surroundings. He slaps the horse several times until it begins to trot by itself east on McCubbins Lane.

Taking Jennie to the main road, Joshua leads her north, towards Elizabethtown. Gradually he falls back, stops, and watches Jennie continue her slow pace north. He waves to her, turns around, and begins walking to Munfordville and the approaching battle.

It's late in the evening of Thursday, 11 September, when Joshua reaches the camp south of Munfordville. He reports to his first sergeant, informing him that the lieutenant and sergeant have been killed by guerrillas and the wagon stolen. He does not mention the chest, assuming the first sergeant knows nothing about it.

Seeing Joshua's poor condition, the first sergeant tells him to go to the hospital that's in the Presbyterian Church. "I'll inform the captain," says the first sergeant, but he never does. In the ensuing confusion and battle, all thought and concern of the chest of greenbacks is forgotten, and the deaths of the lieutenant and sergeant become part of the casualties of the next several days.

Joshua's bruises and cuts are tended to and he is told to take a bath in the makeshift facilities in the back of the church. A platter of beef-stew and potatoes with hot coffee is brought to him in the bed assigned to him. "Get some rest and report to your company tomorrow afternoon," the doctor tells him.

That morning after a breakfast of beans, hardtack and coffee, Joshua takes paper and pencil from his bedroll and writes his aunt and uncle:

> "Dear Aunt Mary and Uncle Hank,
> I am near Munfordville and sorry I cannot come to see you it being so close. We expect to have some fighting to do soon. I am all right. Get somethin' you need with the two five dollar greenbacks. I love you and miss you.
> Faithfully yours,
> Josh"

He wraps the two greenbacks in paper and slips them in between the folded letter.

After a lunch on Friday, 12 September, of pickled pork, Yankee beans and coffee, Joshua reports back to his company which is located inside Fort Craig, the earthwork that contains about 300 men. He receives his first musket.

Joshua is welcomed back by his comrades who, not knowing

what his two-day leave was about, ask him no questions; and he, not wishing to discuss it, merely raises his hand in recognition. "Finally!" he says, holding up his musket, and changing the conversation.

The men Colonel Wilder sent out to scout have brought him information that Confederate General Bragg has crossed the Tennessee River with 30,000 men. They provided him with the number of artillery pieces Bragg has, and inform him that Bragg is within fifty miles of Munfordville.

The previous year Confederate forces had destroyed one of the piers of the railroad bridge across the Green River, immediately south of Munfordville. Union forces established a pontoon bridge later that temporary replaced the 1,000 feet bridge and by late 1862 had rebuilt a wooden substitute pier.

Union General Buell, who had followed the Confederate forces departing Kentucky in 1861, had given up his offensive against Chattanooga, changed his base to Nashville and now raced to intercept General Bragg before he could reach Louisville.

A lawyer without military training, except the training he had during the eighteen months he had served since entering the military service as a private of artillery in April 1961, Colonel Wilder was popular with his companions who elected him captain. Now as colonel, he commands 2,600 men at Munfordville, 478 of who are unarmed, with orders to defend and maintain the railroad bridge over the Green River.

This is the situation during the afternoon of 12 September 1862, when Joshua and several others, released from the hospital, march to Fort Craig, a redoubt ordered constructed by Colonel Wilder.

Joshua looks across the land as they approach the entrance to the redoubt, which he figures is about halfway between Munfordville and the railroad bridge. South of the fort, facing the river, he sees three rifle pits, semicircular in form and terminating in a strong stockade. The fortifications are so constructed that they are protected from artillery fire by the nature of the ground. Entering Fort Craig, Joshua guesses that with the soldiers in the rifle pits and those in the fort there are over 3,000 Union troops.

In this, his first battle, the test that separates "the men from the boys," Joshua hides his uncertainty by bravado: "We'll kick them 'Secech' outa Kentucky and send 'em back to Tennessee!" he joins the rest of his comrades in yelling. The dirt wall is reassuring, and the ditch around the wall, that he observed when entering, makes this redoubt, he anxiously convinces himself, impregnable.

The next twenty-four hours of waiting and watching Confederate movement in front of them churns the ever present opportunity for rumor to spread. "They're getting ready to attack!" and "They're retreaten'!" and "We're gonna be s'rounded!"

The order is given to "fix bayonets." Sudden shouting and firing comes from the river. "We're bein' attacked!" is repeated down the line of men standing against the earth wall. Joshua looks at the fine point of the eighteen inch bayonet he has just fastened to the barrel of his musket, and remembers what the old, regular army sergeants told him: "If ya can't pull it out ov 'is body, pull the trigger."

The Confederates attack, yelling, shouting, their standard bearer leading in front. Shooting randomly from the top of the earth wall, the young Union recruits pick their target before firing. Joshua sights a tall man holding his hat atop his sword, rushing towards the redoubt. He takes careful aim at the man's chest, holds his fire for a moment, while continuing to breath steadily, and then he pulls the trigger. The figure throws up both hands, the sword and hat falling to the ground, as the body, instantly killed by a bullet through the heart, spurts blood from the mouth and continues to run a moment longer before tumbling to the earth.

"Good shot, soldier," says the sergeant, passing by and seeing the Confederate officer fall. Joshua feels pride in his action and begins to find another target. Suddenly he sees the face of Sergeant O'Conner! What's the difference between killing someone with a bullet and being proud and killing someone else with a blow to the head and feeling guilt? This momentarily crosses his mind before he sees three Confederates fifty yards in front.

Joshua points with his finger. "You get the one on the left, Bobby, and I'll get the one on the right," he yells to private Robert John on his left. "Tossup for the middle one!" he adds. He takes aim, holds for a second, and then fires. The Confederate soldier on the right falls instantly, a bullet through his throat; the middle one, two seconds later with a bullet through his forehead; and the one on the left, shot through the thigh.

The Confederates come within thirty yards of the fortifications and then, after a terrific volley, retreat. In this ill-timed charge the

Confederate officers presumed the Union forces to be half of what they were and lose their lives as well as a tremendous amount from the rank and file. Amazingly, the recruits under Colonel Wilder, the majority of whom had never before been under fire, held their ground in the face of a determined Confederate advance. Joshua smiles at Bobby and notices a bullet hole in his own shirt sleeve.

The next morning Bobby points out to Joshua the flag of truce that emerges from the Confederate lines. It wasn't until later that morning that the men in Fort Craig learned that Confederate General Chalmers demanded their unconditional surrender, adding that the Union forces had made a gallant defense of their position, and that it was time to prevent further bloodshed.

Joshua and the rest of the men yell with joy when they hear that Colonel Wilder replied: "I can hold my position against any force that you can bring; at least, I will try to do so." They prepare themselves for another attack, this time with confidence added to their prayers.

Two days later Joshua and the rest of the Union forces become aware of being surrounded by General Bragg and his army of 30,000 and are not surprised to hear early on the morning of Wednesday, 17 September, of their surrender to the Confederate superior forces by Colonel Wilder.

At six that morning Joshua is one of 4,000 Union soldiers who march out of the fortifications with colors flying and field music playing to surrender to General Buckner, whose home, Glen Lily is only a few miles from Munfordville and to which Union General Cook has attached a no trespassing order.

Being far from his base, General Bragg does not wish to be encumbered with prisoners and, therefore, paroles the entire force of Union troops, allowing them to retain their side arms, personal property, and rations for four days. To prevent them from carrying information of his command ahead of him, he requires that all of them report to Bowling Green. There, meeting with Buell's army marching from Tennessee, they reach Louisville five days later with Joshua suffering a severe case of dysentery.

Buell's army is quartered southwest of Louisville in fields west of Twelfth Street and north of Broadway (also called Prather). Near Eighteenth and Broadway Joshua lies in an army hospital that is composed of a dozen Sibley conical tents, each capable of holding twenty men. He is in the Dysentery tent, which contains twenty-five soldiers, each suffering from gripping pain and unable to keep down the little food they are able to eat.

Three days after drinking a cup of boiled oats mixed with water and sweetened with double refined loaf sugar every half-hour, Joshua regains his normal strength and is ready to return to his unit. He takes no notice when a sergeant speaks to him: "I understand you're good with mules." "Yep," replies Joshua.

That evening Joshua is informed that he has been assigned to the 6th Kentucky Volunteer Infantry, a unit in dire need of teamsters—men who know mules. Dressed in a clean uniform, his money belt, containing the box of matches and five dollar greenbacks, tied around his waist, and extra clothing rolled in his bed roll, a freshly shaved Joshua walks with Sergeant Gustave Weis to the headquarters of the 6th Kentucky Infantry, a half-mile from Louisville.

Sergeant Weis had been in the Feet hospital tent and met Joshua at the same time both reported to the hospital office, where Gustave was ordered back to the 6th Kentucky Infantry and Joshua was assigned to Company F of the 6th Kentucky.

Four inches taller and three years older than Joshua, Sergeant Weis assumes the "big brother" role with him. His close-cut black hair, bushy moustache, and bright brown eyes enhance his military bearing, while his broad grin and smile, and his "Kum, mine brudder, ve go together!" assures Joshua that he has found a friend. Joshua instantly likes Sergeant Gustave Weis.

"Der 6th Kentucky ist made up ov immigrant Goemans mostly from Louie-ville—four kopanies of dem," Gustave tells Joshua. Joshua strains to understand Gustave's words as he tells Joshua more about the 6th Kentucky, how it was a consolidation of three separate organizations, each of which had hoped to become a separate regiment but could not raise the required ten companies.

The other seven companies, relates Gustave, are made up of local farmers from Henry, Oldham, and Shelby counties, and some natives of England, Ireland, and Scotland. "I kom from Shelby county, vere my vater and mutter brought me fifteen year ago ven I was little kid," adds Gustave.

The regiment received its brutal baptism of fire at the battle of Shiloh last April, suffering 103 casualties. After garrison duty in

Murfreesboro, Tennessee, they marched to Louisville last week. Gustave points to his feet. "Day schtopped marchen at Mufreesboro, got big und red," he says, with a big smile.

Gustave takes Joshua to the Company F headquarters of the 6th Kentucky. "Varren," he greets First Sergeant Warren Libert, "Dis ist mine friend Joshua, who belongs now to kopane F. You do what Sergeant Libert tell you, Joshua. He good man, good soldier. You lucky, Joshua. No immigrant Goemans in F, only American speakers." He pats Joshua on the shoulder. "Auf Wiedersehn!" he says and leaves.

From the next room a soldier shouts "Joshua!" He jumps out of his desk chair and, all smiles, rushes to Joshua. "John!" exclaims Joshua, as they both hug each other.

A clerk of company F, Corporal John Tafel is a friend and old schoolmate of Joshua. Since it is Sunday and the normal routine is relaxed, John asks First Sergeant Libert if he can show Joshua around after recording Joshua on the Daily Report. "Take the morning;" says Sergeant Libert.

It has been over a year since John and Joshua last saw each other (a few days before John enlisted), and they tell each other what each has been doing since then. Joshua skips all references to the two days away from camp. After taking Joshua to the second platoon tent of Company F (John is in the headquarters platoon tent) and letting Joshua put his equipment on the cot assigned to him, John takes Joshua to a tent that serves as a recreation facility for the soldiers and where they can purchase items from different peddlers. They buy two fried apple pies and sit down.

"When we go back to headquarters, ask Sergeant Libert to put you on Guide Duty," says John to Joshua. "When you're on Guide Duty, you wear an arm band with corporal stripes around your arm and take recruits through their chores. This takes place at regimental headquarters, so you're not on any company work list." Joshua listens, wondering why he should do this, but says nothing.

"Regimental headquarters doesn't keep a list of the names for those acting as Guides, doesn't even count the number that report each day."

Joshua's expression tells John that he doesn't get it. "As a Guide, you're on no daily roll-call," says John, "and you and I go into Louisville for the day!"

"Oh!" says Joshua. "But won't I need a pass?"

"Our scribe will provide that," says John. He gets up and takes Joshua to another tent.

John explains that the scribe is able to forge anything and is an expert on passes. There's always a scribe in every company as well as a firer, who mysteriously and magically provides fire, particularly on the march. The trader always has the cooking utensils or other small items a soldier needs and can't get. Besides a barber and joker being inevitably in every company, there is the professor, who "knows it all" but is not much at fighting. The scribe joins these in the unofficial, but necessary, coterie of providers for soldiers. John, realizes Joshua, is the company's unofficial promoter, schemer, and wire-puller.

John takes Joshua to the company supply tent, where Supply Sergeant Graff is always to be found, particularly on Sundays, when serving as the unofficial company trader is easier, and performing as scribe is safer.

A blank pass is taken from a box on Graff's desk. "Spell you name for me," Graff asks Joshua. A minute later, Graff hands Joshua the pass.

When John begins to pay him, Graff lifts one hand and shakes his head no. "You owe me," is all he says. Joshua puts the pass in his pocket after reading to himself: PASS Louisville. Private Joshua Applegate From: 7:00 A.M. 29 September to 7:00 A.M. 30 September First Sergeant Warren Libert, Company F. 16th Kentucky.

Later that afternoon, John and Joshua return to company headquarters. Joshua speaks to First Sergeant Libert: "Sergeant, I've been in the army almost half a year and would make a great Guide for the regiment."

Sergeant Libert, putting down the Local Louisville Journal Newspaper, yells to John, who has gone to his desk in the other room. "Put Applegate on the Guide list."

An hour later, John tells Sergeant Libert he's finished all the reports and asks if he can take the day of leave due him tomorrow into Louisville. To sweeten the request, he adds a last word. "I'll bring you back a flask of Kentucky Dew."

Sergeant Libert makes out a pass for John and hands it to him. "Have a good time, Johnny," he says. "And come back sober—and in one piece," he adds.

Early the next morning, Joshua removes six five dollar greenbacks from his money belt and folds them neatly into his right pocket. Before breakfast and before Sergeant Libert calls the morning formation, Joshua and John begin the half-mile walk to Louisville.

Although eleven forts with earthen breastworks had been constructed in a semicircle around Louisville, the threat of a large Confederate army under the command of Simon Bolivar Buckner approaching Louisville in September had created panic among its inhabitants and martial law had been imposed. All males between the ages of 18 and 45 had to enroll for military drills, and persons entering and leaving the city had been required to have passes. General Nelson had ordered women and children to be sent out of Louisville.

With the arrival of General Buell's Army of the Ohio, euphoria settles over the booming city with a 100,000 troops now guarding its bulging store houses. Known as the City of Flags, Louisville also becomes The Gateway City, because of the large Union troop movement by rail. Louisville is in a state of celebration, and Joshua and John are ready to celebrate.

"How about breakfast, Joshua?" asks John as they saunter towards Louisville.

"I'm ready!"

"There's a boardinghouse on Seventh Street near Green Street. It belongs to a Mrs. Emma Willich." says John.

"It's a restaurant too?"

"No. But we'll make it one for us this morning, Josh."

Joshua sees a slight grin on John's face that approaches a smirk, a sign, Joshua has noticed, when the promoter and schemer appears in John. The boulevard of trees and fine Gothic style homes on Seventh Street astonish Joshua, who has grown up among mostly single storey, frame houses.

John points across the street to a white frame, two-storey house with three windows on each side of the white, paneled door. They walk across the street, and enter through the open iron gate as two well dressed gentleman exit the house.

A small sign in black lettering reads "Room and Board, Mrs. Emma Willich." John lifts the brass door knocker and slowly, deliberately, taps three times.

A woman wearing an apron over a pale yellow dress with a lace collar and buttons up to the neck opens the door half-way. Full figured, her salt and pepper hair tied in a bun on top of her head, her piercing blue eyes study both John and Josh momentarily, and then in a soft but firm voice she speaks. “I have no rooms available.”

Before she can close the door, John takes one step closer, lifts his hands in a “welcoming” gesture, with the right one slightly touching the door, keeping it open. “Do I have the pleasure of speaking with Mrs. Willich?” he asks. Yes, she is Mrs. Willich. “Mrs. Willich, Joshua and I”—he likes to mention the old Bible name—“seek only breakfast.”

“I only run a boardinghouse, not a restaurant,” she says. John takes another short step and presses firmly on the door.

“Mrs. Willich, ma’am,” says John, lowering his voice to a softer tone, “we haven't had a good home cooked breakfast in almost a year. Joshua and I have this one day to visit Louisville, and we left our quarters before having breakfast. We'd be much obliged for any vittals you can scrape together.”

"You‘ll have to eat in the kitchen,” she says. In the corner of his eye, John observes a Negro woman clearing the empty plates and cups from the large dining room table.

Their request is granted. Now to embellish it. “A fried egg or two with coffee would be a feast,” says John.

“A little sow belly, would be nice,” says Joshua.

“We have only steak,” says Mrs. Willich. She folds her arms. “It’ll cost you fifteen cents. Fifteen cents for each of you,” she says.

Joshua grins. “A bargain for us, Mrs. Willich,” says John, tilting his head. She unfolds her arms, opens the door, and John and Joshua step into the vestibule.

“You can wait in the parlor while Sadie sets the kitchen table,” she says, pointing to the parlor before walking into the kitchen.

All the better, thinks Joshua: Served right from the stove.

John and Josh sit rigidly in two French Empire chairs, careful not to scratch the white and gold frame or blemish the blue cotton upholstering. John notices the only painting in the parlor is of a handsome gentleman hanging above the fireplace and sees the single golden cross hanging on the wall at the other end of the parlor.

Joshua watches the calico cat asleep on the divan in front of the fireplace. Fifteen minutes later, the Negro woman comes into the parlor. "You all can come into the kitchen, now."

Mrs. Willich is in front of the wood store. She flips four fried eggs onto a platter and lifts two juicy steaks with a large fork from a frying pan onto another platter. A large bowl of fried potatoes sits in the middle of the kitchen table. Sadie pours coffee into each of their cups as John and Joshua sit down to the table covered with a freshly ironed red-and-white checkered tablecloth.

"Finish the dining room, Sadie;" says Mrs. Willich. "I'll get the biscuits." She opens the oven and removes two trays of hot biscuits. She removes the biscuits from one tray and places them on another platter along with a small bowl of freshly churned butter.

"Shouldn't we give a blessing, Josh?" says John. Startled, Joshua immediately recovers his gentle manner. "Yes of course, John."

"Thank you, Lord, for this breakfast, so generously prepared for us by this kind lady. Protect us in the coming days and bless this home. Amen," says John.

Matured, middle aged boarders are part of Mrs. Willich daily life. These two young boys are a refreshment, a change in the daily routine of preparing two meals a day for six men and cleaning their rooms. She sits down at the kitchen table, something she never does with the boarders during breakfast or dinner.

"Who is the fine looking gentleman in the portrait over the fireplace?" asks John, as he takes another biscuit and spreads it thick with butter.

"My husband. He's a lawyer."

"He appears to be in uniform," says John.

Mr. Willich had been Zachary Taylor's lawyer. Emma fondly remembers the time he and she attended the wedding of the Taylor's daughter Sarah to Jefferson Davis, sadly dying three months later; but she says, "He was a captain in the State Guard. He served in General Taylor's administration when he became President."

"Then you've lived in Washington, Mrs. Willich," says John.

"I stayed in Louisville and Mr. Willich went to Washington. In fact Mr. Willich remained in Washington after President Taylor's untimely death after only fifteen months in office."

Their baby died at birth. It was a boy. Mr. Willich consoled his wife, assuring her that they would have another child. Two years later they did, but it also died at birth. It too was a boy. This time Mr. Willich said nothing, and when the offer to go to Washington came, he expressed his pleasure by quickly accepting. Mrs. Willich said she would remain in Louisville.

Mr. Willich, remaining in Washington after the death of President Taylor, wrote to Emma that he needed her in Washington, and came home during Christmas. The next year he wrote, "Why don't you join me in Washington?" He visited Louisville the following two Christmases, and then stopped.

In March of 1861 Rudolph Willich wrote his wife Emma that he had been commissioned a colonel in the Confederate Army and had moved to Montgomery Alabama, the new Capital of the Confederacy, to serve in the War Department. "If you wish, you may join me in Montgomery," he wrote. This was the last time she heard from him.

"Is he there now, Mrs. Willich?"

"Yes," is her single reply.

The boys sensed that this is not a pleasant subject for Mrs. Willich and remain silent, while they take a second helping of fried potatoes. She gets up from the table and picks up an empty platter. "I'll get you hungry boys more fried eggs." She can't tell these two young Union soldiers that her husband serves in the Confederate War Department.

She is not conscious of it, but these two young boys have become the two boys she lost at birth, for they would be about the ages of John and Joshua. It's not the physical presence of John and Joshua, but the idea of other persons. Her heart has moved from the particular—her two dead sons—to the general, to the idea of two other persons. It's the difference between loving a person and then just loving.

Her mind, deeply under the influence of the idea, image, and emotion of this change from feeling love for someone to just being love itself, brings a calmness, a peacefulness she has never experienced. She finds herself in a state of quiet, almost passive, enjoyment.

Suddenly, without warning, she finds herself wrapped in a flame-colored cloud. For an instant she thinks of fire, some sudden conflagration in Louisville. The next instant she knows that the light is within herself. She has touched the empyrean, paradise, the Kingdom of Heaven.

Just as suddenly Emma looks at the two boys, restraining her desire to hug them, and unconsciously wipes the tear sliding down her cheek.

"You must be very proud of your husband," says Joshua.

Emma says nothing and begins to fill their cups with fresh coffee.

"We must be going, Mrs. Willich," says John. "We are most thankful for this excellent breakfast." He takes three nickels from his pocket and hands them to her. She places them on the table, as Joshua also fumbles in his pocket, not wanting them to see the greenbacks. He removes the small change from his pocket and hands her a dime and a nickel. Bemused, she places the two coins with the three nickels. Joshua and John pick up their hats and walk to the door.

"I'll be back in a few minutes, Sadie," she says as she follows behind John and Joshua. "I'll walk out to the road with you."

There is light conversation about the good breakfast, the weather, but Emma Willich cannot say to these two young soldiers that they have become her two sons, as they begin walking north on Seventh Street, and she must restrain her desire to hug them. Turning down Green Street, John and Joshua turn around once more and wave. It is not until they disappear down Green Street that Emma turns around, closes the gate, and thinks, I have many sons! She walks with a slight skip back towards her house.

It's ten o'clock and downtown Louisville is filled with hundreds of soldiers, walking, mingling, bartering with the peddlers and merchants, and watching the girls walk by. The wide streets, with three and four storey buildings on each side, bewilder Joshua, who thinks he must be in Paris or London. John sees two first sergeants talking in front of the Louisville Hotel. He motions for Joshua to come with him to the two sergeants. John speaks to the taller one.

"Sergeant, we've only got today in town. Any suggestions?" asks John.

Both sergeants take an appraising look at these two young boys before the taller one speaks. "Well, there's the Burlesque Show, a museum, and lots of special shops along Main Street." Had the boys been a little older the sergeant would have mentioned some of the better saloons. "Watch out for pickpockets," he says.

"What about Billy Goat Strut?" asks John.

The sergeant reacts to this as a father reacts the first time his son asks where he came from. "It's an alley, Corporal." As a surrogate father, the sergeant says, "You two don't want to go there. Especially at night."

Suddenly two young girls, well dressed, each with long black hair, approach John and Joshua. "Want to come to a party?"

"There!" says the sergeant. "You've just come to town and are invited to a party."

The girls' smiles and youthful body movements contribute to the immediate "Yes" response from Joshua and John. "Follow us," say the girls, and they do, eagerly.

They walk down Fourth Street to Walnut Street and approach the side entrance to a church, a sudden disappointment to both Joshua and John. A small sign over the door way reads: Walnut Street Baptist Church.

The Gothic structure is brick covered with stucco to simulate stone. The steeple is one of the tallest among a number of church steeples in Louisville. They notice two soldiers entering the door and hear a number of voices in the large basement room of the church. They enter.

Soldiers are talking with girls, while matronly women serve behind two tables with plates of cookies, cakes, and candies, and one table with a large glass punch bowl and numerous glass cups. "This is a daily affair in our church for soldiers visiting our city;" says one girl, while the other pours two cups of a pink punch for John and Joshua. Sipping the punch, they decline the cookies offered them by the first girl. "We just had breakfast, thank you," says John.

Joshua and John meet Pastor Wilber Flexner. "You'll be at the ten-thirty service?" asks the small figure in black. John and Joshua hide their surprise with a faint grin and slight nod—a nod that can mean yes as well as no. The pastor turns to speak with a gentleman, after saying, "Don't forget, boys, ten-thirty." While the two girls go to the kitchen for more cookies and punch, John and Joshua slip quietly out of the room and return as quickly as possible down Fourth Street and back to Main Street.

Instead of returning to the Louisville hotel area on Main Street, they turn right and walk the five blocks to the magnificent Galt House. Replacing the first Galt House built in 1832, the second Galt House of five stories has more than 250 rooms, and has become the meeting place for army officers.

John and Joshua blend in easily with the numerous enlisted men and officers who share the sidewalks with a lesser number of civilians. "Let's go in," says John. Joshua slows his steps, looks straight up to the ceiling and turns his head in full circles, mesmerized by the paintings on the walls and ceiling and by the tall Corinthian columns running down both sides of the two storey lobby. He apologizes to the several army officers he bumps into and, seeing John walking to the back of the lobby, hurries his steps.

John stops and draws Joshua's attention to a tall army officer standing by the staircase talking with another army officer. "That's General Nelson," says John. He's called "Bull."

"I can see why," says Joshua. "He must be six foot four. Must be over 300 pounds."

"I think the officer he's talking with is General Jefferson Davis," says John. To the disbelieving look on Joshua's face, John smiles. "He's Jefferson C. Davis, no relation to the Confederate president." They hear the loud confrontation between Nelson and Davis.

"General Nelson," yells General Davis, "I want to know why you disgraced me by placing me under arrest?"

"Do you know who you are talking to?" snaps General Nelson. "Go away, you damned puppy, I don't want anything to do with you."

Spellbound and standing near the hotel desk, they watch General Davis walk towards them and grab a calling card. "Did you hear that damned insolent scoundrel insult me?" says Davis to two officers standing near the hotel desk. "I supposes he don't know me; I'll teach him a lesson," he says , and walks back to the stairs throwing the wadded card into Nelson's face.

With the back of his hand, Nelson slaps Davis's face. With eyes afire, he heads back to his room, leaving to avoid further difficulty.

Davis meets Captain Gibson, who is about to enter the dining room. "Do you have a pistol?" asks Davis.

"I always carry the article," says Captain Gibson. He hands it to

Davis, warning him. "It's a hair-trigger."

Livid, compounded with indignation, mortification and determination, Davis follows Nelson up the stairs. "Halt!" he yells. Nelson turns and approaches Davis. "Not another step farther," commands Davis. He looks into Nelson's eyes and fires from a yard away, striking Nelson above the heart.

Nelson continues walking up the stairs and then falls. Davis returns the pistol to a startled Captain Gibson and leaves the lobby. No one stops Davis, Joshua notices. No effort is made to arrest him. Davis merely walks away, as if nothing has happened.

"We better leave, Josh," says John. As they push their way through the growing crowd, they hear Governor Morton speaking with several men in uniform. "I saw it all. If Davis hadn't acted as he did, he would have deserved to have been shot himself."

How, Joshua wonders, is killing someone because of an insult different from killing someone to save one's life? Is it because of the great separation between a private and a general, or the honor afforded a military officer to avenge an insult, or just the military necessity in a time of war? Whatever guilt Joshua's reasoning has ascribed to his conscience, it is now less.

John and Joshua leave the Galt House and walk back in the direction of the Louisville Hotel, without talking. When they get to Fourth Street, John motions for Joshua to join him and go down to the wharf, a final escape from the tragedy they have witnessed and a change from the bustling activities of merchants and peddlers on Main Street, to the hard laboring stevedores, unloading military cargos from dozens of paddle wheelers lined alone the shore south to the falls of the Ohio River.

The clatter of dozens of ox-drawn wagons, moving to and away from the river over the cobblestone surface that separates the row of buildings from the Ohio River, provides a steady rhythm that eclipses their vision of the shooting. Suddenly the rhythm becomes melodic: four young Negro boys, one playing a drum; another, the spoons; a third a washboard; and the fourth, a bent trumpet. Joshua drops a nickel in the tin cup in front of the four youngsters.

"Are you hungry, Josh?" asks John.

"Shucks, yes," says Joshua.

"Let's go to that saloon on Fifth Street," says John, and they do.

Although it is not yet noon, the saloon is crowded. A sign on the bar states: Free Food with Nickel Glass of Beer. Both John and Joshua have their beer and now decide what to put on their plate: a hardboiled egg, large pickle, two slices of German rye bread with mustard, onions, and a slice of ham, and cheese in between. Finding no empty table, they stand at the bar.

After consuming the last morsel on their plates, they order another beer. John is describing his best fishing story and accidentally hits the bearded soldier next to him with his arm while demonstrating fly casting. The bearded soldier turns around and pushes John away from the bar.

"Who da ya think yur pushin around, sonny?" he says.

John, regains his composure, puts his hands up. "Sorry, friend. No harm intended."

"I ain't no friend a yours, pretty boy," he says, taking a swing at John.

John steps aside and comes down with his fist on the bearded man's neck, stunning him momentarily. Shaking his head to regain his senses and stroking his beard in a moment of concentration, he grabs a bottle from the bar and raises it over his head glaring daggers at John.

Instantly Joshua pushes John away, pulls the knife from his sock, and confronts the shaken man with his knife pointed at his heart. "Put the bottle down. We don't want any trouble."

The next few seconds seem minutes. "Ah," he says, turning to the bar, "Jus a bunch of smartass kids," and drops the bottle onto the bar. Joshua and John begin to leave, but not until John takes his last sip of beer.

"This day of fun and relaxation isn't turning out to be exactly that," says John. "The marquee across the street says there's a two o'clock burlesque matinee. It starts in fifteen minutes. Let's see it, Josh, and we might get some fun and relaxation."

"I'll buy the tickets," says Joshua.

He buys two seats in the front row, and receives back four one dollar bills for his five. A tumbling act reminds them of army exercises, a sword swallower reminds them of army food, a juggler reminds them of carrying all their equipment on a march, and the two clowns' antics remind them of the daily drudgery of marching. Only the ventriloquist proves funny and only the quartet singing "My Old Kentucky Home, Good Night" provides relaxation, if not nostalgia.

They saunter down Main Street, occasionally stopping to gaze into the woman's apparel store; going into Shafer's candy shop, with its candy marble jars arranged in mosaics; buying two cents worth of jelly beans; and, crossing the street, buying two cream puffs from Jake Martin's small bakery and grocery.

Between Fifth and Sixth Streets is a narrow alley, and as they pass it, a tall man wearing a long overcoat whispers to them: "Postcards? French postcards?"

Both John and Joshua have heard about those erotic pictures made possible by William Fox Talbot's patented process that made multiple copies possible, permitting a near limitless number of prints to be produced from a glass negative. Paris soon became the center of this trade, and by 1860 had over 400 photography studios, most of them profiting by selling illicit pornography to the masses, who could now afford it.

Traditionally, an academie was a nude study, which had to be registered with the French government and sold only with its approval, but the realism of a photograph made many of them inherently erotic. The models' poses had to be held very still for a long time, resulting in the standard pornographic image from one or two or more people engaged in sex acts to a solitary woman exposing her genitals.

Soon, pictures could be bought near train stations from traveling salesmen and women in the streets who hid them under their dresses. In the case of the tall man accosting John and Joshua, the pictures were in a dozen inside pockets of his overcoat, under four categories: genitals for the top three pockets on his right side; acts for the lower three; nudes for the top three on his left side; and sweet for scantily dressed girls.

Being healthy young men, John and Joshua listen to the man's pitch. "Gentlemen, I have the latest pictures from France. Here!" (showing a genitals picture) "Behold the delicious mystery of Venus."

Their shocked expression tells the man to put the picture back in his pocket, and replace it with one from the acts pocket.

"Or you may prefer to look." Startled by seeing what had been whispered in their ears by older boys when they were youngsters, John and Joshua both feel a revulsion and body excitement simultaneously.

The man takes a photo from his nude pocket. "Such a loving girl or boy, if you prefer." John and Joshua both react together; pulling back at the sight of the latter.

Astute to the desires of his customers, the man knows they will go for his last category: sweet. He pulls four pictures of beautiful young girls, wearing heavy make-up and scanty dresses. He holds the four photographs up with his dirty fingers and shows two missing teeth with his smile.

John grabs two of the pictures and so does Joshua. "How much?" they ask.

Normally, the less erotic sweet pictures are five cents and the most erotic, the genitals, is twenty cents. "Twenty cents. Each," he says.

Joshua reaches in his pocket, but John takes him by the arm. "We're not interested," he says, pulling Joshua away.

He wants to barter realizes the man. Very well. "You are two fine looking soldiers. For you, ten cents each."

John shakes his head, no, slowly stepping away with Joshua.

"Five cents. Each," laments the man, reconciled to his normal price.

John and Josh each immediately hand the man two nickels and smile as he gives them the four pictures.

They stroll among the pedestrians on the sidewalk, engrossed in masculine fantasy. Eventually, before crossing the street, they put the photographs in their shirt pocket.

"What about having dinner at that French restaurant, John?" asks Joshua.

"You mean Delmonico's," replies John. "They'd be expensive."

"I'm buying. You'll be my guest, John," says Joshua, trying not to be sentimental, but wishing to convey the importance of John's friendship. "Then we'll go to the Folies."

John's serious expression causes Joshua to add, "My treat."

"Joshua, I'm not going to be able to pay you back for a year."

"I don't expect you to, John."

John raises both arms. "All right!" he says, and they amble to Delmonico's Restaurant, talking, saluting officers, and observing the girls. John wonders about Josh's apparent affluence but says nothing. Some enlistments came with an immediate bonus. That might be

Josh's case.

It is five-thirty when John and Joshua walk through glass doors opened by a Negro doorman, and enter Delmonico's Restaurant. Joshua and John, being the only enlisted soldiers among formally dressed couples, senior military officers, and gentlemen of authority, are observed but ignored, for Louisville and its citizens welcome the protection from any Confederate threat.

John and Joshua wait behind a major and his lady, as the maitre d' glances at his list of reservations. After taking the major and his lady to a table, the maitre d' returns, apprehensively observing John and Joshua to be a private and corporal, and very young. Lowering his deep voice even lower, he asks, "May I help you?"

"We'd like dinner for the two of us," says John.

"Do you have reservations?" asks the maitre d'.

John hesitates and then says, "No."

"We have no tables available without a reservation. I am sorry," says the maitre d'. He says this as gently as possible for a six foot man, not because John and Joshua are not welcome in Louisville, but because these two enlisted men are very young for such an assemblage of older, important persons. While the maître d' speaks, Joshua takes the role of five and one dollar greenbacks from his pocket.

The maître d' observes Joshua unravel the fives and ones. Joshua pulls out two, crisp one dollar bills and, holding them in his left hand, points to a table in the corner. "Isn't that table available?" he asks.

The maitre d' and Joshua look at each other, and Joshua smiles slightly, moving his hand with the two bills in front of the maitre d'.

"Yes! The gentleman is correct. That table is available." He takes the two bills, shoves them into his pocket, removes two large bills of fare from the stack on the desk, and asks John and Joshua, "Please, follow me."

He opens one of the large menus, first offering it to Joshua, and then the second to John. "Bon appétit!" he says, snapping his fingers for Albert to serve them.

The young gentleman must be from a well-to-do family the maitre d' reasons, returning to his desk. Or he may be the son of a ranking officer. Even they never handed him more than a dollar.

There are four soups, two fish, five relishes, ten vegetables, fifteen kinds of confections, cakes (some with fancy French and

Italian names), and ten entrees, including: saddle of venison with currant jelly, red-head duck stuffed plain, wild goose with pot wine sauce, and bridge of buffalo tongue a la Godar.

John sees Joshua in a somewhat different light than he did moments ago. Joshua's self-confident demeanor surprises him as much as the maitre d'. Knowing one has access to a fortune creates self-assurance, and this is true for Joshua. John waits to see Joshua's reaction to the bill of fare, the size of a Medieval manuscript.

"There's a lot here, John." He speaks of the food, not of the price. "Why don't we ask the waiter what he would recommend?" He folds his menu and defers to John.

"Waiter!" says John. Albert places two chilled glasses of tomato juice with a lemon slice on the rim in front of them. "Yes sir." he says.

Twice their age, Albert's only son has just enlisted in the Union army. Albert's pleased to serve these two young gentleman in uniform, normal diners being his own age or older and several social steps higher. Aware that the large Bill of Fare is initially intimidating, Albert wonders if they will ask his assistance in ordering.

"It's Albert, right?" asks John.

"Yes sir."

John likes being called 'sir' but does not dwell on it. "What would you recommend?" asks John, holding the bill of fare in front of himself.

"I would suggest beginning with the consommé, and then the pulled greens with Roquefort cheese dressing. For fish, I would suggest the kippered salmon. For your entree, the chef's special rib of beef with Poivards sauce. It comes with julienne potatoes and buttered asparagus tips. Our pastry chef has prepared charlotte russe for this evening, topped off with Punch au Rhein."

Both John and Joshua shake their heads, yes. "Fine." says, John.

"Do you have any champagne?" asks Joshua.

"Yes, sir, we have a fine wine cellar. I'll have the wine steward come to your table," says Albert.

"Is there anything else?"They shake their heads, no. Walking to the kitchen, Albert motions to the wine steward, "Champagne, for table two," he says, before entering the swinging doors.

The wine steward comes to their table and holds a bottle wrapped in a white napkin in front of Joshua and John. "This is our house champagne—an excellent vintage," he says.

Joshua again defers to John. "We'll have it." says John. The wine steward pops the cork, smells it, and then lets John smell it, "A fine bouquet." says the steward. Not sure what all the smell of the cork is about, John merely shakes his head, yes.

The wine steward slightly fills a champagne glass and hands it to John. John is not sure what he is supposed to do with a glass slightly filled with champagne. "The taste, sir. It's aroma."

John takes a sip. "Fine!" he says.

The wine steward fills the long-stemmed champagne glass behind each of their plates and has the bus boy remove the other four wine glasses from the table. He places the chilled champagne bottle, still wrapped in a white napkin, into the wine bucket sitting on a tripod, which the bus boy has placed by their table.

John and Joshua take their glasses and toast each other, the glasses sounding a soft 'ting'. "To our success," says John. "To our good fortune," says Joshua.

Joshua wonders why there is so much silverware set at each of their plates: an odd shaped knife back of their plates, and two knives, three spoons and three forks aside their plates. After each course is served, certain silverware is removed. Joshua guesses they are removed because he and John will not need them, just as the glasses were removed after they were served champagne. One army canteen cup serves as a soup bowl, coffee pot, and plate!

Finishing the charlotte russe, they feel stuffed like a sow looks just before giving birth to a litter of eighteen piglets, and they can't believe that Albert is placing another dish in front of them: cheese, small crackers, and grapes. "Would you like coffee?" he asks.

They each answer, no, and spread a small slice of cheese on a cracker. Surely, their dinner is over, but what is this golden bowl of water for, that Albert places in front of them? Several small pink rose leaves float on the water.

A satisfactory rapport having been established between them and the waiter, Joshua speaks to Albert, who places a silver tray on the table with the bill facing down. "What is the bowl of flower water for?" He does not say "Albert" again, in deference to his age.

"For your fingers, sir," says Albert.

John and Joshua dip their fingers in the rose water, wiggle them a few seconds, and then wipe them dry on their napkins. They look at each other and laugh. Army life is so different!

The two meals are $1.50 each and the champagne is one dollar. Joshua puts a five dollar bill on the silver tray. A few seconds later, he takes a quarter from his pocket and places it on the tray. He wants Albert to know they have appreciated his service and his understanding of two young country boys.

He takes two one dollar bills from his pocket and writes on both: "Galt House October 1, 1872, Joshua Applegate." He gives one to John and says, "You sign both of them. Keep one for yourself and give me back the other."

A five minute walk takes them to the Follies. The ticket seller is suspicious when Joshua requests two seats in the orchestra, but the suspicion changes to surprise when the young army private hands him a five dollar bill, the cost for two orchestra seats.

The theater is nearly full, and eight patrons on the right of the first row in the orchestra have to stand up to let John and Joshua reach their seats: a major and lieutenant colonel with their wives, and two couples in formal dress. The orchestra, twice the size of the band at the burlesque, begins, allowing John and Joshua a moment to marvel at the red satin curtain with golden fringe at the bottom, and the faux-baroque, white theater interior with golden trimming. The crystal chandelier, a massive eight foot wide collection of several thousand glass beads, hangs from a ceiling painted to look like clouds against a blue sky.

The five different theater price sections are discernible by the people and their dress, sitting in the sections. Students and enlisted soldiers are in the cheapest section, the 25¢ back of the balcony section; while non-commissioned officers and laborers sit in the 50¢, other half of the balcony. Lieutenants, clerks, and sales persons view the stage from the back of the theater, the $1.50 section; and captains and formally dressed store managers, with their ladies, carry on conversations in the middle $2.00 section.

It is only in the first three rows of the orchestra, the $2.50 section, that field and occasional general officers, with government officials in formal attire, sit. Like the stamens of a orange lily, John and Joshua reside in the middle of the elegant attired orchestra patrons.

The curtain is drawn and the most spectacular line of girls prance in rhythm to the orchestral music in nine exotic costumes, each a different color. Five foot tall Ostrich feathers, arranged in a semi-circle, adorn their heads, and long satin cloaks of matching color, fanning out as they dance, reflect the hundreds of tiny, colored glass beads adorning the cloaks. The eyes of both John and Joshua stare ahead without blinking, never have they seen more of the feminine body, and never in such magnificent apparel.

After anxiously waiting for the intermission to end, John and Joshua discover each succeeding performance reveals more of the feminine body and less exotic dress. In the finale', fifteen scantly dressed girls dance, shuffle, hop, tap, and shimmy, before separating into two parallel lines. They stretch their hands to a tall, blond, bare breasted girl, wearing only a g-string, sashaying towards the audience. John and Joshua are the first to applaud when the curtain comes down and the last to stop.

"That was all right, particularly the end, don't you think, John?"

"Sure do!" says John. "I could see that over again but we better find a hotel for the night."

The Franklin House, The Russell Hotel, The Louisville Hotel, and the Galt House, all the hotels in Louisville, are filled for the night. It is getting late and they are too tired to walk back to camp, something best not done late at night. "I've got an idea, Joshua," says John. "Do we still have some money with us?" (He means do you Josh, have some money left.)

"Yes," said Joshua, curious as to why John asked.

"Come with me," says John, going in the direction of Second Street and Washington Street.

This was not Billy Goat Strut, but the girls under the gas lights are no different than the "ladies of the night" lined along the narrow alley of that name. What is John thinking!

As they walk along dimly lit Washington Street, John ignores the "inducements" from the prostitutes old enough to be their mothers as well as the hustler's whose ugly features, unnoticed by older "hurting" men, dampen any youth's desire. In the shadows of the doorway, a tiny figure stands next to the brick building, her arms folded, and a shawl wrapped around her neck to keep out the chill in the air. John stops in front of her.

"Do you have a room?" he asks.

Slightly over five feet tall, she steps out of the shadows and under the gaslight, keeping her dark black hair and soft, pink face covered by a hood. Keeping her head down, she whispers "Yes, I do."

"How much?" asks John.

"Twenty-five cents, sir."

"How much for two?" He points to Joshua. "The two of us?"

"Fifty cents, sir."

"How much for all night?" asks John.

She steps back in horror! "All night?"she asks, but more as a disturbing statement.

"No, you don't understand," say John, laughing. "We only want a place to sleep tonight. Nothing else."

"Breakfast, perhaps?" interrupts Joshua.

"For the two of you to sleep tonight? Two dollars. And twenty cents for breakfast for the both of you. "

"What do you say, Josh?" asks John.

"The best two dollars and twenty cents we'll ever spend," says Joshua. The "we" is only a convenience of speech.

"Where do you live?" asks John.

"Five blocks down Washington Street," she says.

"What shall we call you, my dear?" asks Joshua.

"Tessie, sir. My name is Tessie Scholl."

"Take us to our bed, Tessie," says John, and she does.

Her home is a shotgun house: a parlor, bedroom, dining room, and kitchen, joined by a hall, running the length of the house. The parlor contains a bed, table, chest, and two chairs, and is lighted by a kerosene lamp. Another bed and a crib are in the bedroom, next to a wardrobe. A cot sits against the back wall of the dining room with a round table and two chairs in the center and a potbellied stove to the side. A wood stove and water pump over a sink take up half of the small kitchen, with the other half containing a cabinet and counter.

An old lady rocking a baby stares at John and Joshua when they enter the parlor. "I live with my grandmother." She goes to the baby and kisses it on the cheek. "Jenny is six months old," she says, taking off her cloak and shawl. "This is your room. Granny and I sleep in the next room with Jenny. You'll have to go out the front door and around to the back for the privy. Turn out the lamp when you go to bed, please. We raise some chickens in the back, so I'll have some fresh eggs for you in the morning."

"And coffee," adds Joshua.

Her grandmother and the sound-asleep-baby go into the next room. "Good night," she says, following them and closing the door.

"Married?" asks Joshua, beginning to undress.

"Probably. She's a sweet little thing," says John, taking off his boots.

"Maybe he was killed," suggests Joshua.

"Well, no matter, it's a tough way to make a living."

Exhausted, they turn off the kerosene lamp, climb into bed, and fall asleep.

A cock wakes Joshua, who raises the window shade and allows a small stream of light to enter. He goes back to bed, not disturbing John, who continues to snore. He places both hands behind his neck and allows the events of the last day to parade before him. He'll remember yesterday and reminisce about everything they did, he says to himself, in the coming months. In the coming years? There's a knock at the door.

It's Tessie, letting them know their breakfast will be ready in a few minutes. Waking up John, Joshua and he dress and step into the dining room. Jenny lies wide awake in the crib. Granny puts two forks on the oilcloth covering the table, and Tessie brings in two plates of sunny-side up eggs and a platter of warm biscuits. She places a jar on the table. "This is special. Apple cinnamon jam. You two have been kind to me, and I want to thank you," she says, before returning to the kitchen.

"We're going to have to hurry to get back by 7:00 this morning," says Joshua.

"Do *you* have your pass with you?" asks John.

Joshua does and hands it to John, who takes a pencil from his pocket and makes a small line by the 7 to look like a 9. "Now you have the time," smiles John. "And Josh, if anyone at regimental headquarters questions you, just say you've been on courier duty. That always stops more questions."

"What are you going to say to Sergeant Libert?" asks Joshua.

"Nothing. I'll give him the pint of Kentucky Bourbon I bought him," says John, which explains his short absence when they were in and out of shops on Main Street.

Tessie joins them at the table. They were right. Her husband was crushed to death by a overturned wagon three months before Jenny was born. Tessie had no where to go but to her invalid grandmother, and their livelihood depends on her.

After a third cup of coffee they tell Tessie that it's time for them to leave. Joshua hands her a five dollar bill. "Buy Jenny something with the change," he says, as he puts on his hat, ready with John to leave through the front door. Tears fill Tessie's eyes and she steps up to Joshua and kisses him on the cheek. "Be careful," she says and walks to the kitchen, wiping her eyes.

A half hour later they reach camp. John (and the pint of Kentucky Bourbon) goes to the company headquarters' tent and Joshua to regimental headquarters, where he is told that the army will leave Louisville tomorrow, and he should report back to his company headquarters, which he does.

"Report to Lieutenant Dodson at the wagon compound, Applegate," says Sergeant Libert. "You're the only teamster in our company that is a muleteer. The other three are horseman—don't know nothin about mules. Teach em fast, Applegate. We march outa here tomorrow."

Yesterday was like a rocket, lighting up the sky and bursting in a glorious spray of glowing sparks before fading back into darkness—a darkness of unknowing, unhappiness, unpreparedness, unreality, unreasonableness, unruliness, unrest, but for Joshua, not unsinfulness.

Joshua Applegate has a secret and can't tell anyone.

CHAPTER FOUR

WEDNESDAY, 1 OCTOBER 1862, 10:00 A.M.

How can it be my duty
To kill someone like me?
If there's a God in heaven,
Please don't let it be.

Our Time is neither linear nor circular but spiral. In linear time our routine of sleeping, eating, and coupling, is like a perpetual calendar, never ending; and in circular time our routine is like the week or month, ever repeating, never ending. Spiraling time, however, is different: we seem to repeat our routine, but actually arrive slightly "higher" than where we began, and with a new awareness. This new awareness results in a curiosity about itself, desperation of its consequences, or a readiness to spin away from the spiral. Joshua Applegate's spiraling journey begins in desperation and ends with a new beginning.

General Don Carlos Buell has reinforced his army with thousands of recruits. On 1 October 1862 he sends 20,000 troops to Frankfort, which, with Lexington, had been captured by Confederate General Kirby Smith, and with the remainder of his army of nearly 58,000, marches to General Bragg's command at Bardstown.

Leaving their encampment outside Louisville, the army of wagons, artillery, horses, mules, and nearly 80,000 men are cheered by crowds of citizens along Broadway, who, once again, feeling safe from Confederate attack, view the march as a parade. Joshua sits on the lead wagon of his company next to Bill Shaughnessy, a veteran of the Battle of Shiloh but a recruit as a teamster, who holds the reins while listening to Joshua explain how to handle mules.

Joshua suddenly stops explaining, seeing in the crowd ahead the two girls, who took him and John to the church, waving and yelling. He turns away, continues his explanation to Billy, trying to pull in his head like a turtle. When the wagon is in front of the two girls they wave their handkerchiefs and yell, "Joshua! Joshua!"

"I think those girls are calling you, Josh," says Billy, interrupting Joshua's explanation about mules. Joshua slowly turns to the girls, now only a few feet from them, smiles, slightly, and waves his right hand, slightly. A few seconds later he resumes his explanation of dealing successfully with mules. Billy concludes that Josh may know how to deal with mules but he "shore don't know nothin about dealin' with women."

Nine hours later and twenty miles from Louisville the army bivouacs along the north side of a small stream. A company fire is lit and the frying pans and camp chests are removed from the wagons with each group of ten men preparing for the evening meal. Joshua explains the difference between a bull fire and a cooking fire to the two recruits in his squad of ten men. "You cook on coals and shoot the bull around leaping flames which will only burn food," he tells them.

The mess cook lays two logs side by side and builds a hot fire slowly until it burns down to coals. Then the frying pan of pickled pork (the fat side of sou-belly) is placed directly on the hot coals as well as a pot of coffee. Beans and rice, onions, and potatoes contribute to a satisfying meal. Joshua looks past the two platoons between his platoon and headquarters' platoon, but sees no trace of John, whom he hasn't seen since their arrival at camp two days ago. He takes out a cigar, and lights it with a long sliver of wood that he stuck in among the hot coals.

Three days later, the army reaches Bardstown, and Bragg with only 18,000 Confederates withdraws to Perryville, a village of 300 on the rim of the bluegrass area in central Kentucky, which has been plagued for months by a severe drought. Buell's army follows and on 7 October the Union troops arrive at Perryville.

Joshua joins the rest of the troops in the search for water and finds local streams, creeks, and wells completely dry. Informed about a small pond, Joshua fills his canteen from the pond, while his fellow troopers wash their feet and socks from the same water. He forces himself not to throw up when he sees a dead mule floating at the other end of the pond.

Joshua notices that Billy Shaughnessy doesn't fill up a canteen. In fact, Billy doesn't have a canteen. Curious, Joshua watches Billy get a canteen drink from privates Cummings, Floyd, and then Alcott, before they fill their canteens. Joshua walks over to Alcott. "How come you give Shaughnessy a drink from your canteen?"

"Billy gave me a canteen a couple of months ago, so I'd have two. Jus' le' me have a drink once in a while, he said. So I do," said Private Alcott.

Privates Cummings and Floyd tell Joshua the same thing, but Cunnings explains: Bill Shaughnessy began collecting lost or discarded canteens at Shiloh, and after giving them as a second canteen to *over* twenty men in the company, he no longer needs to carry his own canteen. Joshua decides that Billy and John need to meet each other, having much in common.

A rumor that Doctor's Creek holds water precipitates a Union effort to take the creek, beginning the first shots of the battle. General Bragg believes that the Union force is a minor one and orders his troops the next day to brush them aside before marching to Versailles and link his command with Kirby Smith's army.

The Union troops, many of whom are new recruits with some never having fired their rifles, hold for several hours, but they are eventually forced back more than a mile. The 6th Kentucky is not ordered into battle, and Joshua waits among the wagons, which are some distance behind his regiment and the fighting.

After fastening the reins to the wagon and pulling the brakes tight, Joshua and Billy stand in the wagon watching the huge white cloud that hangs over the battlefield, and hear the rapid discharge of guns that sound like a volcanic uproar. Private Davis in the wagon next to them suddenly shouts, "Cavalry!"

Joshua turns around and sees several dozen Confederate cavalrymen at the top of a rise in the land a thousand yards away, galloping towards them. The rebels draw their sabers and Billy yells, "Get under the wagon!"

Billy and Joshua jump out of the wagon and roll under it, while the other teamsters run ahead in panic towards the rear of their regiment and the battlefield. The Confederate cavalrymen race between the wagons and cut down the slowest teamsters. Then Billy rolls out from under the wagon, jumps into it, and grabs the nine-foot length of wagon chain under the seat. Some of the men of the 6th Kentucky regiment see the Confederates and open fire, compelling them to abruptly turn around and race back, towards the line of wagons.

Joshua rolls from under the wagon, grabs his carbine, and, jumping into the wagon, kneels behind one section. The Confederate cavalry, still brandishing their sabers, begin to yell as they return to the line of wagons. Joshua aims and fires at them as fast as he can during the few seconds before they reach the wagons. He sees Billy standing forward to the left of their wagon whirling the chain.

With too little time to withdraw their pistols, the Confederates see Billy just in time to avoid contact with the chain he whirls in a menacing circle above his head. They pass through the wagons and head back to the rim of the hill they left five minutes before. Joshua fires several more shots before jumping down from the wagon. Billy may not turn out to be a top teamster, concludes Joshua, let alone pass for a muleteer, but he sure is worth having around when trouble begins.

Victorious in the fighting north of Perryville, the Confederates learn that nearly 40,000 Union troops did not participate in the battle. Outnumbered three-to-one, the Confederate army withdraws to Harrodsburg, leaving their dead and most of the wounded behind. The 6th Kentucky and its brigade pursues the withdrawing Confederates as far as London, Kentucky, while the wagons and teamsters not killed or wounded by the rebel cavalry, follow. Joshua hears that John had been assigned as a courier for the brigade during the battle.

The following day, with Union forces now concentrated around London and soon to push towards Danville, Joshua searches for John at headquarters tent during afternoon mess. He asks several of the headquarters' personnel whom he knew where John is, but none of them know, other than he had been acting as a courier for brigadc headquarters. Sergeant Libert would know.

Sergeant Libert puts his pencil down and leans back in the army chair. "Tafel was killed," he says

"Are you sure?" asks Joshua. The sergeant nods yes.

"Where is he?" asks Joshua.

Aware of Joshua and John's friendship, Sergeant Libert stands up. "Joshua," he begins, using the first name as a sign of condolence. "John was acting as a courier. A courier that was near him said an exploding shell hit him. There was nothing left to bury."

Without saying a word Joshua nods his head and leaves Sergeant Libert, the tears trickling from his blurring eyes as he hears John, "Just say you're on courier duty."

That evening Joshua writes a letter to John's mother.

Near Danville 10 October 1862

Dear Mrs. Tafel,
I am sorry to have to tell you that John was killed the day before yesterday. He was killed instantly and did not suffer. When I last looked at him, he had a happy face. He was a good friend. I will miss him.

Very truly yours,
Joshua Applegate

The Confederates win a tactical victory at Perryville in pushing back both ends of the Union battle line; but they endure a strategic defeat by withdrawing from Kentucky. The hope for a Confederate Kentucky is permanently ended. Also ended is the expectation of gaining thousands of Kentucky recruits.

General Buell is replaced by Major General William S. Rosecrans, who reorganizes the Army of the Ohio. Renamed the 14th Army Corps, it soon becomes known as the Army of the Cumberland and follows Bragg into Tennessee. Reaching Nashville in late October, the Army of the Cumberland encamps there through Christmas, and Joshua receives an unexpected "Christmas present."

Joshua is told to report to Sergeant Libert who informs him that he is to train the new company recruits. "They're country boys, Applegate. They're big, vulgar, wild, and nasty; and General Headquarters wants them trained to be disciplined solders ... by next week. Any questions?"

"No, Sergeant," says a dubious Joshua.

"Go over to the parade grounds and report to Sergeant Weis. He'll assign a squad of recruits to you," says Libert.

"Is that Gustave Weis?" asks Joshua.

"Yea, I think so," says Libert. "Get going."

Joshua turns and lifts the flap of the tent. "Oh, Applegate! You're Corporal Applegate now," says Libert.

Joshua, who has his rifle and bayonet with him, sees Sergeant Weis standing in front of a dozen young men, who are in an indifferent civilian "at ease" stance, and listen to but ignore what Sergeant Wise says.

"Now boys, ve can continue dis drill after dinner, even mitout dinner and through der night. It's up to you," says Sergeant Weis, turning the squad over to the corporal behind him. Weis sees Joshua and walks towards him.

"Joshua, mein fruend!"

"Hello, Gustave. I've been assigned to train a squad."

"Ja, I know. I recommend you," says Sergeant Weis. "Kom! I take you to your squad."

Twelve tall, lanky, young bodies lounge around a single tree on the parade ground, swearing, laughing, cursing, and giving Joshua a country evaluation.

"Fall in, men," commands Sergeant Weis. After stretching, scratching, and yawning, twelve disheveled young men line up before Sergeant Weis and a corporal their own age.

"Der yours, Corporal Applegate," says Sergeant Weis. "Do vatever you need to do."

Telling men that they will continue drill on the parade ground through dinner and through the night if necessary may work fine for Sergeant Weis, but not for someone their own age. Besides, Joshua has no intention of drilling through dinner, and certainly not through the night. Joshua stands erect but relaxed in front of the men, taking a moment to look at each one without saying a word.

"A ... ten ... shon!" commands Joshua. Nobody moves.

"By the order of the commanding general it is my right to command this squad," says Joshua in a quiet, reasoning manner. "And it is necessary for you to obey my commands." He withdraws the bayonet from its scabbard and attaches to his rifle.

"I shall repeat the order, and if it is not instantly obeyed, I shall run the man nearest to me through the body and will proceed, right to left, as long as my strength supports me and as long as you do not obey my commands."

Joshua stands at attention, his rifle at his side.

"A... ten ... shon!"

The twelve young men straighten up and follow all of Joshua's commands. Two hours later Joshua removes the bayonet from his musket and dismisses the squad. It is not until all the men are gone that Joshua smiles.

On 16 December 1862, Rosecrans advances from Nashville, Tennessee, against Bragg at Murfreesboro; and on December 31, 1862, Bragg's Army of the Tennessee attacks Rosecrans near Murfreesboro.

North of Murfreesboro, Stones River zigzags from north to south. Prodded by Grant and urged by Lincoln, Rosecrans marches his 42,000 troops of the Army of the Cumberland northeast along the Nashville Pike to confront Bragg's 36,000 Confederates of the Army of the Tennessee. Criticized for abandoning Kentucky after the battle of Perryville, Bragg vows to hold the line at Murfreesboro and places his forces astride the river, intending to attack the Union left on 31 December 1862. Rosecrans plans to attack the Confederate right the same day.

Wearing corporal stripes and no longer a teamster, Joshua eats breakfast before his company prepares to attach, when suddenly they hear the roll of thousands of muskets and the heavy booms of cannon that become thicker and faster. The Confederates are the first to attack.

Panic grips the Union men who push their breakfast and cooking gear aside and rush, yelling, to the rear. Joshua calls out. "Stand your ground men!" But except for the officers and sergeants the entire body of troops becomes a mob, pushing, yelling, and running.

Looking towards the center of the Union line, Joshua sees General Phil Sheridan rally his troops and hold the center from becoming a rout. The Confederates' relentless assaults, however, press Sheridan back toward the turnpike, where Rosecrans rallies troops near his headquarters.

In a cedar grove called the Round Forest, but which the men in Joshua's platoon name "Hell's Half Acre" Joshua conceals himself behind a fallen tree, firing in the direction of rebel fire. During the next hour, an eternity to Joshua, heavy firing is followed by silence and then a repeat of heavy firing. During a time of silence, he hears the sound of a single bird and watches the breeze ripple through the leaves of the forest.

To his right, a hundred yards away, a single rebel, dressed in grey and holding his musket with both hands, steps from behind a tree and begins walking in the direction of Joshua, but unseen by those on Joshua's left and right. With each step the rebel scans the terrain in front of him from right to left, lifting each foot slowly through the tall grass.

Joshua is so surprised by this foolhardy Confederate, that he lifts his eyes from the sight of his musket and watches as the soldier continues his snail-like pace. At half the distance, Joshua can see the rebel's thick mustache, his long black hair hanging beneath his squashed hat, and a slight reflection of light from his glasses.

Spellbound, frozen with disbelief, unconsciously Joshua places the barrel of his musket on the fallen tree he lies behind and lowers his right eye onto the sight. At twenty yards he can see the ruddy features of the man, and even that his eyes appear blue.

The confederate stops. Slowly, he moves his head from right to left, and then back to the center, directly in the direction of Joshua. Joshua feels their eyes have locked on each other and wonders why the rebel does not drop or run, but his finger pulls the trigger, and the rebel slumps down, like a handkerchief falling gracefully from the hand of a woman, and with a tiny red hole in his forehead.

Joshua can't understand how he can kill someone he doesn't know with such ease of conscience, so different with Sergeant O'Conner. He didn't hate this confederate, he didn't know him, but he hated O'Conner, a hatred that had to kill. The thought is forgotten in a moment as Joshua prepares for another attack.

With massive infantry and artillery around the grove, the Union forces withstand the Confederate attacks. The next day the contracting Union lines are strengthened; and Confederate General Breckinridge, ordered by Bragg to take the high ground, is stopped by devastating cannon fire.

The line of men which Joshua is part of is ordered forward. They rush through trees and brush, dodging sporadic rifle fire. Before the line of men drop to the ground and conceal themselves behind trees and stumps, Joshua stumbles on a root. He falls down and his cocky French style hat falls from his head, with a round hole through the top back of his hat and out the lower back part.

His face, bruised and scratched, and his left knee, aching and swelling, Joshua uses the butt of his musket to stand up on his right leg, while the pain in his left leg increases the more he stands on it. He picks up his hat and notices the two holes made by a minie ball. Aware that if he had not stumbled the moment he did, the minie ball would have gone through his brain, Joshua whispers, "Thank God!"

Twenty paces ahead, Private Jack Head turns around and yells, "Are you alright, Josh?"

Too overcome with emotion, with his close brush with instant death, with the sudden realization that life is a joy, Joshua can only shake his head yes and lift his right arm holding his musket, and begin walking towards Private Head.

"You're hurt," says Private Head, "Tough luck, Josh." Private Head helps Joshua catch up with the line of moving troops and is baffled by what Josh says.

"I've never been happier, Jack!"

This brush with death sparks within Joshua a beginning harmonization with the vibrations that sustain all matter. The next day, the 3rd of January 1863, General Bragg withdraws his Army of the Tennessee from Murfreesboro, beginning the year on a ominous note for the Confederate cause. More than 9,000 are buried by both sides. Bragg does not command the respect of his subordinate officers, who denounced his leadership and strategy, but his close friendship with Confederate President Jefferson Davis helps him retain his post in Tennessee.

In the withdrawal of the army from Stones River at Murfreesboro, Bragg notices a straggling soldier. "Don't you belong to Bragg's army?" he shouts.

The soldier does not recognize Bragg. "Bragg's army?" responds the soldier. "Why, he's got no army! One half of it he shot in Kentucky, and the other half has been whipped to death at Murfreesboro!"

Joshua soon hears about Frances Clayton, the Minnesota housewife who fought at Stones River. When her husband John enlisted in a cavalry regiment, she put on trousers and enlisted alongside him. The story has it that she fought in a number of battles, including the Union capture of Fort Donelson, and learned "all the vices of men," including drinking, swearing, gambling, and enjoying a good cigar. When her husband John was killed at Stones River, she is said to have stepped over his fallen body and kept fighting.

Through the spring of 1863 Union General Rosecrans and Confederate General Bragg take the opportunity to rebuild their armies, while their superiors focus on Vicksburg. Rosecrans settles his army in central Tennessee with headquarters in Murfreesboro, and Bragg marches his army to Chattanooga.

Rough log cabins are built to hold twelve men and the issue of flour provides the one highlight in an otherwise cold and snowy army routine—Flapjacks. Water, grease, and salt are added to the flour to make a batter, which is then cooked in a pan. Flipped out of the pan when they turn brown, flapjacks and a hot cup of coffee make building, hauling, drilling, and marching tolerable for Joshua and his platoon. When one of their numbers discovers a lean steer and kills it, the feast is enhanced by sprinkling gunpowder on it to replace the lack of salt.

In February Joshua's company is ordered to Woodbury, a small town twenty miles from Murfreesboro, to demonstrate a "show of force." The frozen roads have become cold and muddy, and the men take off their shoes and socks, tying them to the end of their muskets. With rolled up trousers, they wade through the cold, ankle-deep mud, whistling and singing.

As evening approaches, they reach Woodbury and settle just outside the fringe of houses surrounding the center of the town. Joshua's squad takes possession of a large barn, from where they can see the Baptist Church of Woodbury just opposite the courthouse. Food supplies having been low, the company has only three ears of horse corn per man. That night the corn is parched in hot coals and salted. The larger portion is eaten with hot coffee, and the remainder is stored in pockets for tomorrow to be eaten on the march when they return to Murfreesboro.

That night Joshua writes to his aunt and asks her to send him new underwear. He has worn his present underwear for three months and it is ready to be thrown away. The moon slips through patches of clouds, shining on the small cross atop the Baptist church, granting Joshua a moment of reverie and reflection, and he puts his pencil down. He ignores his aching jaws and sore gums and teeth from the horse corn.

No longer do thoughts of Sergeant O'Conner come to his mind, but Joshua's dreams, when remembered, picture hideous creatures pulling him into black rivers or pushing him down bottomless holes. Gazing at the cross on the church, Joshua recalls back home hearing Pastor Beckman's sermon about "streets paved with gold" and he thinks about his eventual return home. As he falls asleep he dreams of two black ravens standing on the sides of a open chest which glistens with thousands of gold coins.

The company returns to Murfreesboro late the next evening, tired and hungry. The last of the parched horse corn was eaten that afternoon and the men hurry to the battalion mess for dinner. Dinner ended an hour ago and the pots and pans as well as the food have been put away. There is hot coffee and corn cakes. Billy Shaughnessy had been assigned to the battalion kitchen to serve his company.

When Billy returns to his squad's cabin, everyone is grumpy about the small amount of food they were served, particularly after a six hour march in cold, damp weather. "Look what I've got!" exclaims Billy, holding up a package the size of a big church bible.

A recent innovation to the food supply for the army is dehydrated vegetables, which come in rectangular compressed packages. Heated with an equal portion of water, one package can serve a dozen men a vegetable, including potatoes, corn, greens, carrots, squash, and, ideally, a mixture of two or more. Billy "requisitioned" a package from the battalion mess, theft not being a consideration, since the army is "one great family."

First the large cooking pot is brought from the supply wagon; water poured in and heated on the single stove in the cabin. "Maybe it'll be a mixture of potatoes and squash," says one soldier. "With greens!" yells another. The unofficial platoon cook removes all the wrapping.

"What is it?" they inquire. The unwrapped, still dehydrated contents, looks like a sold block of compressed white straw. One of the men leans closer, sniffs, touches, and scrapes off a piece. "Onions!" he yells.

The illusions of hot vegetables vanishes, and the hunger pains somewhat abate, but for weeks afterwards, none of Joshua's squad eat onions or vegetables mixed with onions.

Morning and evening formation and drill consume less than two hours of the day and assigned duties another two hours, so that half the day is available for sleeping, resting, playing checkers, horseshoes, poker, baseball, and gambling. Pinochle has been introduced into the county two years before, and sergeant Monahan in Joshua's company has bought two regular decks of cards from the sutler in order to create a pinochle deck.

A pinochle deck consists of 48 cards: two each of the ace, king, queen, jack, ten, and nine of each of the four suits. The object of the game is to bid a certain number and then to reach that score or more. Certain combinations of cards (a king and queen of the same suit, or a run of ace, king, green, jack, ten of the same suit) have point values.

The queen of spades and jack of diamonds is called pinochle and has a point value of 4, while double pinochle has a point value of 30. The odds of holding double pinochle are rare but valuable in points.

Sergeant Monahan and several other non-commissioned officers are playing pinochle in a Sibley tent, a conical tent patterned after the tepees of the Plains Indians which could accommodate twelve to fifteen men for sleeping and twice that many for recreation—in this case, gambling.

Late afternoon, two hours before evening mess, with all formations and most duties completed, gambling becomes a main activity in camp. Joshua finishes playing checkers and decides to see what all the commotion is at the table of non-commission officers.

"We're 42 points ahead. That'll cost each of you 21 cents," says Sergeant Monahan to Sergeant Murphy and Corporal Slocum.

"Is that pinochle you all are playin'?" asks Joshua.

"Yea it is," says Sergeant Monahan, pocketing his 21 cents. "Do ya know how to play?"

"No," says Joshua.

"We'll teach you," says Monahan.

"Take my seat Josh," says Corporal David Slocum. "You might be luckier than me."

Joshua takes Slocum's seat and listens as Sergeant Monahan explains the game of pinochle. "Sergeant Hopper and I are partners and Sergeant Murphy is your partner, Applegate. The side with the most points after each game wins. For each point the winners have over the losers, they get one penny. Got it?" asks Monahan. Joshua shakes his head yes.

"You can help Applegate, Davie," says Monahan to Corporal Slocum, and begins to deal three cards to each consecutively.

Joshua has a marriage (a king and queen of hearts) worth 4 points, four kings of different suits (worth 8 points) and two queens-of-spades and two jacks-of-diamonds, which is double pinochle and worth 30 points, for a total of 42 points.

Josh's partner, Sergeant Murphy passes, and so does Sergeant Hopper, Sergeant Monahan's partner.

"How much do I have to bid?" asks Joshua.

"At least 16," says Monahan. "If no one bids, I, as the dealer, have to take the bid for 15."

"Well, I'll bid 45," says Joshua.

Monahan and Hopper laugh. "Well, I guess you're gona hafta learn the hard way, Applegate," says Monahan. "Let's see your meld?" The puzzled look on Joshua's face brings further instructions from Monahan. "Your meld! Layout the cards that are points." Monahan can't decipher the odd expression on Corporal Slocum's face.

Joshua places the king and queen of hearts face up on the table. "That's 4," says Monahan. Then the four kings of different suits. "That 8 more," says Monahan.

"A total of 12," says Joshua.

"Yea, Applegate," says Monahan. "But you better have more meld than that."

Joshua places two queens-of-spades on the table and next to them, two jacks-of-diamonds. "Isn't this 30 points?" asks Joshua, confident enough to know he has a "good hand" but too inexperienced in the game to know how unusual it is to hold double pinochle the first time a person plays the game. "That's a total of 42 points," says Joshua.

"Talk about luck of the beginner," says Monahan.

Joshua and his partner easily win and each receive 21 cents.

All four, including Corporal Slocum, laugh and comment on "beginner's luck." This time, Joshua's partner, Sergeant Murphy, deals.

Joshua is dealt four jacks of different suits and double pinochle again, a total of 34 points. This, being Joshua's first time to play two successive games of pinochle and to be dealt double pinochle in both, doesn't impress him as being unusual, something that probably has never happened before and probably will never happen again. He bids 45.

Monahan and Hopper burst out laughing, putting their cards on the table, face down. "You're not thinking, Josh," says Monahan, reverting to his first name, an unconscious sign of respect. "You're pushin your luck."

Joshua melds his four jacks and his double pinochle.

There is no laughter. No one smiles. Sergeants Monahan and Hopper sit with eyes wide open and an expression of shock.

A silence comes over the players, a silence of wonder; for all except Joshua appreciate that they'll never experience a pinochle game like this again. No one will.

Joshua and his partner each win 18 cents. "You can take my place, Slocum," says Monahan. "That's enough pinochle, for me," he says, handing him the deck. "You can give me the deck later, but I doubt I'll be playing much pinochle." The others, besides Joshua, concur, and the game ends.

Like most young men, Joshua learned "the facts of life" from older boys. He had been warned against "fallen women," not knowing exactly what that meant, and frightened in his youth regarding "misuse" of his own body. He had heard in whispers and been shown through pointing fingers young men who had contacted "the French disease," something one "got" from fallen women as well as from those who had the French disease. Cautioned to be careful when with those with the French disease, he had been scared to even be near a fallen women, but again was not sure how to know when a women was fallen. Rather than becoming more enlightened in the army with these facts of life, he became more confused.

After shaving himself on a mid-spring morning and then going to the latrine to relieve himself, Joshua notices a reddish, inflamed spot on his private parts. The French disease!

But he was still a virgin. How did this happen?

This might keep him from someday becoming a father! The disabled and disfigured men who had been pointed out to him flashes through his mind. Oh no! He'll ask his platoon sergeant, Sergeant Richard ("Dick") Stonebrenner.

In his thirties, six-foot tall, barrel-chested, with an insatiable sexual appetite for fleshy women, Dick Stonebrenner radiates a charm which seduces women and commands men. Not only does he "get things done" but he inspires others to do the same. Stonebrenner is Joshua's image of a big brother. He approaches Sergeant Stonebrenner immediately after morning formation.

Affectionately called "Stoney," Stonebrenner is called "Big Dick" behind his back, a play on the double meaning of his physical size and his womanizing. Joshua always refers to him as Sergeant Stonebrenner except in personal conversation.

"Stoney," begins Joshua, "I need to go on sick call. I got a reddish spot on my dong." Joshua's naive but innocent manner and his willing attitude in his army duties has impressed Stonebrenner into looking after this naturally good individual, a goodness admired by Stonebrenner but a goodness impossible for the likes of him. Stonebrenner's expression is one of surprise.

"No, Stoney, I haven't had relations with any girl," says Joshua. To be sure, he adds, "Or woman."

Personally pleased to know "his boy" has not fallen, Stonebrenner smiles. "Get Sergeant Libert's O.K. to go to the field hospital," he says. "The doctor probably won't believe you, Josh," he adds. This statement is believable in Stonebrenner's circle but not in the class to which Joshua is destined. Joshua is in that group of men for whom sex has no limitations, but he is not of it. In his limited experience, however, his present world is the entire world.

Joshua walks to the company headquarters tent, agreeing with Stonebrenner; not only won't the doctor believe that he "hasn't had relations" but he may laugh.

Like Sergeant Stonebrenner, Sergeant Libert judges Joshua to be one of the few "good boys" in the company, and shows not only the same surprise that Stonebrenner did at first, but—and this bothers Joshua—the same disappointment.

Sergeant Libert says nothing when he writes out a slip for Joshua to go to field hospital, and Joshua can not explain when disappointment in him is not spoken of but only facially expressed. He takes the slip and hurries to the field hospital.

Major Charles Thomas Conrad has been a doctor for thirty years. With graying hair, a thin moustache, and a bedside manner that still remains after two years of army service, Major Conrad listens to each patient as a person and not as number in an army unit.

Joshua is last in a line of twelve men standing before the small desk at which Major Conrad sits. Joshua wishes the doctor would stick to medical questions and drop the personal ones about "Where's your home?" and "What did you do before enlisting?" Unhurried when Joshua steps before him, Major Conrad lifts his eyes from the note he writes at his desk, observes a nervous Joshua, and smiles. "What's the problem, son?"

"I have a reddish spot on my ... private parts," says Joshua.

Doctor Conrad learned years ago that looks can deceive, for this young man appears an individual capable of controlling his sexual appetites. Now, after thirty years of practice, his expression is non-judgmental. "Drop you pants," he says.

"How long have you been exposed?" asks Doctor Conrad after observing the reddish spot.

"You may not believe me, Doctor, but I've never had relations with a girl."

"Sure, I believe you!" says the doctor. He begins to write a prescription.

The most welcome words! Joshua is of this group (represented in Doctor Conrad), which appreciates that there are men for whom sex is a natural expression, not to be abused, but for now Joshua is not in this group.

"Give this to the pharmacy. Apply the salve twice each day. It's just a little irritation. It should be gone in a week," says Doctor Conrad. He leans back in his chair, an indication of a personal comment. "This war will be over sometime soon, young man. Keep waiting until you're back home."

Joshua's company has been ordered to return to Woodbury, and his squad returns to the same farm and barn for their quarters. The middle aged sergeant in the company platoon, whom Joshua knows only as "Deacon," comes to the barn and speaks to Joshua, the only one there that evening, the day before Easter.

"Corporal," he begins. "Several of us are going to the Baptist Church early tomorrow morning at seven o'clock for Easter Services. I'd appreciate you telling your platoon. What's your name, corporal?"

"Applegate, Sergeant Deacon. Joshua Applegate."

"I'm Sergeant Micah Bellmeister, but everyone calls me Deacon. I'm a deacon in my church back home in Danville. You come along tomorrow morning, Joshua."

"I ain't no Baptist, Sergeant," says Joshua.

"Makes no difference," says Bellmeister. "Easter is for all Christians. We'll meet at headquarters tent at 6:30 tomorrow morning. I'll be looking for you," says the sergeant, as he leaves Joshua.

The next morning Martin Broderick is the only one from Joshua's platoon who arrives with him at the company headquarters tent, where eight other men are talking with Sergeant Bellmeister. "It's time for us to leave," says Sergeant Bellmeister. They walk down the road to the church and wait outside the entrance.

Three steps lead to the doors of the church, a faded white clapboard structure twice as long as it is wide with a cross and spire. A dozen families have already entered the church while several other families and individuals are walking to it, suspiciously glancing at the eleven Union soldiers with muskets, standing to the side of the steps.

A youngster, rushing to be with his family in the church, is stopped by Sergeant Bellmeister. "What is your pastor's name, young man?" he asks.

His eyes darting among the weapons, the youngster says, "Pastor Farthingham!"

"Go tell Pastor Farthingham that I wish to speak to him."

The young man does not ask who "he" is. The blue Union uniform is name enough. "Pastor," says the youngster, grabbing the elbow of Farthingham, "There's a blue belly outside that wants to talk with you."

Pastor Farthingham stands slightly higher than he is wide. His red bald head shines from the sunlight, and a trickle of perspiration slides down his cheek, a result of the same sun as well as the message he was given. The little remaining hair he has becomes a gray band behind his head from ear to ear. Not knowing why he has been called out, he stops at the church doors, allowing him to "look down."

"May I help you?" he says, hoping it is help these soldiers want.

"We wish to attend your Easter Service," says Sergeant Bellmeister. "We must keep our weapons with us, you understand."

This is a situation never discussed or mentioned in the seminary. Farthingham takes it for granted that "wish" means "intent" and makes no objection. "Are you Baptist?" he asks, a legitimate question under the circumstances.

"Two of us aren't, but we're working on that," replies Bellmeister.

“All right,” says Farthingham, relieved. “Follow me.”

Sixty men, woman, young girls, and children fill half the pews, but there are no young men. The eleven soldiers march behind the pastor down the aisle, and all heads turn and watch as the soldiers sit on the first bench on the right, after Pastor Farthingham motions with his hand for the three boys to move.

Joshua is a member of no church, but he did occasionally attend the Methodist Church in Munfordville with his aunt and he recognizes two songs and is familiar with most of what the pastor does and says. When Pastor Farthingham invites the congregation to come and partake of the bread and wine, Joshua does not join the nine soldiers who do, but remains in the pew with Martin Broderick, whose family, but not he, are Congregationalists.

Joshua notices pretty sixteen year old blond, blue-eyed Clara Jane Sterling, daughter of Martha Sterling, in the choir. During the third time he looks at her, she looks at him, before he turns his head. In that moment the spark of life unites them momentarily.

The service is nearly over except for a few words from the minister before he gives the benediction. He encourages all members of the congregation to attend the Sunrise breakfast prepared by the Ladies Circle and served in the hall behind the sanctuary. “All are welcome,” says Farthingham, suddenly realizing this includes the eleven Union soldiers. This might prove a dilemma.

From the back of the church, in the last pew, rises a young gentleman dressed in the gray uniform of a Confederate officer. He supports himself with a cane and holds his left arm in a sling. “Pastor!” he shouts, in a firm, deep, commanding voice.

Pastor Farthingham looks to the back of the church. “Yes, Lieutenant Cooper,” he says, fearful of what might now occur.

“I invite my brother soldiers of today to join me for breakfast on this Easter morn.”

There are gasps, sighs, and grunts, and Farthingham seizes the moment and immediately gives the benediction. The congregation hesitates to exit the sanctuary through the two back doors that lead to the congregational hall, when Joshua and the other ten soldiers stand up, Sergeant Bellmeister speaks up “We shall wait and enter with the lieutenant.” to the relief of Pastor Farthingham. The congregation cautiously departs the sanctuary through the two back doors.

A ten year old youngster, running ahead of his family, stops in front of Sergeant Bellmeister and places his arms on his hips. “Are you a damn Yankee?” he asks.

Sergeant Bellmeister laughs and replies, before the boy’s astonished father can grab him by the arm and rush him to the hall. “I am a Yankee, young man, and I’ll be damned if I’m anything else.”

Three rows of three tables with benches are covered with white linen table clothes and tableware. On a large table next to the side wall rest jars of jams and jellies, warm biscuits, fresh churned butter, hot coffee, and dried fruits.

Lieutenant Cooper points to the middle table in the middle aisle with his cane. “We’ll sit at this table gentlemen,” he says. Mrs. Sterling, who has observed Joshua, the young soldier with the dark brown eyes and dark wavy hair that hangs down to his shoulders, glancing at her daughter during the service, now sees Clara Jane intends to sit next to him. She steps in front of her daughter and sits herself next to Joshua, and Clara Jane sits on her other side.

After Pastor Farthingham gives the prayer, six ladies from the Ladies Circle come from the parsonage into the hall with steaming bowls of scrambled eggs.

The men and women sitting at the table with the lieutenant and the eleven Union soldiers, each with their muskets by their side, ask them questions. “Where are you from? Do you have a family? What did you do at home?” But all mention of the war is avoided. Two of the ladies motion to Mrs. Sterling. She gets up and speaks a few words with them, before they exit the hall, still talking.

“Wou1d you like some strawberry jam?” asks Clara Jane. When Joshua says yes, she extends her hand holding the jar to him, moving a few inches closer. He reaches with his right hand and clasps his hand around the tiny, soft, white, slender fingers holding the jar, speaking and hearing inwardly a lifetime of words before taking it from her.

“Well, men, it's time for us to return to camp,” says Sergeant Bellmeister. Joshua and his companions stand up and thank everyone. Clara Jane stands up and steps closer to Joshua, while inconspicuously extending her hand. Continuing to talk, Joshua lowers his left arm and their two fingers touch. He doesn't even know her name.

The next morning the company moves out of Woodbury back to camp at Murfreesboro.

By late Spring the boredom of the daily routine of army life is broken when the troopers discover they can purchase bay rum, the fragrant and medicinal liquid distilled from the leaves of the West Indian bayberry, from sutlers—not as a cosmetic or a medicine but as a drink. Shouts of "ki yip" echo through camp when this oily, greasy, unpleasant but intoxicating liquid is drunk. The sutlers are soon forbidden to sell bay rum by general headquarters. The discovery of a still soon provides another substitute for the forbidden bay rum—moonshine.

Billy Shaughnessy considers straggling—unofficial foraging—not only profitable but enjoyable, even when his lieutenant frowns upon it. On a Sunday in late spring, Billy strays a good distance from camp, following a small stream that meanders through open fields and thick woods. His patience is rewarded when he discovers a little old whiskey still fully equipped for active operation. There is a supply of "mash" on hand, and all other essential ingredients for turning out whiskey. The possibilities are endless, but he needs help.

Billy persuades eight from his platoon to join in the production of "Tennessee moonshine," as well as two privates of Joshua's platoon. This secret operation takes a great deal of planning, in scheduling operations within the daily routine of army duty, preventing interference from headquarters, and limiting and controlling "customers." An unforeseen event nearly destroys the entire operation.

A small detachment of Union cavalrymen comes across the still while the men are working it. Not wishing to share or lose the still, Billy grabs his rifle and summarily arrests the cavalrymen. Befuddled but amused, the cavalrymen accept a "pardon" if they behave themselves and depart, which they do. The still and equipment is immediately moved to a more secluded location.

For the next two months, before the army prepares to leave Murfreesboro, the four platoons of Billy's company are surreptitiously supplied at a reasonable price with a moonshine that is limpid and colorless as water but burns like fire. The jug of this elixir that periodically appears at battalion headquarters stops all inquiries from division headquarters into any "drinking problem" and enables the still to produce moonshine with no interruptions.

In the middle of June 1863 orders to prepare to move out come from general headquarters. General Rosecrans intends to advance his Army of the Cumberland against Bragg's Army of the Tennessee around Tullahoma, a town 30 miles south of Murfreesboro.

Joshua packs his knapsack with new underwear, soap, towel, comb, brush, looking-glass, tooth brush, paper and pencil, envelopes, pen, ink, cotton strips for wounds, needles and thread, buttons, fork, spoon, and knife, and oil-cloth rolled together with two blankets and fastened to the top of his knapsack, his Sgian Dubh knife always concealed behind the top of his sock. When packed correctly, this 25 pounds rests comfortably on his back.

He takes a five dollar bill from the diminishing roll of greenbacks concealed in the money belt his aunt made for him and includes it with the letter he has written her and his uncle, something he does each month. The precious box of matches is no worse off for the grueling wear it receives cushioned against Joshua's stomach.

On June 24 the 6th Kentucky remains at Murfreesboro while the Army of the Cumberland marches towards Tullahoma and five days later outflanks Bragg's Army of the Tennessee, forcing him to withdraw from Tullahoma to Chattanooga. Instead of praise, Rosecrans receives a stern message from Secretary of War Stanton urging him, after the Union victories at Gettysburg and Vicksburg, not to "neglect the chance to give the finishing blow to the rebellion."

Relentless pressure makes Rosecrans overeager and he closes in on Chattanooga in late August. Union artillery open fire on Chattanooga from across the Tennessee River, once again outflanking Bragg and forcing him to abandon the town without a fight on the 7th of September. Five days later the 6th Kentucky boards a train for Chattanooga, jubilant with the prospects of ending the war.

After withdrawing southward into northern Georgia, Bragg is heavily reinforced and challenges the overextended Union forces along a creek called Chickamauga, a Cherokee name meaning River of Blood.

The 865 able officers and men of the 6th Kentucky leave the buildings they had requisitioned and the structures they had built and lived in during the months they were stationed at Murfreesboro with ambivalent memories, but anxious to join in what they expect is the final battle of the war. It isn't until late in the evening that they begin the march to the train station, where a locomotive with a string of boxcars has gotten up steam.

The spirit of the men is high at first and they rattle on among themselves, describing what they intend to do after they are discharged, the girl they intend to marry, and the farm they intend to buy. As the march continues and the weight of their equipment begins to cause shoulders to ache, conversation ends and fatigue oozes through their bodies.

It is late at night when they arrive at the station. Heavy clouds shroud a dark, moonless night and the comments of the officers "Where are we going?" and "Who's in charge?" are not reassuring. The men march in single file along the station platform entering a boxcar until it is full and then moving to and entering the next car.

The station platform is the length of four box cars and allows Joshua and the men in his company to board the cars by merely stepping into them, while the remainder of the regiment must lift their equipment and themselves three feet up to the floor of the box cars. The sliding doors in the center of each boxcar are open.

Tired and uncertain, Joshua starts to enter the second car when a calm, soft inner voice says, "Don't get into this boxcar; get into the next one," which he does. He steps over several men, already stretched out from fatigue, and starts to turn left and go to the front end of the box car where Jim Nickols and Everet Janke are sitting. They are in Billy Shaughnessy's squad and not Joshua's, and Joshua, not seeing Billy, decides not to go there.

He looks towards the opposite sliding door, which is open, and places his equipment there. When he slumps down, he sees the outline of Martin Broderick. Mart Broderick is Joshua's age; and coming from Elizabethtown, Kentucky, he is Joshua's near neighbor and friend. Joshua's eyes close and the rhythm of the ta-ta-tun ta-tat-tun of the wheels quickly puts him to sleep.

The same sound, ta-ta-tun, ta-ta-tun, that put Joshua to sleep now awakens him early in the morning, just before the sun casts orange streaks of light through the trees atop the mountains of southeastern Tennessee. The morning is crisp and most of the men are still sleeping. Joshua gets out his pencil and a piece of the thin writing paper that he bought from a sutler to write to his aunt and uncle.

He is impressed by the beauty and size of the mountains and writes, "Our knobs is nothin' to these Tennessee mountains, and there's more of them." He asks his aunt to send him a box of her homemade fudge. The cookies she mailed two months ago took a month to reach him, and they had been "jostled around so much that they was all crumbs."

During the last ten miles the tracks have begun slowly to descend from the mountains to the valley below, and the train has begun to pick up speed, which Joshua notices as he puts his pencil down and looks out the open sliding door. He estimates the train is travelling sixty miles an hour as it finally reaches the level ground of the valley.

The farms are becoming more numerous and he waves back to a farmer who waves his hand excitedly up and down. A minute later two more persons wave their hands as if they were trying to tell him something. Such friendliness surprises Joshua and he again waves back.

Suddenly he hears the hu-hu-hu-hoo-hoo-hoo-hu-hu-hu sound of the train whistle again and again and wonders what it means.

The frantic engineer, suddenly aware that his train has been switched to a side track on which sit two locomotives, prays to God that the SOS signal of three short, three long, and three short sounds will be understood in the few remaining seconds before the train crashes into the two stationary locomotives.

Joshua returns to his letter when he suddenly feels a slight jolt of the boxcar, then another, another, and then a series of jolts that slowly, like watching the moon move through the branches of a tree, lift the corner end of the boxcar closest towards the engine up slowly into the air so that the floor of the boxcar tilts at a 45 degree angle, and the back and side of the lifted corner split open as if two huge hands casually pull them apart. With the final jolt the boxcars settle, like the slight final movement one feels when a wagon stops moving.

From the first jolt to the final bump takes less than a minute, and Joshua becomes, during that time, a spectator watching two sides of the boxcar diagonally opposite him splinter, rip, break, and emit the chilling sound of thick wood being ripped apart. Unaware of what has happened, Joshua's first thought is that this is another army foul up.

What happened was far more than a foul up. Tragedy resulted when two events of no consequence happened simultaneously: the train brakes were faulty and the switch from a side track to the main track had not been pulled.

The side of the boxcar that Joshua sat by is lying at a 45 degree angle with the ground, and the floor becomes a wooden "hill" that he and the other unhurt men climb up in order to exit through the split between the walls of the boxcar. The side with the other sliding door has becomes a partial roof and the open door, a opening to the sky.

At the top of the "hill" Joshua has to jump eight feet to the ground, and the first thing he sees on the ground ten foot from him is a complete brain resting on the ground, three feet from the blue face of Jim Nickols, the back of whose head had burst open when he was thrown from the boxcar and hit an iron side rail.

A few feet from the body of Jim Nickols lies Everet Janke, whose mouth, bloody and toothless, has been hit by a board from the splintering corner of the boxcar. Joshua sees Sergeant Gustave Weis, who is standing near Nickols.

"This is serious!" is all Joshua can think to say.

"It is vorse tan battle. All at once. Bitter git used to it, Josh," says Sergeant Weis.

Joshua looks at the locomotive that pulled the boxcars. It has smashed into the locomotive on a side track that had another locomotive behind it. The heavy weight of the two stationary locomotives was sufficient to cause the speeding train and boxcars to stop almost instantly in the collision, and the twenty-three boxcars behind began a concatenation of twenty-three devastating jolts that diminished with a final insignificant bump.

From where he stands, the collision of the locomotives appears to be one twisted mass of iron parts with the first five boxcars piled up upon each other as they were hit in the series of jolts and stops until the last of the twenty-three boxcars came to a stop. The boxcar that Joshua did not get into had turned sideways and was squeezed to half its size between the boxcar in front of it and the boxcar Joshua did get into.

A quick glance into the boxcar startles Joshua. The bloody parts of nearly forty bodies seems unreal. One survivor sits on the ground, a large gash in his right thigh has nearly severed his leg and a sergeant is helping him to apply a tourniquet. Except for heeding that inner voice, Joshua realizes he would have been in this boxcar.

In a semi-state of shock, but not physically hurt, Joshua walks down the line of the first five boxcars, the second piled on the top of the first, the third on the top of the second, and the same for the fourth and fifth car, and sees several men crawl out of them. Most injuries are serious and require a doctor, not a medic; and Joshua, looking around the dozens of injured soldiers, is at a loss as to what he, unhurt, can do to help. He walks among the dead, which number in the dozens, and the injured, uttering a silent prayer.

He walks around what had been three locomotives, which he now sees as a mound of twisted steel, belching steam and scalding water. Among the injured he notices a number of bodies with both legs severed. He realizes that they were sitting on the boxcar floor with their legs dangling over the edge, and when the boxcars began to jolt and push, the sliding doors acted as guillotines, slicing through unprotected legs. Joshua turns around and walks back to the boxcar he had been in.

He sees Mart standing by the boxcar and calls his name, pleased to seem him safe and unhurt.

"What can we do, Mart?" he asks.

"I don't know, Josh. I was worried about you. I knew you were near me when it happened."

Sergeant Weis walks over to Josh and Mart. "Get de rest of our company that ain't injured and report to der captain inside der train station," says Weis. Two hours later the 825 men, including Joshua and Mart, who are not injured, march 20 miles to Chattanooga, now in Union hands.

The rumor spreads throughout the regiment that the engineer was a Confederate agent and deliberately ran into the locomotive after another Confederate agent opened the switch from the main track to the side track.

The engineer is a Union sergeant who had operated locomotives for the Louisville and Nashville Railroad Company before enlisting in the army and is familiar with this rail through southeastern Tennessee. The long slow decline of over ten miles allowed the momentum of the train of twenty-three boxcars, filled with over 900 men, to build up more speed than the unchecked brakes could handle. The brakeman applied the brakes as best as he could, and the engineer knew that level ground would be reached in a few minutes, and the closed switch would continue the train on the main rail.

It wasn't until the locomotive was suddenly on the side track that the engineer realized the switch had not been pulled. With seconds remaining before a collision, he pulled the whistle and, just before the collision, he and the and brakeman jumped from the train.

Unfamiliarity with the Confederate locomotives and boxcars and the lack of a yardmaster familiar with the rails is not the cause of the tragedy, but a simple misunderstanding of the new technology is.

Sergeant Fredrick Stabler, who had learned the International Morse Code in Germany in 1855 after it had been created and based on the American Morse Code in 1848, had been assigned to the Signal Corp after his enlistment, where he learned the American Morse Code.

Created in the 1840s by Samuel Morse and made functional in 1844 when the first ever telegraph "What hath God Wrought!" was sent from Washington to Baltimore, all commercial telegraph was seized by an act of congress in 1862. The army used the Morse Code, which Morse created first as marks on paper and then as clicks to be heard.

Number 6 in the International Code is the same as number 8 in the American Code, except the dash in the International Code is longer:

International Code number 6 (— * * * *)
American Code number 8 (- * * * *
Sergeant Stabler intended to telegraph the following:
A R I V E 6 A (arrive 6 AM)

But Sergeant Stabler, still retaining the International Code in his mind, inadvertently telegraphed International number 6, which Sergeant Quincy McCulloch at the other end read as number 8 of the American Code. Sergeant McCulloch considered the extra length in the dash due to a new telegrapher and informed the yardmaster that a troop train would pass through at 8 AM.

When the two locomotives were shunted to the side rail at 6:55 that morning, to be sent to Murfreesboro immediately after the troop train arrived, the switch engineer, having been informed that the troop train was not due until 8 AM, believed he had more than sufficient time to walk the ten minutes to pull the switch. The misunderstanding (8 AM instead of 6 AM) proved fatal.

Five minutes after the two locomotives had been shunted onto the side track, the troop train, travelling sixty miles an hour, passed the switch and continued speeding towards the two stationary locomotives, less than a mile ahead. The farmers along the track, who tried to warn the men in the boxcars of the impending collision, stood in horror as they heard the eerie train whistle become the sound of thunder and watched the engines collide into a mingled mass and the box-cars twist like the withering tail of a dying snake.

The men of the 6th Kentucky, including Joshua and Mart Broderick, who marched from the train wreck to Chattanooga, camped in the open and ate the meager provisions that they were able to obtain from other units. Two days later, on the 15th of September, 1863, they marched two-hours south to join the Union forces stretched along the Chickamauga River. Assuming the rebels were on the run, General Rosecrans hopes to corral them.

More a creek than a river, the Chickamauga divides the Union army on the west from the Confederate army on the east and proves a source of drinking water for both sides. A few Confederate attempts to cross the creek does not discourage Joshua on 17th September from filling several canteens while being concealed behind tall grass under a shade tree next to the creek.

"You got any extra salt, Yank?" Joshua sees only a patch of gray behind the tall grass on the opposite side of the creek, from where the question comes.

"I might have," Says Joshua.

The figure in gray stands up, raising both of his arms. He's young; Joshua's age. "I ain't had no salt for weeks, Yank. I got some sugar." Joshua stands up, holding his musket with both hands.

"You wouldn't shoot me would ya, Yank?" says the rebel, in a humorous tone. Joshua lowers his musket.

"I ain't had no sugar in a long time," says Joshua. "Ya got some with ya?"

"If you got some salt with ya," replies the young rebel.

Joshua reaches in his shirt pocket and pulls out a small bag. "Here!" He holds it up.

The young rebel lifts up a small bag. "Whatja know? Sugar. Meet you halfway?"

Joshua nods his head yes and they both step into the creek, and with their muskets slung over their shoulders, wade through the shallow water towards each other.

They meet in the middle of the creek, with each holding a bag at their side. They scrutinize each other for several moments, and then, at the same time, they exchange the two bags.

"Where ya from ,Johnny?" asks Joshua.

"Mississippi. Where ya from, Yank?"

"I ain't a Yank. I'm from Kentucky," says Joshua.

"Lordy, man!" says the rebel. "You a Southerner! You should be fighten' with us!"

Joshua ignored the implied question. "All hell's gonna let loose round here soon, I fear," says Joshua.

"Yea, Kentucky." says the rebel. "Well…" he begins and extends his hand.

Joshua extends his hand. "Good luck. Mississippi," says Joshua.

They shake hands and lock eyes for a moment of comradeship, before turning around and walking back to their separate sides. Joshua puts the bag of sugar in his shirt pocket and picks up the filled canteens.

Bragg sends Confederates across the creek the night of the 18th and begins a furious battle the next morning. The battle becomes "guerrilla warfare on a grand scale" and the woods along the Chickamauga are filled with "ghastly mangled dead and the horribly wounded."

The next day a quarter-mile-wide hole in the Federal lines proves disastrous when Confederate forces launch an attack and pour through the opening. Joshua and the men of the 6th Kentucky are in line facing the attacking Confederates. The platoon sergeants are behind the line of men, ready to prevent anyone from panicking and running to the rear, while the captains and lieutenants are in front.

Holding their muskets with bayonets facing the rebels, the line moves forward step-by-step. The distance is too far for the sporadic firing from the Confederates to be effective, but as the distance narrows, the casualties increase.

"Keep low," Joshua shouts to Billy Shaughnessy on his right.

"The bullet's not made with my name on it!" boasts a defiant Billy Shaughnessy.

"On the double!" yells the captain. The line begins to shout and run as the captain stumbles and falls with a bullet through his right eye. The first lieutenant raises his saber in the air. "Come on, men!" he yells.

Running as hard as he can, Joshua keeps ahead of the line and sees Billy slightly ahead of him. Suddenly, a cannonball takes Billy's head off and Joshua is shocked to see the body continue to run for another second without the head before tumbling to the ground.

He gags and vomits while forcing himself to run. The line wavers. The lieutenant is shot. In an instant the remaining men in the line stop, turn around, and run to the rear, while the sergeants yell, fire over the men's heads, and then fall back themselves.

Rosecrans retreats, while General George Thomas's corps shields him from pursuit. Thomas holds the rebels off until nightfall and skillfully withdraws his forces, earning the name, "Rock of Chickamauga" Five days later, on 24 September, Rosecrans withdraws from Lookout Mountain, which Bragg immediately occupies. He places artillery on Lookout Mountain and halts traffic on the Nashville and Chattanooga Railroad, forcing the Union to haul food and ammunition overland.

Hemmed in at Chattanooga by Bragg's tight grip around the· city, morale among Union forces plummets. Soldiers are on quarter-rations. They tear down houses and use the lumber for firewood, to build shacks, and to construct fortifications. Joshua decides to do a little straggling.

He follows the Tennessee River north on the east side for two miles and comes to a farm house untouched by the acquisition of livestock by the army or the pilfering by roaming soldiers. Joshua, his musket slung on his shoulder, walks to the woman hanging clothes on a line.

Joshua, like other simple backwoods people of his time and locale, expresses his feelings in a natural, homely way, without any display whatever of extravagant words or feelings. "Afternoon ma'am," he says, tipping his hat with his finger.

Alarmed, she pulls the shirt she was about to hang on the line towards her bosom. The soldier is a young boy, the age of her own son, she decides. He's alone and his greeting is disarming, if not friendly, without the gun slung over his shoulder. She says nothing, but nods her head.

"Would you have any fresh eggs, ma'am?" asks Joshua.

Is that all he wants, she wonders? She visualizes her son, Michael, in his gray uniform, asking someone the same thing. She mellows slightly from being an antagonist to being a mother. "Is that all you want?" she asks. Her tone is not hostile but inquisitive.

"Yes, ma'am. My two buddies and I ain't had fresh eggs neigh on to a year." says Joshua. "Six would do us just fine."

She puts the shirt, she had been holding, back into the basket by her feet and motions for Joshua to follow her. "Where are you from?" she asks, as they walk to the chicken coop, near the barn, opposite the house.

"Kentucky, ma'am. Near Munfordville," replies Joshua. He had seen that the shirt she had held was a man's shirt, and as he followed her, he observes the house and the barn and sees no one.

She stops at the chicken coop and notices Joshua scanning the buildings and the distant field. "My husband and I live alone here. He's out in the field," she says. She opens the door to the chicken coop . "Give me your hat," she says. Seeing Joshua's surprised look she adds "To put the eggs in." Joshua notices that she has put eight eggs into his hat.

In Joshua's mind she is less an opponent than she is his aunt and in her mind, Joshua is less an enemy than he is her son. "Would you like a scrambled egg biscuit?" she asks. Her offer is sincere and might encourage his early departure.

"Yes, ma'am, I'd sure like that," he says

She spoons a scoop of fresh lard in the hot skillet and pours two cracked eggs over it. She motions for Joshua to sit down at the table and two minutes later puts a scrambled egg and biscuit sandwich on a plate before him. Significant things of the day are better not mentioned. "What's your name?" (Joshua.) "How long have you been in the army?" (Almost a year.) And "Is that a picture of your son?" (Yes, that's our son Michael.) "Have you had a good crop this year?" (Yes, but Union troops have taken most of it.) These questions are more easily handled. After savoring the last bite of egg and biscuit, Joshua takes a dollar greenback from his money belt and hands it to her.

"Union money!" she exclaims. "I don't want to touch it."

"I ain't got no other money, ma'am," explains Joshua. "Could you use some matches?"

Yes she could. From the crushed box in his money belt Joshua removes three matches and hands them to her. He ties his kerchief into a bag and carefully places the six eggs in it. "We'll be moven' in ta Georgia soon, ma'am. I doubt you'll be bothered anymore." he says. Again, tipping the side of his hat with his finger, Joshua gets up from the table. Not sure what to say, they each nod. Ten minutes later, Joshua sees a man in the field turn around and look in his direction. Joshua lifts his hand and waves.

That evening Joshua places the six eggs on the top of a half barrel in the small shack he, Mart, and Harry Carrol have built among dozens of other shacks. He explains to them that tomorrow morning, Sunday, he will prepare for them a fresh egg omelet.

Early the next morning Joshua borrows a mess kit for a skillet from Mart's personal commissary, and a tin cup, which had contained some exotic food that Mart bought from a sutler, to hold the eggs after they are cracked.

He makes two slits opposite each other into the end of a long stick and inserts two three-inch thin pieces of wood into the slits. Placing the end of the stick with the prongs into the cup that contains the cracked eggs, Joshua spins the other end of the stick rapidly between his two hands, and soon a golden liquid bubbles in the cup, ready to be poured into the hot skillet. A very hungry Mart contributes salt and pepper, and a very pleased Harry provides ground coffee beans. Delmonico's could not do better, thinks Joshua.

Three days later a sudden deluge of cannon balls exacerbates the Confederate strangle on the Union troops. An unexploded shell falls through the tent of a sutler and buries itself partially in the ground. Terrified, the sutler rushes out of his tent and runs north, never stopping while laughing troopers watch. Unattended, the tent soon is overwhelmed by dozens of men, and soon all the sutler's wares, the wines, canned hams, fancy condiments as well as army shorts, sweaters, pins and needles, disappear. That evening Mart offers a bottle of wine and a can of meat to Joshua and Harry.

A month after the battle at Chickamauga on 16 October 1863, Lincoln appoints General Ulysses Grant as commander of all union armies in the western theater and asks that Rosecrans be relieved of his command in Tennessee. Grant replaces Rosecrans with George

Thomas, who is soon reinforced with 10,000 men from the Army of the Potomac under Joseph Hooker and several divisions from the Army of the Tennessee led by William Tecumseh Sherman.

Ten days later the perilous wagon route is replaced with a new and faster "Cracker Line," so called for the hardtack crackers of the soldiers' diet, that allows 30 freight-carloads of goods to be hauled to Chattanooga daily.

Joshua is told to find a wagon to bring supplies to his company. There is little to be found among the remaining houses that have not been torn down for timber and fuel. Many of the civilians who did not flee the town live in shacks that are described by one reporter to be likened to the "worst tenements in New York City." Joshua sees a wagon that can be pulled by two men, in the rear of a house still standing and still occupied.

He knocks on the door. An old man and women come to the door. "I want to borrow you wagon," Joshua tells them. Too old to have left their home, hoping that by remaining they may prevent it from being torn down, the scared couple can only stare at Joshua, understanding that "I want to borrow your wagon." is a statement of fact, not a request. Seeing the fear in their eyes, Joshua feels more embarrassed than imperious. "I'll bring it back," he says, smiling as much to placate himself as to reassure the old couple.

"I borrowed this wagon from an old couple and told them I'd bring it back," he tells the sergeant in charge of moving the supplies. That evening he returns and sees the wagon had been tossed into a deep gully, filled with debris. At midnight, he returns and pulls the wagon from the gully, pulling it to the old couple's house and taking it behind the house where he originally found it.

By 23 November Grant decides to test Bragg to see whether he is prepared to stand and fight. He orders the Army of the Cumberland to stage a demonstration in the valley below Missionary Ridge, which runs north and south, two miles east of Chattanooga.

Never has such a spectacle of war been witnessed in the Western theater. Joshua feels he is in a great pageant when he and the rest of the 6th Kentucky parade through the valley with the Army of the Cumberland and some of Hooker's division. Bugles blare, drums thunder, and cadence calls ring out. General Sheridan on his black mount prances back and forth in front of the Confederates on the ridge. He holds his flask high, and then takes a drink.

Suddenly Joshua and those demonstrating, proud of their new commander, General Thomas, and eager to demonstrate their valor to Grant, transforms a "peaceful pageant" into a real fight, when they turn and go on the attack. Southern sharpshooters at the base of Missionary Ridge open fire but the Union troops keep racing uphill, driving the rebels from the outcroppings of the ridge and send a galvanizing jolt that rallies all the Union troops.

The next day General Hooker's fresh Union troops drive the weary Confederates from Lookout Mountain. The next morning a U.S. flag flutters above Lookout Mountain, and Grant asks General Thomas to test the mettle of the rebels who are entrenched at the center of Missionary Ridge.

The Army of the Cumberland, with the 6th Kentucky in the middle, comes under heavy artillery, but overruns the entrenched Confederate positions in the valley and surges up the hillside in an impulsive charge. Like buzzing bees, flying lead hisses past Joshua who joins in the new battle cry: "Chickamauga! Chickamauga!" and continues the charge uphill.

From the corner of his eye Joshua sees to his right a young officer of the 24th Wisconsin pick up the regimental flag from the fallen sergeant, and carry it forward, rallying the men with "On Wisconsin!"

The young officer is 18-year-old Lieutenant Arthur MacArthur, Jr., who volunteered at 16 and obtained his commission with the help of his father, a prominent figure in Milwaukee. Older soldiers learned to respect this precocious leader of men after first making fun of the "baby adjutant." Young Arthur MacArthur is awarded the Medal of Honor for his heroics at Missionary Ridge.

The line surges forward and continues yelling. Joshua runs behind the captain who suddenly staggers and falls to the ground, handing his raised saber to Joshua, who grabs it as if it is the golden ring at the merry-go-round. He looks back and yells, "On Kentucky!" Thirty feet from the crest of the Confederate line atop Missionary Ridge, Joshua is shot through the fleshy part of his right leg, just above the knee. He falls, holding the saber in the air, still yelling. A moment later the 6th Kentucky is one of five regiments to reach the crest of Missionary Ridge. It is the afternoon of November 25,1863.

In the hospital, Joshua receives a piece of a Confederate state flag from his platoon: a red and white strip of cloth with the partial word "ssissi" on it. He also is visited by a colonel in a battered felt hat and an oil-cloth "slicker" splashed with mud. The colonel pins a medal on the hospital pillow next to Joshua's head. "For bravery and leadership, corporal. Your heroic act helped in the capture of the ridge, my boy."

During the week Joshua is in the hospital, he writes to his aunt and uncle.

> "We changed things at a place called Missionary Ridge, just east of Chattanooga. I got a little scratch on my right leg durin the fightin and now get to play off in the hospital. Old Glory flies over most of Tennessee now. What's left of the Confederate states is just a patchwork of territories shrinkin each month. Some colonel gave me a medal.
>
> All my love,
> Joshua"

He encloses a five dollar bill.

Three days after Joshua went into the hospital, the 6th Kentucky is dispatched to Knoxville, which Confederates attempt to retake after being driven out by General Ambrose Burnside's Army of the Ohio two months earlier. The town had voted against secession and welcomed the Union forces. Discharged from the hospital four days later, Joshua rides in a supply wagon to Knoxville where Mart has found good winter quarters for the two of them—a small, deserted shop.

The shop produced Confederate uniforms and was abandoned in early September when the Union army entered Knoxville. Two extremely cold nights in army tents, just outside of the town, had encouraged Mart to find better accommodations. The shop, secluded within a residential area, was locked and boarded, and the three carved, wooden letters CSA fastened to the door had been smeared with excrement by Unionist citizens. Mart found an unlocked window, crawled through it, and discovered piles of gray material, eight sewing machines, and eight work tables.

The next morning his squad and Sergeant Emmert's squad took up quarters in the shop, making comfortable beds with layers and layers of gray fabric. Joshua closed the door to the small office in the back of the shop and nailed on it a scribbled note: "Corporal Broderick and Corporal Applegate."

Mart cleaned the CSA letters and turned the C ninety degrees to the left to form a flat U. He painted the bland letters red, white, and blue, from cans of paint he found stored on shelves in the shop. The following day he found a wild flower lying on top of the three letters.

Mart takes great pleasure in showing Josh their new quarters and the two beds. Mart had cut eighteen-inches off each of the legs of two work tables that he had brought into the office and then had stretched dozens of layers of gray fabric on the table top to make a softer bed than ground. But it was the stove in the corner that held Joshua's attention.

"A stove!" said Joshua. "No more cold nights or cold meals. This is livin', Mart!"

"We can cover the walls in gray, Josh, and cover the window with gray curtains. Why, hell, we can make bed comforters and fillum with straw. There's cartons of gold braid that we can decorate things up with. Ain't we lucky, Josh?"

The desk that had been in the room became their table with, of course, a gray tablecloth, which, when soiled, would be replaced by a new gray tablecloth. Two crates, upholstered in gray, served as chairs.

Each day, after formation and marching, Joshua and Mart devote their free time adding to the comfort of the room. Half of an old barrel serves as a basin, and a bucket of water, hanging from a rafter, can be tiled by pulling a rope to supply a small, medium, or full stream. The eight parts of the legs that had been cut off became pegs nailed to the walls to hold clothing and cooking utensils.

One night loud human voices are heard yelling in the far distance. Joshua and Mart walk outside and listen for a few minutes and decide the laughing and yelling is a party. They shrug their shoulders and go back inside and notice that no one else is in the building. They shrug their shoulders again, and go back to sleep.

In the middle of the night both Joshua and Mart wake up when someone starts beating on their door. Suddenly the door opens and there, his glazed eyes staring into space, stands Lemuel. The smell of alcohol fills the room.

In a stupor, the normally quiet and reclusive Lemuel stumbles into the room, bumps into the table, knocks over a chair and claws at the stove pipes that lead outside. In his present state of mind, he doesn't hear Joshua or Mart yell at him and continues to stagger around the room. At six-foot, two-inches and over two-hundred pounds, with big hands, Lemuel is too much for them to handle. If they did get him out of their room, he'd either hurt himself in his dazed state or end up in military jail; so they decide to stay outside their room and lock Lemuel inside to sober up.

A half hour later the disruption in their room stops and members of the two squads begin hobbling one at a time into the shop and fall on their beds. Now the entire shop smells like a brewery.

Before the sun rises, Joshua and Mart unlock their door and enter. Lemuel is stretched out on the floor, with the several sections of the stove pipe scattered over the room. They shake Lemuel, who is in a deep sleep, but finally wakes up.

"What am I doin here?" asks Lemuel. He cannot understand why his inflamed hands show signs of touching something hot and why his head pounds inside.

"You slept the night in our room," says Mart. "You have to go back to your own quarters." Joshua and Mart help Lemuel to get up and direct him out the door. He turns around.

"Ya all keep a messy place," he says, and staggers off.

That morning a number of men do not show up for the company formation. Sergeant Libert reads an order: As of this day no alcohol of any nature will be tolerated within the confines of this company. Anyone bringing any alcoholic beverages into the confines of this company will be court marshaled. Anyone not able to perform his duty due to intoxication shall be fined a month's pay.

Sergeant Weis tells Joshua and Mart what happened. In the home of a Confederate army officer, the third platoon discovered a wine cellar filled with over a hundred bottles of imported wine. The celebration that night by a majority of the men in the company resulted in one gun-shot wound, two stabbings, and fifteen men requiring medical attention. "Dees Inglish sons doesn't know how to trink wine," says Sergeant Weis. "Good Rhine wine vasted."

Joshua, Mart and the members of the two squads quartered in the shop, help the local residents repair some of the minor damage caused to their homes and the church during the fighting. Mrs. Mattie Pringle, the wife of Pastor Pringle, invites the two squads to Christmas morning service and the meal following, in appreciation for "all the help the kind members of your company have given in repairing our church and many of our homes," she tells Joshua. On Christmas morning most of the invited men attend service and come for the meal.

To serve a congregation of over twenty families and the men of the two squads, the ladies of the church have set up three tables to hold the trays of foods to be portioned out to those in line: mashed potatoes, dressing, peas, fried chicken, coffee, apple, peach, and pumpkin pies, and hot biscuits, an inch and a half thick and as big and round as a woman's hand—a fulsome woman.

At home, Joshua's aunt tried to have chicken every Sunday, and always pleased Joshua when it was fried chicken. Joshua is behind Mart, as they line up among the members of the church, and holds a plate in one hand and eating utensils in the other. They each are given a heaping serving of mashed potatoes with lots of brown gravy, dressing, and peas by the ladies, anxious to show their appreciation by "piling it on their plates."

The last woman to serve is Mrs. Pringle, who uses two forks to place a large, golden brown breast on Mart's plate. Joshua swallows the anticipated taste several times and smiles when he hears Mrs. Pringle. "I've kept these two succulent pieces for you, Joshua," she says.

Joshua holds out his plate and Mrs. Pringle places what she considers the most succulent part of the chicken on it: two necks. She smiles; Joshua gasps. Her tender manner assures Joshua of her good intentions, and he gains his composure. "Thank you, Mrs. Pringle," he says.

"Go back for seconds, boys," announces Pastor Pringle. Most of the men do, but Joshua can't, with two uneaten necks still on his plate.

"You haven't eaten your chicken," comments the soldier across the table from Joshua.

"I don't like necks," says Joshua.

"That's the best part!" says the soldier.

"You want mine?" asks Joshua.

"Shore do!" The soldier spears one and then the second neck with his fork.

Joshua gets up and walks to the table with the tray of chicken. Everyone has been served and only one woman stands behind the tables. "I'd like a breast, please," he says.

The lady looks at what remains of the chicken. "I'm sorry, they're all gone. But there are two necks!"

Young, single soldiers have a different problem than old married soldiers, like thinking about a fruit that has never been tasted. Jacob Prentice is one of those old, married soldiers, and he is grumpy all the time, except for the last two weeks. Now Jacob Prentice smiles, whistles, and arrives at his bed in the shop minutes before the morning bugle sounds.

It soon becomes common knowledge within the two squads. The green grocer is a middle aged man who is married to a much younger woman. He has made an arrangement with Jacob that will solve his problem and satisfy both his wife and Jacob at the same time. Jacob now smiles, the wife now sings, and the green grocer no longer needs to try.

One of the old soldiers is Ben Sturgel, whose small farm is outside Munfordville. Ben has ten children and enlisted to escape going to jail for operating a still. Being that Joshua is also from Munfordville, Ben takes him to "be one of his own." Short, skinny, and agile as a squirrel, Ben is a good soldier, except when he gets drunk.

"Joshua! You better come over to the third platoon's quarters," says a member of the third platoon. "Ben's drunk and threatens to shoot everyone with his musket. We can't do anything with him."

Joshua hurries to the third platoon quarters where he finds Ben in the middle of a circle of soldiers, slumped over and holding his musket. Ben turns to Joshua and in a playful, not hostile, tone says, "Don't ya fool with me, Josh, or I'll shoot ya."

"Now why would ya wanta do that, Ben. I'm practically your own kin," says Joshua. "Hand me your weapon, Ben." Joshua reaches for it, and Ben sheepishly lets go. "Go to sleep, Ben," says Joshua. Ben does and Joshua turns to leave. "Call me, if you need me again," he says.

To keep in shape, the company goes on a ten mile march around Knoxville. They learn that when they return there will be a grand review by the Inspector General, Colonel Randolph Rutledge, a graduate of West Point.

Immediately upon returning, the company lines up for inspection. They are tired and nervous, feeling that this West Point colonel looks down on them as ragged volunteers. The colonel looks at each soldier critically as he comes opposite each one, and each soldier brings his piece into the prescribed position, but the colonel takes no musket.

When they reach Joshua the commanding officer whispers to the colonel, "This is Corporal Applegate, the one that led the company up Missionary Ridge." The colonel stands in front of Joshua, looks him in the face, scans his uniform, and then stares into his eyes without saying a word.

Erect, looking straight ahead without moving his eyes, Joshua begins counting his breathe to keep his heart from pounding as the colonel continues the review.

Reaching the end of the line, the colonel says something to their commanding officer who smiles. The colonel turns, sweeps his hand to the men, and yells, "Good Soldiers!"

In March 9, 1864, Lincoln appoints General Grant to lead all Union armies and replaces him with a close colleague, General William Tecumseh Sherman, as leader of Union troops in the West. The two generals will work in tandem. Grant makes his headquarters in the field with the Army of the Potomac under the command of General George Meade, and Sherman, acting in coordination with Grant, consolidates his command of three armies: General Thomas's Army of the Cumberland, General James McPherson's Army of the Tennessee, and General John Schofield's Army of the Ohio.

On May 4, 1864, Grant sends the Army of the Potomac south across the Rapidan River in a campaign against Robert E. Lee in Virginia, and three days later, Sherman launches his 100,000 men against Confederate General Joseph Johnston in Georgia. Grant plans to hammer Lee frontally, while Sherman prefers to encircle Johnston with his three armies while advancing to Atlanta.

The 6th Kentucky returns to Chattanooga and embarks on the grueling campaign into Georgia.

Three days into Georgia, Joshua becomes part of the team under Lieutenant Prather, ordered to requisition horses. Covered with dust, their blue uniforms appear gray. The group of ten men gallop to the farm of Curtis Tuttle, who stands on the veranda of his spacious home.

"We're requisitioning ten of your horse," says Lieutenant Prather as he writes out a requisition slip.

Far from expecting Union troops, Mr. Tuttle assumes the officer and men with him are Confederate soldiers, which is confirmed by their "gray" uniforms. "You all have already taken ten of my best horses, Captain," he says. Mr. Tuttle believes the officer's insignia is a lieutenant's but, patronizingly, he promotes him a rank higher.

"That was Confederates," says the lieutenant. He bends down from his mount and hands the requisition slip to Mr. Tuttle. "These ten horses put you in a neutral position," says the lieutenant, smiling at his attempt at humor.

Mr. Tuttle looks at the slip. "Ain't you all one of us?"

"No, Sir, we're Union troops;" says the lieutenant, pulling the reins of his horse and leaving a bewildered Mr. Tuttle.

"Sarah!" yells Mr. Tuttle, rushing into the house. "The Yankees are in Georgia! God helps us!"

"Just take ten, Joshua," says the lieutenant. Joshua starts to salute when the lieutenant holds up his finger. "But the best ten," he adds.

Joshua has never seen a farmhouse like Mr. Tuttle's, or a farm like his. The white, framed structure of two floors has a porch with six white columns across the front of the house, and there are three out buildings besides a large barn. Ambling through the one of three fenced in fields that contains grazing horses, Joshua points out certain ones, which are then bridled and made ready to accompany the team back to camp.

Leaving the Tuttle farm and house, Joshua wonders if there's enough money in the chest to buy land and build a house, maybe a house as fine as this one.

Two days after the armies of Thomas and Schofield went head on against Johnston's initial line of defense at Rocky Face Ridge, the 6th Kentucky camps there and Joshua decides to do a little straggling.

Past the sounds of the camp, Joshua follows a narrow path along a small stream and sees a farmhouse snuggled within a circle of tall trees. He walks around the house, and then up to the back door, which is open, and calls out. "Hello!"

Other than the sounds of some goats and a cow, no sound disturbs the silence of a pristine, sunny morning deep at the base of verdant mountains. He knocks on the screen door.

No one answers. The screen door is unlatched and Joshua walks in. A quick search of the small, four room house reveals no one there. He goes into the parlor and looks up the chimney. He's right. Several feet above the fireplace hang three smoked hams. He cuts them down and ties them together. Seeing a pencil and scraps of paper on the kitchen cabinet, he writes: "US Requisition: 3 hams" and leaves it on the table.

That evening the first platoon invites the second platoon to a banquet of smoked ham and fried potatoes.

That next afternoon the camp is visited by two small black youngsters, one pulling a cider barrel and the other carrying a tray of pies.

"Got good fresh lemnade here, Yanks," says the one pulling the barrel. Two wheels have been attached to the barrel, half-full of cool water, squeezed lemons, and a sprinkling of sugar. Five feet tall, about twelve years old, the youngster is a true salesman. "I'ms da only lemnade man round here, and its only a penny a cup."

"Da lemnade go good wit one a my pies," proclaims the other black youngster, shorter and younger than the first. "Dayz jus two pennies each."

Soldiers, and particularly American soldiers, are pushovers when it comes to children, and Joshua and those in the camp gather around the two boys, enjoying youthful energy and refreshing southern talk.

A group of men dig into their pockets for two pennies to buy an apple pie, made from buckwheat and dried apples fried in rancid butter and sprinkled with sugar, while Joshua and a dozen others line up for a drink of lemonade from the single tin cup attached to the barrel.

After the two youngsters make a number of sales, and have two pockets full of pennies, Private Charlie Myer takes one of the Confederate dollar bills from the wad he found and hands it to the boy who sells pies, pleased at the opportunity to obtain change in Union currency for the worthless Confederate money.

"I'll take five pies and give you four cents for each one for this dollar and the 80 cents change."

"I's ken't do dat, boss. Only take Union money. But I gib youz ten pennies fa dat wad in your hand."

The Confederate money is worthless to me, thinks Charlie, but ten US pennies is ten US pennies. Charlie nods his head yes and gives him the wad of Confederate bills. Slowly the youngster counts out ten pennies, and Charlie wonders how this young black boy learned to count.

Joshua, who watched the entire transaction, smiles at the cleverness of the boy: Confederate bills are worthless in the north, but they are still worth ten cents on the dollar in the Confederate south.

Two days later the 6th Kentucky marches through the village of Dalton, past a house that is only several feet from the road. The two dozen biscuits on the tray taken out of the stove and placed on the windowsill to cool disappear one by one in synchrony with the men passing by. When the cook notices the missing biscuits, she shakes her head and smiles, and places a second tray in its place.

Joshua has observed the disappearing biscuits from the rear of the marching men and dreams of spreading strawberry jam on the one he will soon grab, but the last biscuit is taken by the man in the front of Joshua's squad and the rest of the men in front of Joshua can only complain at their loss.

Joshua, on the other hand, is more enterprising, and steps to the window as he passes by. "We're out of biscuits!" he yells and steps back in line, to the cheers of the men behind him.

"A stolen biscuits tastes good, but the taste of one not stolen lingers," says the philosopher in Joshua.

After a skirmish the middle of May at the town of Resaca, the rebels are forced to fall back to the south, towards Atlanta. Sherman's forces are half way to Atlanta in twelve days. He intends to avoid costly frontal attacks and moves around fortified Allatoona Pass, where Johnston's troops have raised breastworks from New Hope Church to the village of Dallas, four miles southwest.

In the last of three days of fighting, Joshua finds himself isolated from his platoon in the tangled woods, which Union troops call the "Hell Hole." Exhausted, he leans against a tree behind heavy bushes. He starts to stand up and move in the direction of the shooting, when he sees movement among the trees fifty yards towards the enemy line. A single Confederate soldier is moving between the trees towards him.

Fritz Schmidt is the fourth generation of German Pietists that settled in Pennsylvania a century ago and drifted each generation farther south until Fritz's father settled in northern Georgia. Fifteen years old, and four inches shorter than Joshua's five-foot-ten, Fritz leans his musket against a tree while he wipes the perspiration off his thick glasses. Separated from his platoon, Fritz moves slowly over what appears to be an animal path through the woods.

Crouched behind thick bushes, Joshua watches every move of this rebel, and whispers to himself: Move the other way. Don't come closer. Don't make me shoot you.

Fritz moves cautiously closer to where Joshua is concealed and stops in front, turning his head, and squinting his eyes in an attempt to see past the green vegetation. Slowly Joshua stands up and points his musket at Fritz.

Their eyes meet and neither makes a move.

Through eons creatures like they have spent an eternity in those few moments when eyes look into eyes in confrontation, and each of their lifetimes, no matter how old, pass by in a flash.

Why do they send out children! Joshua says to himself. His musket is pointed directly at Fritz's heart. One movement and Fritz knows he's dead. They communicate silently in a spaceless, timeless world of primitive awareness.

Joshua nods his head to the right. Fritz nods yes and slowly steps back. Another step and then another. He turns around, waves his left hand while he holds his musket with his right hand, and walks to the Confederate line.

Fritz reaches an open space and Joshua, aware that some Union soldier may see him and shoot at him, says, "Run!" Joshua fires in the air and Fritz runs!

Fritz reaches the woods from where he came, and Joshua relaxes his hold on his musket, feeling both exhausted and elated. "He was just a kid!" says Joshua.

On June 4, a month after the battle at New Hope Church, Sherman approaches Kennesaw Mountain and notices grey-clad officers surveying the field. Unaware that Johnston and two of his corps commanders, Polk (who is also a bishop) and Hardee, are among the party, Sherman orders artillery to fire on them. Hardee and Johnston take cover but Polk is killed.

The Confederates had called Polk the "Fighting Bishop" and the Yankees called him the "Devil's Bishop." When Joshua and the men of the 6th Kentucky hear that a cannon shot had crashed through Polk's chest, they celebrate by shouting, "We killed the bishop! We killed the bishop! At Kennesaw Mountain, we killed the bishop." Joshua is not sure if this is proper and does not join in the shouting.

Fighting continues around Kennesaw Mountain for twelve days until Johnston is flanked and forced to pull back and abandon Marietta on June 27. Sherman is now within fifteen miles of Atlanta. The more Sherman is faulted for missing opportunities to destroy Johnston's army, the more his forces come nearer to Atlanta. Joshua and the other troopers rally to Uncle Billy and his successful encircling tactics.

The 6th Kentucky occupies the plantation of Senator Titus Clarborne, the radical Southern secessionist, now Brigadier, in General A. P. Hill's 3rd corps of the Army of Northern Virginia. Joshua and Mart take over one of the small rooms on the third floor attic away from the officers and where they are free to apply their artist inclinations on the white, plastered walls of the room.

Claborne's home is spacious, the dining room alone able to serve two platoons at the table. The imported furniture and mirrors are thrown outside, the red velvet curtains are used as blankets, and the two fire places on the first floor are fueled by several hundred books in Claborne's once handsome library. Joshua keeps the copy of *Moby Dick*.

Joshua pulls guard duty on the third day for two hours on and four hours off. His second two-hour duty begins at twelve midnight at the entrance, a hundred feet from the house. Two tall stone columns with medieval gargoyles atop, stand at the entrance to the house, a hundred steps down a winding path from the country road.

A cluster of small houses line the road near the entrance, and a small brick chapel in the center of a cemetery across from Joshua remains empty and dark as Joshua stands with his back to one column, allowing him to look past the other column, down to the small village. The moonless night and the occasional howl of wolves makes Joshua's two hours of guard duty not only unpleasant but also scary.

Except for the sounds of crickets and night owls, a quiet, ominous feeling clutches Joshua's heart, and he attempts to lighten the moment: "Someday I'll tell my grandchildren about this creepy night, and laugh." A cold chill crawls up Joshua's spine when he hears faint footsteps on the country road.

He holds his musket with both hands, ready to fire. He doesn't move when a dog, the size of a goat, walks past Joshua without noticing him. The night is cold but perspiration forms around the brim of his hat. He relaxes and would like to smoke his cigar, but doesn’t dare reveal his presence with the glowing end. An hour of his guard duty has elapsed.

With his back still next to the column, he stares down the country road towards the dark houses, when he suddenly sees something crouching and crossing the road from the opposite side to his side. It’s a human, he can tell from the faint outline. Should he shout “Halt!” Shoot over the figure’s head? It’s probably one of the men returning after a “visit” to one of the houses. The figure is lost in the shadows. It has to be one of the men returning to the house, prays Joshua.

Joshua is relieved from duty and falls asleep during the next four hours. When he is awakened again for two hours of guard duty, the first rays of the morning sun cast fine lines of yellow light along the ground, and the menacing columns of that night become the enchanting entrance to a make-believe palace. The figure that crossed the road must have been one of the men returning to the house. The following day the 6th Kentucky is ordered to march to Atlanta.

The long line of men march over muddy, red Georgia clay with their company wagons behind them. Joshua rides next to the driver of their first platoon wagon, nonchalantly smoking his cigar as the present “lighter.” Lighters provide the source for fire when needed, and cigar smoking provides the easiest way to continue a source of fire and the most enjoyable.

The muddy, red clay road becomes a small river of wagons, horses, cannons, and men, floating slowly southeast to Atlanta. A drizzle stops and the sun warms Joshua’s heart more than his face. The road follows the curve around a hill on the field to their right, and the driver points to the erect officer, sitting calmly astride his black stallion atop the hill. “There’ s Uncle Billy,” he says.

The death of his son Willie eight months ago has changed Sherman. Where he had always been concerned for the well being of his men, now a fatherly concern is apparent; and where he had always demanded obedience to orders, now a tone of understanding for human frailties is also discerned.

He is idolized by his men as "Uncle Billy," and with the death of his son Willie, he begins to address the young men of his command informally as "son."

Joshua notices that Sherman chews on an unlit cigar clamped between his teeth. When their wagon comes within hearing range of General Sherman, Joshua yells out. "Need a light, General?"

"Yes I do, soldier," says Sherman, seeing Joshua holding his lit cigar up in the air.

Joshua jumps off the wagon and hurries to Sherman. He holds his cigar up to Sherman, who bends down and inhales through his cigar until it lights and then takes the cigar from his mouth. "What's your name, corporal?" He asks.

"Applegate, Sir. Joshua Applegate, General."

"Joshua! Well, that's a good omen. Bringing down the Confederate walls!" says Sherman. Joshua, not well versed in Bible stories, doesn't understand and Sherman changes the subject. "Where are you from, son?" he asks.

"Kentucky, General. Munfordville, Kentucky."

"Down the road from Fort Duffield," replies Sherman. Momentarily he recalls the events that have propelled him to become the general leading an army into Georgia. In that moment Joshua ventures a question.

"General, when are we going to be able to go home?"

"Are you a farmer, son?" asks Sherman.

"Hope to be when I get back to Kentucky."

"You'll be planting corn next Spring," says Sherman. He puts his cigar in his mouth and pulls the reins of his stallion right. "Good luck, Joshua," he says, returning Joshua's salute with a touch to his hat.

"You, too, General," says Joshua. He runs to catch up with his wagon, anxious to tell everyone about his conversation with General Sherman.

Joshua and the men of the 6th Kentucky participate in the shelling around Atlanta in a counterclockwise direction to cut off all avenues into the town. On August 19 they are ordered from the entrenchments in front of Atlanta to guard vital railroads in Chattanooga, and on September 2 are given garrison duty at Bridgeport, Alabama. Two months later they move to Nashville, Tennessee, to be mustered out of the army.

Joshua hears that Sherman marched into Atlanta on September 2 and reads in a local paper: "Grant walked into Vicksburg, McClellan walked around Richmond, and Sherman is walking upon Atlanta."

He also reads that Jefferson C. Davis, the man who murdered General Nelson at the Galt House in Louisville, has been promoted to major general and is given command of the 14th corps. He murders a man in cold blood and then gets promoted! Joshua thinks of Sergeant O'Conner, whom he murdered, of the enemy soldiers he killed, and of the young Confederate with thick glasses whom he allowed—no, encouraged—to run away.

The last members of the 6th Kentucky are to be mustered out of the army in Louisville, but if any wish to depart the train near their home, they can be mustered out in Nashville, but will not receive their pay then. It will be mailed to them later.

Joshua has three months pay and the bonus due him, which is less than $400.00. He is mustered out in Nashville on the morning of January 2, 1865. One bundle of fives in the chest is worth more than his entire mustering out pay.

The train that leaves Nashville that afternoon holds hundreds of Union veterans, including Joshua. They smile, joke, laugh, thankful that they have come through the horror of the last three years—that slow drizzle of daily, weekly, monthly routine, and the sudden storm of battle. They can smile, joke, and laugh because the storm has ended and the clouds no longer hide the sun, and for a moment they are free from the night of dreadful memories.

The ritual of farewells repeats itself at each stop the train makes at each town and crossroads along its track from Nashville to Louisville, each time reducing its human cargo one by one of gracious souls, who suddenly realize the comradeship that made possible their survival ends with the wave of their hand.

Traveling slower than usual and stopping dozens of times, the journey takes twice as long as normal. The bridge over the Green River, just south of Munfordville, had been destroyed early in the war by the Confederates, but was repaired a year later by the Union.

Early in the morning of the next day, the train stops before crossing the bridge and waits, while Joshua Applegate jumps from the train. The conductor waves to the engineer to start again, the whistle blows twice, and the train resumes its journey, while Joshua continues to wave until the last car of the train merges into the horizon and the yells and laughter of his brothers-in-combat fade away.

Nostalgic at finishing the last sentence of this book of his life, Joshua turns from the track and begins walking to the home he left nearly three years ago, ready to read the first sentence of his next volume. The crisp winter morning keeps him awake and the sleepy countryside lulls him into a euphoria that dismisses the pains of yesterday and beckons him to the joys of tomorrow. The bodies and the chest in the cave, for the moment, are forgotten.

Joshua crosses the bridge and follows the river to Amos's Ferry, and then past the old Embry Creek cabin that he had been raised to believe was the oldest structure in Munfordville. Main Street is quiet, except for a faint hum that comes from the Presbyterian Church, a block farther north on Union Street.

Still serving as an army hospital since the winter of 1861, the church holds several patients now. Joshua turns in the opposite direction on Union Street and heads north through the remains of the 1862 headquarters of the Union occupation encampment that had held as many as 40,000 soldiers of McCook's Second Division. Two miles farther he sees the light of a kerosene lamp by the window of an otherwise dark house that is shrouded in a faint, blue mist. It is his aunt's and uncle's home, the one he left three years ago.

Joshua Applegate's life-changing experiences as a soldier in the army follow the parable of the seeds that fall among the rocks, onto poor ground and onto fertile soil. They have been sown within a receptive soul but need cultivation before they can blossom and bear spiritual fruit.

CHAPTER FIVE

TUESDAY: 3 JANUARY 1865 6:30 A.M.

We think we are a sinner
And find it's all a dream;
How could a God in heaven
Ever be that mean.

One of God's greatest gifts is our ability to change, and from that ability to change emerges the forgiveness of incurred sins for which our soul hungers. The change can be as easy as turning around, from seeing the moon set in the west to seeing the sunrise in the east. But the change is also different as day is from night. This gift, always available to us, is often ignored, but eagerly embraced by one in despair, as a drowning man eagerly reaches for a floating log. The sins of theft and murder, hidden deep within a cave, are simultaneously buried deep within the soul of Joshua Applegate. It is for him to reach out and accept God's gift.

It is 6:30 in the morning, too early to knock on the door. He stands twenty feet from the house and yells. "Uncle Hank! Aunt Mary!" and waits. The light moves from the window and shows through the open space when the door slowly opens.

"Joshua?" The more whisper than voice brings an overpowering joy to Joshua's heart.

"Aunt Mary!" he yells. He drops his pack and runs to the door.

Overwhelmed by the angelic love coming from his aunt, Joshua lifts her small frame, unashamedly cries, and, for the first time in his life, feels the joy of heaven.

"Where is Uncle Hank?" He died this past September. Silence says more than words. "I'm glad the lamp was lit. With the night and the mist, it helped," says Joshua.

"It's burned there every night for the last three months, Joshua, since Jake Cummings returned home after being discharged." She caresses his cheek after starting a fire in the stove and places the coffee pot on it.

Joshua relaxes in "his" chair, next to the one that had been his Uncle's. He marvels that the vision he had of his home had always been in black and white, but he sees it now in color. He is not yet twenty-one, and all his trials and challenges of youth are behind him. All tomorrows are his, and rightly so.

He drinks two cups of coffee and spreads fresh churned butter and peach jam on the hot biscuits piled on the plate, next to the scrambled eggs, fried hominy, and four strips of crisp bacon. His thoughts drift to the chest in the cave, its contents, he reasons, rightly his. Warm and full, he falls asleep the instant his weary body falls on the bed that Aunt Mary has heated with a bed warmer. She takes his shoes off and drapes a cover over his still uniformed body.

The first rays of the morning sun come through the window, and she lifts the chimney to blowout the lamp. She stares at the sleeping figure of her nephew, tossing and turning, not adjusted to sleeping on a bed. His mumbling about "being rich" she takes to mean the beginning of his new life; and his outcry, "had to kill him," a nightmare from the last two years. She is correct, but not in the way she assumes.

It is late in the morning when Joshua finally awakens from a deep, but troubling sleep. His concentration is upon the chest in the cave, it's contents, and the opportunities this handsome fortune makes possible; but, like a flickering flame, the image of the murdered sergeant appears as a recurring moment of darkness in the light of such a fortune.

Over coffee and biscuits sprinkled with brown sugar, Joshua relates some of his experiences of the last two years. "I'm gonna buy me some land and build a house and have a fine farm all by myself, and all for myself, Aunt Mary," he says.

He stands up, withdraws the last five dollar greenback from his money belt, and hands it to his aunt. "I shore do appreciate the money belt, Aunt Mary," he says. He takes out the partially crushed match box and removes most of the matches, handing them to her. "Rich people use these. Now you can , Aunt Mary." He hugs her and kisses her on the cheek. "You were the only one to write me all that time."

"What are ya goin ta do today, Josh?" asks Aunt Mary.

"I got some business to take care of, Aunt Mary. I'd like to borrow old Ned," says Joshua.

"Do ya want the wagon, also, Josh?" asks Aunt Mary.

"The horse will do just fine," says Joshua. "I need to borrow the lantern and some rope, Aunt Mary."

Aunt Mary hands him the lantern on the table and tells him there's rope in the barn. She's puzzled by this request, but says nothing. Fifteen minutes later Joshua rides Old Ned the five miles to the hole.

The sun has melted the light dusting of snow, and the entrance off McCubbins Lane that Joshua and Sergeant O'Conner had taken to the cave two years ago is covered by tall grass and thick bushes with no indication that anyone has been there since. The pile of brush and twigs still lie on the frozen canvas covering the hole.

Joshua ties Old Ned's reins to a tree. He lifts the frozen brush and twigs off the canvas and then pulls the canvas off the supporting branches. Over two feet in diameter, the hole has dead, yellowed grass along its rim, giving it the appearance of a gaping mouth with whiskers.

He lights the lantern and ties an end of the rope to the handle, and slowly lowers it into the hole. The disfigured face of Sergeant O'Conner has an unnatural appearance. The skin appears artificial and the side of the head that had been crushed in from the blow has formed a dark red crust where the eye had been. The body lies where it fell, twisted like a rag doll that a child throws in a toy box.

Next to Sergeant O'Conner's body lies the body of Lieutenant Henry, his head a mass of dark red congealed blood and his arms and legs, spread out from his body. His saber, slightly out of its scabbard, lies next to him. Four feet from the bodies rest the chest, closed as Joshua left it.

Joshua pulls the lantern up and unties it and Old Ned's reins. He leads Old Ned through the trees and underbrush to the cave entrance. The dirt he had piled atop the rocks is scattered below, leaving a small opening into the cave made by small creatures.

Joshua removes the dozen smaller rocks sitting atop five large ones. With the rope around the pommel of the saddle and the other end around a large flat stone, Old Ned pulls it down to lie flat. After one more large stone is pulled flat, Joshua is able to enter the cave, after tying Old Ned to a tree and lighting the lantern again.

The quarter mile through the cave to the hole contrasts with the last time Joshua walked through it as a dirge contrasts with a march. Ten minutes later, the patience of two years is rewarded. The lantern lights up the chest. He steps to it, averting his sight from seeing the two bodies. He opens the lid, lets it fall back, and, leaning back himself, sighs. "There must be a hundred bundles!" he says aloud. "Maybe more!"

There appear to be more bundles of ones than fives. He takes a bundle of ones and three bundles of fives, squeezing them into his pockets. He closes the lid and sees the body of the lieutenant.

Joshua turns the lieutenant's body over and pulls it several feet from Sergeant O'Conner's body. He places the body on its back, its arms next to its side, and the legs stretched out together. He pushes the saber fully into its scabbard and lays it long ways aside the lieutenant's body. A white scarf is hidden under the lieutenant's uniform. Joshua pulls it up around the lieutenant's neck to cover the congealed blood.

From the lieutenant's jacket pocket Joshua removes the lieutenant's name tag, glances at a letter signed "Angelica", reads an unfinished letter by the lieutenant, and notices a note to a paymaster. He folds and sticks them in his jacket pocket. He decides to see if Sergeant O'Conner had a name tag. He did. Joshua puts it with the other papers in his pocket. Joshua is repulsed by the face of Sergeant O'Conner: Part of his nose and ear have been chewed off by small creatures, but the face of the lieutenant seems not to have been.

Joshua looks up to the hole, which is about nine feet from the rough floor of the cave. He decides he'll build his house over the hole and attach a ladder. Money is no problem; privacy is. He must be discrete in spending the greenbacks, and he must not allow his actions to stir up curiosity. His desire to be alone for awhile will be accepted in the community. But first he must have title to the land.

Using a thick branch as a lever, Joshua lifts the two large stones to cover the entrance and places the smaller stones on top. He decides to bring a shovel next time and fill all the small crevices to prevent any creatures from getting into the cave.

The wagon is in satisfactory shape, except for the two years of vines that entwine within its wheels. He harnesses it to Old Ned who easily pulls the wagon out of the grove and back to the hole. Placing new branches across the hole, he places the canvas on top of them and throws new brush over it.

Joshua ambles back home revelling in the joy of discovered treasure and the expectations of youthful dreams. Tomorrow he will visit J.M. Talmadge and buy fifty acres of his land. But first, he wants to see the expression on his Aunt Mary's face when he hands her twenty five-dollar bills.

At his aunt's house, Joshua dismounts and lets Old Ned saunter to the barn by himself. He opens the door and sees his aunt bent over the wood burning stove. He sniffs the aroma coming from the skillet and pots on the stove. It's been most of the day since he had breakfast. "Something smells mighty good, Aunt Mary," he says, giving her a kiss on the cheek.

She puts her hands up before him. "Don't look! I've got a surprise for you, Joshua. Go wash up."

"First I gotta unsaddle Old Ned, Aunt Mary," says Joshua. "And I got a surprise for you." He rushes out of the house humming a tune. If she asks where I got so much money, I'll say its bonus money, he thinks to himself.

She doesn't ask. She holds the twenty greenbacks in both hands; her lips parted, her eyes in rapture, as if she were looking at heaven's golden streets. Tears slide down her cheeks. She sits down at the table and gently lays the bundle of greenbacks down. "These past two years has been hard, Joshua. Thinking of you, praying for your safe return, helped keep us going. Hank and me never had no children of our own, and when you came to us, you were our gift from heaven.

"Since I didn't birth you, mothering you was different; you was mine, and yet, not truly mine. When your Uncle Hank died, you were all that I had. I thought I'd have to sell the farm. I wished to keep it for you," She picks up the greenbacks. "I only prayed for your safe return, not wanting to bother the Lord with my money problems; but He's granted my prayer and my wish.

"But this is old women's talk!" She gets up and puts the greenbacks in a box by the cabinet. "It's time for your surprise." Like a magician, Aunt Mary arranges the simmering, frying, and bubbling ingredients in the pot, skillet, and pan, cooking on the wood store, into a feast that Joshua has dreamed about for two years. With pride, a smile, and love, she places the plate in front of Joshua.

"Smoked ham and red-eye gravy with grits and hot biscuits!" yells Joshua, Tying the large white napkin under his chin.

"They was your favorites, Josh," says his aunt.

"Still are!" were the last words Joshua spoke before finishing two helpings of biscuits, grits, and, red-eye gravy. The smoked ham is minus five hearty slices: one by his aunt and four by himself. He takes a cigar from his bundle and lights it with a sliver of wood stuck down into the stove. He sits back into the chair, relaxed, at ease. "I'm going to see Martin Talmadge tomorrow morning," he says.

Jose´ Martin Talmadge owns Twelve Oaks, the 1,500 acre plantation north of Munfordville, near Glen Lily, Alyett Buckner's plantation. Neighbors, both Alyett and Jose´ Martin Talmadge's father, Jacob, were also enthusiastic supporters of the two great leaders in the cause of South American independence: Simon Bolivar and Jose´ de San Martin. Consequently, when Alyett Buckner named his son Simon Bolivar Bucker, Jacob Talmadge named his son, six months later, Jose´ Martin Talmadge.

Jose´ Martin Talmadge calls himself Martin Talmadge and signs his name, J. Martin Talmadge. He is pleased to be called Jose´ when it is pronounced correctly in Spanish—/HO-SAY/—but he avoids those in Hart County, Kentucky who unknowingly or derisively call him /JOE-SEE/.

Martin Talmadge married Elizabeth Louise Hubbard when he and she were 18. The Hubbard family, for which Hubbard Street in downtown Chicago is named, own property in the center of Chicago, which is of substantial value. This has allowed Martin Talmadge to increase the land inherited from his father and to build Twelve Oaks, his manorial, English Tudor style home. He is a director of the Louisville and Nashville Railroad.

An admirer of George Rogers Clark and his brother William, Martin Talmadge named his first son William Clark Talmadge and his second son, born a year later, Rogers Clark Talmadge. In November of 1861, William enlisted in the Kentucky Home Guard, which was friendly to the Union; and his prodigal brother Rogers, avowing to be eighteen, enlisted in the Kentucky State Guard, which was friendly to the Confederacy.

Badly wounded in the Battle of Shiloh in April 1962, William Clark Talmadge discovered that his brother Rogers Clark Talmadge's unit (The Orphan Brigade of Confederate General Simon Bolivar Buckner) had also fought at Shiloh.

He learned from a wounded Confederate prisoner that Rogers Clark had been blown to pieces by an exploding shell during the battle.

Before dying from his wounds ten days later on April 16 , 1862, William wrote to his father: "Your darlin Rogie was killed during the battle at Shiloh, Papa, but did not suffer. Remember, he was my darlin too."

William's body is buried in the family cemetery at Twelve Oaks and next to his headstone, which reads "William Clark Talmadge 1843 1862 USA," is another, which reads "Rogers Clark Talmadge 1844-1862 CSA." The mound over William's body is the only difference between the two graves.

The deaths of her two sons devastated Elizabeth Louise Talmadge, who now confines herself most days to her bedroom. Her husband, whose strength she depends on, is reconciled to the loss of his sons and heirs; but the business drive that has brought him greater wealth has mellowed and become philosophical, instilling compassion. Where before he would consider what he might gain from a person, now he considers what he might offer the person.

Wednesday morning Joshua shaves, trims his long, wavy dark hair to shoulder length, and puts on his uniform which his aunt has cleaned for him. He slides one bundle of fives in one pocket and another bundle in his other pocket. He doffs his hat to his aunt and kisses her on the cheek. "Ned and I'll be back for dinner, Aunt Mary," he says, hurrying to the barn.

Joshua's uncle Hank had worked a short time for Martin Talmadge's father as a young man, before he began breeding and selling mules himself. Some years later Martin Talmadge bought two mules from Hank Bonger. When Hank Bonger brought the mules to Twelve Oaks, he also brought his nephew. Joshua unleashed the mules from the back of the wagon, while he observed Martin Talmadge and his uncle conclude business. He thought Mr. Talmadge looked like some English lord.

Joshua noticed the two boys, William and Rogers, ride from the barn towards him. Each of the three, not yet in their teens, characterized his personality in his comment.

"Those mules look like good work animals," said William.

"But you can't ride 'em like a good horse!" says Rogers.

"Not if the mule don't wantja to," says Joshua.

A few moments of young boys' talk, and William and Rogers galloped away, while Joshua helped his uncle lead the mules to a near pasture before returning home.

Now, riding a horse, Joshua enters the narrow lane that leads to Twelve Oaks, The house, with it's gabbles laced with black wooden strips against white plaster and it's hand-blown leaded, speckled windows, reminds Joshua of the house in a picture hanging in the Galt House. Three years ago, he would have ridden to the back of the house, but he cavalierly tethers his horse at the entrance of the house, strides up the brick walk, and raps three times on the door.

Having a thousand dollars in one's pockets contributes to one's self-esteem. His three knocks are not answered. This time the three knocks are louder and spaced farther apart. Rebecca, a black woman in her forties, an orange bandanna wrapped around her head, abruptly opens the door, scans the figure of Joshua quickly, and looks him straight in the eye. "Yes?" she asks, coldly.

"I have business with Mr. Talmadge. I'm Joshua Applegate, Hank Bonger's nephew."

She observes the screen door is hooked. "Wait here," she says. She remembers Hank Bonger, when he worked for the Talmadges. She closes the door slightly as she leaves. Proud of her Hebrew name, Rebecca does not answer to "Becky" from other blacks nor from the members of the Talmadge family. A minute later she returns, opens the door wide, and unlocks the screen door. "Mr. Talmadge will see you shortly. He asked me to show you into the parlor."

Resplendent in French-style furnishings, it is the 10' by 18' rug that captivates Joshua's attention. Small, ornate design-like flowers form a line along each of the four sides of the pale green rug, separated only at the middle of each end of the rug, like an entrance through a gate in a flourish of brilliant colors and geometric designs. A huge diamond of intricate composition and colors spreads half way from the center of the rug towards each of the four gates.

The rug enchants Joshua, mesmerized by its dazzling colors, with meandering vines leading his eyes through complex motifs and ornate forms mutating into exotic flowers. A panel in the wall to Joshua's left opens.

The panel, an intricate part of the wall's design, is the door leading into the hexagonal office of J. Martin Talmadge. Of average height. Martin Talmadge's thin body and his white coat and trousers make him appear taller. A full head of wavy black hair is complimented by a black goatee and a thin, extended Napoleon III moustache. Black eyes that once sparkled before the tragedy of his sons now appear misty. His once haughty stance has become an amiable stoop. Talmadge enters the parlor. "Mr. Applegate?" he asks.

Joshua stands up and extends his hand. "Yes, sir. I'm Joshua Applegate, Mr. Bonger's nephew." He deliberately avoids saying "Hank Bonger."

"I was sorry to hear of your uncle's recent death, Mr. Applegate," says Mr. Talmadge, wondering if that is the cause of his visit.

"Thank you, sir. I'm here on business. I want to buy fifty acres of your land at the corner of McCubbins Lane and the creek."

Talmadge notices the corporal stripes on Joshua's uniform. "Come into my study, Joshua." Talmadge says. Is the maturity of a young man who has experienced several years of war speaking, or is it the dreams of a young boy? wonders Talmadge. Either way, Talmadge is reminded of his sons, particularly Rogers, who resembled Joshua.

The library is a hexagon with three sides being bookshelves and the other three sides, windows extending to the floor. Half the study (making up the three shelves) is within the house, while the other half (comprising the three windows) extends out from the side of the house and forms a bay window, overlooking a garden.

A table-like desk and swivel chair are in front of the three widows, and two upholstered, red leather chairs sit facing the desk. A large world globe stands just to the right of the desk. Mr. Talmadge points to one of the chairs for Joshua to sit in and, turning the other towards the first chair; sits in it rather than behind his desk.

"I was discharged three days ago, Mr. Talmadge. I want to start farming. I want to be alone for awhile. I want to buy those fifty acres at the corner of your property."

The thought of selling any portion of his land would have been out of the question before both his sons were killed, but now, with no descendants, life and property take on a different meaning for Talmadge. Talmadge tests whether the youth of dreams or the maturity from experience wishes to buy. "Why not rent the land? I'd consider a ninety-nine year lease," says Talmadge.

Joshua shakes his head no. "I want to own it, Mr. Talmadge. I'm ready to pay you for it now."

This comment surprises Talmadge. The young man probably received a bonus with his discharge, reasons Talmadge. The acreage Joshua wants to buy is unproductive, rolling, and of little value to whatever usage Talmadge might wish to do with the surrounding acreage. Another test.

The land should sell for seven or eight dollars an acre. "Very well," says Talmadge, "I have to have ten dollars an acre. Five hundred dollars for fifty acres."

"Done!" says Joshua.

Startled by Joshua's response, Talmadge sits in amusement as Joshua withdraws a stack of greenbacks from his pocket. Innocently he looks at Talmadge. "These are all fives, Mr. Talmadge," says Joshua. He begins counting and placing ten greenbacks in separate stacks. After finishing the tenth stack, Joshua sits back and sighs. "That's five hundred dollars. I'd like to begin putting up a cabin on the land tomorrow, Mr. Talmadge."

Except for the youthful impertinence of his son Rogers, Talmadge sees both Joshua and Rogers not only look alike but act alike. His older son William, on the other hand, had the blond hair of his mother's family and certainly their quieter, more genteel manner. Talmadge writes out a receipt for the five hundred dollars with approval for immediate usage of the land and hands it to Joshua.

"I'll have my lawyer arrange for the survey, title, and recording at the court house," says Talmadge. He takes string from his desk drawer and ties the ten bundles together. Standing up, he says, "Come back in about three weeks for your deed." He walks to the panel of books on his left, removes several books (revealing a small safe) opens it, and places the bundle of greenbacks in it, and then spins the knob closed. A man with a hoe appears at the near window.

"Excuse me a moment," says Talmadge, as he opens a door that is also part of the window to the left of his desk. He steps out into the garden and follows the man down a brick path.

The three bookcases are made of mahogany with shelves reaching the nine-foot ceiling. Joshua figures all three bookcases must contain hundreds of leather bound books. He gets up and walks to the middle bookcase, where the door is. The titles and authors are foreign to him: Abalard's *History of Calamities*, Hobbes' *Leivathan*, Julian's *Against the Christians*, Machiavelli's *The Prince*, Emerson's *Essays*.

He stops. Emerson! He is familiar with that name. He remembers being impressed with what some captain said to his men, "Your spirits may be raised by a military victory but as Emerson said in his *Essays*, 'Nothing can bring you peace but yourself.'"

He opens the book to the first essay, *History*. At the bottom of the page he reads, "Of the universal mind each individual man is one more incarnation." and is not sure what that means. He turns to the essay titled *The Over-Soul* and reads, "That unity, that Over-Soul, within which every man's particular being is contained and made one with all other." makes him uncomfortable and causes him to think. "Made one with Sergeant O'Conner?" Talmadge enters the study.

"Well, I see you have found something interesting from my library," says Talmadge. Lifting up the book held by Joshua so that he can read the title, Talmadge exclaims, "Emerson! A excellent choice, Joshua. "Would you like to borrow the book?"

"Yes I would, Mr. Talmadge." says Joshua. "I'll bring it back when I come for the deed in three weeks." Joshua grabs his hat from the chair and walks to the door with Mr. Talmadge behind. When they step into the parlor, Joshua stops and turns to Talmadge.

"You sure have a beautiful rug, Mr. Talmadge. It reminds me of a garden."

"That's what it represents, Joshua. It's longer in its relation of length to width than most oriental rugs. That's why I bought it—it fits in our parlor. See? This is the garden of paradise," says Talmadge, pointing to the large diamond design in the middle. "And the four ends of the rug are the four entrances into paradise: through body control, through love, through wisdom, and through a spiritual life." A figure descends from the stairs into the vestibule.

"Rogie!" exclaims the figure. Dressed in a Chinese kimono, Elizabeth Louise Talmadge walks towards Joshua and embraces him. "Rogie ! Rogie! My own dear Rogie! You've come home!"

Bewildered, unsure what to do or say, Joshua does not move except to look at Mr. Talmadge, who gently takes his wife's right hand and removes it from Joshua's shoulder. "This is Mr. Applegate, Elizabeth."

"Oh?" she says, removing her other hand from Joshua's other shoulder and stepping back.

"Rogers is no longer with us, my dear," says Talmadge. The black woman who met Joshua at the door enters.

"Rebecca, will you take Mrs. Talmadge to her room." He looks at his wife. "You need to rest, Elizabeth."

"Come on, Dearie; Beckie will help you to your room," says Rebecca, helping Mrs. Talmadge ascend the stairs to her room. Mr. Talmadge places his arm on Joshua's shoulder, as they walk to the vestibule.

"Both of our sons were killed at Shiloh. Their deaths have been greatly unsettling for my wife," says Talmadge.

"You have my deepest sympathy, Mr. Talmadge. Surely they're in heaven and know that their sacrifice has saved our Union," says Joshua attempting some consolation. But Mr. Talmadge merely replies, "Yes," and does not mention that only William fought for the Union.

Joshua dons his hat and puts his finger to the rim. "In three weeks," he says, and walks to his horse.

Old Ned walks a slow pace, which satisfies Joshua who has much thinking and planning ahead. First, he'll cover the hole with a floor of a cabin he intends to build, and the he'll build a hinged "cellar-type" door over the hole.

He'll open a savings account in the Munfordville Savings and Loans Bank, one in a bank in Elizabethtown, and one in the new bank he saw in Louisville in 1862, The Liberty National Bank and Trust Company.

He will open each account with several hundred dollars and periodically add to each account, so that gradually, without creating any suspicion, a large number of green backs can be disposed of during the following years.

It appeared that the top layer of greenbacks in the chest were five dollar bundles and the lower layers appeared to be all ones. There might be as many as 200 bundles of which possibly 40 bundles are fives. That would be $20,000 in fives! The remaining 160 bundles, if only one dollar greenbacks, would be $16,000. There might be as much as $36,000 in the chest! He'll check his calculations tonight.

He will count the money in the chest later, because the two bodies made him extremely uncomfortable that afternoon. It is safer to leave the bodies in the cave. Removing them would be difficult and might be noticed: the cat would be "out of the bag" so to speak.

That evening, Joshua did the arithmetic and was satisfied that his earlier calculations were correct: an estimated $36,000 in the chest. He told his aunt that he bought the old wagon, because he needed it to haul material to build a small cabin on the land he purchased. He'd like to buy old Ned.

"Heavens, Josh! Old Ned's yours," says his aunt.

"Thank ya! Then I'll be leavin' early tomorrow morning, Aunt Mary, right after breakfast. I'm goin' to buy a good deal of lumber and it needs to be hauled to my land." He liked the sound of "my land."

Pulling the wagon. Old Ned hauled the cement for the foundation and the lumber for joists and flooring of the cabin at a slow pace. Not wishing to draw attention to the construction, Joshua did not cut down any heavy brush or small trees until he was deep into his fifty acres, and then only steps away from the hole. He untethered Old Ned and let him graze on the tall grass.

After clearing the dirt several inches away from the hole, Joshua constructed a larger square, cement wall, three inches high, around the hole and fastened a 4x4 board atop each of the four sides of the wall.

He fastened two eye-hook bolts into opposite boards. The ends of a rope ladder (to be made later) would be fastened to the eye-hooks, allowing the stretched ladder to be several inches within the edge of the hole.

He made forms for ten cement posts, also three inches above the ground, for the foundation of a 10 by 18 foot floor for the cabin.

He filled the forms with concrete the following day and built a wooden top with hinges to fit over the hole.

Joshua cut three straight branches, two to three inches in diameter, from the large oak near the hole and got eight eighteen – inch "steps" for the rope ladder. Cutting in half the twenty-four feet of rope that he had purchased, he fastened one rope around the end of a bolt and the other rope around the end of the other bolt. Continuing this for the remaining seven steps one-foot apart, Joshua made himself a nine foot robe ladder that dangled into the hole. Shaky but sturdy, the rope ladder allowed Joshua to easily go up and down through the hole.

Each morning before the sun rose, Aunt Mary had jumped out of bed to made Joshua a cheese, onion, and chopped-and-dried tomato sandwich to take with him, and then had cooked him three scrambled eggs and four strips of bacon for his breakfast. She wanted his breakfast ready when he awoke and his lunch ready when he finished breakfast, for during the past four days, Joshua left the house at sunrise and returned at sunset.

During these four days, Joshua completed the floor, attached the ladder to the board, fastened the hinges of the door covering the hole to the floor, and concealed it with the folded canvas. Each day he had purchased a wagonload of lumber and on the third day had met Charlie Brumley, who had gone to school with him.

Charlie, married with two children, couldn't pay his thirteen-dollar rent, and had no food for his family. Joshua fumbled in his pocket and pulled out a roll of one dollar greenbacks. Telling Charlie to hold out his hand, he counted out twenty. Smiling and crying, Charlie told Joshua he didn't know when he'd be able to pay him back.

"I don't expect you to, Charlie. Just promise me you won't tell anyone that I gave you this," said Joshua. Embarrassed, when Charlie attempted to kiss his hand, Joshua again reached into his pocket and pulled out five more greenbacks. "Buy your kids a gift from me but don't mention my name. OK?" Charlie could only nod yes; he was too overcome to speak.

Old Ned may not have noticed, but had someone been sitting next to Joshua in the wagon, he would have heard Joshua whistle and sing all the way to the cabin site. Beguiled by the pleasure in giving,

Joshua experienced the true value of abundance, and that evening wrote in a small notebook Charlie's name and the amount he gave him.

Joshua completed building his cabin during the next two weeks. The hinged top over the hole is north of the ten foot wide sides of the cabin with a door three feet from the northwest corner. A single window lets light in from the south, and a pot bellied stove sits in the southeast corner of the cabin. Rafters allow for storage and a folding bed provides more space during the day. It is time to go to Twelve Oaks and get the deed to his property.

The hour ride to Twelve Oaks on Old Ned is at a leisurely pace, allowing Joshua the opportunity to plan, reflect, dream. His visit this time is business and he decides he will go to the rear of the house this time, like a family friend. He raps gently on the screen door, enters when Rebecca turns around from the stove. "Good morning, Miss Rebecca," he says.

Taking Joshua's entrance through the back of the house as a sign of family acceptance, Rebecca asks him to come with her to the parlor, after which she goes to find Mr. Talmadge. Talmadge arrives several minutes later, finding Joshua standing in the middle of the rug engrossed in the design in its center.

"Good morning Joshua. Still fascinated by the rug?" he asks.

"Yes. Good morning Mr. Talmadge," replies Joshua. He holds up the book he has in his hand. "I was wondering if Emerson would say paradise is not an end?" Letting Joshua explain his comment, Talmadge says nothing. "In his essay on circles, Emerson said every end is a beginning,"

"An interesting question, Joshua." Talmadge points to the panel door into his study and they enter.

"That question has been asked since the beginning of history." He points for Joshua to sit down. Joshua hands the book to Talmadge who sits behind his desk.

"Thank you for loaning me the book, Mr. Talmadge," says Joshua. "What do you think Emerson would say?"

"Well, Emerson was a student of the East. There are those who believe there is nothing after death, and there are those who believe in a paradise soon or in the future after death. Emerson would probably add a third possibility: the soul's return in another human role."

Joshua says nothing, absorbed in the significance of Talmadge's response. Not wishing to pursue the trend of the conversation, Talmadge reaches into his deck drawer and removes a paper.

"Here's your deed, Joshua." he says, handing it to him.

Joshua looks over the deed, folds it and puts it in his pocket. "I've finished my cabin and will move into it in a few days," says Joshua, proudly.

Talmadge gets up and walks to the shelf of books on his right. "There's another book you should read." He searches for a moment and removes a small book which he hands to Joshua. "Thoreau was a little older than you when he moved to Walden Pond and lived there by himself for several years. He worked hard, like you have. He writes in *Walden* about conscience, not self-interest. It is a wise and earthy book, but witty."

Thanking Talmadge for the loan of the book, Joshua leaves the study with Talmadge behind him. Stepping on the rug in the parlor, Joshua stops and turns to Talmadge. "Mr. Talmadge, I notice that you have seven old oak trees along the road to Twelve Oaks. There aren't any oak stumps. Why do you call your home Twelve Oaks instead of Seven Oaks?"

"Seven oaks doesn't have the right sound, Joshua," says Talmadge. "Twelve does." Seeing from Joshua's expression that this is an insufficient reason, he continues. "In the series of ancient folk tales the title, The Thousand and One Nights sounds enchanting, charming, poetic, while The Thousand Nights doesn't."

Joshua, nods his head yes. "I see," he says, but he doesn't. He puts his finger to the tip of his hat and leaves, baffled by the reasoning of someone who is certainly an intellectual.

During the next several months of 1865, Joshua had a barn and privy built, a well dug, his pond stocked, and his entire fifty acres fenced in. Joshua has cured the mangy pup, a mixture of Welsh Terrier and Collie, that whimpered outside his cabin one wintery night. His once starved body now round and full, Buddy is more than a name, having become Joshua's constant companion sleeping at the foot of his bed each night, except on very cold nights when he snuggles in front of the stove. Joshua attempts to train Buddy to help with the goats he has added to the farm.

At sunrise the day after Joshua had moved into his cabin, he entered the cave through the hole and took out fifteen bundles of one dollar greenbacks from the chest. He deposited three bundles in a new savings account he opened at the Munfordville Savings and Loans Bank. The 10:30 A.M. Louisville and Nashville train took him to Elizabethtown where he deposited another three bundles of greenbacks in a newly opened savings account at First Citizens, and two hours later boarded the 12:30 train to Louisville, where he deposited four bundles in a new savings account at the Liberty National Bank and Trust Company.

Before leaving Louisville on his return home Joshua visited the private banking firm of A.D. Hunt and Sons and purchased $400 worth of Louisville and Nashville Railroad stock with four bundles of ones. Joshua intends quietly to add to the deposits and purchase stock three times each year. He kept the last bundle of ones and enjoyed a late lunch at Delmonico's.

To friends, acquaintances, and even strangers whose sad financial problems seemed endless, Joshua gives money, the amount depending on the "depths of misery," and the only requirement, that the recipient not mention Joshua's gift to anyone. He writes every name and amount in his "Gift Book."

He decides to attend the auction of the estate of wealthy deceased bachelor Wilber Pierce described on the poster in Stratton's Drug Store window.

A 4-foot by 6-foot Oriental rug catches Joshua's eye and he continues to bid for this perfect cover for the hole. The next offering is a 5-foot by 7-foot companion oriental rug that would be perfect on the floor of his cabin. Bidding against two women, Joshua bids a dollar higher after each of their bids. When the younger woman stops bidding, the other woman glares at Joshua. "Young man, I want that rug!" she exclaimed.

"Ma'am, so do I!" said Joshua, with a mocking bow.

Joshua begins bidding on the 20-by-36 inch table with drawer and chair, which he visualizes sitting on the rug over the hole, but no one else bids. He then bids on the damask red drapes with a golden rose pattern and the other two bidders stop after their second bid. Those bidding with Joshua for the Chippendale yellow satin chair stop after their third bid. Joshua's determination in his immediate and quiet bidding delights the crowd, who applaud after he had purchases the table, drapes, and the Chippendale chair.

If they had known where this young man intended to place these exquisite furnishings, they would have smiled. Had they seen the five nails in the corner next to the cabin door serving as a wardrobe, they would have laughed aloud.

In late June Aunt Mary became very ill and passed away a few hours after Joshua arrived. In settling her estate, Joshua discovers that her debts exceed the value of her property. He retrains Old Ned and takes Billy, the beagle hound that he has grown up with, to his spread.

Billy tolerates Buddy's playful antics, but after fourteen years of farm life, he no longer can step up into the cabin. He stops eating and drinking, lying along the wall near the stove. Buddy seems to understand and merely snuffs around Billy's head, while Joshua strokes him and whispers softly to him. On a crisp morning, when Joshua gets out of bed to stoke the fire in the stove, he pets Billy only to feel his cold, taut body.

Later that morning, Joshua wraps Billy, his "Old Buddy," in a sheet, and buries him in a spot he had cleared of trees and brush a number of paces' walk south of the cabin.

His Aunt Mary's death affected Joshua in a totally different way than had the deaths of his comrades in combat. Even as her body was lowered into her grave, Joshua felt she was standing beside him; and when he walked away from the grave, he felt her loving presence caress him. Surprisingly, he felt happy, not sad. It's not that she loved him but that she loves him. He decides that next Sunday he'll go to the church near Salt River road—The Church of John the Baptizer in the hamlet of Perryville.

The minister of the Church of John the Baptizer is Jeremiah C. Trumble, a 42-year old ex-Union infantry officer, recently discharged from active service and newly reinstated as pastor of the church. Trumble began the church after the Baptists divided into southern and northern groups in 1845, mainly from tensions related to slavery. Too deep within the South to join with the northern group, and opposition to slavery preventing them from joining the southern group, Trumble, then a 23-year old Baptist minister, and ten families began their special church.

Six-foot four-inches, robust, strong, black hair with a tinge of gray at the temple's, Trumble wears a black eye patch over his right eye, which had been pierced by a splinter of shrapnel during the battle of Atlanta. Always smiling, Trumble never meets a stranger; and when the smile is big enough to show his white teeth, women sigh and men stare, all mesmerized by his charm, wit, and persuasiveness.

The unpretentious church is a little wider than Mr. Talmadge's parlor and twice as long. In the sanctuary two doors at the side of the choir and pulpit lead to what Joshua assumes is a meeting room. He arrives early, before Mr. Schultz the greeter begins his greetings and sits by the outside isle in the third of eight pews. Soon a stream of families begin to arrive with the youngsters skipping down the isles through the two side doors, and parents scattering to predetermined pews. The gentleman of the couple that sit in front of Joshua turns around to welcome him and introduces his wife, and is followed by the couple that sit behind him doing the same.

An older couple shuffle their large frames down the narrow space in front of the pew Joshua sits in. The woman, whose plump daughter is soon to be twenty, sits next to this handsome young man who is alone. Enquiring whether this is his first visit to "our church," she learns that it is, and that he is single, a veteran, and owns a farm. Satisfied, she begins planning how Hester, her daughter, might properly meet the young Mr. .... (what is the name?) ... Appleton, just as the organ music begins and the sudden hush of buzzing conversations ends.

The service and music brings warm memories to Joshua of attending church with his aunt and uncle when he was a youngster. But it is the minister that shakes him out of his nostalgia and opens the hidden cave within Joshua's soul.

"Mose's declaration 28 centuries ago to the people of Israel, that as a nation sows so shall it reap, is true for each of us today: What you have sown you shall reap," yells Pastor Jeremiah C. Trumble.

The image of Sergeant 0' Conner flashes before Joshua's inner vision, and he braces his body, suddenly thrust from the light of the sun to the dark of the cave. Then reprieve. "But Jesus'll help ya ," cries Trumble, "but you gotta save your own soul!"

After the benediction, the congregation of forty-eight souls line up along the two outer isles and the center isle to greet Pastor Trumble, who has positioned himself squarely at the entrance to the church. Joshua is in the last isle to greet the pastor and he stands behind a tall gentleman who had been greeted as a guest. The tall gentleman shakes hands with Trumble and introduces himself.

"And where are you from, sir?" asks Trumble.

"Lexington," says the gentleman.

"The heart of bluegrass country!" exclaims Trumble. "I too, am from God's gift to Kentucky—those rolling fields of blue carpeting. Visit us again, sir." The gentleman puts on his hat, bowing his head slightly and says he shall.

It is difficult to compare the lush fields of the distant bluegrass country with the holey ground of his local cave country, and Joshua struggles with a feeling of inferiority when Trumble turns to face him. "I'm Joshua Applegate. I have a farm on the holey ground just east of here."

"Holy Ground! What a wonderful name for a farm!" exclaims Trumble. "And Joshua! A great Hebrew name like mine—Jeremiah. Visit us again, Brother Applegate."

Joshua assures Pastor Trumble that he will. He has a question to ask him: How do you save your soul?

The next Sunday Joshua attends church and hears the answer to his question during the sermon. "If you would save your soul, sisters and brothers, repent!" exclaims Trumble. "And what does John mean when he yelled 'Repent' to the Israelites? He meant change your ways! And change begins with baptism."

"Baptism of fire!" comes to Joshua's memory of the battles he fought in. One enters as a boy and comes through as a man. Not physically, reasons Joshua, but inwardly. The change, the redemption, is inward. No matter what he does or thinks, the opportunity for change is always there.

He should have refused to cooperate with O'Conner, but then O'Conner would probably have killed him. He could have walked back to his company and left O'Conner asleep, but by then Joshua was an accomplice. If only he could wake up and say, "It was all a dream."

But Jefferson C. Davis, after murdering Nelson, was promoted! It's not the killing of O'Conner that continues to bother Joshua. He was justified in doing that, and that's over. Suddenly Joshua realizes it isn't over! The lieutenant is not buried, and O'Conner as a human being is entitled to a proper grave. Change! How can he change that?

Hester's mother insists that she and her father wait in front of church to see if the nice looking young man arrives for Sunday services. He does. He nodes to the mother's morning welcome, walks up the four steps to the entrance, and then to the same pew he has occupied the last two Sundays. Encouraged by her mother, Hester enters the church and sits next to Joshua, followed by her mother and father. "Good morning, Mr. Applegate," says the mother. She obtained his name from the pastor. "I'll say no more. We, Hester's father and I, do not wish to disturb young people's conversation. Isn't that right, Cyril?" The father nods his head yes. "I remember when I was young and conversed with so many young men, that I lost count. I remember that our best conversation occurred shortly after church service. But I'll say no more." The organ music begins, and Pastor Trumble takes his seat in the high-back chair in front of the pulpit.

Hester is not a good conversationalist. "That's a beautiful hymn." "Yes, it is." "Pastor Trumble has a powerful voice." "Yes, he does." "The flowers in front of the pulpit are beautiful." "Yes, they are." And all this time, Joshua is captivated by the most beautiful girl he has ever seen, sitting in the other section, closer to the pulpit. Her profile glows, as if a halo surrounds her golden hair. She looks in Joshua's direction and for a moment her blue eyes and Joshua's dark eyes meet.

Frances Rose Seymour has come from Nashville to live with her aunt at the dire request of her father, the only brother of her aunt. A major of cavalry in the Confederate army, Francis Seymour's plantation and home were sacked during the war, but not burned. Nashville society now caters to young Union officers, and Fanny—Frances Rose's preferred name—is the honey in a hive of dozens of them. With the death of his wife last year, Major Francis Seymour, whose stare alone commanded obedience, cannot control his twenty-year old daughter. For her sake (for the sake of all those Union officers!) he implored his sister to "take this uncontrollable girl off my hands, and find her a strong willed husband, for God's sake!"

Her slim figure gives the impression that she is taller than her five-foot five-inch height, and her angelic face is enlivened by biting her lips so they are redder and pinching her cheeks so they are rosier. With men, she intentionally steps closer in conversation, and unobtrusively accentuates her words with a gentle touch of her finger on the back of a man's hand. Removing sweets just before they are tasted excites her, and suggesting with body motions what young men seek and old men dream, makes her teasing an art. A spiritual descendant of ancient Greek Maenads, Fanny reflects the soul of a suppressed Victorian lady, "pining for her demon lover."

At the end of the sermon and before the benediction, Pastor Trumble informs the congregation of the auction lunch the following Saturday. For those guests, he explains that the women of the church prepare a basket lunch and the man bidding the highest gets to eat the lunch with the woman who prepared it. The lunch, he explains, will take place in back of the church, where the noise of the town is less disturbing.

"You can meet at my farm!" says Joshua, raising his hand.

"Holy Ground!" yells Trumble. "Only the pristine sounds of nature! Excellent! Thank you Brother Applegate. The auction lunch will be at Brother Applegate's farm – Holy Ground—this coming Saturday afternoon."

Hester and her mother are pushed aside by members of the congregation, thanking Joshua for offering his farm for the auction lunch and asking directions to it. Finally the crowd is gone and Hester and her mother are alone with Joshua. Hester has difficulty opening a conversation, but not Fanny. Standing by herself under the single tree in front of the church, she speaks before Hester can think of something to say.

"Mr. Applegate?" The southern accent and femme fatale intonation sounded: /'Mea-sta A-pl-gay-t?/ , a lure only for catching males. Joshua turns from Hester and walks ten paces to Fanny.

"Do you like fried chicken, Mr. Applegate?" asks Fanny.

"Yes!" Said Joshua. "Yes, I do."

"The breast?" says Fanny, heaving a sigh that exposes the cleavage of her breasts.

"Breasts? Oh! Yes. Chicken breasts. Yes. I love ... chicken breast." The words stumble stutteringly out of his mouth.

"There'll be more breast than you can eat, Mr. Applegate," says Fanny, "If you bid high enough." She turns and walks to catch up with her aunt and uncle. "Bye!" she says with a slight wave of her long fingers.

Joshua had finished digging a root cellar three days before the auction lunch that Saturday, and had cleared a sizable portion of the slopping hill that led down from the cabin to the creek below. All that would be needed for a great festival would be a sunny day, and the day of the auction was one of the hottest so far that year.

The smaller rug he had purchased at the auction covers the door over the hole, and the table and chair sit atop. The larger rug brings the only "charm" possible to the cabin, with the exception of the Chippendale chair and drape. To ensure no one enters the cabin, he locks the door, after first pulling the elegant drape over the single window—the ornate furnishing might be noticed and a request to see them inside would prove embarrassing.

Besides the eight married couples, two widowers, three widows, and Pastor Trumble (his wife had died while he was in the army), there are six young bachelors and six young maidens, two of which are Hester and Fanny Rose. Pastor Trumble begins the auctioning by observing the seventeen assorted baskets, piled high with food.

"Our women folk have outdone themselves. Under this basket top I see a bowl of golden fried chicken and this basket has a pie with strawberries oozing through the crust. Men. I can't wait to begin the feast. It's up to your bidding. And remember, a large bid is a compliment as well as a contribution to our church. Now what am I bid for this cornucopia of mouthwatering vittles in this basket with a yellow ribbon attached."

All baskets are identified with one or more colored ribbons, to be sure that each husband buys his wife's cooking. Part of the festivities is for another husband or a widower to make one bid on a basket not his. An unwritten rule forbids anyone other than the husband having the final bid. The three widowers (including Pastor Trumble) bid on the three baskets prepared by the three widows.

After the adult bidding, ten adult couples scatter among the shade trees, waiting for Pastor Trumble to begin the much anticipated bidding for the other six baskets, prepared by the other six young women., including Hester and Fanny Rose. Widow Clemens, whose basket Trumble bought, stands next to him, pleased as a newly crowned princess.

The six young bachelors, including Joshua, if favored by one of the young women, are subtly informed by her what color ribbon is tied to her basket. Hester wears the same red and white ribbon in her hair as is tied on his basket. With each of the six bachelors being "a favorite," Fanny has gone to each of them and. puckering her lips, said "Blue!" and pointed to the sky blue ribbon in her hair and to the basket on the table with a bright sky-blue ribbon.

With the completion of three auctions, Pastor Trumble lifts up the basket with the sky blue ribbon tied to the handle. He lifts the end of the blue and white checkered tablecloth. "The tallest slice of chocolate cake I've ever seen!" he says. "Who'll start the bidding?"

"Twenty five cents!" The instant bid is from a recent graduate from West Point, Lieutenant James Sterling. At home for a three month furlough before leaving for one of the newly created forts west of St Louis, Lieutenant Sterling is dressed in his tight-fitting uniform. His dark, cropped hair and piercing dark eyes command the attention of men and the homage of women.

Jarred by this sudden competition, Joshua immediately feels umbrage and, as if withdrawing a pistol from his side, fires back, "One dollar and twenty-five cents!" before anyone else can bid. No third party does.

Not sure what such a jump in bidding means, the lieutenant, slightly less confident, yells, "One dollar and fifty-cents!"

"Two dollars and fifty cents!" yells Joshua.

The congregation understands this is no longer friendly bidding; this is a duel.

"Whose basket?"

"Fanny Seymour's!"

"Oh!"

"Three dollars!" yells the lieutenant not as loud and not as assured. With this bid, he has less than a dollar in change.

"Four dollars!" says a confident Joshua in a softer tone as if he were putting a pistol back into its holster. Trumble looks at the lieutenant, who after a few moments shakes his head no. "Going once! Going twice! The basket is bought by Mr. Joshua Applegate." says Trumble, handing it to Joshua, who has grabbed Fanny by the hand.

Joshua and Fanny spread the tablecloth under a large oak tree among three young couples where there is little conversation but much eating; and Joshua discovers that three chicken breasts are the most he can eat, after finishing the slice of chocolate cake.

A half hour after the last auction (Hester's basket, bought by Lieutenant Sterling), the married couples begin to leave, and Fanny's aunt tells her to be ready soon to join them. Joshua tells Fanny he'd be pleased to take her home later. Their conversation, being limited within the group they sat with, Fanny touches her aunt's arm.

"Auntie, Mr. Applegate has kindly offered to bring me home later."

Her aunt looks in the direction where Joshua is sitting, and then at Fanny. "Another hour Frances, no later." There's not much a person can do that they shouldn't in an hour her aunt concludes.

A whole hour to do what we couldn't do around all those other people, says Fanny to herself. "You said you have a pond Joshua. I'd like to see it."

The innocent request germinates romantic thoughts of being alone with this beautiful, welcoming girl in Joshua—just as Fanny intends. His hermetic life is anxiously shed and he quickly agrees to "show her my pond."

A small dirt path meanders back of the cabin for several hundred steps, some so slippery that Fanny has to hold onto Joshua, and gradually it becomes necessary for Joshua to hold her, not her hand. They reach the circular pond, which is fifty feet across. Joshua removes the branches from a grassy spot near the edge of the pond. He's glad he brought the tablecloth.

Fanny slides down on the tablecloth, her blond hair falling around her head like a halo. Joshua lies down beside her, touching her cheek. He kisses her and gently places his hand on her breast. Slowly she reaches over and just as gently removes his hand. "Your hand can not linger, until a ring's on my finger," she says, smiling like Alice's Cheshire cat.

Joshua lifts himself on one elbow. "Do you want to go back?" he asks.

Fanny sits up and pushes Joshua back on to the covering. "No, you dear boy," she says, kissing him on the lips and sliding on top of him.

Ten minutes later, Fanny now underneath Joshua, pushes him off. "We better go. My aunt said an hour." They walk back to the cabin saying little, holding hands. A half hour later Joshua helps Fanny out of the buggy. "I'll go up the walk by myself, Josh." says Fanny.

"See you Saturday?" asks Joshua. "Another picnic?"

Fanny nods her head yes. "I like your pond," she says, blowing him a kiss with her fingers.

Joshua carries the basket that following Saturday from the buggy, which was as close to the pond as they could get Old Ned to pull them, to the same bewitching carpet of green and true to her word, Fanny has prepared another lunch of fried chicken, biscuits, potato salad, fresh fruit, and two slices of her aunt's apple pie.

"I've brought something special," says Fanny, flapping two ends of the tablecloth and letting it float to the ground. Joshua sets the basket on the cloth and kisses Fanny on the neck. She snuggles her head next to his. "Look in the basket," she says.

Joshua lifts the lid of the basket and sees a small bottle. He takes it out. "Is this it?" he asks. Fanny nods her head yes. The label on the dark bottle reads "Doctor Markham's Elixir of Youth." Joshua smiles. "Aren't we young enough?"

"You are, Josh, for sure," says Fanny. "Take a sip."

Joshua pulls the cork out and sniffs. "It's whiskey!" he says and takes a taste. "That's good old Kentucky bourbon whiskey, Fanny. "I learned that much in the army."

Fanny's aunt and uncle, strict Baptists, not only were teetotalers but never had any alcoholic beverages, other than medicinal, in their home. The one exception was the whiskey Fanny's aunt used to preserve her holiday fruit cakes. It was called "the preservative" never "the whiskey." The dark brown cakes, full or preserved fruit and nuts, are sprinkled with "the preservative" periodically and always covered with several layers of cheesecloth, which are saturated with the preservative.

It isn't that they are hungry, for it is part of an inherent ritual that eating occurs first and merriment follows. The two small glasses Fanny included in the basket assure her that the beverage is part of a picnic, not of a saloon.

Two young people can transform eating into merriment. Fanny bites into a fresh apple, licking her lips and handing it to Joshua. They toast with the tingling of two full glasses, then one glass is shared, and finally, the upturned empty bottle is tossed with laughter into the pond. Half the food remains in the basket while Joshua and Fanny stretch out on the tablecloth holding hands, laughing, giggling, slipping into an intoxicating, false world of pleasure and gratification.

Suddenly Fanny gets up. "Let's go swimming!" she says. She takes off her shoes and stockings, unbuttons her blouse and tosses it with her skirt onto the tablecloth.

Joshua, entranced in his stupor, watches Fanny skip to the pond and wade in up to her hips. "Come on in, Josh. It's warm," says Fanny, inching closer to the deeper center of the pond. He removes all his clothing except his shorts. He is not in such a stupor as to reveal what his shorts now conceal.

The water slows his walking towards Fanny, and she splashes water at him as he nears. He reaches to embrace her and she jumps into his arms. She bites him on the neck before releasing him and swims towards the bank of the pond.

Confused by her swimming away, Joshua follows and stands over her, as she lies on her back, resting on her elbows. "Is something wrong?" he asks.

Fanny motions with her left hand for him to come closer. When he does, she puts both hands on his shoulders and pulls him next to her. She hugs him tightly so the fresh scent of her spellbinds the confused, but hopeful, Joshua.

The warm sun and languid summer air conspire to send both into a light sleep. They wake a half-hour later, his body "spooned" against hers.

"We can get married next week." says Joshua.

Fanny sits up. Her playful game has become serious. Delay; but not end. "Sweet boy, before that happens I must have a home. A beautiful home. A large parlor, a spacious dining room, kitchen," And to assure the playing continues: "And bedrooms upstairs."

Undaunted, Joshua agrees much to the chagrin of Fanny. An understood agreement becomes Joshua's contract of future marriage. As they leave Holy Ground, Joshua considers the things he must do to begin construction of a house, while Fanny confronts the confinement in "settling down." It takes a long time to build a house, she concludes.

Joshua draws a plan of the house he has in mind and the following Monday shows it to Peter Schönbachler, a carpenter and member of the Church of John the Baptizer. Schönbachler agrees to build the house with the help of his two sons Willie and Franz for $1,500 with Joshua supplying all the material.

The drawing is of a two story, frame house with a central hall and a kitchen attached to the cabin. Sliding doors separate the kitchen from a dining room. A parlor is on the other side of the hall where a stairway leads to the second floor. Fireplaces are in the dining room and the parlor.

The rest of that week Joshua hauled cement and sand, water from the creek, and stacks of lumber to the cabin. By that Saturday, when Joshua brought Fanny to Holy Ground for "another picnic," Schönbachler and his sons had begun forming the trench for the thirty-by-forty foot foundation.

Joshua and Fanny "picnicked" in the cabin, where they could close the drape and lock the door.

The next Saturday Schönbachler and his sons were nailing the last of the flooring when Joshua brought Fanny to Holy Ground. Joshua, absorbed in the construction of "his house," spent half the time they were at Holy Ground showing an indifferent Fanny the three rooms, two fireplaces, the hall and vestibule, and the stairway.

"The chicken will be cold soon," said Fanny.

"We can eat here," says Joshua. "You get the basket from the wagon and I'll fix a place for us by the cabin. We can watch Mr. Schönbachler and his sons finish the foundation." This, their third picnic, did not include "picnicking," much to Fanny's displeasure.

During the follow two Saturdays Joshua showed Fanny the construction later in the afternoon, without a picnic basket; and the two Saturdays after that, Joshua was too busy helping Mr. Schönbachler to bring Fanny to Holy Ground, seeing her only at Church the following two Sundays.

By early September the Schönbachlers' were finished and Joshua had completed plastering the walls. He had missed seeing Fanny and looked forward that Sunday to taking her to see the roofed house and nearly completed first floor rooms. He oils his hair and combs it back with no part, shaves a six-day beard, and slaps his face with spicy toilet water. The new suit he wears will be his wedding suit. He pictures himself walking down the aisle, and Fanny, all spruced up in white, smiling at him. She will say "I do" and then he will, and Pastor Trumble will pronounce them "man and wife." Life is wonderful, and he has never been so happy.

He arrives at church later than usual and is surprised at the serious expression of members when he bids them "Good morning!" They nod back, and in a sudden somber mood, respond with a woeful "Good morning." He searches for Fanny and her aunt and uncle, but they are not there. He sits in his and their regular pew, and is puzzled by the different, almost strange, look from those sitting near him.

While the organ music begins the morning service, Joshua keeps glancing back. After, what seem hours, Pastor Trumble gives the benediction, and every conceivable reason why Fanny is not here has entered Joshua's mind. Except one. When the parishioners line up along the isles, Joshua lingers back, wanting time to speak with Pastor Trumble.

Trumble bids the last parishioner "Good Morning!" He looks at Joshua, and his perpetual smile disappears. "Joshua," he says, in a tone of consolation.

"Where's Fanny Seymour?" asks Joshua.

"She left for St. Louis. With Lieutenant Sterling."

Like a hawk shot by a farmer, Joshua, who has been soaring in the clouds, crashes to the earth.

"Would you like to come to my office?" asks Trumble.

Five seconds pass. "No," says Joshua. "I have some things to do at Holy Ground," he says, putting on his cap.

Trumble puts his arm around Joshua's shoulder as he begins to leave. "You can come to my office anytime, Joshua. And you're always welcome at my home ... even after midnight."

Joshua gets on Old Ned, who, sensing the despair in his master, instinctively begins the trip back to Holy Ground. On the upper shelf built in the corner of the cabin next to the door, sits a cigar box given to Joshua when he had returned Thoreau's *Walden* to Martin Talmadge. It had contained a gift of six Havana cigars, but now serves as the depository of those unimportant things which Joshua is unable to throw away. Among these things, Joshua tosses the daguerreotype of Fanny in a coquettish pose and a frayed blue ribbon that had been tied to a basket.

Joshua continues his regimen of work, but it's pleasures have become tonics to forget. He completes the dining room fireplace and converts the room into his bedroom. Finding diversion in auctions, Joshua buys two four-poster beds. one is placed between the front windows in his new bedroom, and the other, is stored in the larger of the two unfinished rooms on the second floor. A hooked-rug, larger than the Oriental rug in the center of the cabin, covers the floor of his new bedroom.

The taller of two mahogany wardrobes fits against the wall opposite the fireplace, and the other is set next to the bed on the second floor. He records the price of each piece of auction-acquired items in a small book and stacks the chairs, tables, mirrors, cabinets, vases, and dishware in the second floor room.

Joshua's natural skills with animals, particularly with mules, earns him the appellation "Doc" among farmers who have an ailing mule, horse, or cow, and parents, whose son's dog or daughter's cat, "ain't actin like it aughta." The dogs and cats are brought to Holy Ground in a neighborly manner, and the "doc's service" is paid for in the same manner: with a bushel of potatoes, a chicken, or a basket of beans. When Joshua is asked to come to see a sick mule, horse, or cow, he receives the next day at Holy Ground a rack of cut wood, a patchwork quilt, one or two piglets, or a smoked ham.

The red fox, that was raiding Joshua's chicken coop, was too beautiful a creature to throw away after he had killed it. He built a frame out of wood and formed the stuffed skin around it after placing two yellow marbles in its eye sockets. A stuffed fox standing on the floor is not the same as a side table next to a chair, and Joshua decided to put the fox in the upstairs room. During the next two years Joshua proudly added a stuffed raccoon, coyote, three squirrels, a hawk with its wings spread out, and his favorite goat, Millie.

Joshua thought of Buddy as more human than a dog and certainly more human than the fox and other stuffed creatures that were beginning to fill the small upstairs room. When Buddy died, Joshua constructed a small box, lined it with a white cotton shirt, and nailed it closed after placing Buddy's body in it. He buried it next to where he had buried Billy, and them hammered two wooded stakes at the top of each grave with "Billy" painted on one and "Buddy" painted on the other.

He buys a small pocket size notebook at Crumb's Store and writes "Cemetery" on the front, listing on the first page the names of both dogs and the date they were buried. He wonders what's the difference between stuffing an animal and burying it? He'd gladly stuff O'Conner, but he'd bury the lieutenant—if only he could.

Joshua lives at Holy Ground, constructing a root cellar, completing the kitchen and parlor, and cultivating a vegetable garden. Except for Sundays, when he attends church services and those eagerly anticipated occasions when he returns a book to Martin Talmadge or meets with Pastor Trumble to discuss some church or congregational need.

Talmadge's wife has died, leaving her husband alone in their large home. Joshua's occasional visits become a joy for Talmadge, who always insists that Joshua never leave without taking "this important book" with him each time he returns a previously borrowed book.

The pattern develops into roughly a visit each month. During one summer visit, Joshua notices Ulysses, a collie and favorite of Martin Talmadge's five dogs, is limping. When Joshua asks Talmadge about the limping, Talmadge replies that Ulysses is twelve years old and getting old.

Talmadge welcomes Joshua's request to look at the leg. A few minutes later, after feeding Ulysses a small piece of meat and talking softly to him, Joshua gently lifts the paw Ulysses holds up. As he rubs his fingers over the webbing between the toes, Ulysses whimpers slightly and pulls his paw back from Joshua.

Continuing with soft words, Joshua feels something inside the webbing between two toes. A slight squeeze and he extracts a thorn. Ulysses turns from Joshua and walks away on all four legs. Two weeks later, Joshua receives a package that contains a leather cigar holder with five cigars in it with *Joshua C. Applegate* embossed in gold on it. A card reads, "Ulysses thanks you."

Reconciliation between Union and Confederate sympathizers is most difficult in Kentucky, one of the border states during the Civil War. A line running from Columbus in the west, through Munfordville in the center, and just north of Cumberland Gap, separates what could have been called the "Confederate State of Kentucky" from the Union, with Bowling Green serving as its short-lived capital. The people along that line are equally divided, if not in action, at least in feeling. On the night of 21 July, Hardbottom's General Store, on the corner of Main and Old Streets in Munfordville, burns to the ground.

The coincidence that the 21st is the fifth anniversary of the First Battle of Bull Run, the opening battle of the Civil War between Union forces and Confederate forces, does not go unnoticed. Jacob Hardbottom, the son of the owner of the store and its new manager, had served in the Confederate Army as a private. The rumor spread quickly in the county that the store had been set on fire by some young, Unionist fanatics.

Jacob Hardbottom, who is two years older than Joshua, came to his defense during a confrontation between Joshua and an older student when they were in school ten years ago. Joshua, a sixth grader at the time, was knocked down by an eighth grade bully. Smaller than the bully, Jacob had pulled him off Joshua and fought with him until the teacher stopped the fight. Jacob had two black eyes and eventually lost sight in one of them. Beholding to Jacob, Joshua was the first to welcome Jacob home, when he was released from a Union prison and returned home to Munfordville a month after hostilities ended.

Joshua visited the Hardbottom home and offered to give Jacob the funds to rebuild and stock the store if he would rename the store Hardbottom & Applegate General Store; and, as long as Jacob or any members of the Hardbottom family owned the business, they would charge Joshua their cost of any item he would purchase. Overwhelmed, Jacob readily agreed, and six months later Hardbottom & Applegate had a Grand Opening.

When Joshua went down the hole to retrieve a sufficient amount of greenbacks, he found the letters C.S.A. followed by an explanation mark, printed in ink on the band around one of the five dollar bundles. This convinced Joshua that the greenbacks had belonged to Confederate sympathizers and had been intended for the Confederate government. It was enemy money that he had found and he now felt justified in believing it was rightfully his.

As with all young romance, a lost love is soon forgotten, for Joshua no longer thought or cared to think about Fanny. He found the company of two wise, older men far more rewarding than the silly conversation with a fickle, self absorbed girl. He marveled at how foolish he had been to "get so involved."

These two dissimilar men, Martin Talmadge and Pastor Jeremiah Trumble, had opened his mind and heart to the marvels of the natural sciences and the wisdom in the Bible. This knowledge unfortunately, does not teach or prepare a young man how to contend with the designs of unattractive, boorish women.

Having made the dining room his bedroom, Joshua had fastened two large sheets across its two windows. Pulling the ends aside in the morning took time and did not allow enough sunlight to come into the windows. He had heard of Mrs. Hannah Hopper a seamstress, when he helped the woman of the church prepare a meal for the outside church festivals during the summer months. The next Monday he went to Hannah Hopper's home in Munfordville.

A small woman, looking much older than her age, her graying hair pulled back into a tight knot, Hannah Hopper answers the knock at her door with a scratchy "Come in!" Sitting on a stool in front of the single window to the room, she lifts her eyes above her glasses without stopping her sewing.

He owns two bolts of green damask material. Can she make drapes for him? She is a "needle woman," but only in making dresses she informs Joshua with a slight lifting of her eyes to take him in. Does she know anyone who make drapes, drapes for large windows? She puts her hands in her lap and raises her head. "My daughters are outside. Ask them." She returns to her needlework, pointing over her shoulder. "In the back," she added ignoring Joshua's "Thank you!"

Among the chickens, dog, and cat, two plump women are hanging wash, and when they turn around to see who is asking for them, their normal oafish appearance becomes absurd. Having a handsome young man ask for them, their toothless smiles, their sudden brushing of their disheveled hair, their attempts to straighten their dirty dresses by pushing against their hefty thighs, and their efforts to conceal the hairy mold on each of their cheeks with their hands, shocks Joshua into silence.

It is drapery makers, not Greek goddesses, he wants. Joshua manages to overcome his surprise and is rewarded with the assurance that Ida and Huldah Hopper are quite capable of measuring, cutting, sewing, hanging short, medium, or long drapes. "And gladly," added Ida, with a sigh. Captain Billy, their handyman, will take them to Holy Ground in their wagon tomorrow. Joshua leaves and Ida and Huldah glow. Huldah will bake him a juicy apple pie, but Ida objects. Huldah the older by two years, hasn't found a man yet, and Ida is not getting any younger. Ida will bake him a pie. They compromise: they will both bake him a pie and let him decide.

The following Monday, Captain Billy hitches up the wagon and places a covered basket containing two hot pies—one apple sprinkled with cinnamon and one peach—under the seat of the wagon. Dressed in their finest, Ida carries a pencil and paper to record the measurements and Huldah, the necessary scissors, rulers, pins, and string. Joshua greets them and is surprised at receiving two pies. He shows Ida and Huldah one of the bolts of green damask material he had bought at an auction in Louisville, its ornate floral design emerging when the sunlight falls on it. The roll of golden cord that he had also bought at the auction will trim the drapes made from the green damask. Ida and Huldah agree to make the drapes for one window for five dollars.

Captain Billy helps Joshua bring a ladder from the barn into the dining room and then returns to the hammock hanging between the two oaks in the back of the house to resume his nap in the shade. Joshua will be in the barn and Misses Ida and Huldah are to let him know if they need anything. A half hour later Ida wakes Captain Billy and tells him to inform Mr. Applegate that they have finished measuring. They will be back with the finished drapes next Monday. Joshua finishes both pies by Friday, confused as to why they brought them. He becomes more confused the next Monday when they bring him fried chicken and ham with raisin sauce.

Joshua kept the ladder in the dinning room (or bedroom which it is) and tells Misses Ida and Huldah that he will be in the barn. He puts the fried chicken and ham on the kitchen cabinet, and Ida takes a large checkered napkin and covers the chicken—"to keep it warm." Annoyed, Huldah takes the large bowl sitting on the cabinet, turns it up and places it over the ham "keeps the raisin sauce fresh." Captain Billy settles into the hammock again.

With Captain Billy asleep and Joshua in the barn, Ida and Huldah stop hanging the drapes in order to satisfy their curiosity: the cabin door is closed and the single window covered. While Ida watches out the kitchen door, Huldah turns the knob on the cabin door. It's locked.

Captain Billy is again awakened and tells Joshua the drapes are up. Joshua pulls both drapes with a quick, energetic pull, closes them, and then opens them again. Pleased, he takes a five dollar bill from his pocket and hands it to Ida, who is closer to him. Ida smiles and Huldah frowns. Next week he'll find thc other bolt of green damask material for them to make drapes for the other window. They tell him how pleased they'll be to come back.

Ida and Huldah have lost the measurements to the first window, and tell Joshua the other window "appears not to measure the same as the first." Joshua thanks them for the plates of pecan fudge and divinity candy they hand him. He takes the two plates to the kitchen and dumps the pecan fudge and divinity candy into a bowl, takes a bite of each before putting the bowl in the kitchen cabinet, and then, going to the barn, puts the two plates on the chair next to the hammock where Captain Billy reclines, while scratching the head of General Sheridan, the aging collie that has replaced Buddy and Billy. Ida and Huldah move the ladder to the second window and begin measuring this third week of "hanging new drapes."

"You can put these plates in the wagon," says Joshua. Captain Billy picks up the two plates and gets up from the hammock. "Miss Ida and Miss Huldah are good cooks," says Joshua to Captain Billy as he begins to saunter over to the wagon. "I don't know why they keep bringing me food," he says.

Captain Billy stops and turns around. "They're sparkin' you, Mister Joshua," says Captain Billy through a grin that shows two missing teeth.

Sparking? A cold chill runs up Joshua's spine. It never occurred to him. No! Had his acceptance of the food and his "Thanks!" encouraged them? He shuttered. He walked to the barn, a man's haven from unwelcomed women.

The measurements are quickly made, and Ida looks out the kitchen door. Captain Billy is sitting on the chair near the hammock, talking to General Sheridan while rubbing him with his foot. In the distance she hears hammering from the barn. She shakes her head yes, and the two sisters scurry up the stairs leading to the second floor.

Ida and Huldah had heard about the young man that lived off McCubbins Lane that bought a lot of furniture at auctions around Munfordville. He must keep it upstairs, and they were determined to see it all.

The stairs and two rooms on the second floor are not completed except for the door to each room. The smaller room on the left at the top of the steps, is stacked with furniture and other items Joshua has purchased at the auctions, while the larger room on the right contains all the animals he has killed, stuffed, and mounted onto frames.

The cloudy day permits little light to illuminate the stairs, and the dirty windows at the ends of each room upstairs further blur the fixtures in both rooms. Assuming both rooms contain furniture and fixtures, Ida and Huldah squint there· eyes as they reach for the doorknob to the room on the right.

They slowly push the creaking door open. Odd shaped furniture is revealed through the dim light. They open the door wider and step into the room. The odd shaped furniture has eyes! Frozen motionless, Ida and Huldah stare wide-eyed at a grinning coyote, a menacing fox, a spread-winged eagle, and a horned animal staring directly at them. Speechless, they rush out through the door at the same time, breathing heavily as they bound down the stairs and out the kitchen door.

They pull Captain Billy from his chair and order him to untether the horse and leave "as fast as you can, Captain Billy!" In the barn, Joshua walks outside to see what all the ruckus is about. Still half asleep, Captain Billy snaps the reins while Ida and Huldah, unlady-1ike, hop into the wagon yelling "Faster! Faster!" ignoring a bewildered Joshua, standing arms akimbo, in front of the barn.

After two weeks Joshua concludes that whatever caused such an abrupt departure must be permanent, and, with his newly acquired wisdom about conniving women, is all the more thankful for it. After all, he got what he wanted: drapes for his window.

The next evening Joshua picks up the book Martin Talmadge had given him three years ago—*Marcus Aurelius Meditations.* He reads into the night, but one sentence, one line in book seven keeps occurring in his mind: "If we lose the ability to perceive our faults, what is the good of living on?" He decides it has been too long since he talked with Talmadge. Sunday he'll go to Twelve Oaks.

Alone, after the death of his wife, Talmadge welcomes Joshua as young friend as well as neighbor, and looks forward to their philosophical discussions. Joshua describes his confusion regarding morality, the good life and attainment of personal virtue, which he considers the province of religion not philosophy.

Talmadge explains that during the time of Marcus Aurelius, Roman religion had no concern with moral problems. Its business was to perform the rites that ensured the Empire's protection by the gods as well as to avert their displeasure. Philosophy was the province of morality and virtue, and Marcus Aurelius' frequent allusions to "philosophy" implied what is now associated with the word religion.

Talmadge and Pastor Trumble, thought Joshua, were like two horses abreast. The *Meditations* meant everything that a religion can mean, a rule for living, a manual of personal devotion. Joshua reflects on his recent conversation with Trumble, that the Greek and Roman gods were metaphors for basic principles or natural laws, and the chief god—Jupiter or Zeus was God. Can religion and philosophy replace loving a woman? wonders Joshua.

Proud to have his name on the general store on Main Street, Joshua also enjoys clerking in it on Saturdays and receiving a small salary. By now he has disposed of most of the greenbacks in the chest either through his three bank savings accounts and minor investments or through his great number of gifts. He intends soon to close the savings account in Elizabethtown and transfer the balance to the Munfordville Bank. Financially, Joshua is "comfortable" Holy Ground is his "paradise on earth" and his minor veterinary work, church activity, and now weekly clerking keep him involved in his community.

He understands the occasional "uncomfortable feeling" lies at the heart of his "paradise on earth" but the other occasional feeling is not the loneliness he thinks it is, but the longing to be loved—and to love. It is then, with a subtle pleasure, that Joshua's subconscious notes that the new clerk Jacob introduces to him one Saturday morning is a thirty-year old woman with auburn hair pulled back in a knot, a gold band around her head, dark brown eyes that glisten, and a figure that Venus would envy.

"I want you to meet Dorothea Shelton Hamilton," says Jacob, as Joshua enters the side door of Hardbottom & Applegate General Store. Dorothea smiles and extends her hand. "She is my cousin, and has come to take care of her mother, my aunt, who is very ill. She has clerked in a woman's shop in Louisville but has no experience in working in a general store. You can help there."

Jacob, married to Judith for three years, recognizes the signs: Joshua and Dorothea shake hands, say the proper words, but their eyes speak volumes. "I'm going home now," says Jacob, knowing the words are heard but not registered.

As Joshua and Dorothea speak together at one level but sense the presence of each other at another level, Jacob closes the side door, comfortable with the thought: "They would make a fine couple."

On the Sunday following their third Saturday of clerking together, Dorothea attends church with Joshua, who proudly introduces her to the ladies of the church and to Pastor Trumble after services. The sudden appearance of envy among the ladies of such a beautiful woman soon changes.

"Mr. Applegate has told me about the good work you generous ladies do through your Church Circle," says Dorothea. "Anyone should be pleased to be part of such important community work," she says. When invited to attend the next Circle meeting, she radiates a joyous smile. "I'd be delighted."

After Pastor Trumble welcomes Dorothea to church and invites her to return, she comments on his sermon. "Pastor, I liked your example that darkness may reign in a cave for thousands of years but vanishes immediately by bringing in light," Pleased, Pastor Trumble adds: "No matter what a Person's defects, they vanish when brought into the light of goodness."

Dorothea's words "darkness in a cave" hold Joshua's attention, and Trumble's words, that defects vanish in the light of goodness, becomes imbedded in his heart and mind. Joshua takes Dorothea's arm walking down the church steps. How fortunate I am, he thinks, to have met this wonderful, good woman, and then says, "You've made a number of friends this morning, Miss Hamilton."

"Do you think so Mr. Applegate?" she says, as Joshua helps her into the buggy.

"I know so, Miss Hamilton."

The next day, Joshua removes all the mounted animals from the room on the second floor. He had found either Ida or Huldah's apron in the room and concluded the sight of the stuffed animals caused their sudden flight. While confident that Dorothea had more grit than Ida or Huldah, he would not take any chances—he burns all of them.

That week after church, Jacob and Judith bring Dorothea to Holy Ground. Judith has prepared vegetables and Dorothea, fried, country chicken. This, being Dorothea's first visit to Holy Ground, Joshua shows her through his house, explaining that some time, when he gets drapes made from the bolt of damask he has for the second window in the dining room, he'll move his bed and chest out and bring the Early American, walnut dining room table with eight chairs down from the second floor.

"I'll make your drapes, Mr. Applegate," says Dorothea. Judith raises her eyebrows. "And Judith will help me. Wouldn't you, Judith?" Judith smiles and nods her head, for Jacob has shared his thought with her about Joshua and Dorothea "making a fine couple."

The bolt of green damask rests next to Dorothea in Jacob and Judith's buggy on their return to Munfordville. There's so much that can be done with that house, thinks Dorothea.

During the next week, Joshua papers the parlor with a pale green wallpaper, which Dorothea picked, and begins plastering the walls of the smaller upstairs room. Joshua and Dorothea take the train to Louisville to buy material for parlor drapes.

They go to A.D. Hunt and Sons Bank, which has become J.J.B.Hilliard and Sons, where Joshua purchases more Louisville and Nashville Railroad stock. They have lunch at the new Galt House that was built four years after the original Galt House burned in early 1865 and was inspired by Rome's Palazzo Farnese. They attend the matinee at Macauley's Theater, before returning home.

During the ensuing weeks, Dorothea makes and hangs flower-patterned chintz drapes in each of the four parlor windows and has Joshua and Jacob bring down furniture from the second floor and placed "in the perfect spot." She makes pillows from the left over material.

Joshua orders wallpaper for the small upstairs room that Dorothea picks out—birds flying on a pale blue background. To Joshua's surprise, Dorothea has him and Jacob move the four-poster bed, the wardrobe, and the rug in the dining room up to the smaller upstairs room. The oriental rug in the cabin is rolled out on to the dining room floor.

"Now, Mr. Applegate," says a pleased Dorothea, "you have a dining room and an upstairs bedroom."

"Yes, Miss Hamilton, it's a nice arrangement," says a reconciled Joshua. Joshua marvels at how quickly and subtly a woman impresses her will upon a budding romance. It has been less than a month since Joshua and Dorothea were gently swaying in the swing on her mother's porch, the sun casting its last rays over the lawn, the country silence broken only by chirping crickets, and her small hand resting gently on Joshua's arm. Joshua turned his head down to Dorothea. With closed eyes she turned her head to him and their lips touched.

Everything important is different now, but nothing about the difference is mentioned. It's understood. Darkness brings it's own special mood and allows, encourages, two people in love to express that love. Joshua helps Dorothea to get out of the swing, takes her in his arms and kisses her on the forehead. "I'll see you tomorrow Dorothea," he says.

"Yes," says Dorothea. "Tomorrow, Mr. Applegate," Some things change in an instant; some things take time.

A month later, Dorothea's mother dies. "Come live with us," said Jacob and Judith, knowing that Dorothea's mother rented the house. "We have more room than we need. You'll have privacy with your own bedroom, bath, and sitting room on the second floor. There's even an outside stairway to your rooms." A week after her mother is buried, Dorothea moves in with her cousin Jacob and his wife.

For the next several weeks Joshua sees Dorothea almost every evening, and half of that time having supper with her and the Hardbottoms. The four play rook, sing songs, and discuss a little business, but Jacob and Judith always manage to leave "for bed" early enough for Joshua and Dorothea to have time together in the parlor.

Dorothea had never expected or wanted to find love after her fiancée died of wounds received in Virginia at the Battle of Five Forks, less than a month before hostilities ceased. He had returned home "to recuperate" but he knew differently and said nothing. "When the war is over," he would say when Dorothea asked when they would marry. Dorothea was doubly elated, therefore, when Lee surrendered at Appomattox, for the end was near. Indeed it was near; he died a week before the final surrender of the remaining Confederate forces east of the Mississippi.

It is Sunday evening, a day and time Joshua considers appropriate for his "intentions." Jacob and Judith both notice a certain anxiousness in Joshua and exchange knowing glances. Earlier than usual, they excuse themselves. "We've been busy this week and are going to retire early," says Judith, kissing Dorothea on the cheek, something she has never done before.

"They're our good friends." says Joshua.

"Yes. They certainly are," replies Dorothea.

"Dorothea ..." says Joshua.

Dorothea immediately notices this is the second time she is called by her first name. "Yes? Mr. Applegate."

Joshua gets up. "Is it too warm in here for you? Shall I open the window?"

Why is it still the custom for the man to propose wonders Dorothea. Over the centuries women have had to learn how to assure men that they think they are doing what they wish to do, and that skill should now be instinctive. "Is there something you wish to say, Mr. Applegate?"

Joshua stops. He appreciates a little help. He's never done this before, and doesn't expect to again. He steps in front of Dorothea, who is composed, self-assured, with her hands folded on her lap. He kneels down on one leg and looks into her gentle eyes, her curved lips fortifying him.

"I own Holy Ground outright, have a savings account of nearly three thousand dollars, own some shares of The Louisville and Nashville Railroad, have a yearly income from the farm, a little veterinary work, and Saturday clerking of about seven hundred dollars." He stops and continues to look at Dorothea.

Her ears, tuned only to hear his proposal, Dorothea's comment is misunderstood. "Go on, Mr. Applegate."

"Well, that's all I got, Dorothea. Maybe a few debts that's owed me."

Dorothea leans forward and takes Joshua's hand. "And why are you telling me this, Mr. Applegate?" she asks in a voice as sweet as honey poured on sugar.

"Why, I want you to be my wife. Will you marry me, Dorothea?"

She takes Joshua's other hand and looks lovingly into his eyes for a moment. "Yes," she says, in that sweet, soft angelic voice.

They both stand up, embrace, and kiss.

Suddenly Joshua steps back. "Should I ask permission from your cousin?"

"That's not necessary," says Dorothea.

"Should we tell them tonight?"

"I'll tell them in the morning, Mr. Applegate."

"Dorothea. Don't you think you should begin calling me Joshua?"

"Yes, Joshua, Oh, yes a thousand times, my darling!"

Dorothea stands on tiptoes and kisses him. Five minutes later, Joshua sings on his way to his buggy, and Dorothea hums going up the steps to her room. To be loved is good. To love is better. To love and be loved is best.

He must conceal the hole. He orders sufficient linoleum to cover the cabin floor and removes the last bundle of greenbacks from the chest, a bundle of five-dollar greenbacks. He decides to keep this bundle of greenbacks. Although he has convinced himself that the money is rightfully his, retaining the greenbacks becomes his testament that he "did not spend all the money."

Into the larger of two cigar boxes Talmadge has given him, Joshua tosses everything that connects him to the cave and the secret it conceals, including the book listing persons to whom he gave money, the last entry being $400 to Tim and Mary Shackelford. He decides to include his knife—he had intended to kill O'Conner with it.

He places two narrow boards across the hole and lays the cigar box on top. Four long nails fasten the hinged door covering the hole securely to the floor. Removing all the furniture in the cabin, Joshua covers the entire floor, including the portion over the hole, with linoleum. He places the rug and table back over the hole, and takes the stove to his second floor bedroom. That afternoon, Joshua throws small rocks on top of the large boulders that cover the cave entrance and then fills in the small crevices with dirt and twigs.

The wedding is to be in November, Dorothea tells Pastor Trumble, when she and Joshua discuss their plans with him. When Trumble asks when Joshua was baptized, Joshua says, "Never been!" Trumble informs Joshua he must be baptized before he and Dorothea can marry. The next church full submersion baptism will be in late October at the creek near the church. Joshua recites a silent pray that it be a warm day.

His prayer is granted. Fall's full colors have reached their peak, and the early morning sun shines fully on the creek. More interested in following the procedure rather than experiencing its spiritual significance, Joshua tries to hold his breath the moment Trumble pushes him under the water. A powerful man, Trumble makes sure Joshua is completely submerged each time. Struggling with each submergence, Joshua relaxes his breath too soon and swallows some creek water before spitting out the rest as Trumble ends with "and the Holy Ghost. Amen."

Trumble takes Joshua by the shoulders and asks if he is all right. Before Joshua can answer he senses a sudden warmth embrace him and feels himself being lifted up. He looks up and the dome of heaven begins to turn. Slowly Joshua is aware of floating up, able to see miles in all directions. Just as suddenly he hears himself speak. "Yes. I'm all right, Pastor," Trumble takes his arm and helps him to the shore.

Joshua wonders whether the three others, who were baptized before him, had the same experience. He doesn't think so. He won't say anything about it to Trumble or Dorothea: it would sound boastful, appearing to be self-serving. He might tell Talmadge, though.

He does. "You've been blessed, Joshua," says Talmadge. "You've been privileged to experience the empyrean for a moment." Joshua's uncertain expression prompts Talmadge to explain. "Jesus taught us to experience the oneness with God that he did. You have, even if but for a moment. Don't let that experience leave you, Joshua." Joshua promises himself to recall the experience every night before going to bed.

In his conscience and mind Joshua no longer feels guilty of murder or theft. The concealed hole gives him a symbol for a rational redemption, a redemption of the mind; but the hidden bodies and chest do not allow a redemption of the heart. Joshua alters his spiritual journey but not the results of his actions.

Sunday, 22 November 1874 begins with a bitter frost that remains through the morning and into early afternoon, when the sun breaks though the clouds and creates meadows of sparkling diamonds. In a simple white dress, Dorothea carries her mother's bible with a pressed daisy from the bouquet Joshua had brought her on the day he proposed. In a new, black suit, bought at Dorothea's insistence, Joshua keeps pulling his collar with his finger to relieve the tightness around his neck, while watching Dorothea come down the isle. When asked by Pastor Trumble for the ring, Joshua reaches in several of his pockets before Jacob, his best man, touches him on the shoulder and hands the ring to him.

Immediately after the wedding, Joshua and Dorothea are driven to the train depot and board the Louisville and Nashville train to

Louisville. Now relaxed, Joshua loosens his tie and opens his collar, sighing. Dorothea touches Joshua gently on his hand with her two fingers. "You're handsome in that tie, my dear. After tomorrow, you may take it off." Except for dressing up fancy, marriage, determines Joshua, is going to be just fine.

This time, at Dorothea's insistence, they stay at the Louisville Hotel, cheaper than the Galt House, but just as nice. Without letting Dorothea know, Joshua has reserved the bridal suit. The bellhop opens the drapes and points to the vase of red flowers on the table. "Compliments of the hotel," He says.

"We'd like breakfast in our room tomorrow morning, Bellhop: Scrambled eggs, sausage, toast, jam, and coffee, Eight A.M." says Joshua, handing him a quarter.

"Nine A.M." says Dorothea. She smells the flowers. "Fresh!" she exclaims. As the bellhop closes their door, she pulls the drapes closed.

The next morning, a waiter, dressed in white raps on the door twice and then a second time. With a robe thrown around his shoulders, Joshua opens the door, allowing the waiter to push the breakfast cart towards the two windows. "Shall I open the drapes?" he asks. Yes. He does and then lifts the silver domes covering two plates.

"Scrambled eggs and sausage," he says. "Shall I pour?" he says, holding the silver coffee pot. No. Dorothea will. Joshua tips him a quarter and he leaves, slowly, gently, closing the door and smiling.

Surprisingly, they are not hungry, but cozy up to each other near the cart to nibble, commune only with their eyes, and speak in their own private language. Joshua yawns and, smiling knowingly with Dorothea, follows her to bed. Three hours later, they stroll down Main Street towards busy Fourth Street.

First, Joshua insists that they have their picture taken. To avoid wrinkling her dress, Dorothea stands and Joshua sits, for what will be their "wedding picture." They go to Shade's Drug Store and buy a penny's worth of each of the dozen kinds of chocolates, each on its own glass tray, and spend half an hour looking at all the books in Rice's Bookstore. They have lunch at the old Bell Tavern on Jefferson Street before buying tickets to Stickney's circus, where Ricards, the clown, tells jokes that their grandfathers heard as youngsters.

Before going to the train station, they look at the silver bracelets, gold earrings, diamond rings, and a glistening pearl necklace in Lemon & Sons window, one of the few fine jewelry shops on Fourth Street. Dorothea touches her wedding ring through her leather gloves. "Which do you like most, Dorothea?" asks Joshua.

"The pearl necklace." She says without hesitation.

"I'll buy it for you!" says Joshua, starting to enter Lemon and Sons.

"No, Joshua," says Dorothea, grabbing his coat and pulling him back. She had observed the tiny price tag attached to the pearls. In fine ink script was written $20.00. That was more money than she earned working at the general store for four Saturdays. "Maybe some day," she says.

It is early in the evening when the train pulls into the Munfordville station and Joshua and Dorothea climb into their buggy at Jacob and Judith's home to return to Holy Ground, as man and wife.

The once placid aura of Holy Ground soon becomes a workshop of activity, when Dorothea, an Aries born on the 24th of March in 1842, begins refurbishing the larger room upstairs and has Joshua construct a fenced-in area for the several sheep she intends to breed into a flock.

Joshua is true to his pledge, and each evening before going to bed reflects on the solitude and comfort of his baptismal experience; but in tired, dispassionate moments, what is concealed in the cave, appears in the shadows of his mind.

"What is bothering you?" asks Dorothea.

"I can't tell you. I'm just one of many worthless sinners," he laments in a moment of despair.

"Never call yourself a sinner, Joshua, because that is the greatest sin against the image of God within you. It is better that you always affirm that you are a child of God, because that is what you are," says Dorothea.

Dorothea has no faults, and in that lays a disturbing fault: In the goodness of her heart, she gladly gives away what she should not. What had first pleased Joshua as being saintly, is approaching being foolish. The tables, chairs, cabinets, cutlery, and tableware are all gone from storage in the larger room on the second floor—gifts to "those more in need than are we, Mr. Applegate." The occasional pig, goat, and chicken, will not be missed. It is two of the four kitchen chairs that become the straw—not of the camel, but of a once understanding and generous Joshua.

Friday evening Dorothea rings the bell for Joshua to come in for supper. After washing, Joshua sits down across from Dorothea before noticing that two kitchen chairs are missing. After praying, he puts two heaping spoonfuls of mashed potatoes on his plate. "Where are the other two chairs?" he asks, adding a ladle of brown gravy.

"I gave them to the Pickerings. They had a fire that destroyed their kitchen and everything in it," said Dorothea, adding a helping of green beans to her plate. The straw did not fall lightly. Joshua lays his knife and fork on his plate and tries to keep the blood from rushing to his face. "This is too much, Dorothea! You must stop giving everything we have away to people we hardly know!"

"We knew the Pickerings before we were married!" says Dorothea. "Besides, we don't need the chairs."

"And when we have guests?" asks Joshua.

"We eat in the dining room, of course!" she says.

Unthinkingly, Joshua takes an untested stance. "That makes no difference. From now on you are to stop giving our things to others." He mechanically beings to eat again, and puts sugar, rather than salt, on his mashed potatoes. Dorothea says nothing more, and keeps pouring brown gravy until the vegetables and beef on her plate look like small islands in a sea of brown gravy. The rest of the meal is eaten in total silence.

This is the Saturday Joshua goes to the store by himself, and he lets Dorothea sleep, as he always does on her Saturday not to work. Not hungry, he warms the coffee that Dorothea uncharacteristically left in the coffee pot, and spreads plum jam over a piece of toast left on a plate in the corner of the kitchen cabinet. She'll come to reason and things will be back to normal when he returns that evening. He hopes.

Ezekiel Stull is waiting for Joshua at the back entrance of the store, holding a umbrella to ward off the tiny flakes of snow, falling to the ground but not sticking to it. Ezekiel had been a clerk for Jacobs' father since Mr. Hardbottom owned his general store, and he now helps out occasionally as well as on two alternate Saturdays in the month.

Joshua is surprised two hours later when Jacob enters. "Go to my house, Joshua!" yells Jacob. "My buggy is outside. Hurry! Dorothea is there with her packed grips."

He hadn't expected this! Unprepared, Joshua responds to Jacob's words, puts on his coat, scarf, and hat and rushes out to the buggy, saying nothing and not hearing—or not caring at the moment—what Jacob says: "Mr. Stull and I will watch the store."

Dorothea is removing the last bit of luggage when Joshua arrives, jumping from the buggy and letting the horse trot to the barn by itself. "Dorothea, Dorothea! What are you doing? For God's sake, stop and talk with me."

She stops, turns defiantly towards Joshua and folds her hands without saying a word.

"Dorothea, please, listen to me," says Joshua. "You may give anything we have away, as long as it isn't something that we must replace. Please, Dorothea, put everything back into your buggy and return to our home." He removes his hat. "I love you, Dorothea. I need you." He rubs his sleeve against his right eye.

Dorothea's stern expression does not change, but after a few excruciating moments for Joshua, she walks to the buggy and places the grip in it, and then returns to the house for the other grips. Joshua continues to stand where he is with his hat still in his hand, as he watches Dorothea, who has not said a word, get in the buggy and leave, waving to Judith, but not to Joshua. As the buggy turns out of sight, Judith tells Joshua to come in out of the cold.

Like a young boy who has been chastised by his mother for something he doesn't consider wrong, Joshua looks pleadingly at Judith. "When you go back home this evening don't bring it up," she says. Joshua nods his head and kisses her on the cheek. The lump in his throat won't allow him to say thanks. Returning to the store, Joshua thanks Jacob, and tells him he can go home now. "Judith is waiting for you," he says. Too experienced in problems of married couples, Jacob does not ask what happened. He shakes his head, the ancient sign of masculine camaraderie, and leaves.

Nothing is said about the incident, but each day for weeks both Dorothea and Joshua have occasions to remember. Gradually the remembrance looses its bitterness and acknowledges its humor, causing each to want to find some way to compensation for what they now consider inappropriate behavior. The occasion comes on a

Saturday when they both clerk at the store, and Liza does the wash, house work, and feeds the sheep at Holy Ground by herself.

Both Joshua and Dorothea notice the four chairs in the window of Clatten's New & Used Furniture Store, a block from their store, but they say nothing to each other. Later in the morning Joshua goes to the bank and on the way back stops at Clatten's. He speaks with Calvin, one of the two Clatten brothers who own and operate the store.

The chairs are exact replicas of their kitchen chairs. Joshua pays five dollars for two chairs and is promised by Calvin that they will be delivered to Holy Ground late that afternoon. He looks forward to seeing the expression on Dorothea's face when they return home that evening.

Dorothea leaves late in the morning to buy two cups of coffee for a noon snack in the back of the store but first stops by Clatten's. She gives Chester, Calvin's brother, five dollars for the two chairs she is pleased to see are exact duplicates of her chairs. Chester promises the chairs will be delivered to Holy Ground before evening. "Tell Liza I would like the chairs by the kitchen table when Mr. Applegate and I return home," she says.

The snow is sticking and there is little business. They close the store exactly at five and bundle up in their buggy. "I've got a surprise for you, Dorothea," says Joshua.

"And I've got one for you," says Dorothea.

They stop the buggy as close to the back porch as they can, in order to carry in the several packages they have brought with them. They each see the extra two chairs and wait to see the other's surprised expression. A moment later, holding the packages, they see six chairs! With a truly surprised look, they each stare at each other, and then, understanding the surprise, burst into laughter.

Liza shakes her head, finding white people's sudden bursts of laughter unusual. She also wonders why they need four more kitchen chairs – there's only two of them.

During the next three years, Joshua shares his conversations with Talmadge and Trumble with Dorothea. Under the influence of these ideas and emotions (recalled from these conversations) Joshua is calm and peaceful, sitting on the porch, watching the stars and moon play games with the clouds. In this state of quiet, almost passive, enjoyment, he suddenly, without any kind of warning, becomes engulfed in light, which he soon realizes comes from within. A sense of exultation, of immense joy, and a flash of spiritual awareness engulfs his heart, as tears well up inside and the sound of rolling thunder echoes in his mind.

Is this what saint's experience? Is this the Kingdom of Heaven that John preached was at hand and that Jesus preached was here? He becomes part of the myriad whirling stars and the source of their creation. He is his soul! What Joy! What Bliss! He is overcome.

A slight wind caresses his face and the sounds of night once again bring him back into this world.

In a timeless, spaceless state, we can never know what something actually is, only what our realization of it tells us it is. In its many aspects, simple persons call their realizations of natural and spiritual forces, gods, and in its unity, God. Of a thousand, one seeks; and of a thousand that seek, one finds. This is the spirituality that, like a silver thread woven within a fabric, immerges into a human soul. In their return, all savior's spirituality becomes other's religion.

The metaphors for the teachings of all saviors are religiously true but not necessarily spiritually true, as the description of an orange is not the same as tasting it. Joshua Applegate has had a spiritual experience. He has tasted the orange that countless saints have described, and now he, a simple man, in his return, may speak of a spiritual experience that for others is religious.

Joshua's spiritual awakening is not sudden, although, if Dorothea hadn't encouraged him to be patient, others would have said of his exuberant change, that he had "gotten religion." His experience is like poking a fork into the yellow center of a poached egg and watching it ooze from its thin membrane and make yellow all that was white.

Where before Joshua walked, now he glides. Where before he smiled, now he glows. Where before he sympathized, now he empathizes. A man who has lived in a black and white world, Joshua now lives in one of many colors.

Dorothea understands. She has always been in the many colored world, the world of love, not sadness. She has also always been in love, not necessarily with· someone, just in love—a condition of being, not of place.

His new awareness, his new abilities, like a gentle stream damned up and suddenly released, may prove dangerous; but Joshua listens to

Dorothea and allows the aura of his exuberance, not his behavior, to attract others.

Pastor Jeremiah T. Trumble dies. The church elders ask Joshua to assume the position of pastor of the church. For the last several years, Joshua has given the Sunday message and conducted the service when Pastor Trumble was away or unable to preach. Dorothea encourages Joshua to accept the position and he does. The annual salary of $275 a year is appreciated but is not his primary, or even secondary, reason for accepting. It is certainly a "calling," but it is also a pleasure.

A small office, attached to the meeting hall behind the sanctuary, has an outside entrance and serves as the pastor's office. He decides to be in his office each weekday morning, to prepare his sermon, meet with members of the congregation, and be of spiritual service to those in need. He writes in the notebook he began in 1875: "A lifetime of errors may be corrected today."

Joshua fits comfortably in his adopted routine with the morning devoted to his pastoral duties, the afternoon to the farm and general business, and the evening to those activities that engender empyreal encounters: music, singing, reading, painting, stargazing.

Most evenings Dorothea plays the piano, which is across from Joshua's desk in the parlor, and they both sing to their heart's delight. Joshua obtained his desk and the piano at the same auction. He likes to read special passages to Dorothea from the books he has collected into a small library, and they like to criticize each other's sketches and paintings. The summer night skies give them the opportunity, not only to find constellations and special stars, but also to transport themselves into the timelessness of moving celestial bodies and the spacelessness of human thought that is able to comprehend its own existence. Joshua and Dorothea live in both the physical and the spiritual worlds.

The flock of sheep has become a small business for Dorothea, and she gives the month's income from it—twenty dollars—to Joshua to put in her "sheep account" at the bank. On such beautiful days as this, Joshua walks the mile to church but since he must go to the bank, he takes the buggy.

The weather is so pleasant that Joshua leaves the door to his office open, letting a refreshing breeze enter and enabling him to see a wagon stop in front of the church and a woman to get off. Putting down a grip as the wagon leaves, she looks at the closed church doors and then towards Joshua's office with its open door. She picks up the grip and walks towards the office.

By the time she reaches the office, Joshua has gotten up from his desk and walked towards the door. A woman who appears to be in her forties, dressed in rather gaudy colors, her stringy, faded blond hair hangs out from a hat that is more appropriately worn in the evening, she stops ten paces from the door. Her left eye droops and her right eye is wide open, causing the pupil to appear to be a miniature bull' s eye of a target.

"You haven't changed, Joshua. A little more handsome." she says, dropping the grip.

"You have the advantage over me. Do I know you?" he asks.

"I'm Fanny," she says.

Far from expecting ever to see her again, and shocked at her appearance, he is speechless. For him to say "You've changed" or "I'm glad to see you" would be rude and dishonest. An uncomfortable silence is broken. Fanny sighs. and changes her weight from one to the other foot. "Well, ain't cha goin ta invite me in?"

"Yes. please do." says Joshua, as he reaches for her grip. "Let me help you." The grip is heavy and he places it inside, next to the door, which he gives a shove to open it all the way. He motions for her to sit in the chair in front of his desk, an arrangement that gives him a feeling of safety from an uncomfortable situation for which he is unprepared. He avoids smiling, and waits for her to speak. "It's been a long time. Joshua," she says as an opening for him to speak. He doesn't, but nods yes, and continues to wait. She leans back, realizing that what she wants will be obtained only by frankness.

"Jamie, you remember Jamie? Lieutenant James Sterling who you outbid? He never forgot that, Joshua. He left me in Kansas City when he went to Fort Sill, to—as they liked to say—'keep watch over the Comanche tribes'. That was the last time I saw him. A year later I heard he had been killed.

"I was on the stage in Kansas city, third in the chorus line. Sang several years at various saloons until my voice gave out, and even played the part of Ophelia in Hamlet. Can you imagine me as Ophelia?" She's told Joshua enough. He can see she is in need.

"Some months ago I received a letter from a lawyer telling me my uncle in Nashville left me some money, and I should come there to claim it. I did last week and signed some papers, but the lawyer said it would be a few weeks before I would receive the money.

"I spent all I had to get to Nashville. A girl I worked with in Kansas city lives and works in Chicago and has a job for me there, but I don't have any money to get there."

The only feeling Joshua has for Fanny is sorrow. This once beautiful creature has become an overly used and abused, disfigured and graceless person. His heart goes out to her, but his mind suggests prudence. The heart is silent but the mind speaks. "How much do you need?"

She leans forward, an old habit that reveals the bosom, but even that is no longer alluring. "Fifteen dollars," she says.

Joshua pulls the two ten dollar bills Dorothea gave him from his right pocket and the several bills and change he has in his left pocket: Two one dollar bills, a quarter, and two nickels. He hands it to her. "Here's twenty-two dollars and some change."

Fanny grabs the bills, looks at Joshua, and folds them before putting them with the change into her small purse."I'll pay you back as soon as I get to Chicago." Joshua shakes his head, meaning repayment isn't necessary. "Thank you, Joshua," she says, her eyes filling up.

"I can take you to the train station, Fanny."

"Homer – he's the one who drove me in the wagon said he'd stop by after making a delivery, in time for me to catch the train. I'll wait for him in front of your church."

"I'll wait with you," says Joshua.

He carries her grip and walks to the front of the church just as Homer and the wagon appear at the bottom of the hill. Before she steps up to the wagon, she kisses Joshua on the cheek. "I made a terrible mistake seventeen years ago. God bless you Joshua."

Joshua watches as the wagon goes up the hill and disappears on the other side. When it reached the top of the hill, Fanny waved. What will he say to Dorothea?

That noon, after he returned home from his office and Dorothea asked him for her deposit slip, he said he had not been able to deposit the money. "I'll explain while we eat," he said, believing dinner to be more conducive to understanding if not tolerance.

Someone— a young woman at the time—he knew fifteen years ago from church, before he knew Dorothea–had visited him at his office. She found herself short of funds and asked to borrow money for a ticket to Chicago. He gave her the twenty dollars and the few dollars he had with him.

"That was most generous of you, Joshua. That must be a terrible feeling to be away from your home with no money to be able to return. What was her name?"

A slight hesitation. "Mrs. Sterling." Joshua is proud of his understanding wife, and is satisfied that his comments are truthful.

"The next time you make a deposit in our account you can take twenty dollars of it and put it in my sheep account," says Dorothea removing the empty plates from the table. She's shrewd also, says Joshua to himself.

Eighteen months later. Joshua receives a letter from the Sisters of Charity Mission in Chicago. It contains a check for $23.00 and a letter from the Mother Superior stating that Mrs. James Sterling had passed away and had requested the Mother Superior to send Mr. Joshua Applegate, Hardbottom and Applegate General Store, Munfordville, Ky. $23.00 from whatever of her funds remained. Fanny had rounded the $22.00 and some odd cents to $23.00.

On his birthday, Joshua receives in the mail a copy of Tolstoy's *War and Peace* and a note from Talmadge. Joshua becomes absorbed in the book and identifies himself with Pierre. He writes in his notebook the words Tolstoy ascribes to Pierre: "Man is created for happiness ... happiness is within him."

During the next two years Joshua visits Talmadge almost every month. A week before he planned to visit Talmadge, Joshua received a letter from Talmadge's lawyer stating that Mr. Talmadge had passed away unexpectedly and had provided in his will that the large oriental rug in his parlor be given to Mr. Joshua Applegate. The rug adds a European elegance to the parlor and pleases both Joshua and Dorothea but its the pattern of the garden and its four entrances that continue to captivate Joshua.

Trumble, thought Joshua, would see the four entrances as the four ways Jesus told the youth to love God: with all one's strength, heart, mind, and soul; while Talmadge would prefer Plato's terms of sensation, feeling, thinking, and intuition. Trumble had been his counselor of the heart, while Talmadge had been his counselor of the mind. He visualizes Trumble and Talmadge at two opposing entrances on the rug, but each leading into the garden of paradise.

Suddenly it occurs to him that his aunt had been the strength in his life. In his mind he places her at the far entrance. There's one more entrance: soul or intuition: Dorothea!

Of course! Dorothea is not only a perfect soul, she has changed him from thinking himself to be a body with a soul to a soul with a body. Dorothea is his fourth counselor. He is so pleased with this discovery, he decides to share it with Dorothea, but at that instant, she comes to the parlor entrance. "Supper's ready!" she says and returns to the kitchen. He gets up and suddenly understands: She knows.

In looking through the 1896 Sears Roebuck Catalogue, Joshua sees their advertisement of Faux Pearls. A price of $2.75 is centered in a bursting star underneath a photograph of a long string of pearls. Can that be correct? wonders Joshua. He remembers the price of the pearls he and Dorothea had looked at during their honeymoon was $20.00. He is not sure where Faux is, but Paris pearls, London pearls, or Faux, pearls are still pearls, and $2.75 is a low price.

Dorothea's recent illness convinces Joshua that a gift of pearls will make her feel better and he orders a strand, with delivery "guaranteed" in three weeks. During the next two weeks Dorothea no longer can stand, and Joshua must help her dress, do some of the cooking, and ask Liza to come to Holy Ground every day.

The pearls arrive on the day before the three weeks ends. Dorothea has worsened. She has lost weight, speaks little, and reclines in a chair on the porch, with a shawl around her neck. Joshua opens the package and holds the necklace up to the light. They don't seem any different than the ones he remembers seeing in Louisville twenty-two years ago. He'll give the pearls to Dorothea this afternoon and not wait until supper.

Holding the pearls behind his back, Joshua walks out onto the porch and stands before Dorothea, who opens her eyes and smiles, but does not move.

"Dorothea, you know I've never been much for fancy talking. And you've always known I love you. You're important to me. But I want to make sure, so: I love you, Dorothea, very much." Dorothea blinks her eyes as her smile broadens. She struggles to lift her right hand off the arm of the chair and Joshua reaches down to touch it, still holding the pearls behind his back.

"I've got a surprise for you Dorothea," He moves his hand in front of himself and grasps the other end of the strand with his other hand. "You said 'some day.' Well, this is that day." She slowly lifts her head up and points her finger at her neck.

"It will be my pleasure, Mrs. Applegate," says Joshua as he moves behind Dorothea and begins to fasten the pearls around her neck. The clasp is not meant for men's hands, and he keeps opening it when suddenly her breathing stops. He knows, but continues with the clasp and in a moment is successful. He walks in front of Dorothea, who stares blankly ahead. "You make them glisten, Dorothea," says Joshua. He falls to his knees and buries his face in her lap and cries.

Dorothea is buried in a plot Joshua had trimmed and cut thirty feet from the animal cemetery. He puts fresh flowers on her grave each morning, and visits her each evening. He depends more on Liza now, and asks the congregation to relieve him of his pastoral obligations.

They do and hire a young minister, Benjamin T. Turner. Turner's contract includes board and meals each month at the homes of different members of the congregation. Joshua offers to have Pastor Turner stay permanently with him at Holy Ground. This, being satisfactory with the congregation, young Ben Turner moves into the upstairs bedroom at Holy Ground. Joshua moves his old cot, stored in the upstairs room, to the cabin and pushes it to its old place against the wall.

Dorothea had converted the cabin into a small pantry where she stored canned goods, kitchen utensils, and, in the Spring, new seedlings, on shelves Joshua had made. Joshua's work table always sat over the hole and still does. He removes the shelves and buys a new stove.

During the next two years Joshua and young Ben converse about politics, the weather, farming, church maintenance problems, parishioner problems, and next Sunday's sermon.

"Ben," Joshua says one morning, "be sure I'm buried on Dorothea's left side. See if you can put my final date on my tombstone."

"Are *you* all right. Mr. Applegate?" asks Ben.

"Yes. Just want to be sure," says Joshua.

The next morning Joshua does not have their breakfast ready. He is still on his cot. “Mr. Applegate!” says Ben. He shakes Joshua gently, but his body is cold, and he slowly lifts the cover and pulls it over Joshua's face.

In his will, Joshua leaves Holy Ground and the rest of his estate to the church. Ben makes sure that Joshua is buried on the left side of Dorothea's grave and the headstone incised with the date of his death. He continues to live in the house until it is sold to Mr. and Mrs. Robert Henry MacDowell eighteen months later.

This world is a stage upon which we, as actors, play many parts. Joshua Applegate's redemption, like a new role, had granted him the forgetfulness of murder and theft and the blessedness of purity of soul. But in the hard world of reality, even when hidden deep within the earth, the spirits of two dead soldiers seek a proper grave, something that can be accomplished through another role and another time for the spirit that was Joshua Applegate.

PART THREE

TRUDY

CHAPTER SIX

SATURDAY, 11 MAY 1935, 6:00 AM

We bury all our sins,
Deep within our minds;
And wonder why our thoughts,
Are evil and not kind.

David's aunt and uncle, Robert Henry and Sarah Lou MacDowell, have reached the age where the structured day provides security and stability, and any deviation from their charted daily duties demands undesired decisions. Both Robert and Sarah are as punctual in their daily chores as is the grandfather clock that stands in their hallway. Their alarm clock is always set for 6 A.M., but Robert, who always wakes up five minutes before it rings, has been up since 5:30 A.M. this morning. A chance discovery by him yesterday requires a different routine today and will affect their day tomorrow and beyond.

After washing, shaving, and combing his graying hair, Robert attends to his morning farm chores earlier than usual so he'll be finished before David comes. By the time he returns to the house Sarah has placed his daily morning soft-boiled egg at his place and checks the biscuits in the oven that she made from scratch.

Their morning greetings do not require spoken words. Robert sits in his chair, the only one with armrests. He cuts off the top of the soft-boiled egg in front of him, sprinkles it with pepper, and spoons out the warm liquid.

Sarah squeezes four oranges with the new contraption Jane gave her: a white bowl with a half egg-shaped protrusion in the center on which she twists a half orange to extract most of its juice. "What will they think of next ?" commented Robert when they received the gift.

A platter of bacon, bowl of grits, tray of hot biscuits and jar of homemade blackberry preserves sit next to a plate of fresh, hand-churned butter on the table. Sarah begins to sit in her chair nearest the stove. "Bob," she says. The tone is that of a mother letting her son know he is not supposed to eat until everyone is at the table. Robert puts his spoon down, lowers his head and folds his hands in prayer. Sarah always vows to serve him his egg last, but never does.

The day before, Robert had begun renovating their pantry, the original structure built by Joshua Applegate, the previous owner of Holy Ground. In separating, lifting, and rolling that part of the old linoleum not under the refrigerator, Robert had discovered a cellar door that had been nailed shut. He had removed the four nails fastening the door to the floor, lifted the unhinged side, and let the door lean against the rolled linoleum. A large cigar box sat on two boards that covered a hole in the ground. Robert had given the box to Sarah who sat it on the kitchen table.

A berm several inches high had been built around the hole—a hole over two feet in diameter. The light from the single window in the pantry had not allowed Robert to see down the hole, and he yelled to Sarah to bring him the flashlight on top of the refrigerator. Sarah had handed the flashlight to him and he had beamed it down the hole.

"What do you see?" Sarah had asked.

"It's a cave. There's a rope ladder attached to the rim of the hole," had said Robert, struggling to see deeper into the cave. "I see several things, but I can't be sure what they are."

"They?" had asked Sarah.

"A chest and what looks like two bodies," had said Robert.

"Two bodies!" had exclaimed Sarah.

Robert had seen the body of Sergeant Pete O'Conner, or what remained of it. Tiny rodents had found their way through the small opening in the cave entrance and had eaten part of an ear and nose. The remaining flesh had become leathery, and the blue uniform had become discolored from mold. A blow to the right side of the head had created a wound that had hardened into a dark red scar.

The rodents hadn't bothered the body of Lieutenant Henry, and it lay and appeared almost as it did nearly three-quarters of a century ago. The folded hands and the supine body contrasted with Sergeant O'Conner's as a baby rabbit contrasts later with its maggot-infested dead body.

The scabbard and sword (placed by the lieutenant's side) and the hands (folded one atop the other on the chest) had suggested a care by someone, while the contorted body of the sergeant (resulting from its ten-foot fall onto the rough rock floor of the cave) had suggested disdain.

What had looked like a chest was partially hidden and farther away from the light of the flashlight than the two bodies, but Robert had seen that the lid was open.

Robert had pulled the rope ladder up. The steps were thick tree branches with each end fastened between the two ropes. He had handed Sarah the flashlight and stood up.

"They look like Civil War soldiers. One has a smashed head and the other, I can't tell," had said Robert brushing off his clothes as he stood up. "Let's look in that cigar box."

They had emptied the contents of the large cigar box onto the kitchen table, and Robert told Sarah what he suspected happened after they had read and looked at two love letters, a 1etter to a Quartermaster, two names on small strips, a bundle of $5 greenbacks, and a list of gifts to individuals.

"During the Civil War battle near Munfordville, the chest containing greenbacks must have been discovered by the Union forces," said Robert. "Probably three soldiers were ordered to deliver the chest containing the money to the army quartermaster in Elizabethtown. Two of them were killed by the third, who then hid the chest and the money in the cave."

"You mean he stole the money?" Sarah had asked.

"Whoever crushed that skull must have stolen the chest of greenbacks and hid it and the bodies in the cave. After the war, he built a house over the cave and spent the money."

"Mr. Applegate?" had asked Sarah.

"Who else?" had replied Robert.

"Shouldn't we call the sheriff, Bob?" had said Sarah.

"I think we should call David first. What's in that cave has been there near a century. Another day won't make any difference. I'll drive down to Fletcher's and phone David at his office to come here early tomorrow morning. Tomorrow's Saturday, so it shouldn't be a problem for him," had said Robert.

Returning from making the telephone call to David, Robert had again looked at the items in the large box. Remembering the smaller cigar box he had found in a chest that had come with the house and which he had put in the back of the bottom drawer of his desk, Robert spent the remainder of Friday evening looking through it. Joshua Applegate's name had been scribbled on the cigar box.

Robert had found nothing in the smaller cigar box relating to the chest or the two bodies, but he had kept a faded sheet of music about Sherman's march to the sea and had put it on the piano. He'd ask Sarah to play it tomorrow.

After breakfast Robert and Sarah continued their conversation about the cave and its contents over several more cups of coffee.

"Would you like a slice of cake with your coffee?" she asks.

"The jam cake?" asks Robert.

"No. That's for the church dinner tomorrow. The yellow cake," says Sarah.

"If it has chocolate icing," says Robert.

"It has. I know your favorite by now, Bob," says Sarah. She gets up, puts two slices of yellow cake on two plates and places them on the table. Robert slices a piece of the cake off the top with his fork, where the chocolate icing is as thick as a piece of bread, and devours it. Suddenly he stands up.

"I'm going down into the cave!" he says.

"No you're not!" says Sarah, getting ready to sit down.

"I have to be able to tell David if there's anything in that chest and if there is, show it to him, Sarah," says Robert, as he gets up. He walks into the pantry and reaches on top of the refrigerator for the flashlight, followed by Sarah.

"I wish you'd wait, Bob. David should be here soon."

Robert ignores Sarah and hands her the flashlight while he steps on the second round of the robe ladder. "Point the light down at me, Sarah. You can hand it to me when I get near the bottom," says Robert.

The last rung of the ladder is three feet from the floor, and when he begins to place his foot on what he thought would be another rung, he loses his balance and falls to the floor hitting his head.

"Bob! Are you alright?" yells Sarah, peering down into the cave. Stunned, he does not answer. Sarah puts the flashlight in her apron pocket and begins to climb down the ladder. Half-way down, the left strand of the ladder rips from the hook and Sarah and the flashlight land on the hard rock floor. At the same time. the rolled linoleum, which has been holding the door in a vertical position, begins to unroll. Pushed by the linoleum, the door slams shut over the hole and the linoleum straightens out, covering the door.

Sarah's yell startles Robert and he crawls to her. "Are you all right?" he asks.

"I twisted my ankle. At least the flashlight is still working," she says, picking it up. She shines the beam on the back of his head. "That's a nasty bump, but it's not bleeding."

"Give me the flashlight, Sarah," says Bob. He beams it at the rope ladder, now hanging from one strand. "We can't climb up this one strand," he says, pointing to it.

"David should be here soon," says Sarah. "We have to wait until he comes."

"He won't know we're down here, Sarah. The linoleum has probably covered the door. I doubt yelling will help," says Robert. "We just can't wait. David might not get here for some time." Robert sniffs the air.

"I felt a slight movement of air when the hole was open and smelled cooler air, but I don't now. I bet the old cave entrance is over there," says Robert, pointing. We can push the rocks blocking the entrance and get out of the cave, Sarah," he says.

"What if David finds the hole and we're not here?" she asks.

"Take off your apron, Sarah," he says and she does. "Fold it like an arrow and point it in that direction," says Robert, again pointing in the same direction as before.

Sarah folds her apron into the shape of a triangle and points one end towards the direction where Robert thinks the cave entrance is. "We better pray that the flashlight holds out!" exclaims Robert. He takes Sarah's hand and beams the flashlight ahead of them into the dark, cool cave. Sarah averts looking at the two bodies.

Above ground the walk to the cave entrance from the house takes five minutes, but the rough rock floor of the cave and the diffused light from the flashlight makes walking a slow, tedious task. Twenty minutes later they see a spot of light ahead.

"See Sarah, light is coming through the entrance," says Robert. "Hold on to my hand. Another minute and we'll be there."

Exhausted, they sit down before the cave entrance, which is closed by several boulders and a number of small rocks on top of them. At the top of the cave entrance light comes through a small opening, made when a small wild creature scrapped away the dirt and twigs between the small rocks. Robert believes he can push the small rocks away and move several of the boulders enough for them to get out of the cave. Suddenly he remembers.

"I forgot to look in the chest!" says Robert.

CHAPTER SEVEN

SATURDAY, 11 MAY, 1935, 12:45 P.M

A cave that's dark a hundred years,
Is lighted by a single flame;
And all the darkness disappears,
And only vibrant light remains.

We are born into a world of magic, where elves and pixies join our play and the fairy folk watch over us in the forest of adults. By our sixth year we outgrow such imaginations on our road to adulthood, and the magic, like the elves and pixies, fades away. What the elves, pixies, and fairy folk teach remains with those few who nourish the child within by seeing through the veil of this delusive world and by communing with the silent rhythms of nature.

Both David and Jane have long ago replaced the magic of youth with the certainty of science, and their intuitive link to the world of Spirit has been replaced by the chance and probability of a hunch. Trudy, however, has allowed the elves and pixies to become the subtle vibrations of matter and the fairy folk to become the hidden energies in all nature. The subtle world of Spirit David and Jane bclicvc in, Trudy knows.

David's question, "What's caused this?" is not intended to be answered. "My gut feeling is that Uncle Bob and Aunt Sarah are all right and before evening we'll all be sitting around the table." Like the pause after ending a chapter of a book and the anticipation of beginning the next, the moment of silence is broken by Trudy. "I'm hungry!" she says.

David says they might as well eat lunch while they wait and think what else they could do. Jane asks him if he'd like some fresh squeezed orange juice. Certainly! She cuts several of the oranges from a bowl on the kitchen cabinet and begins to squeeze them on the new device she has given Aunt Sarah. When David says he had wondered what that odd shaped dish was for, Jane told him their store had ordered a case recently and sold all of the squeezers within two weeks.

David notices the jam cake on the counter. It's tall enough to be a five layer jam cake—his favorite. David takes the knife Jean had used to divide the oranges, cuts out a good "man-size" slice, puts it on a plate he takes from a shelf in the kitchen cabinet, and sets it on the table in front of the chair he had been sitting in. He finds a fork in the top drawer of the kitchen cabinet.

Trudy is in the pantry and holds the German potato salad her mother had put in the refrigerator and the six slices of bologna David had bought at Fletcher's Grocery in her hands, as she continues to look into the refrigerator.

"I don't see any holey cheese in the refrigerator, Mom," she says.

"Holy cheese!" says David. "Don't tell me Holy Ground farm has holy cheese."

"It's Swiss cheese, David. Trudy liked the holes in Swiss cheese and called it holey cheese when she was young and still does," says Jane.

"Holy cheese!" says David. "H-o-l-e-y, not h-o-l-y. This is cave country. It's holey ground."

"What?" says Jane. "Oh! H-O-L-E-Y, not H-O-L-Y."

"Exactly! We've looked on the first and second floors but not under the house," says David.

"A cellar?" asks Jane.

"Right!" says David.

David and Jane go into the parlor, but Trudy puts the bologna on a plate and then puts it and the potato salad on the table. She saunters to the pantry and finds the four nails she had seen when she was at the refrigerator. She picks the bent nails up and looks for equal size nail holes in the linoleum. She sees a number of nail heads protruding from the surface of the linoleum but no empty holes.

She lifts the end of the loose linoleum and sees the door, which is even with the wood floor. She sees two nail holes in the unhinged side of the door and a nail hole in each of the two adjacent sides. She puts her finger in the notch at the end of the door and lifts. The door rises slightly but is too heavy for her to lift further.

David pulls the other end of the oriental rug (as he did the opposite end) back onto the floor, after having lifted it up to look at the floor and finding no cellar door. In the vestibule, hall, and under the stairs, Jane finds nothing indicating a cellar. Trudy walks into the parlor and stands before her uncle, who is looking where the walls and the floor meet.

"Uncle Dave?" she says. He looks up. "I think I've found it," she says.

David stares at Trudy for a moment. "Where?" he asks.

"In the pantry," says Trudy.

David and Trudy walk down the hal1. "Trudy says she's found it, Jane, in the pantry," says David. David and Jane follow Trudy through the kitchen into the pantry. Trudy pulls the linoleum back and points to the door.

"I pulled up on that little notch and lifted the door a little, but it's too heavy for me," says Trudy.

David puts his finger in the notch and lifts it several inches before letting go. "Hand me that screwdriver, Jane," says David, pointing to the screwdriver lying on the floor. He lifts the door again and sticks the screwdriver under it. David pushes down on the handle of the screwdriver and lifts the door up so that he can put his hand under it and pull it open.

David pushes down on the roll of linoleum until it cracks and collapses on to the floor, allowing the door to fall on top of it and keep from covering the hole. He looks on top of the refrigerator for the flashlight, but it's not there. "Trudy, go up stairs and get the flashlight from the small table between the beds," says David.

David stands over the hole. "It's not a root cellar. It's deep. A good size cave," says David. "Take a look, Jane."

"Uncle Bob? Aunt Sarah? Are you there?" yells Jane, into the hole. "They must be down there, David. But they don't answer." The sudden fear for her aunt and uncle's safety causes Jane to raise both her hands to her lips. Trudy returns and hands the flashlight to David. David kneels by the hole and beams the light into it.

"Here's one end of a rope ladder. It looks like the other end is torn. That looks like a body ... in a blue uniform ... another body, twisted ... same blue ... the head looks like a mask, a big red spot on one side. That looks like a triangle by the second body. It's blue. Jane? Look at it. What is it?" David hands Jane the flashlight.

"That's Aunt Sarah's apron," says Jane.

"May I look?" asks Trudy. Jane hands her the flashlight.

"It's pointing in that direction," says Trudy, pointing with her finger.

"They were here," says David. "Both of them must have gone down the ladder before one side became loose. They must have the flashlight they keep on the refrigerator and started walking towards that old cave entrance blocked with stones." He yells out, "Uncle Bob! Aunt Sarah!" He hears only the hum of the refrigerator motor.

"The ladder in the barn should be long enough to reach the floor of the cave. I'll get it." says David, starting for the barn and telling Jane to open the pantry window.

Five minutes later, David shoves the ladder through the pantry's single window, which is opposite the hole.

"I'd like to be sure it's tall enough, before I slide it down the hole," says David.

"Here's Uncle Bob's yard stick hanging by the refrigerator," says Trudy. She measures the ladder. It's a nine foot ladder. "Let me measure how deep the hole is, Uncle Dave," says Trudy. She looks into Uncle Rob's workbench that he had moved near the window. She removes a ball of twine and unscrews a large nut from a bolt.

She ties the end of a long piece of string onto the nut. Dropping the nut down the hole, she holds her fingers around the string where it touches the rim of the hole, pulls the nut and string up, and blackens the string with a pencil where she is holding it. She stretches the string three times along the yardstick. "Just under nine feet," says Trudy.

"The ladder's long enough," says David. He begins to lower the ladder into the hole.

Trudy's measurement of the cave's depth is correct, but she held the string at the edge of the hole. The rock floor, where the nut sat during the measuring, begins to slant down. The center of the rock floor directly under the hole, therefore, is two inches deeper than nine foot.

As David pushes the ladder down the hole, he grasps the ends and stands over the hole, slowly lowing the end into the hole. His hands come opposite the rim of the hole but the ladder is not touching the rock floor. He lowers it further until his hands are below the rim and the ladder touches the bottom.

He relaxes his body while balancing the ladder with one hand. "This isn't going to work," he says. "If I let go, the ladder will fall towards the rim and just miss touching it. I'll have to pull it up." He attempts to pull it up but the weight and his awkward position do not allow him to. The ladder slips from his grip and it falls onto the cave floor.

"Well, we can't climb down," he says. "They're probably at the cave entrance," says David "We better go there. They may need help. We can drive there in Uncle Bob's truck."

Tired from digging out the dirt, twigs, and rocks blocking the cave entrance, Robert had set down next to Sarah. They both see the light and hear the noise coming from the hole. They yell, but their voices are not as forceful as they used to be and are drowned out by the refrigerator's motor.

"Give me your hand, Sarah," says Robert, rejuvenated. "Hope this flashlight holds out while we walk back on this rock floor. Thank God they found the hole."

David, Jane, and Trudy get into the truck and head for the cave entrance. Half-way there the truck stops and will not start again, and they begin walking towards the cave entrance. At that moment, ten feet below ground, Robert and Sarah are walking away from the cave entrance and towards the light coming through the hole.

Robert and Sarah see the ladder on the rock floor. "It must be too short," says Robert as he and Sarah avoid looking at the two bodies.

"We're here!" he yells. "We're down here!" he yells again. "They must have seen your apron." He smiles. "They're probably at the entrance by now." He looks at the ladder, and then glances at the open chest.

"This is not the time to be looking into that chest," says Sarah.

"Two birds with one chest!" he says. He picks up the two bands lying in the chest and puts them in his pocket. "What ever greenbacks these bound are gone." He begins sliding the chest towards the rock floor directly under the hole.

"What are you doing?" says Sarah. "You can get that chest later. Let's get out of here first!"

"Be patient, my love," says Robert. "That's what I'm getting ready to do."

He pulls the chest with its lid closed directly under the hole. Lifting the ladder, he balances it so that one end sticks through the hole. He lowers it slightly so that the bottom two legs then rest on the chest. "It is not the steadiest, but I'll hold the two ends on the chest and you start climbing Sarah, very slowly."

Two minutes later Sarah pulls herself out of the hole. Reaching as high as he can, he hands Sarah, who reaches down into the cave, the flashlight. "Beam it on the steps, Sarah." Three minutes later, she helps Robert pull himself out of the hole.

They hug each other, smile, and walk into the kitchen.

"Well, I know what was in the chest," says Robert, slumping into his chair. "I'd sure like a fresh cup of coffee Sarah. And maybe a fresh slice of cake."

"Right after I get the Witch Hazel from the bathroom for that bump," replies Sarah.

CHAPTER EIGHT

SATURDAY, 11 MAY, 1935, 2:30 P.M.

Fill with dirt
Such **holey** ground;
Thus, no one's hurt
On **wholly** ground.

Then purge it of
The evil found;
And what's above
Is **holy** ground.

Walking through a newly plowed field, you pick up an arrowhead and wonder who was the last person to hold it before you and when. With Joshua Applegate's death, when the two bodies and the chest in the cave are discovered no longer matters. On the other hand, because of the imbalance that his sin has created, who discovers them does matter in the timeless realm of Spirit, and it is not just chance alone that has brought David Crist to Holy Ground.

On the way from the cave entrance to the house, Trudy runs ahead of Jane and David. "I'll tell them we'll get a ladder so they can climb out of the cave, Uncle Dave," she says. Approaching the house from the back, she hears voices in the kitchen, but cannot understand what they are saying. She doesn't see General Pershing. Concerned, she waits for David and her mother.

"Someone's in the kitchen, Uncle Dave. I heard them talking. And I don't see General Pershing," she says.

Telling Trudy to wait with her mother, David approaches the house. He hears talking and soon recognizes Bob and Sarah's voices. He motions with his hand for Jane and Trudy to come and then hurries to the kitchen screen. "Uncle Bob! Aunt Sarah!" he yells, followed by Jane. "You're all right!

"Thank God!" she exclaims. Trudy notices General Pershing in the corner licking a piece of yellow cake, and being stroked by Uncle Bob.

"Someone took a slice of my jam cake!" says Sarah.

This abrupt change of conversation changes David and Jane's anxiety to laughter, and they sit down to the table.

Aunt Sarah sees nothing to laugh at. "I baked that jam cake for tomorrow's church dinner. Now it's ruined," she says. Uncle Bob looks at David and raises his eyebrows.

"Well, we might as well ruin it a little more, Aunt Sarah. I'll take coffee with my slice," says David.

Not amused, Sarah gets the jam cake and cuts it in half. She can take half a jam cake to church Sunday, but not a whole cake with one slice missing. She places the rest of the jam cake on a plate and places it on the table.

"Eat what you want," she says. David, Jane and Trudy each take a slice.

Robert explains how they managed to climb out of the cave. "I see you've looked through the two cigar boxes, David," he says. "You've seen the two bodies?"

"Yes, Uncle Bob. They appear to be in uniforms."

"They're Union uniforms, David. Civil War uniforms. I guess you noticed the bundle of five dollar greenbacks?"

"Yes, printed in 1862. Where did you get it?"

"Mr. Applegate—he built our house, you know–must have killed those two in the cave. Did you see the chest?" David nods his head yes. "It must have contained a lot of those bundles of greenbacks, like this one that was in the large cigar box. My guess is Applegate killed them to keep the money for himself."

"And he built the house—well, the pantry, over the hole?" asks David.

"Yep, and went down the hole whenever he needed money." says Uncle Bob. "Shouldn't we call the sheriff?"

"I will soon, Uncle Bob," says David.

"What about that bundle of $5 greenbacks?"

"Is there any identification on or in the chest?" asks David.

"No," says Uncle Bob.

"Then I wouldn't say anything about it. It's yours. It's on your property," say David. "I better call the sheriff now."

"Will he remove the two bodies today?" asks Uncle Bob.

"He'll order the coroner to remove the bodies after he investigates," says David.

"That's Ed Sipes. Why don't you call Ed at the same time," says Uncle Bob. "I'd like those bodies removed today. Sarah? Give David Ed's telephone number."

David gets up to go to Fletcher's Grocery and use the telephone, and Uncle Bob asks Trudy to put the items on the table back into each of the two cigar boxes. "Would you like that knife, David?" asks his uncle. "Trudy, hand David that knife," he says. "Maybe Bobby would like it."

David takes the knife, pulls the blade from the sheath and pushes it back in. He puts it in his pocket.

"Yea, maybe," says David. He thinks, maybe he'll keep it, as he leaves for Fletcher's Grocery.

"Did Bob and Sarah return yet?" asks Mr. Fletcher.

"Yes they did, Mr. Fletcher. I'd like to use your telephone again," says David, not wishing to spend any time talking with him. With a wave of his hand, Mr. Fletcher said yes, moving closer to the telephone, wondering what this call is about.

David first calls his wife, explaining that he will be home late in the evening, and not to wait dinner for him. Then the sheriff's office.

"Sheriff, this is David Crist. My aunt and uncle are with us now. They're all right."

"You only had to call me if they didn't return by five o'clock, Mr. Crist," replies the sheriff. His emphasis on didn't, indicates his displeasure with another disruption from this troublesome lawyer.

David ignores the rudeness. "They discovered a cellar door that led to a cave. They both went down into the cave and the cellar door closed, keeping them from returning and kept us from finding them," continued David.

The sheriff is not interested in the details of the aunt and uncle's senile problems. “Mr. Crist ...” begins the sheriff, but is interrupted by David.

“That's not why I'm calling you. They found two bodies in the cave.” David waits. Sheriff O'Connell does not like surprises or to lose control of events. He has trained himself to take a deep breath and not react to surprise. Two bodies? He inhales and nonchalantly replies. “I'll send my deputy over.”

With a smile of satisfaction David says “He may need a rope ladder to descend into the cave.” The sheriff hangs up.

David calls the coroner. “Mister Sipes?” asks David.

“This is Ed Sipes.”

“This is David Crist, Bob MacDowell's nephew,” says David.

“How is Bob? I missed him at lodge meeting,” says Mister Sipes.

“He' s fine. He discovered a cave under his house and found two bodies there.” says David.

“Oh!” says Mister Sipes.

“They were Civil War soldiers.”

“Have you called the Sheriff's office?” asks Mister Sipes.

“Just before calling you. He's sending a deputy.” Says David.

“That would be Billy Whitiker. He'll inform me officially later.”

“My uncle hoped you'd be able to remove the bodies today,” says David.

“We should be able to. I'll send Harry and Gilbert over. If the bodies are Civil War soldiers, it shouldn't take Billy long to give them permission to remove the bodies,” says Mister Sipes.

“Mister Sipes, they'll have to use the cave entrance to remove the two bodies,” says David. “It's about a hundred yards into the cave where the bodies are. Several large boulders block the cave entrance. They'll need a crowbar.”

“Very well. Tell Bob I'm glad he's all right, and I look forward to seeing him at lodge meeting next week,” says Mister Sipes.

David hangs up the telephone and starts to leave the store. Mr. Fletcher is looking at him, his countenance pleading for details. He heard “sheriff,” “bodies” “Mister Sipes.” David hesitates. Why not? He looks at Mr. Fletcher.

“My uncle discovered a cave under his house and in the cave he found the bodies of two Civil War soldiers. Thanks for the use of the telephone, Mr. Fletcher," he says. He leaves Mr. Fletcher, whose eyes and mouth are wide open.

Billy Whitiker arrives at Holy Ground fifteen minutes after David returns. A slim young man with large brown glasses, Billy is the opposite of Sheriff O'Connell. All smiles, he holds a chain ladder in his hands. "Sheriff said I'd need this," he says to David.

David takes Billy into the pantry and shows him the hole. "I'll need it by golly," he says. He takes the flashlight hooked to his belt and beams it down the hole. "Yea. I see two bodies." Seeing the two eye hooks, he connects the chain ladder to them and lets the eight foot ladder fall through the hole to dangle at the bottom. He turns to David and gives him the flashlight. "You point the light on me, Mr. Crist." He climbs down and before touching the rock floor reaches for the flashlight.

David hears commotion in the house and sees two men following his uncle into the kitchen. "The men from coroner's office, David," says his uncle.

Billy has completed his investigation, and David helps him climb out of the hole. Billy sees Harry and Gilbert. "You guys can remove the bodies. They've shrunk a lot. Not much weight."

David sits in the coroner's truck with Harry and Gilbert to show them the way to the cave entrance, passing by his uncle's truck on the narrow road through the wooded area. The three of them quickly remove two large boulders with the crow bar. David waits while Harry and Gilbert place the two bodies in special bags and carry them to the truck. Fifteen minutes later, they, Billy, and the bodies of the lieutenant and the sergeant are gone from Holy Ground.

"What will they do with the bodies, Uncle David?" asks Trudy, standing next to Uncle Bob.

"Try to locate their families. Otherwise, the bodies become wards of the state. As the land owner where they were found, Uncle Bob, they could be buried here."

"If they can't find the families, I'll see that they're buried in a pine, cloth covered casket and buried in our cemetery. David, see if there isn't a good place in our cemetery where they could be buried."

While he's still at Holy Ground, David agrees to take a moment and look for a place in the cemetery. Saying she'll go with him, Trudy decides some bright flowers in the kitchen will bring some cheer, and she takes the small rose sheers hanging in the pantry, while her mother tends to the minor injuries of her aunt and uncle.

David and Trudy walk to the cemetery with Trudy cutting flowers along the way. The two tombstones behind the two graves are incised with the date of birth and death and name of Mrs. Applegate and, Mr. Applegate.

Mr. Applegate's grave is covered with poison ivy and goose berry bushes, but tiny yellow violets are scattered through the green carpet over Mrs. Applegate's grave.

Holding a bunch of flowers, Trudy extends her hand to David, who accepts them with a slight nod. David tosses part of the bunch onto Mrs. Applegate's grave while attempting to avoid stepping into the prickly goose berry vines and poison ivy covering Mr. Applegate's grave, but he is unsuccessful and drops the remaining flowers.

Upset at first, David smiles at the thought that the spirit of Joshua Applegate is restraining him. He ask Trudy for the rose sheers and cuts himself free from the prickly goose berry and poison ivy tendrils.

Seeing the tendrils and aerial roots covering Mr. Applegate's name, David takes the knife from his pocket, removes it from the sheath and scrapes away the tendrils and roots, once again exposing the incised name.

Our minds are in the world of matter, but our hearts are in the world of matter and the world of Spirit simultaneously. In the presence of human death and nature's greenery, David contemplates both worlds and contrasts the life of Joshua Applegate with his own. In this moment, for the first time in his life, David intuitively senses the world of Spirit as real and the world of matter as illusion.

David and Trudy return to the house, when Trudy tells David to stop a moment while she removes several vines and tendrils still clinging to his pants legs. Ten seconds later, she holds the last tendril up for David to see. "You're no longer entangled, Uncle Dave," she says.

Resuming their walk, David thinks to himself: With the two bodies gone, Applegate's moral obligation ends, and now this can rightfully be called holy ground.

EPILOGUE

LATE SUMMER, 1935

The flight of cranes
Is always straight;
Unless disharmony
Is of late.

David discovers that Lieutenant Robert Patrick Henry's father, George Henry, was the second son of Gideon Henry. When Gideon died near the end of the Civil War, his estate and financial holdings were willed to his first son, Joseph. Shortly thereafter, George, his wife, and daughter Patricia moved to Louisville. David learns that George Henry, his wife, and daughter are buried in Cave Hill Cemetery in Louisville.

Patricia and Robert were twins. In visiting the grave site with his wife Ellen and son Bobby, David notices that the obelisk tombstone has the names Patricia Beth and Robert Patrick incised under the larger name Henry, above and centered on the base of the tombstone. Under Robert's name is incised "November 28 1838 September 11 1862" and underneath, are the capital letters MIA. David explains to Bobby that MIA stands for "missing in action." The twin sister had died in 1868, and David assumes that the family moved to Louisville shortly before then.

With the certification of the Hart County coroner, that the body found in the cave is that of Robert Patrick Henry, David is able to obtain Cave Hill Cemetery's approval to have the body buried in the family plot. David is also able to arrange that the letters MIA be removed and "Battle of Munfordville" incised in their place.

Pleased with David's success in obtaining permission to bury the lieutenant with his family and the sergeant with his Union comrades, Uncle Bob gives David the bundle of $5 greenbacks to cover the costs of disinterment, transporting the bodies by train to Louisville, and the charges of Cave Hill Cemetery.

The following Memorial Day David, Ellen, and Bobby, place flowers on Colonel MacDowell's grave. They stop by the Henry plot and see that the lieutenant's body now rests with his mother, father, and twin sister in their family plot, and the letters M I A have been replaced by "Killed in the Battle of Munfordville September 1862."

All three walk silently among the white stone markers perfectly lined up, row after row. They walk across the narrow road and read the words underneath the raised letters "CSA" at the top of a large stone, while a Confederate flag flutters above.

Uncle Bob completes renovating the pantry, nailing the door closed before covering it with new linoleum. General Pershing dies, and, to be militarily neutral, the new hound pup is named Admiral Byrd.

Aunt Sarah now plants flowers in the cemetery—around both the human part and the animal part.

Trudy is to play the part of rich Mrs. Throckmorton in her high school's play "The Victorian Americans" and asks Aunt Sarah if she has any costume jewelry that she can wear. Aunt Sarah hands Trudy her ivory inlaid jewelry box and tells her to look through it.

Trudy finds a huge purple stone at the end of a long hairpin, a bracelet with six green gems, golden earrings, sparkling rings with different colored stones, but it is the necklace wrapped in a piece of silk cloth that holds her attention. She goes to the mirror and fastens the pearl necklace around her neck.

"Aunt Sarah. Could I have these pearls?" she asks.

"Of course you may," says her aunt.

"I mean to keep, Aunt Sarah," says Trudy.

Aunt Sarah notices the pearls compliment Trudy's dark eyes. "I found them wrapped in a silk cloth, hidden in the corner of the top shelf in the pantry when we moved into our house. I've never worn them, they just did not feel 'right'. You're certainly welcome to have them." Trudy thanks her aunt and walks to the mirror again, before going outside to see why Admiral Byrd is yelping.

To keep the young pup from traipsing off, Uncle Bob has tied one end of a long rope to a tree and the other end to a collar, which is fastened around Admiral Byrd's neck. As a result of his playful antics, he's become a yelping bundle of "rope and puppy." Petting him, speaking softly to him, scratching him under the chin, Trudy calms him and slowly unentangles him.

Relaxed and thoughtful, Trudy sits in the hammock, while Admiral Byrd bounces around, nips at her fingers, and then snuggles under the hammock and falls asleep. With the pearl necklace still around her neck, Trudy stretches out in the hammock and watches a flight of sandhill cranes fly straight over Holy Ground.

In Darkness
one comprehends the Light;
In Light
one feels the soul.
Not in having or using,
but in being the soul.
Alone,
It finds its source;
And with patience
and solitude,
It merges,
not in time or space,
But through entanglement.

####

IN MEMORY

So very young.
Not yet twenty;
And listed as
Killed in action -
World War II.

The Quiet of
ROBERT JOHN,
The cleverness of
JOHN TAFEL,
The dedication of
JACK HEAD,
The sharpness of
WARREN LIBERT,
The shattering of
NICK, and
The German,
FRITZ SCHMIDT.
Live again,
In these pages.

###

AFTERWORD

The author wishes to acknowledge the following list of literary works and their respective authors for the tremendous assistance they were in the writing of this book. *~Ed.*

Views Of Louisville Since 1766, Ed. Samuel W. Thomas.
The Kentucky Book, by Wade Hall.
Mythology, by Edith Hamilton.
Encyclopedia of American History, Ed. Richard Morris.
An Encyclopedia of World History, Ed. William L. Langer.
Kentucky's Civil War 1861-1865, Ed. Jerlene Rose.
The Civil War Time, Ed. Richard Stengel.
Atlas of The Civil War ,NATIONAL GEOGRAPHIC, Ed. Neil Kagan.
Nothing But Victory, by Steven E. Woodworth.
Breckinridge, by William G. Davis.
A History Of Currency in The United States, by Alonzo Barton Hepburn.
Civil War Household Tips, by Maggie Mack.
Detailed Minutiae of Soldier Life in the Army of Northern Virginia, 1861-1864 by Carlton McCarthy .
Union Army Camp Cooking 1861-1865, by Patricia B. Mitchell.
Memoirs of General William T. Sherman, Volumes I and II, by William Tecumseh Sherman.
The Story of a Common Soldier in The Civil War, 1861-1865, by Leander Stillwell.
The Land Before Fort Knox, by Gary Kempf.
Don't Know Much About Mythology, by Kenneth C. Davis.
War and Peace, by Leo Tolstoy.
The War Lovers, by Evan Thomas.
Cosmic Consciousness, by Richard Maurice Bucke, M.D.
Meditations, by Marcus Aurelius.
Simon Bolivar Buckner: Borderland Knight, by Arndt' M. Stickles Chapel Hill; Durham, North Carolina; 1940.
The Battle of Munfordville, Hart County Historical Society, Munfordville, KY., 1984.
Indiana's German Sons: Baptism. of Fire at Rowlett's Station, by Michael A. Peake, Hart County Historical Society, Munfordville, Ky., Ed. Tres Seymour, 1997.
An Artist In Treason, by Andro Linkletter.

ABOUT THE AUTHOR

Karl F. Hollenbach was born in 1925 in Louisville, Kentucky. He received his B.A. and M. Ed. from the University of Louisville. His esoteric and metaphysical articles have been published in Japan and England as well as the United States. He and his artist wife live on Dunsinane Hill Farm near Fort Knox, Kentucky.

Additional information about the author may be found at http://BooksAuthorsAndArtists.com and on the Books, Authors and Artists Facebook page at https://www.facebook.com/BooksAuthorsAndArtists

by Karl F. Hollenbach

A JOURNEY TO THE FOUR KINGDOMS

Amazon Kindle ebook: http://amzn.to/YCQpwJ
Amazon paperback: http://amzn.to/15l16Ig
CreateSpace paperback: https://www.createspace.com/4136583

ANECDOTES AND SPECIAL NOTES

Amazon Kindle ebook: http://amzn.to/16pgHtU
Amazon paperback: http://amzn.to/10Dmb1v
CreateSpace paperback: https://www.createspace.com/4278307

SCROOGE AND MARLEY

Amazon Kindle ebook: http://amzn.to/XWgQPs
Amazon paperback: http://amzn.to/WFEoXJ
CreateSpace paperback: https://www.createspace.com/4055049

PATTON: MANY LIVES, MANY BATTLES

Amazon Kindle ebook: http://amzn.to/XIjvsm
Amazon paperback: http://amzn.to/WFENtl
CreateSpace paperback: https://www.createspace.com/4097702

MANSIONS OF THE MOON (formerly ERICIUS)

Amazon Kindle ebook: http://amzn.to/1gYq8p6
Amazon paperback: http://amzn.to/1f8r2yy
CreateSpace paperback: https://www.createspace.com/4428046

FRANCIS ROSICROSS
Amazon Kindle ebook: http://amzn.to/1klGlGu
Amazon paperback: http://amzn.to/1d3pzIi
CreateSpace paperback: https://www.createspace.com/4521941

HANDBOOK – APPLYING METAPHYSICAL PRINCIPLES IN TEACHING
Amazon Kindle ebook: http://amzn.to/Ysuo3o
Amazon paperback: http://amzn.to/Y1O6Df
CreateSpace paperback: https://www.createspace.com/4035946

THE GREAT HAWK
Amazon Kindle ebook: http://amzn.to/Z9TCo5
Amazon paperback: http://amzn.to/1513XGb
CreateSpace paperback: https://www.createspace.com/4044068

THE RIGHTEOUS ROGUE
Amazon Kindle ebook: http://amzn.to/12QAMWD
Amazon paperback: http://amzn.to/13CHeiD
CreateSpace paperback: https://www.createspace.com/4247817

THRICE TOLD TALES
Amazon Kindle ebook: http://amzn.to/17YzgH5
Amazon paperback: http://amzn.to/14wpXZV
CreateSpace paperback: https://www.createspace.com/4280447

THRICE TOLD TALES: LARGE PRINT EDITION
Amazon Kindle ebook: http://amzn.to/1jBITzW
Amazon paperback: http://amzn.to/1eblTEg
CreateSpace paperback: https://www.createspace.com/4614310

HOLY GROUND
Amazon Kindle ebook: http://amzn.to/1lTsnv2
Amazon paperback: http://amzn.to/1fLaHkS
CreateSpace paperback: https://www.createspace.com/4727103

How to Contact Karl F.:

Goodreads:
http://www.goodreads.com/search?utf8=%E2%9C%93&q=Karl+F.+Hollenbach&search_type=books

Publisher's Facebook:
https://www.facebook.com/BooksAuthorsAndArtists

Amazon's Author's Page:
http://www.amazon.com/Karl-F.-Hollenbach/e/B00B36VS38/ref=sr_tc_2_0?qid=1363387919&sr=1-2-ent

Where to purchase books by Karl F. Hollenbach:

Please see the Amazon and CreateSpace links under each title above.

YOUR REVIEW IS IMPORTANT!

We appreciate your support for Karl F.

In advance, we are very grateful for your review of any of his works. Please post a review, with your analysis, thoughts, and ideas at:

Amazon: http://amzn.to/1lTsnv2

Goodreads: https://www.goodreads.com/book/show/22096270-holy-ground

Karl F. Hollenbach, as author, interviews David Crist, a main character in *Holy Ground.*

Author: Thank you Mr. Crist for answering some questions today, which I hope will enlighten our readers.

David Crist: My pleasure, sir.

Author: First I have to confess to a personal question, "Why are you an attorney when other occupations would, perhaps, be more easily understood?"

David Crist: A very good question, sir. I am compelled to be part of the process which balances all things. I must; I am driven to assist the closure to events and happenings, reward and punishment in the grand scheme of all things.

The part I am bound to play may be miniscule or major, but I am required by a power greater than I to seek, to help find resolution.

The not-inconsiderable assistance I provided in *Holy Ground* is evidence of that ingrained trait. That trait, or compulsion, would easily lead any person to become an attorney.

Author: You know from the third chapter of *Holy Ground* that Joshua Applegate's experience at the cave explained the disappearance of your aunt and uncle.

David Crist: Yes. It proved that what we (my cousin Jane and her daughter Trudy) surmised from certain bits and pieces of evidence we discovered in the two cigar boxes to be true.

Author: You had never met Sheriff O'Connell before, yet felt almost instant hostility.

David Crist: I've met and dealt with his type. Arrogant, humorless, oppressive.

Author: Any similarity to Sergeant Peter O'Conner?

David Crist: I know Sergeant O'Conner from what is written in Chapter III and noted several times in the following two chapters.

Both are unpleasant characters who don't hesitate to abuse their authority.

Author: Is that all?

David Crist: Are you suggesting a connection between Sheriff O'Connell's disfigured face and Sergeant Peter O'Conner's crushed in face?

Author: Yes. Also, their names. O'Conner and O'Connell.

David Crist: As a lawyer, I'd say "coincidence."

Author: And personally?

David Crist: I feel a certain affinity with Joshua after becoming aware of his life in chapters three, four, and five. There may be more than just coincidence, something like the entanglement mentioned in the beginning of the book.

Author: Is Joshua guilty of theft and murder?

David Crist: As far as "theft," a military court martial probably would have found him guilty, but I doubt so if brought before a civilian court. I did, as you know, suggest to my uncle not to report the five hundred dollars in greenbacks.

As far as murder, in his defense his lawyer would stress self-defense. A court might make a judgment of manslaughter, but hardly murder under the circumstances, recognizing it was war time, preparation for battle, and definitely a valid case of self-defense.

Author: The three parts of *Holy Ground* are entitled David, Joshua, and Trudy, with each part having two or more chapters. Why do you think these three parts are given these three titles?

David Crist: Well, I'm virtually the only character in the first chapter and play a significant part in chapter two, both chapters comprising Part One of *Holy Ground.*

All three chapters of the Second Part are Joshua's biography.

The Third Part, entitled *Trudy*, is different. She has an unusual role, being a "wise" youngster. With regards to entanglement, I think Trudy is some agent for an entanglement between Joshua and me.

Author: You seem hesitant to say "reincarnation," you being a reincarnation of Joshua.

David Crist: Remember, I'm a lawyer, neither a scientist nor a philosopher. The debate continues whether consciousness immerges into a body or emerges from a body. If the former is true, then reincarnation is one explanation.

Author: For the sake of argument, do you think Trudy is the reincarnation of a character, or someone else, from the Civil War?

David Crist: Yes. Dorothea, Joshua's wife.

Author: Ah! Dorothea Applegate was instrumental in Joshua's redemption but was not able to bring closure to the reaping of what Joshua had sown in the cave. Now, as Trudy, she influences events so that both the lieutenant and the sergeant are buried properly, bringing to a close the results of Joshua's transgression.

David Crist: Well said. There's a hint of scientist and philosopher in you.

Author: Merely traits of a good interviewer. Thank you, Mr. Crist for illuminating us on many points.

David Crist: My pleasure, sir. I hope you will see to it that I appear again, in another book, perhaps in another life.

##

Karl F. Hollenbach, as author, interviews Pastor Jeremiah Trumble, a supporting character in *Holy Ground*.

Author: Pastor Trumble, is Joshua guilty of murder?

Pastor J. Trumble: Responsible for killing, but not guilty of murder, young man. It was war time, in fact the beginning of a major battle.

Author: Do you think a court martial would convict Joshua?

Pastor J. Trumble: Danged if I'da cared what any court would conclude when they are meeting in comfortable surroundings and the safety of peacetime. The event happened at the same time both the northern and southern armies were preparing for battle.

Author: Well, what is your personal opinion, Pastor? Was Joshua guilty of poor judgment: going along with Sergeant O'Conner's plan and then letting his rage cause him to kill O'Conner?

Pastor J. Trumble: One at a time, young fella. It t'waren't easy for Joshua to refuse to help hide the chest of greenbacks in the cave without ending up being killed by O'Conner, which, in fact, nearly happened. Joshua's compliance with Sargent O'Conner's scheme was a mixture of self-preservation and the enticement of wealth, no easy decision on the brink of battle and the persuasiveness of a matured, cunning man who also had rank and authority over a boy not yet seventeen.

Author: You're saying ... ?

Pastor J. Trumble: Ya can't tell a starvin' man to not steal bread.

Author: That's understandable. What about killing Sergeant O'Conner?

Pastor J. Trumble: Joshua had little choice. They could hardly compromise and "start over again." They were too deeply involved, and eventually, before Joshua would "talk too much," O'Conner would have to kill him.

Author: Why couldn't Joshua go around O'Conner and walk to Munfordville?

Pastor J. Trumble: Whatever Joshua would tell his sergeant on returning would only implicate himself, and if O'Conner returned, he would, as I just said, he would have to get rid of Joshua before he talked too much.

Author: If I understand you, then, you feel Joshua is not guilty of theft and murder?

Pastor J. Trumble: Not in the spirit of the law.

Author: What would you have done, had you been Joshua?

Pastor J. Trumble: Cut his throat and spend and distribute the greenbacks as he did, and not report the remaining treasure to the authorities, as David Crist advised his uncle to do.

Author: Thank you, Pastor, for taking the time to answer some questions for my readers. I expect they will discover insight into a few of the characters, from your answers.

Pastor J. Trumble: My honor, sir. May God bless and I wish you a good day.

##

Karl F. Hollenbach, as himself, interviews "the author," of *Holy Ground.*

Karl F.: Where did you get the idea for Holy Ground?

Author: I had written a short description of an individual going into his aunt and uncle's home and finding two warm cups of coffee but no sign of them. Some years later I decided to use the description to write a short mystery, and over time "thought through" the plot. In time, the plot for a short story evolved into a full length novel.

Karl F.: I'm familiar enough with Civil War history to know some of the story that takes place during the Civil War is true. What about the rest of the story?

Author: The major Civil War events are factual: dates, places, commanders (both North and South), and even lesser officers. I did a tremendous amount of referential reading to make the scenes and characters as historical as possible. The *Afterword* lists those works.

Most of Joshua's experiences during his visit to Louisville, and even his march to Georgia, are based on personal experiences and visits.

A number of characters that have a "cameo" appearance are individuals I've known who were killed during World War II. Their names are listed in the back of the book, in the "*In Memory*" section.

Karl F.: You say you started off wanting to write a mystery, which the mysterious disappearance of David's aunt and uncle is in 1935. But the abrupt change—virtually a biography of Joshua seven decades earlier—borders on being a morality story.

Author: The last thing David says in Chapter Two is "What caused this?" He is referring to the disappearance of his aunt and uncle. Events in Chapter Three explain their disappearance, and the remaining biography of Joshua in Chapters Four and Five hints at the relationship between Joshua and David, two total strangers three generations apart.

Karl F.: I think it is more than just a "hint." In the preface portion of your book, you define "entanglement," which may be a subtle suggestion of reincarnation. But I understand entanglement to be concerned with space, not time, and David and Joshua do not share the same time.

Author: Time and space are one, according to Einstein—space-time, you'll recall. A reader, with some awareness and some understanding of reincarnation, may conclude that David is a reincarnation of the soul personality that had been Joshua Applegate. The soul that was Joshua sinned and that same soul as David helped redeem itself.

Karl F.: I don't understand.

Author: Every action has an equal and opposite reaction.

Karl F.: That's Newton's Third Law.

Author: Yes, a physical law. But also, an effect for every cause. You eventually reap what you sew.

Karl F.: Ah! Karma!

Author: Right. David killed Sergeant O'Conner and only total justice is figuratively attained with the proper burial of O'Conner, something Joshua could not accomplish.

Karl F.: What about the theft? Joshua helped in stealing the greenbacks.

Author: Steal from whom? A court would have to decide. But Joshua's many gifts of the money to those in need probably redeems him in most readers' judgment.

Karl F.: Is there a message in your story?

Author: Yes. Nature is just, with every cause eventually having an effect.

Karl F.: A punishment?

Author: If there's a lesson to be learned from the effect.

Karl F.: So, there is good and bad karma?

Author: There are pleasant and unpleasant lessons.

Karl F.: I'll start being more careful.

Author: You're learning!

##

Made in the USA
Charleston, SC
10 June 2014